Flatline

JUDY McDONOUGH

Judy McDonough

ebook: 978-0-9911930-4-2
paperback: 978-0-9911930-5-9

Cover Design and Interior format by The Killion Group
http://thekilliongroupinc.com

For my daddy.

I think of him every time I smell original ChapStick in the black tube. Old Spice. Strong coffee. Beer. Menthol cigarettes. When I hear Johnny Cash, George Jones, or George Strait. When I see the Navy AD rating or someone chopping wood or burning leaves. When I eat biscuits and gravy or perfectly cooked pancakes that are fluffy in the middle and crunchy on the edges. I see him in my youngest son, the way he walks, talks, the witty things he says, and even some of his facial expressions. I miss my daddy every day, but I cherish those rare nights when he visits me in my dreams.

Bud Loyd
March 20, 1943 - February 17, 2012
Rest in peace.

To those who have lost loved ones. I hope you can find comfort in knowing they're still around you. Whether it's in the form of a dream, animal, song, smell, or a gentle breeze across your face, they're watching out for you.

ACKNOWLEDGEMENTS

Jennifer Bray-Weber. Thank you for everything. You are the blanket to my Linus, the net beneath my tightrope, the rum to my Coke, and you have taught me to believe in myself. Thank you for being the voice of reason when I write crazy stuff that is too "out there" to be reasonable. May you see many sparkling rainbows in your future. :-)

The Killion Group, Inc. Your ability to reach right into my head and put my ideas together into such beautiful designs and bring them to life will never cease to amaze me. Thank you for all your help.

Nina Cordoba. You are truly the Query Fairy and I bow at your feet offering endless praise and Cadbury Creme eggs.

My street team and Beta readers. Thank you for reading my stories, catching my mistakes, for loving my work and promoting me wherever you go.

My family. I have been a crazy loon this past year. Moving, adjusting, rewriting, more moving, revising, editing, rewriting, more revising, stressing, not cooking, not cleaning, not sleeping. . . This saga finally has its happy ending. Thank you for not giving up on me.

My writer friends. Thank you for your guidance, support, encouragement, critiques, promoting and sharing, workshops, co-insanity, and fun.

My nurse friends, Charray Ellis and Carrie Grandfield, thank you for your input about specific trauma injuries and how it would affect the patients. Dr. Kimberly Neathamer-Guillory, thank you for answering my bazillion OB/GYN questions.

My military cousin-in-law, Derrick Spires. Thank you for getting back to me so quickly and sharing your knowledge of the Middle East so my information and descriptions weren't way off.

Silver-Hart, LLC. Scott Silverii and Liliana Hart. Thank you for providing this great company with its industry, law enforcement, and public safety professionals for me to ask questions and get speedy, accurate responses.

My readers. Thank you for supporting me and loving my work. I do this for you.

ONE

"Please, God, let them be okay." Caroline prayed for her twins as she lay in the hospital bed for the second week in a row. Her eyes studied the monitors beside the bed. She was ready to have her babies and go home, but twenty-eight weeks wasn't quite long enough.

Her phone rang with a familiar tune, and Caroline released an exasperated sigh.

"Hey, Momma. Before you say a word, I'm fine. The babies are fine. We're all fine." This was what seemed like Emily Fontenot's five-thousandth phone call since Caroline was admitted to the hospital and put on bed rest. "They're taking great care of me. Stop worrying."

"Stop worrying?" Emily Fontenot snorted. "Right. That's like telling a dog not to pant. You're my daughter, and I'll be praying every second of the day until you and those babies are safe and sound."

"Well, hopefully you'll have to wait a while longer to see them." Caroline watched the needle scratch across the rolling paper of the NST monitor that detected the babies heartbeats. Non-stress tests were common while on bed rest, and everything looked okay, but she couldn't help but feel that something was wrong. One of the babies kicked in agreement.

"Has the doctor said anything new?" Emily asked.

"Now that I've finally decided what I want to do with my degree, Dr. Breaux said I can start shadowing the nurses in the maternity ward when I'm ready." Caroline knew her mom was fishing, and hated lying to her, even if it was a lie of omission, but she didn't want to worry her any further until she knew something concrete.

"Not the doctor I was referring to, I was talking about your OB, but that's great, honey. Don't rush into a job, though. I'll be happy to babysit, but you need to make sure you're ready to be a working mother. It's a tough job. Trust me." Emily's breath hitched, "And you miss out on so much during the early years."

"Mom…"

"Focus on a safe and successful delivery first, okay?"

"We're fine. Strong heartbeats all around. Plus, Ochsner has a level three NICU, so if they come early, they'll be in great hands." Caroline nervously eyed the monitor again. Maybe she was paranoid from the unexplained bleeding, but her instincts were usually spot on, and right now they were screaming. Caroline reassured her mother a few more times and ended the call, relieved to be off the phone. She loved her mom dearly, but was glad she'd stayed in Golden Meadow rather than coming with her to the hospital in New Orleans. Emily was a worrier, and Caroline didn't need more stress than she already had, nor did she want to needlessly worry her mom if everything was okay. She knew Emily Fontenot wouldn't be able to stay quiet if anything happened. Silence truly was golden.

Caroline smoothed her hand across her distended belly. She would miss this. The flutters and rolls, the hiccups at night after she ate a large bowl of ice cream, even the wallops to her full bladder. Well, maybe not that part.

The pregnancy had been smooth, aside from Caroline being the size of a barn, but the cramping and bleeding that started two weeks ago still hadn't stopped. It wasn't a lot of blood, but enough to have Caroline's doctor concerned. Losing too much blood could endanger her, and if she lost any more amniotic fluid the babies could suffocate. Therefore, she'd been on hospital bed rest receiving painful steroid shots nearly every day to help the development of the babies' lungs in case an emergency cesarean was needed. At least she'd been able to spend the Thanksgiving holiday with family in the bayou before coming up to New Orleans, or *town*, as her family referred to it.

Cade's exuberant smile greeted her as he held up a lovely bouquet of yellow flowers. "Hey, beautiful. How ya feeling?"

"Other than a numb butt and stiff legs, I'm okay, I guess." Caroline looked away so he wouldn't see right through her. If Cade knew she was worried about something he would never leave her side or get any rest.

"You sure?"

She nodded and motioned to the flowers. "Those for me?"

"Yes," he smiled. "I thought about getting certain colors to celebrate the sex of the babies, but I figured you wouldn't like that very much."

"You figured right. We don't have to spoil the surprise for everyone else just because we know." She smiled. "Those are perfect. Yellow is bright and happy." She glanced out the window at the gloomy winter day. "Right now we could all use a little sunshine."

He kissed her forehead and grinned. "You are my sunshine. My *ornery* sunshine," he sang. "Your mother is going crazy wondering if she's having grandsons or granddaughters. She's asked me every day for the past two months to let her in on the secret."

"It'll just make it that much sweeter when she gets to see for herself."

Cade's eyes sparkled with humor. "Mean. Just plain mean." He chuckled and held her hand. "You ready?" She nodded. "Scared?"

"A little. I know they'll probably have to do a C-section, and I'm not looking forward to being cut open, but, considering the alternative of squeezing two pineapple-sized babies out of such a small opening, I'm okay with it."

"Maybe they'll be cantaloupes," he said, winking.

Caroline laughed, though it didn't feel genuine and Cade noticed. A janitor passed by her room pushing a bleach mop, and distracted the moment. The sting of powerful antiseptic invaded her senses allowing Caroline to look away to cover her nose. She didn't want to worry him with her unexplainable fears. He'd been strong, weathering anything life threw at them, but she didn't want to reveal how truly frightened she was about her impending delivery. Or the unshakable gloom that had recently settled on her shoulders.

She drew in a breath, "As long as they're healthy, I don't care what size fruit they are. My body will heal."

"What's that?" Cade gestured to a gold chain lying on the bed beside her.

"Oh, someone sent it with a bouquet of flowers." She picked it up and flipped the solid gold, coin-shaped medallion over in her hand to study the design. "I don't know who, but it's really pretty. Mesmerizing, even." The cross on the back resembled crosshairs. "I thought it was the emblem of a Saint, so I've been rubbing it and making wishes like crazy." She snorted, but when she looked up, Cade's expression shocked her. He jerked it from her grasp with a scowl and studied it before his fingers closed tightly around the gold and squeezed. She thought it might shatter in his fierce grip.

"Who sent this to you?" he growled out the words like an angry grizzly.

Stunned by his reaction, she could only sit with her mouth gaping open.

"Tell me where you got it," he said quietly. His anger was almost tangible as he drew in a slow calculated breath and looked up. "Now," he said with a raised brow. His hardened expression frightened her.

"I told you, I don't know. There was no card with it. Cade, what's wrong?"

"When?" His voice was barely audible as he whispered through clenched teeth while glaring murderously at the golden pendant.

She shrugged, "Yesterday. Maybe the day before."

"When exactly, Caroline?" Cade tore his hands through his hair in frustration. "When did you touch this damned thing?"

"I don't know." Her hands trembled from his tone. What was his problem? "I touched it when I found it. I thought you sent it at first, but there was no card. I assume it came from family or friends. Cade, what's wrong? I don't understand. What's with the extreme revulsion to a simple necklace?" She held her palm out for it. "It's pretty." He sat for several moments quietly staring at the object, choking it as if it had murdered his entire family, and he refused to hand it to her.

She dropped her hand to her lap. He clearly didn't want her to have it. But why? "I like it. Have you seen it before? Do you know what it is? Is it the crest of a Saint? For protection?

Health?" His silence infuriated her. "Tell me something! You're just sitting there. What's wrong?"

Finally, he spoke without looking at her. "Nothing," he mumbled as he shoved it into his front pocket. He smiled, but it was clearly forced. "It's okay, love. I'll take care of it."

Unconvinced, she dropped the subject anyway. When Cade decided not to discuss something, he was a vault and it was a waste of energy to probe him for more. "You kind of freaked me out. You okay?"

"It's nothing. Sorry. I'm just a little anxious. I'm ready for you and these angels to be home with me. That's all." He kissed her double-decker belly that had blocked the view of her feet for the last two months.

"Well, relax. So, is it a Saint's medallion?"

"Definitely not a Saint." He leaned close to her face, kissing her forehead, nose, cheek, jaw, and neck until her heart raced in anticipation. His supple lips finally brushed hers as he whispered, "You relax, Mrs. Beauregard." He kissed her into a stupor, adding, "Don't worry about a thing except resting and letting everyone pamper you."

"Beau. A minute?" Cade's best friend, Matteo DeLuka—Runway, as his friends called him—peeked around the door frame. His shoulders were as rigid as his voice.

Cade started toward him, but Caroline grabbed his arm.

"No, please stay. Whatever he has to say, I want to know, too. Especially if it has anything to do with me."

Runway glanced cautiously at Cade and tilted his head.

"Caroline, I. . ." Cade stammered. He was acting very strange, and Caroline's intuition was on high alert.

"Please. I want to know what has him so stressed out." She glanced at Runway. "You see my best friend more than I do. Is Kristy okay?"

Cade shrugged and nodded for him to continue. Runway took a deep breath and stepped into the room carrying a small gift bag.

"Kristy's doing wonderful. She sends her love." His sharp eyes studied her. "How are you feeling?"

"Fine," she snapped, annoyed he was beating around the bush. "Peachy. What's up?"

Runway had been in Louisiana to help protect the Fontenot family since Caroline's graduation party last year where her younger brother, Remy was shot. She thought he'd gone back to California last month. Now her heart thundered against her ribcage at what could possibly have him back in town and this serious.

Runway spoke softly, focusing solely on Cade. "As you know, since Mr. Fontenot filed for divorce, April's been in New Orleans. She's pissed that he's divorcing her and has her lawyers working overtime to fight back. She's trying to take him for all she can. Anyway, she's walking the line, living a clean, risk-free life, thus proving her involvement in the attempts on your family is impossible. She's obviously the prime suspect in your brother-in-law's shooting, even if she didn't pull the trigger, but there's not a trace of evidence to implicate her or connect her to the unexplained things that have happened to Caroline."

April had been the stereotypical wicked stepmother since Caroline showed up on Eddie's doorstep. If looks could kill, Caroline would already be rotting away in the Fontenot family vault next to her ancestors. Aside from being hateful to her, April was nasty toward everyone Caroline cared about. April's hospitality and kindness didn't extend past her own nose.

Caroline struggled to hide her dislike for the woman at the mere mention of her name.

Runway's lips pressed into a thin line. "We can't pin her for anything, but I've done some recon over the past few months."

He cleared his throat and glanced at Caroline before continuing. "She changed her routine two weeks ago. Yesterday, at her yoga class where she usually stays for an hour, she came out after only twenty minutes. She sat in her car, unmoving, for about fifteen minutes, then drove to a Catholic church."

Caroline snorted, surprised the church didn't burst into flames.

"She seemed rushed as she ran through the rain into the building," he held up the gift bag, "with this." Runway scowled, his dark brows shading his mint-green eyes. "It was hanging on the door handle when I got here just now." He nodded at Caroline, "I hope you don't mind that I checked it out." He handed it to Cade, "Easy, man," he warned. "She's been busy."

Beau peeked in it, closed it quickly, and cursed as he threw it back to Runway.

Unfazed by Cade's reaction, Runway continued. "Obviously, I can't be certain, but I believe this is why the bleeding started when it did."

"What?" Caroline said. "What is it? Tell me." She'd been right to be uneasy. Something *was* off.

Cade breathed deeply, squeezing his eyes closed, and kissed her forehead before turning his back with clenched fists. Caroline searched Runway's face for an explanation. Runway pursed his lips as he presented a palm-sized burlap doll with auburn hair wrapped around its waist and two red-tipped pins stuck precisely where her womb would be.

"Voodoo?" Caroline searched Cade's face for answers, but he wouldn't look directly at her. *Why not?* "If this is why my bleeding started then why is it just now showing up? If April is responsible, why now? Why not whenever she made it?"

"It's a message," Runway said. "Like a game of Poker," he offered. "She's raising the stakes."

Caroline tossed the doll back to Runway like it had zapped her. "No. Just no. That's ridiculous. It can't be what's wrong with me. A stupid doll couldn't have caused my bleeding. Voodoo's not… There's no. . . That's not possib—"

"Damn her!" Cade snatched the doll from Runway and squeezed it.

"Cade," Caroline gripped her chest and struggled to breathe. "Cade," she gasped. Her heart raced against the crushing weight of her lungs. The pain unbearable. He didn't hear her. "Cade. . ." she choked out again, but he still didn't respond.

Runway heard and reached for Cade's arm only to grab thin air as Cade jerked away from him and paced the floor. "Beau," he said, not realizing Caroline's twisted face was from actual discomfort.

"No. She's messed with the wrong guy. I will end this. She's done." He brushed his fingertips over the red metallic balls of the pins protruding from the womb of the voodoo doll as Caroline cringed from the excruciating pain. "Go to hell, April." He ripped the pins out and threw them across the room.

Caroline shrieked and gripped her swollen belly. Shrill alarms blasted through the small space, and Cade rushed to her side as she arched her back and cried out. The searing pain in her abdomen silenced any coherent thoughts.

"Oh no, Caroline! Oh God. What happened? Runway, get somebody in here now!"

Fire ripped through her lower torso, permeating across her chest and extremities as she tore at the sheets in agony. The fetal monitors showed powerful uterine contractions, but the babies' heart rates were dropping. No! She couldn't lose her twins! Panic stuttered her thoughts. What could she do? How could she stop her body from rejecting what she loved most in the world? *Oh please, God, help me.*

"Talk to me, baby. Please. You gotta tell me what's happening. What can I do?" His eyes darted between her and the flashing screens next to the bed.

Was someone murdering an animal, or were those terrible screeching cries coming from her own mouth? "My babies! They're dying!" Sobs wracked her with the desolation and certainty of her words. They hit her like a tsunami slamming against the beach. "Get them out!"

"Where the hell is everyone?" Cade bellowed again. "Can't y'all hear this?

Get in here, something's wrong!"

Sweat rolled down the side of Caroline's throbbing temple. What had gone wrong? She'd obeyed every single order the doctor gave her. She panted hard trying to catch her breath while the world around her fell away. Pain in her core morphed into a strange burning sensation spreading all the way down to her toes. This wasn't right. Not one of her baby books described this as part of labor. It was all wrong. She refused to believe this was all because of a stupid voodoo doll.

A foul metallic taste washed through her mouth, cutting off her air. The pain, the burning, didn't matter. Her babies needed oxygen. Nothing made sense in her disoriented, distracted mind. Concentrating hard, she sucked in a small amount of fresh air through the putrid waste coating her throat and tongue.

“Caroline,” Cade said, snapping her back in the moment, “look at me.” His breath warmed her face. “Don’t you give up! They’re gonna take care of you and the babies, okay? Do you hear me? Stay strong and keep your eyes on me.”

“I love you,” she whispered in pants through her pain. Fluid gushed from between her legs and drenched the sheets.

“Somebody get in here now!” Cade shouted for the nurses as he frantically searched Caroline’s body for further signs of distress. The stinging heat running through her lower half was replaced by numbing cold.

"Cade. I can't feel my toes. My legs!” Another powerful contraction scorched through her followed by that strange warmth centered between her legs. “What’s happening to me?” Pressure built in her lower abdomen until she thought her insides would explode. She pushed up on her arms in time for a sweet, pleasant rush. Relief. She breathed easy for the first time since Cade pulled the pins.

Relief was momentary, however, as an ever widening circle of red spread across the bed linens. Blood. More blood than could be possible came out of her. She gawked at it in horror.

“Oh, no! No, no, no,” Cade cried.

“Sir, you have to back up. Please go out in the hall.” The nurse shoved him out of the way as she pushed the call button next to Caroline’s head. “Page Dr. Guillory. We need an OR STAT. Room 302 is hemorrhaging and needs an emergency C-section.”

“Please! Save my babies! Don’t let them die!” She screamed at the nurse, but the woman wouldn’t look at her. Why was this nurse ignoring her? She said it aloud, right?

“Caroline, please, stay with me. Don’t leave me.” His voice came from above her head now. Why was he talking crazy? Why in the world would she ever leave him? The doctors and nurses were here working on the babies. She was fine, just sleepy.

"Her blood pressure's dropping."

Cade's hands were on her face. "Please, baby. I need you. You're my everything, do you hear me? Stay with me."

"Sir—"

"I'm not leaving her. I'm staying right here."

Peace engulfed Caroline. Calm. Warmth. The commotion had settled, and Cade's pleading played a background melody to a high-pitched, solid, steady tune she'd heard before.

"We're losing her. I need a crash cart," a distant cry exclaimed.

The need to react danced around her, but the hypnotic pitch—a steady hum like a gentle breeze rustling across crisp autumn leaves—wouldn't allow it. Peaceful. Her body, warm again and light as air, floated toward a blinding light. She must be sedated now. That was it. A lovely hallucination. One she didn't want to end.

TWO

"I'm coming, baby." Cade darted through the coughs and sneezes in the Emergency Room using his guitar as a bull dozer. Caroline loved it when he sang to her, and that's just what he intended to do. Last fall when she moved back to Golden Meadow, she'd asked him to write her a song. "I'll do it later," he'd always said. Later never came, and now he didn't know if she'd even hear him.

He caught a glance of his reflection while passing an open restroom. Exhaustion pulled at his features. Staying up late and waking up early to perfect this song had him running on fumes, but it wouldn't stop him from singing to her all day if he must. The hospital chaplain recommended talking to her regularly to create a roadmap for her to find her way back. Cade snorted. He'd dress in tights and do the Irish jig if it meant she'd come back to him.

He'd texted Runway to tell him where he was headed, and his best friend waited in the lobby on Caroline's floor. Cade had witnessed every look, grimace, or blush Matteo DeLuka could make with his ebony eyebrows after their Navy SEAL team nicknamed him "Runway" for emulating an Italian super model, but Cade's scalp prickled with Runway's current solemn expression. His reluctance to let go immediately from his brotherly hug was a sickening indication that something was wrong.

"What's up?"

"You look like hell. Have you slept at all?"

Cade shrugged impatiently. "A few combat naps. I'm fine," he snapped. "How's Caroline?"

Runway released him and stepped back, keeping his hand on his shoulder. "She's still out, but the doctor didn't look happy when she asked for you. Pretty sure Caroline's status is the same, but prepare yourself in case it's something with the babies."

Cade's stomach plummeted to his knees, and tunnel vision swirled through his eyes. "Well, let's go find out before I lose it." When they arrived at the nurses' station in Labor and Delivery, Dr. Guillory frowned over a patient chart. Light brown hair fell into her eyes, but her welcoming smile disguised her fatigue. Praised as one of the top specialists in her field with a warm bedside manner, Cade figured he was about to experience firsthand her skills with relaying bad news. He took a deep breath.

Her brow creased as she took in his haggard appearance, but Cade only focused on the chart in her hand.

"Mr. Beauregard, may I speak with you for a moment?" She lead the way carrying the chart she'd been scribbling in, which Cade assumed was Caroline's, and, judging by her tense expression, she didn't have good news. Dr. Guillory motioned for him to sit as she walked around the large mahogany desk to her black leather chair. It was the principal's office all over again.

"Before we go over Caroline's test results, Mr. Beauregard, there are some things I need to tell you."

His stomach churned. Cade tightened every muscle in his body to contain the earthquake from his core. She smiled, but it didn't reach her eyes.

"Your daughter is doing well. She's breathing on her own, her heartbeat is strong and steady, and her weight is balancing around three pounds, two ounces. We're keeping the feeding tube intact so we can be certain she's getting enough formula, and she'll need to stay in the NICU for a while longer, but I think she'll be just fine."

"And my son?"

The doctor's vigilant eyes didn't leave his. "Caroline's bleeding was caused by placental abruption. The placenta shears off of the uterus wall causing bleeding and painful contractions. It's a risk factor with someone carrying multiples. Because each baby had their own placenta, I believe your daughter was stronger because hers was thoroughly intact. Caroline's bleeding had been minimal because only a portion of your son's placenta had detached, but not enough to show up on the tests."

She cleared her throat and stared at the folder as if garnering the courage to continue. "We think the rest of it detached yesterday causing the sharp, tearing pain and massive bleeding." Her eyes found his again and grounded him in place, though the room spun. "We're not sure exactly what caused it. Sometimes a quick jerky movement or a fall can do it, but she was lying in bed."

Cade gripped his head and rubbed his brow, mentally cursing himself. He knew exactly why it happened. "The baby?" he asked.

She shook her head, and Cade didn't know it was possible to hurt even worse.

"I'm so sorry, Mr. Beauregard. His heart was just too weak and he passed away this morning."

Her lips moved, but her voice only echoed behind the freight train crashing full speed through his head. In his slow-motion state of shock, he noticed random things. The jagged cuticle that Dr. Guillory furiously picked at on her right thumb. The nicked corner of the extravagant desk, the computer monitor flashing pictures of a healthy baby boy. Her concerned, manicured eyebrows peeked in the middle revealing a few forehead wrinkles. No amount of compassion or sympathy would make his son breathe again. His solid control teetered on the edge of mass destruction.

"I tried to call you, but I didn't think it would be appropriate to leave this news in a voicemail."

Cade swallowed back his tears. He needed to speak, but the frog in his throat complicated things. He coughed. "Do you know why his heart was weak? Did he have a murmur or something? I mean, there had to be some cause or reason for his heart to just stop beating, right?"

"His condition was more critical than your daughter's. He was much smaller than she was weighing only two pounds. Because his placenta was separating, he wasn't getting the appropriate amount of oxygen needed for proper organ function. . ." Cade tuned out her clinical terminology as the grief crashed down. This was his fault. He should have left that doll in the bag instead of reacting. He should've gone after April when he first found out who she really was and forced her to tell him everything—why she lied, why she was after his family, who she was working with. Then he could have stopped her before she had a chance to hurt anyone else.

He was either stupid or cursed. Or both. He knew it. He was incapable of caring for another human being. The list of fatalities he'd left in his wake had him wishing he'd died while serving his country overseas. An honorable death far away from the possibility of hurting—or killing—someone else he loved. Cade's heart fell. If only he'd listened to Caroline's cries before pulling out those damned pins! He needed her to wake up so he could tell her how sorry he was, and that he was the reason their son had died.

Dr. Guillory released a frustrated sigh that momentarily snapped him out of his shame and self-loathing. "He had what we call 'late decelerations' indicating fetal distress. It's very common with large abruptions. . ."

How would he explain this without crushing Caroline even more when she woke and learned their son didn't make it? ". . .and the baby would exsanguinate, or bleed to death. . .resuscitative measures to the mother. . .but Caroline wasn't contracting."

She touched his arm jerking him from his guilt. "I'm terribly sorry for your loss, Mr. Beauregard. In all my years, all my deliveries, I have never seen anything like this."

Cade knew why. Voodoo curses probably weren't on the OB/GYN curriculum in med school.

Cade's mind swam with all of the medical jargon, and his voice twisted with the knot in his throat. His next question cracked out in a whisper.

"Caroline?"

Dr. Guillory's voice softened. "Unfortunately, a complication to placental abruption is something called Disseminated Intravascular Coagulation, or DIC. It's not limited to pregnant women as it can occur in men, non-pregnant women, and children, though it's worse regarding pregnancy due to the placental site being an open, bleeding wound. It's a pathological—"

"Dumb it down for me, Doc."

She pursed her lips. "She's stable now. Her complications are treatable and shouldn't be long term. We're lucky she was already here in the hospital when this happened, allowing us to quickly deliver the babies and treat her properly."

Lucky. That was debatable. Cade dropped his face to his hands.

She stood and walked around the front of her desk and leaned against it directly in front of him. "She's still in a coma, but she's going to be okay." Her familiar smile he'd grown accustomed to over the weeks did little to reassure him. "Her brain activity is normal. Now all we have to do is wait for her to return to us. This could be a good thing. Her body needs time to properly heal and rest."

Cade's throat burned with pent up emotion. Something squeezed his heart and throat to the point he thought he might implode. If not for the stinging pain burning a hole in his chest he'd have bet this was only a bad dream. But it wasn't. He'd caused this extraordinarily real nightmare. Not a day of his life would pass when he wouldn't regret that split second of impulsive anger. And now he may lose his wife, too.

"I'm sure you'll agree that Caroline wouldn't rest if she were awake right now."

Her words threw him over the edge, and the pain conquered the grit.

Cade bawled like a baby in front of this woman who waited patiently while he sobbed uncontrollably in her office. The barking sounds penetrating the small space sounded foreign to his own ears, he couldn't imagine her thoughts as she awkwardly patted his shoulder. He didn't care, though. His life—his reason for trudging through each miserable day to come—crumbled before him.

"She'll come back. Just keep doing what you've been doing. Talk to her," she motioned to his guitar case, "even better, sing to her. Caroline's body and spirit have been through a lot. She simply needs a path to get back to you, so give her one. She's got a bittersweet package waiting for her, the loss of one child, but the joy of another. Your love and support will get her through this difficult time. You have a beautiful, healthy daughter, Mr. Beauregard. Embrace that."

He nodded and swiped the tissue down his face. "Thank you, Dr. Guillory. Can I see my babies?"

"Both of them?" she asked.

He nodded.

Disapproval strained her features. Perhaps she thought Cade wouldn't be able to handle it, but this was something he needed to do. He needed the closure. "I don't know if—"

"Please," Cade whispered, focusing hard on her face with the most compelling look he could manage. She wasn't convinced. "I need to see him. Please. I know it will be difficult, but I need," his breath hitched, "I need to say goodbye."

The doctor's face relaxed. "Certainly. Come on, I'll walk you over there."

Cade avoided eye contact with Runway as he walked out of the office. Runway squeezed Cade's shoulder to comfort him though he didn't know what happened, but Cade couldn't tell him right now. All Cade could manage was a nod as they followed the doctor. This agony surpassed Jenny's death. He thought he'd never experience anything worse than the mind-numbing grief he endured after his pregnant ex-girlfriend died while carrying his son. Cade took responsibility for her accident and, ultimately, their deaths. But now, knowing without a doubt he was the cause of his baby's death, he'd fallen into the belly of hell. The gaping hole in his chest ached. In Afghanistan, he'd watched his friends die in his arms, but even that didn't compare with the grief of losing another child. Another son.

When they approached the NICU, Cade's raw nerves twitched, allowing minimal control of his facial expressions. He mustered enough strength to make it through. A quiet pained sigh escaped Runway when she brought the small covered box over to them. It could have been take-out from a restaurant, it was that small. She cautiously set it down on the table in front of Cade and studied his face, likely gauging his control. She asked the nurses to step out and give them a minute.

"Mr. Beauregard, are you sure you want to do this? Anyone with a heart will understand if you don't. You won't be weak or less of a man if you don't want to look."

His conflicted face twisted before his jaw set while staring down at the box. "No, I have to do this. I didn't get to see my first. . . I want to see him." His gaze flicked to hers filled with sympathy and compassion. "Please, Dr. Guillory. I need to see my son."

Runway stood quietly by his side with his hand on Cade's shoulder. Cade was grateful for the physical contact, leeching from his best friend what little strength he had left. When she opened the box, the bones in Cade's body turned to rubber. Every ounce of energy instantly drained from his body leaving him weak and limp. The world stopped spinning and time stood still. His eyes froze on the beautiful, perfect, tiny face.

Peaceful and calm, his son's eyes rested in an eternal sleep. His perfect, miniature features reflected Cade's own face, strangling him with a pain he'd only imagined existed. His ears rang, and he dropped to his knees as the breath in his lungs whooshed out in a strangled sob. Runway knelt beside him and wrapped his arm around Cade, pulling his face to his chest. He broke down and wept harder than he'd ever allowed himself in his twenty-eight years. He didn't care how it appeared, Cade was grateful Runway caught him when he fell howling into his arms. Dr. Guillory's sniffles harmonized with the rhythmic sobs convulsing through Cade's body.

Once Cade's sobs subsided, Runway helped him to his feet without releasing his hold. Cade took another glance at the sleeping angel and lost it again. He spun around, and, recognizing his anguish, Runway gripped him tightly in a brotherly embrace. Cade held on to him for support with a painful, bruising grip.

Runway's strength kept him sane. Cade squeezed him harder as his sobs intensified. Matteo DeLuka was the only person he'd ever known who would drop everything and fly across the country, the world even, to help him, and Cade completely took him for granted. He didn't deserve Runway's loyalty, but he was grateful for it.

"Why does God not want me to have a son?" Cade bit his bottom lip in misplaced anger. The metallic tinge of blood reminded him this wasn't just a horrific nightmare.

"I don't know, brother. But He did give you a daughter who needs her father. Pull yourself together, man. Caroline needs you, too."

"I can't lose her, Runway." He swayed his head side-to-side, slowly, "Either of them. I can't go through this again. I'm not strong enough."

"Yes you are. And you're not alone. I've got your back, and you have a great family to help you through this." Runway hugged him tightly. "Your girls are going to make it, Beau. But you have to believe it. Be strong for them."

This was one of many times they'd depended on each other to make it through hard times. Shortly after they'd graduated BUDs training to become Navy SEALs, Cade stood by Runway when his parents died. He'd let him pound his chest like a punching bag to release his anger and grief until Runway felt better.

Cade straightened his clothes and wiped his face with his shirt.

"Squared away?" Runway asked.

He nodded his thanks to Runway who silently returned the understanding. Cade turned to Dr. Guillory who was wiping her nose with a crumpled, nearly disintegrated tissue.

Cade drew in a ragged breath, his cheeks puffing as he blew it out. "Thank you, Doctor. I'd like to see my daughter now."

She smiled and nodded as she carefully closed the lid to the tiny cardboard coffin. "I'll see to it he is in the right hands, Mr. Beauregard. Again, I'm really sorry. Let's go see your daughter."

Runway clapped his hand roughly on Cade's shoulder and pulled him close to kiss the side of his head. "I love you, bro."

Cade nudged him with his elbow and smirked. "Thanks. I love you, too. Now let's keep that mushy crap to a minimum."

Runway flashed a face-splitting, boyish smile as he punched Cade's arm back. "You know you dig it."

"Seriously, though. Thanks for being here. I can always count on you, even after all those years I refused to stay in touch. I'm really sorry. I should've called. Blood or not, you're my brother."

"Forgiven. The road goes both ways, you know. I hope you can forgive me for not tracking you down and making you talk to me." Cade agreed and cursed the stupid, ever-present lump in his throat again. Runway placed his hands on Cade's shoulders so they were eye-to-eye. "This crazy thing called life—nobody said it was easy." His playful crooked grin didn't disguise the tough times he'd endured at such a young age.

Another slapping hug, and Cade mumbled their all-too-familiar Navy SEAL motto. "The only easy day was yesterday."

"Hooyah, brother. Let's go see your baby girl."

Getting access to enter the crowded NICU was like being screened to go into a hazmat situation. After showing identification to prove Cade was the father and Runway was his guest, they scrubbed their hands and arms up to their elbows, then used antibacterial foam. Next, they draped sanitary gowns over their clothes, covered their heads with hair nets, and secured masks over their faces. A nurse led the way to a clear incubator with a pink tag labeled "Baby Beauregard." Cade's wounded heart swelled, crowding the butterflies flapping in his stomach. She was the size of his hand with wires and tubes all over her, but she was the most beautiful sight he'd ever laid eyes on. And she was his. Cade smiled at Runway who grinned just as big.

"She's cute, huh?"

Runway nodded. "Oh yeah, dude. She's beautiful. . .a tiny little princess. Does she have a name?"

"No, we couldn't agree. We wanted to wait and get a good look at them before we chose permanent names. You know, to see what they looked like, and which names fit them best."

Through a mixture of wonderment and fear, Cade asked the nurse if he could touch her. He wasn't comfortable holding her yet, all fragile and riddled with wires, but he wanted to put his hands on her.

"Yes, sir. Just place your hand through the holes on the side here." The older nurse's maternal presence set him at ease. Cade gingerly inserted his hand into the delicate area, and lightly rested his palm on her tiny, orange-sized head. Runway put his hand through a hole on the other side and touched her frail little legs that weren't much bigger around than his fingers. How could something, a human being, so small and delicate be alive? The rapid beeping from her heart monitor proved her strength.

"She's a fighter like her mother." Caroline would want to be here with him right now seeing their precious baby girl for the first time. Confident that his daughter was in good hands with the motherly-type nurse, Cade needed to see Caroline. He'd left his guitar in Dr. Guillory's office and they headed back to the Labor and Delivery floor. The pain from losing his son tormented him, but seeing his daughter, and hearing her powerful heartbeat stirred something deep within. It inspired him.

April Fontenot, Ana Morales, or whatever the hell her name was, had better hope she didn't cross paths with him any time soon. He couldn't promise complete control over his hands that currently itched to break her neck. Cade's son was dead while his daughter fought for her life in an incubator, and his wife was lost and wandering aimlessly somewhere in her unconscious mind while he sat on his thumb waiting for a miracle. April did this to his family. She dug something up that he thought was long dead, and his new mission in life was to make her pay dearly for her crimes.

Cade's gruff, menacing voice exuded his deadly warning. "Runway, if you see April before I do, keep her away from me. I might just kill her with my bare hands."

Runway watched him, searching for an ounce of humor in Cade's eyes. He must have realized the sincerity of his threat. Runway nodded. "I've got your back. Always."

Cade grabbed his guitar and made his way to Caroline's room. His sharp eyes scanned the halls, secretly hoping April would show up and give him the opportunity to squeeze the life from her. It was a hunger. A bloodthirsty desire that he hadn't felt in a very long time.

THREE

"Hello? Anyone out there?" Caroline drifted down the halls of the dark hospital. Silently floating from one hallway to the next, she was unsure what she was searching for. Why were all the lights off? Something, unease or doubt, gnawed at her. Where was everyone? Had she missed something, or someone, she needed to find? It was as if the eerie, vacant hospital had been shut down. No beeps from monitors, no staff chatting, no phones ringing or babies crying. She'd never witnessed anything this strange. Surely this was a dream. Hospitals never closed, right?

Her body felt strange. Light and airy, but also tired. And her easily-distracted mind was even more spaced out. Like she was back in college pulling all-nighters with zero sleep, forgetting something important like pants. The ominous silence in the desolate hallways reminded her of when she used to watch *The Twilight Zone*. She peeked around corners waiting for the scary monster to jump out, but there was consistently nothing. Literally a dead zone. Where was everyone and why couldn't she focus? She stopped scouting the unusually empty halls and tried to solve that mystery. Perhaps the scatterbrained sensations would dissolve if she could figure out where she was.

Movement caught Caroline's attention, drawing her in that direction. Her body resisted her mind's urgency and continued at its leisurely, haunting pace. Faint beeping of a heart monitor reached her ears. She closed her eyes to focus, allowing her body to follow the muted sound, and when she opened them again, she'd landed in a patient's room. The bed was occupied by a young woman who looked remarkably like herself. She was sleeping, or perhaps in a coma. Pale with dark circles beneath her eyes, her lips were white like her skin, and she was connected to a plethora of tubes and wires. The only sounds were the steady whooshing of the breathing machine and the rhythmic beeping of the heart monitor. Awareness tingled down her spine and she was officially creeped out. This was all wrong. Something had happened. Something terrible. Who was this patient, and where was everyone else? Where was *she*?

Caroline turned to call out for someone, anyone, but froze mid-breath. Directly in front of her, standing within reach, was a solid figure of Rachel, her great, great, great grandmother. She wore the same white nightdress she had worn in all of Caroline's dreams two summers ago. The warm inner glow emitting from her like a children's glowworm toy set off alarms in Caroline's abstracted mind. A chilling realization. *I must be dead.*

Caroline peeled her gaze from the bright, beautiful figure and glanced back to the sickly girl in the bed.

Was that her? If so, her heart was still beating, and she wasn't dead. What the. . .? Caroline turned back to Rachel who ogled her in wonderment. A proud, maternal expression.

"Rachel? Why are you here? Why am *I* here? Am I dead, dreaming, or hallucinating?"

Rachel's flawless adolescent face transformed from admiration to reassurance as she smiled. "Hello, Caroline. You are not any of those things. You are stuck in the Astral realm of unconsciousness. Your body has suffered trauma and you need to get your soul back inside it before too much time passes." She paused, tilting her head as she regarded Caroline. "You look much like I did."

Against all her efforts, Caroline could not remember what happened to cause her to lose consciousness. Why couldn't she remember? She struggled to keep the rising panic from her voice.

"What happened? I can't remember anything." She glanced back at the shriveled shell of her body. "Why am I so sick?"

In her own obvious bemusement, Rachel ignored her questions and stared blankly at the walls. This outer realm of unconsciousness must be screwing with their ability to focus. Though, Caroline had to admit, even panicked she still held an overwhelming sense of peace. A very tranquil sensation for which she was thankful. To have been only eighteen when she died, Rachel's spirit seemed older, more mature as she maternally caressed Caroline's cheek with her ice cold hand.

"You are a beautiful young lady. I am proud of all you've accomplished. Your strong, fighting spirit will help shield you, and he can do no harm if your faith remains strong. I'm not finished with you, darling, but for now I must protect you." Rachel drifted to the bedside, studied Caroline's empty human shell, and brushed her fingertips across Caroline's cheekbone. "I try to distract him, but he's very powerful," she whispered. "Caroline, you must reconnect with your body before he does." Her calm timbre diminished as she urged, "Please, Caroline. Go. Go before he finds you here." Her eyes flickered, frantically glancing around the room. "Go. Now."

"Wait. What? Where do I go? My body is right here. Before who finds me? George? Can he do that? Why is he trying to hurt me?" The panic seeped through the tranquility.

"Wait, Rachel! I have more questions. I need your help. How am I supposed to get back into my body? What do I do?" She observed her frail body and sighed. She didn't learn anything about this in nursing school.

All alone now with no idea how to get back to her body, Caroline racked her brain to remember what had happened before she wound up in the hospital near death. Rachel mentioned her husband. Cade. He must be the person she was searching for earlier. Why couldn't she concentrate? This was incredibly frustrating.

What happened with Cade that put her in here? As she approached the bed, an ache radiated through her abdomen. The padded midsection beneath the sheet hit her like a freight train. Her babies. April's voodoo doll. The pins. Cade pulled out the pins and. . .oh! The pain! Where were her babies? Where was Cade? Oh, Cade. . . His pleas for her to stay with him echoed in hallows of her memory, and she had failed. Oh, no. She had to get back to him.

There was movement just outside of the room. A shadow flitted through the already obscure hallways. Chills prickled her neck. She needed to find a way to get back with her body. She lay down on top of her empty vessel and tried to push her way back in, but that didn't work.

Though she desperately wanted to, she didn't scream, fearing the ominous shadow—no doubt George Callahan's spirit—would find her. Her ex-fiancé Trevor's great, great, great, or

“G3” as Cade referred to it, grandfather had killed Rachel, and now he was after her. Caroline didn’t understand his fixation. Why skip so many generations after Rachel? Was it because she strongly resembled her G3 grandmother? No matter, George was after Caroline. And her weak spirit stranded in an unknown realm she never knew existed couldn’t protect her. Caroline scurried up to the head of her body and put both hands on each side of her vessel’s face hoping to mentally will herself back. When that wasn't successful, there was only one thing left to do. Unsure if it would work, she had no other choice.

Caroline dropped to her knees beside the bed and prayed. She begged God to bring her back, preferably with a healthy body, to her family. She prayed for her babies to be okay, and for the strength to find her way back to them and Cade. After whispering, “Amen,” she instinctively looked up, her gaze colliding with a familiar set of large, piercing, crystal blue eyes framed by stringy, chin-length black hair. George Callahan casually leaned against the door frame flicking a large silver coin across his knuckles. His attractive pale face possessed the same bone structure as Trevor, only more angular with a sinister edge. He flipped the coin into the air before he caught it and flashed an evil grin.

“Hello, dollface.”

FOUR

"You're late." Kenneth Callahan scolded his son. "I told you to be here an hour ago. Where the hell have you been? Not with your little whore, I hope."

Trevor cracked his neck. "She's not a whore, Dad. Don't ever call her that again." His father had been riding him for weeks about his relationship with Jessica ever since she moved from Louisiana into his Chicago Penthouse flat six months ago. He'd never imagined hooking up with another southern girl, but she'd proven herself after curing his wicked hangover the night he'd started seeing ghosts.

"That's what you said about the last girl who had you by the balls." Kenneth snorted and made a rude gesture with his hand. "Guess you didn't learn your lesson. You bring the prints I need for the O'Malley project?"

"Yeah." Trevor slapped the rolls of blueprints onto his father's desk just as his phone vibrated. He checked the caller I.D. and frowned.

"Uh-oh. The wife? She's starting with that shit early. Better nip it now and train her right." Kenneth's brash laughter filled the room.

Trevor rolled his eyes as he walked out of the room. “Shut up, Dad.” Jessica wasn’t his wife, but he knew she was frustrated that he hadn’t presented her with a rock yet. She’d all but picked out the ring and left hints everywhere. His phone, his office, his pillow, hell, she’d even taped an advertisement for Tiffany & Co. above the toilet. He was in no hurry to drop to one knee considering it hadn't worked out so well for him last time with Caroline.

They were really perfect for each other. Sexual frustration was nonexistent, and sometimes she wanted it when he didn’t, which was completely unheard of for him. Jessica Robicheaux was nobody’s “little woman” in the bedroom, either. She commanded it, and more often than not, had her way with him. Of course, he didn’t mind. What man didn’t want to be dominated occasionally? But when she told him what to do, how to do it, where and when, it became more like a job than pleasurable sex. He missed the way Caroline would blush and shiver at a simple intimate touch. Jessica was impossible to seduce.

Trevor took a deep breath and slipped into a conference room a few doors down from his dad’s office before answering quietly.

“Yeah, what’s up?”

“Hey. It’s Beau. You sound stressed. No problems with our deal, I hope.”

“Nope. I’m good. How’s Caroline?”

“She’s fine.”

Maybe he’d imagined it, but the change in the gardener’s normally arrogant tone caught his attention. “Great. Put her on so I can talk to her.”

The only reason Trevor agreed to Beau’s harebrained idea was for Caroline. He understood why Beau had asked him for help. Kenneth Callahan owned all the land around the Fontenot plantation, and Caroline would want to live near her newfound daddy. The gardener had no choice but to offer to buy some of that property.

Of course, dear old dad would never sell it to a Fontenot. But Kenneth Callahan was all about business. Trevor tricked his father into signing the deed, along with a stack of papers for another deal, and sold the land to Beau's father right under Kenneth's nose. He'd suffer for it later, but what was done was done, and Trevor refused to be controlled by a family feud that should've ended over a century ago.

He smiled with satisfaction knowing that Caroline would have to think of him every time she admired her home. He would forever be on her mind in some way or another, and that made it all worth it. Trevor was probably the only, and by far the best, architect Beau knew. Besides, it was the least he could do for Caroline after the underhanded things his father did to her family. Setting up Trevor and Caroline's relationship with underhanded intentions, and hiring a hit man to off the family Patriarch over a silly vendetta isn't easily forgiven. As much as Trevor hated to admit it, his father would've succeeded with his plan if Beau hadn't interfered.

"That's not gonna happen."

"Why not?" The vein in Trevor's forehead pulsed with his rising temper.

"You don't need to talk to her to do your job. This is our agreement and has nothing to do with Caroline."

"I'm designing her house. It has everything to do with her. What's the real reason you won't let me talk to her?" Silence. "What's going on?"

"Nothing."

"You're lying."

"Drop it, Callahan. It's none of your business."

Trevor's jaw twinged. Something was wrong. He was used to Beau's vague responses regarding Caroline, but this was different. "Is she okay? Has something happened?"

"Nothing you need to worry about. Caroline is not your concern anymore."

"Listen closely, you backwoods dick," he hissed. "Caroline was mine first, and just because she didn't end up with me doesn't mean I don't still care about her. We were best friends before you rutted your ugly snout in the pig pen. If she's hurt or in danger, I want to know about it."

"The only person she's in danger from is your father. And hopefully he's as clueless about this plan as Caroline is?"

Trevor shoved his hand through his hair and clenched his jaw to keep from spewing the curse words on the tip of his tongue. This dude really pissed him off. "Of course." He lowered his voice. "I haven't told him anything. My staff is working on it under the radar." Trevor swore under his breath. "Seriously, tell me. Is she okay?" The delayed response tripped every alarm in his body.

"I told you. She's fine. Any updates? When can we start construction? Do you need anything else from me?"

Trevor stewed. This coonass was keeping something from him, he'd bet his firm on it.

"No. The land is in your father's name now and the blueprints are with my drafting department. I checked with them this morning. They were having issues with the elevation and flood plain requirements because of the marshland. I'll call you as soon as I hear anything else."

"Tell you what. . .email me. I. . .may not have signal to take your call for the next few days."

"Dude, I'm not stupid. I know you're not telling me something." Trevor's phone creaked from the pressure of his grip. "If I help you only to find out you double-crossed me, I will rip your balls off and shove them down your treacherous throat."

"Lay off, Callahan. I'm not double-crossing you." Beau let out a frustrated sigh. He sounded exhausted, and Trevor desperately wanted to know what this bastard was hiding. "Look, I know you're risking a lot by working with me, and I appreciate your help. Trust me, it wasn't easy for me to ask you for anything. I realized when you were down here last summer that you are not your father, and it's not fair for me to judge you based on your family." His voice hardened, "But leave Caroline out of this. Just email me when they're ready, okay?"

Pens bounced off the conference table as Trevor slammed his palm to the wood. Two passing women yelped in surprise and Trevor ignored them, speaking through clenched teeth, "Don't you get it, asshole? Caroline is the only reason I'm *doing* this." He squeezed his eyes closed, sucked in a calming breath, and pressed his forehead against the cool wall. "Just tell me she's okay." Another long pause set his teeth on edge.

"She will be. I gotta go."

Trevor chucked his phone on the table, tore his hands through his hair, and stared at a knock-off Monet painting for several long minutes while sorting through his rage, worry, and confusion. What the hell did he mean by that? *She will be.* Why couldn't that arrogant shit just tell him what the hell was going on? He stooped to pick up his phone and stomped back into his dad's office, fuming and cursing that cocky son of a bitch's pompous attitude. Beau didn't realize just who he was dealing with.

"What's got your panties in a wad?" Kenneth pulled his reading glasses off and zeroed in on Trevor's hostility. "Was that your girlfriend?" Trevor ignored him. "What, is she PMSing?" he mocked. When Trevor still didn't acknowledge his nosy attempts, Kenneth grew angry. "Son, I don't take too kindly to being ignored. If that bitch is coming to my office to raise a stink because she broke a nail I need to—"

"Stop." Trevor held his hand up. "Don't even go there, Dad. You don't have a. . ." He paced the room while carefully selecting his response. He didn't want his dad snooping around, and if he pissed off the ever-nosy, untrusting Kenneth Callahan, that's just what he would do. "Jess is on a Caribbean cruise with her parents. She's not coming anywhere near here for another two weeks. Relax." Trevor breathed and rubbed the back of his neck. He chuckled thinking of Jessica showing his dad just how worried she'd be about a broken nail. She was practically a MMA fighter. She'd jack him up and have him begging for mercy.

"So who was it then?"

"One of my clients. A complication with an ongoing project, that's all."

"What kind of complication?"

Why wouldn't he just let it go. "Nothing I can't handle," Trevor muttered.

He tuned Kenneth out and focused on his cell phone to check his email. He would browse flights to New Orleans later when he wasn't in his father's office. If Beau wouldn't tell him what was wrong with Caroline, he'd go down there and find out himself.

"Where's the party, boys? I thought you high-end executives were supposed to be living it up here in Chi-town."

Trevor's skin crawled as his gaze fell on the miserable face from his past. A face that screwed everything up for him. What the hell was April Fontenot doing in his dad's office?

FIVE

"Come back to me, love." Cade pressed his lips to Caroline's forehead hoping for a response, and, with the painful absence of one, he sank into a nearby chair. "Where are you, sweet girl? Why can't you wake up?" He squeezed her hand and waited for her to squeeze it back. Nothing.

"Dammit, Caroline!" He jiggled her shoulders before finally dropping his face into his hands and sobbing. In all the risks of childbirth, he never imagined this would happen. At least he hadn't lost her, for that he was thankful. But he didn't exactly *have* her, either. That was almost worse than the alternative. So close, yet so far away.

He wouldn't give up. Caroline was a fighter, as was he. If he had to come to the hospital to read, talk, or sing to her every day just in case she heard his voice, he would. Eating and sleeping were pointless, anyway. He wouldn't rest or enjoy a savory meal until he could have both of his girls alive and well by his side. Until then he would alternate visiting the NICU and Caroline's room.

Cade scanned his wife for any sign that she was present. Maybe she was simply locked in her body and couldn't find her way out. Her eyes were closed as if she slept peacefully, and her skin, though pale, was smooth and warm to the touch. Physically, she was okay. So why wouldn't she just wake up? Cade swore under his breath and pinched the bridge of his nose to release the tension. He couldn't remember the last time in his life he'd talked this much. He'd told stories and sang to the empty walls more in the past few days than he'd spoken to any human being in the past ten years. It didn't matter, though. He'd do whatever it took to get Caroline back in his arms.

He had to admit it was pretty fun to get a rise out of Callahan. There was method to his madness in asking him to help design his and Caroline's new home. Cade gambled on Trevor's propensity to buy Caroline's affection when he'd offered to pay handsomely for the property that Kenneth Callahan had purchased two years ago. And if Trevor was invested in the property, maybe he could keep his daddy from targeting it further. It didn't hurt that the cocky bastard was actually a pretty skilled architect.

Cade had done his research, and Trevor was highly regarded throughout the Midwest. He'd won awards for his help in designing well-known skyscrapers for Fortune 500 companies in Illinois, Indiana, Wisconsin and Michigan. Still, Cade had to keep Trevor at arm's length. He didn't need or want him getting attached to his old flame and moving in. Though she'd never admit it, Caroline still had a soft spot for Trevor.

"Dude, you look like hell. Go home. Shave, shower, and sleep, or when she wakes up you're going to scare her right back into a coma with one glance."

Runway's lopsided grin and snide comments would've normally gotten a rise, or at the very least a chuckle out of Cade, but he wasn't in a joking mood. It had been too long since he'd seen Caroline's smiling face, held her close, heard her laugh, or felt her touch. He stayed positive and strong on the outside, but on the inside he was terrified.

Cade shook his head. "I'll sleep when I'm dead."

Runway eyed him thoughtfully. He was sizing him up to see if Cade was losing it. To see if he was falling back into his post-Jenny depression. "Okay. At least go home and shower so the nurses can stand to come in and check on her." Cade glared at his friend's amused face, but it didn't faze him.

"Any news on April?"

Runway shook his head. "No. I've been watching her, but she's keeping to herself and her routine. She's clean as a whistle. Still no record of Ana Morales, though. Completely wiped clean like she never existed as anything other than April Jones Fontenot." Runway moved to the other side of Caroline's bed across from Cade to catch his eye. "Beau, if she's up to anything, she's doing it so we can't pin it on her. I've got some surveillance equipment set up and two guys watching her when I'm not there. If she sneezes we'll know it."

"Good. I talked to Eddie last night, and he hasn't heard anything from her, either. Since their divorce was finalized they haven't exactly been on speaking terms. The only reason they acknowledge each other's existence is because of their daughter, Claire. She's a student at the University of New Orleans now, and has decided to live with her stepmother just to spite her father." Cade huffed. "Like a spoiled teenager. She and my cousin broke up just before Christmas, and now he's acting strange. Don't know if it's a broken heart or what, but he won't answer my calls. My aunt said he rarely comes home anymore. She's worried he's mixed with the wrong crowd." Cade clenched his teeth and rubbed his hands down his face. "My fault, too. I introduced them. I've screwed everything up."

"Beau, you can't—"

"Anyway, Troy, my contact with NOPD, is putting some feelers out, and will call me if Marcellino or his cronies make any moves. So far he hasn't heard anything about the mafia leader, April, or Ana Morales." He scoffed, curling his lip. He rubbed his chin thoughtfully, and his brow furrowed. "That bugs me because April's not the type to lay low. She's sneaky, but also compulsive, and I can't imagine her just leaving things alone." Cade tightened one of the strings of his guitar and mumbled, "She's not as smart as she thinks she is. She's up to something, I know it. And I'm gonna stop her before she has a chance to scratch that itch."

"I'm with you, man, but you need to be on your A-game. And the only thing that will help with that is rest." Runway sniffed. "And a shower."

"Dude, really? You sound like my mom."

Runway held up both hands, palms out. "You stink, man. I won't lie to you. Some scalding water and a bar of soap would work wonders."

"Ha. Ha. That's funny." Cade returned to tuning his guitar. "I'll pretend I haven't suffered your stink before." He strummed the chords.

"I'm serious, Beau. Go home and freshen up. Let the hot water relax your muscles and clear your mind. You'll be a lot sharper if you do. I'll sit with her while you're gone. I promise I will keep her safe, and if she wakes up you will be the first person I call."

"I know." Cade glanced at the clock on the wall above Runway's head. "I'm waiting until one o'clock to visit my baby girl one more time before I go anywhere. You can meet me back here at two and then I'll go shave and shower. I'm not sleeping, though." Cade studied Runway's dissatisfied face and smirked. "You look like you could use forty winks, yourself. What have you been doing? Kristy's not here, so I know it's not that."

Runway shrugged, all joking aside. "Keeping an eye on my brother." He squeezed Cade's shoulder. "You bleed, I bleed, remember?"

Cade nodded. That was the end of the conversation as Runway backed out of the room and left him with his music.

He yawned and rubbed his eyes. He certainly could use a good night's sleep, but that wasn't on the itinerary right now. The cluster of ten-minute combat naps like he used to take in the field had given him enough fuel to adequately function, but they were far from satisfying. He had way too much on his mind to sleep soundly, anyway.

He pulled his phone from his pocket and flipped through the pictures he'd taken earlier of his sweet baby girl. Apart from the wires and feeding tubes, she was perfect. A beautiful little angel. Angel. Cade squeezed his eyes shut as the anguish seized his heart. His son's tiny face flitted through his mind, and he swore, angrily brushing the tears away. His son that he would never hold. The grief-stricken rage pulsing through his body was unbearable. He drew in a deep breath and picked up his guitar.

Singing kept him sane. Mostly. It kept him from losing control. From hitting rock bottom while his world crumbled around his feet. Cade breathed deeply while he strummed the chords, and closed his eyes more calmly this time as he plucked a new melody he'd been working on for Caroline. Hearing his wife's and daughter's pulse was the only thing giving him hope that things weren't over yet, even if it *was* from a damned machine. As long as those precious beats created his rhythm, he would provide the melody to reach out to them.

SIX

Frozen in fear, Caroline stood next to her comatose body and peered into the threatening blue eyes of George Callahan's haunting spirit. She squeezed her eyes closed trying to convince herself she was only dreaming, but when she opened them, he was still there. And smiling wickedly.

"Why won't you leave me alone? Why are you trying to hurt my family?"

He tilted his head to one side as if considering her questions. "Dear girl, I thought you were intelligent. It's quite simple. Your family betrayed mine. I won't rest until I have my revenge."

"Killing Rachel wasn't revenge enough for you? You should have been hanged for murder, but you weren't." His eyes narrowed, emphasizing his evil essence. Caroline swallowed her fear and kept talking. As long as she spoke, he wasn't trying to kill her. "Why me?"

He laughed quietly, the sound rattling her psyche. "Don't you see? You are the ultimate revenge, Daddy's pride and joy. It's an additional prize that you strongly favor your beloved grandmother. I shall enjoy ending the Fontenot family, starting with their long lost heiress." Caroline took a few steps away to distance herself from him.

He slowly moved toward her, his menacing baritone voice chilling the sparse air between them. “Your father is the head of the Fontenot family. He is my target. You are simply a means to an end. Once I dispose of your spirit, your body will be nothing but a corpse for your weak, broken father to mourn." He glanced at her body lying in the hospital bed. “That is when I will end this once and for all. . .nice and slowly. He will suffer the way my family has suffered because of the swindling, egotistical Fontenot pride, and my legacy will reign supreme.” His brow knitted and the corner of his mouth twitched. “Ah, you are much like the woman for whom you were named. You’ve flustered and distracted me." His face hardened, his blue eyes cold and penetrating. “Well, dollface, that ends now.”

Rachel’s words echoed in Caroline’s head. *As long as your faith is strong, he can’t get to you.* While feverishly praying for a chance to find her way home, she conjured the courage to stall him.

“Your legacy?” she spat her disgust. “Kenneth Callahan is a coward. You must be proud."

George’s piercing eyes narrowed. “Kenneth is a disgrace, but I’m working on that.” George’s eyes narrowed while his mouth curved up on each side like the Joker, adding to his villainous quality. “He’s coming around, and so will his spineless son.” His evil grin spread. “They will succeed. The Callahan blood runs deep.” His steely glare hardened even more. “My legacy will continue with everything the Fontenot family has worked toward. Everything they stole from my family will finally be where it belongs.”

“You know what I think?” She stubbornly raised her chin. “I don’t believe this has anything to do with revenge for a double-cross. I believe you were in love with Rachel. You loved her, didn't you?"

He grinned, almost adoringly. "Indeed. I loved her, and she loved me." He fidgeted and muttered, "She simply didn't realize it. But I saw the way she watched me when I would accompany my father to discuss business with Jefferson, his so-called partner. Traitor. I would have persuaded her if that greedy mongrel Fontenot hadn't forbidden her to see me!"

Caroline's heart raced when his pacing neared her position.

"I refused to allow the betrayal. I took matters into my own hands." His vile snicker turned Caroline's stomach. She wished she could disappear back to the time when she couldn't actually *see* the evil spirit haunting her, much less interact.

She'd only begun another prayer when her thoughts were captivated by guitar music echoing through the empty hallways. Confused, she glanced at George to see if he heard it, too. He stood motionless as they listened to the muted melody. The smooth, refreshing tone of Cade's voice filled the room. Caroline nearly burst from relief. He was singing to her. Calling for her. Cade had once told her she was his lifeline that dragged him from the darkness, and now he was hers. She clung to his voice as he rescued her from the terrifying darkness imprisoning her mind. An anchor, her steadfast rock, leading her home.

"No!" Rage flashed across George's features. He lunged for Caroline but she jumped backwards, narrowly escaping the clutches of his frenzied grasp. "I will never stop. I will not rest until my revenge is complete."

"You will *never* have your revenge. Burn in hell where you belong," she spat. The room spun faster, and faster, shaking her bearings. Caroline covered her face and sank to the floor, concentrating on the pleading words of the man she loved begging her to come back to him.

When her equilibrium leveled again, Caroline opened her eyes to the same hospital room. Reaching for her hand, her fingers disappeared confirming the lack of connection. Disappointment flooded her. She wasn't *all* the way home yet. At least she was one step closer.

If the darkness she'd just escaped was the outer realm of unconsciousness, then she must have found the inner realm. The astral reality, or was it etheric? Lucinda, the Creole woman she'd met at a voodoo shop on her honeymoon had been working with Caroline to develop her sensitive abilities. She'd mentioned this once, but Caroline couldn't remember the particulars. Hadn't Lucinda said in the etheric reality spirits could be right in front of your nose?

Caroline studied the sallow face of her listless body. Sunken cheeks, dry lips, and no color. She looked dead.

The music stopped, turning her attention to the solemn, defeated man behind her. Cade slumped over his guitar with his head on his arms, his shoulders trembled with the sobs absorbed by his shirt. Caroline's spirit crumbled. She wanted to hold him. How could she let him know she was here now? To reassure him that she was still with him? Caroline tried lying on top of her body again. Nothing happened. She wasn't sticking. The topic of spirit/body separation wasn't exactly on the syllabus in nursing school, and she hadn't had time to cover this in depth with Lucinda.

While forcing her scatterbrained mind to concentrate on reconnecting with her body, Cade started singing again, and she recognized something about the lyrics. She'd never heard this song before, but the familiar words resonated in her memories. A warm glow infiltrated her spirit, and the corners of her eyes tingled. It was the strangest sensation, like she should be crying, but nothing came from her holographic eyes. While Cade played his guitar and sang to her, she realized why the lyrics were familiar. Between his ache for her return, and his need for her loving touch, recognition of his wedding vows intermingled within the verses. At that moment, it became clear the depth of sadness surrounding his spirit. She sat beside him and studied his face while he softly sang his new song.

Despondent and grief-stricken, his once-sparkling eyes were now tired and stressed. He needed to shave, his wrinkled clothes were days old, and she didn't miss the deep tension lines around his mouth. He seemed ten years older.

How long have I been in a coma?

Tears streamed from his puffy eyes, slowly drifting down his cheek, and disappearing into the new growth of his scruffy whiskers. Caroline realized what a selfish, spoiled brat she'd been up to this point. For two years she'd only focused on her own desires, uncaring of his needs. Carelessly risking their relationship, testing his patience and tolerance by demanding he open up when he clearly didn't want to. All those times she'd pitched a fit about him not telling her his deepest, darkest secrets, now seemed trivial and annoying.

She bristled at the memory of her self-centered behavior when she dragged him into Lucinda's voodoo shop. Voodoo was the one thing he despised most in his life, and she had used his love for her against him by ignoring his wishes to leave it be and making him accept it. She'd known he wouldn't let her go in the shop alone. Shame washed over her. She'd been horrible.

This broken man was her husband. The man who loved her unconditionally. She wished she could go back in time and change the way she'd behaved, but she couldn't. She could only be thankful that he'd put up with her this long and accepted her for the way she was. Caroline vowed, if she got out of this mess, that she'd never be that ungrateful bitch again.

She wanted to hold him and tell him she was here, and how sorry she was for the way she'd treated him. For pushing him to confront the saddest event in his life and face his grief while on their honeymoon…forcing him to accept her friendship with Trevor, her ex-fiancé, knowing full well she'd lose her mind with jealousy if he wanted a relationship like that with his ex. What was she thinking? Cade was amazing. Would she be as forgiving of him if their roles were reversed?

As he approached the chorus she was spellbound. He poured his heart out and had no idea she could hear him. He struggled getting through the song, making the last word nearly impossible to comprehend as he choked it out in a sob. Caroline noticed a tear slowly making its way down the temple of her body's pale face until finally puddling into her ear. Hope surged through her. Her spirit must still be somewhat connected to her body if she was physically able to react to her feelings. The energy of her blood thrumming through her veins was almost palpable.

Cade's voice was barely above a whisper as he spoke with his head in his hands, but it may as well have echoed in the barren room. "Caroline, I'm scared." He raised his face, and the broken look in his weary eyes nearly shattered her. She'd never seen Cade this upset about anything, and for him to admit that he was scared. . .that spoke volumes about the gravity of this situation. "Please come back to me, baby. I love you. I can't go through this alone. I need you. *We* need you."

He squeezed her body's hand, and Caroline studied her fingers, marveling at the unusual tingling sensation. Like pins and needles when her foot would fall asleep, only adding tiny electric shocks that skittered across her palm. "Please, love, follow my voice and wake up. I'm nothing without you."

Placing his guitar in the chair, he stood at her side and smoothed her hair with his trembling hand. "Find the strength, Caroline. I am an empty shell without you by my side. Please hurry back to me. I know you can hear me, baby. I'm waiting for you." He pressed his forehead to hers. "I can't lose you. I'm sorry. If I would have thought before acting, I would never have touched that demon doll."

He kissed her tenderly, and Caroline rejoiced with the tingle of her own lips, even in spirit form. They had a connection like no other. She needed to find her way back into her body, and back to Cade, immediately.

Footsteps outside the door startled her, and Runway casually walked into the room. He looked somber. What was going on here? She wasn't dead. Her heart was still pumping, so why did it seem like they were at her funeral? Runway took a step back when he realized he'd interrupted Cade's intimate moment.

Cade tilted his head, cleared his throat, and mumbled, "No, it's okay. I'm finished."

Runway sank down into one of the chairs near the bed. "Beau, she's going to come out of this."

Cade rested his forehead on his clasped knuckles like he was praying. "She has to. I don't know if I can live without her."

Runway shifted forward resting his elbows on his knees with his hands clasped. Staring at his entwined fingers, he asked, "I hate to sound like a broken record, but have you slept at all since this happened?" Cade shrugged. "Beau, talk to me, man. I'm worried about you. This type of thing, it can bring back some of the. . .symptoms, and I recognize the look on your face that you're trying to hide from everyone else."

Symptoms? Symptoms of what? Depression? Caroline vaguely remembered him mentioning a therapist after he separated from the Navy, but she didn't push for more.

Cade rubbed his face and sat back in the chair. "I can't sleep. Too restless. I've tried, probably got a few hours here and there." Runway's doubtful expression proved he wasn't buying it, and Caroline appreciated his valid concern. "A couple of times I heard a noise and jumped up in the defensive position ready to rip someone apart. It's not as bad as it was, but it's only been a few days. I'm alright."

"How about dreams? Nightmares? Any tremors?" Runway asked. Cade shrugged again.

Runway nodded solemnly. "Beau, have you told her about—" Cade answered with a shake of his head before Runway finished. "Don't you think she'd want—"

"No." He spat, glaring at Runway. Caroline's jaw dropped. What the heck didn't she know? "What's your problem, man? What do you want me to do? Drag Caroline into my hell? Every dark, tragic, painful detail." Cade's chest heaved as he pursed his lips for emphasis. "Just. . .no."

Runway's words echoed in the vast emptiness of Caroline's flighty brain as she tried to process what she'd heard and Cade's reaction to it. When had he started having night tremors?

"She needs to know, Beau. It's part of who you are. She loves you more than anything, and she can help you get through this."

Cade vehemently shook his head. "No. No way. Forget it, Runway. I'm not going to subject her to my misery. I'm handling it." Cade thread his fingers through Caroline's. "Dragging her through the darkness of my past won't help anyone right now.

She's going to have enough pain when she wakes up." He squared his shoulders and warned, "Just drop it, alright?"

Runway nodded and glanced toward the voices outside the door. Caroline's mom and dad walked in with grave expressions on their aged faces.

Emily rushed in. "Oh, Cade. I'm so sorry. We all are. It's just. . .it's just too much to. . ." Emily peered down to Caroline's dreadful shell. "She'll come out of this, she has to. She can't bear to let you down. I know she'll make it back soon."

His smile was weak. "Thanks, Ms. Emily. I sure hope so. I don't think I can handle losing her, too."

Caroline's heart ached for him. If she died, then Cade would have lost the only two women in his life that he ever passionately loved.

"She will. Just remember when you feel that God has given you more than you can stand, it's time to kneel." When Cade didn't respond, Emily studied his weary face. Caroline couldn't contain her amusement as her mom morphed into bossy-mother-mode. "Caden Luke, you are dead on your feet. You let Eddie drive you to the house right now and get some rest. It'll be no good for anyone if Caroline wakes up to you as a patient in the room next to her. Eddie and I will stay here with her until you can make it back."

Caroline glanced at Eddie, his firm lips pressed together in a hard line, his gaze saturated with immeasurable pain. He suffered as much as Cade, like he could burst into tears at any moment. Caroline was desperate to comfort them.

"She'll be fine," Emily continued. "I'm sure she's not going anywhere for a while."

"Yes, ma'am." Cade glanced at Runway and smirked. "My parents are planning to come up here later this evening after my dad gets off work. I should probably make myself a little more presentable before my mom sees me like this. You wanna take a walk to the NICU with me before I go?"

Emily's face lit up. Caroline's brain had been alarmingly disjointed in spirit form, she'd completely forgotten about her babies. She now urgently wanted to see them. But was straying from her body a good idea? While in the outer realm with George, they were both in this room, so the possibility of George still being close and having access to her vulnerable body was quite worrisome. She must figure out how to get back into her body permanently. Knowing she'd want to hold her babies, it would be best to wait to see them in person. As Cade, Eddie, and Emily filed out of the room, Runway stayed behind taking Cade's seat by her bed.

"You guys go ahead. I'll stay here with Caroline." Caroline smiled, thankful for the protection.

Runway gracefully moved around the room. To anyone not paying attention, it appeared as though he adjusted the flowers in an arrangement behind her bed, but he swiftly and discreetly slipped something between the stalks. His nimble fingers expertly untangled a mass of thin, transparent cords and wires. When he had one free, he pulled a pocket-sized electronic instrument from his jacket and threaded the wire through it. He pressed a few buttons, removed the wire, and then wove it into the greenery of the plant. Why was he bugging her room?

When he finished, he pulled a chair up next to the bed to sit and hold Caroline's hand. Strangely enough, she felt nothing when he touched her. It just verified the immeasurable connection with her husband. His velvety, slightly-accented voice filled the silent room with a calming sense of Italian serenity, and his mint green eyes brimmed with concern.

Caroline's anxiety eased while he spoke, and, though she knew it didn't matter, she listened quietly without interrupting.

"Hey there, *bella*. You've really got us all worried, you know. Beau is a walking time-bomb. He's one of the strongest guys I know, but everyone has a breaking point, and he can't be far from his. He's overcome some serious tragedies in his life, but this one, as you all say, takes the cake." He took a deep breath, leaned closely toward her head, and gently brushed his hand over her hair. "Can you do me a favor? Can you come back soon? For Beau? I've known him for a long time, and I've been in some rough situations with him, but I've never seen him break down like he did today. Not after Jenny, or even what happened in Afghanistan. I'm here to support him, but he needs *you*, Caroline. Your mom and dad need you. We all do." He sat back in the chair resting his hand on her forearm. What exactly happened in Afghanistan?

"Kristy sends her love. She wanted me to let you know she would be here already, but she has a medical appointment tomorrow. She'll be here in two days, and she demanded you be awake and ready for her. She insisted. I'd listen to her if I were you."

Caroline smiled. She knew just how bossy Kristy could be.

Runway sighed, and dragged his fingers through his silky dark hair. His voice quieted.

"She's carrying my baby, you know."

What? Caroline was floored. How could Kristy, her very best friend, keep a secret like this from her?

"It's a boy." He smiled before pursing his lips. "She wanted to be the one to tell you. Please don't tell her I said anything. She'd kill me if she knew I ruined the surprise." He released a short burst of laughter. "I'm going to be a father. That's something I thought would never happen to me."

Caroline crossed her arms, raising an eyebrow, still miffed that Kristy hadn't told her she was pregnant.

"I know she's waiting for me to propose, and I want that more than anything, but it's just...she's special to me. I need her to know that I want her to be my wife because I'm in love with her, not because she's carrying my child, though I'm thrilled beyond reason about that." That explained a lot. Why didn't he share this news with Kristy? She would understand.

"You see, Caroline. I need you to hurry back to give me some insight into the female mind. You know Kristy better than anyone. You could help me figure out the best way to knock her off her feet."

Caroline rolled her eyes. Right now, uttering those simple, life-changing little words would do the trick. "Men," Caroline huffed. "Totally clueless sometimes."

A knocking on the door frame drew their attention to Emily's distressed face. "Am I interrupting you?"

He stood. "No, ma'am. I was just confessing my problems to Caroline. I guess it's good that she can't hear me or I would be in trouble with Kristy."

Caroline's mom tilted her head and gave her signature I-wouldn't-be-so-sure look. Caroline knew that look well. "I don't know that she *can't* hear you. There have been reports for years about coma patients waking up and remembering things people said to them when they were out. That's why the doctors want us to talk to her." She shrugged, and her eyes glistened with tears as she smoothed the blanket over Caroline's feet. "You know, just in case. We can hope for that, anyway."

Runway pulled Emily into his arms and hugged her as she cried into his chest.

Caroline was baffled. Her mother just saw her grandchildren. Shouldn't she be happy? The abounding grief wore on Caroline's spirit. The urge to rush to the NICU to see her babies niggled her. Why was everyone she loved so sad? Surely it wasn't because she was in a coma. It wasn't like she died. Caroline scowled. There had to be something else. She had to see her children. It was a risk she had to take. Never mind the dangers of leaving her body. She would be fine while Emily and Runway stayed in the room.

Caroline left in search of her babies.

SEVEN

Unsure how to get to the NICU, Caroline wandered around until spotting a sign in the right direction. Her gut was on the spin cycle as she approached preemie-central. Was it possible for a spirit to hurl? The back of her neck and arms tingled as a frisson of fear ascended her spine. If she'd been in her body, the hairs on it would surely be at attention. Caroline's intuition screamed warnings, but why? She bypassed the cleansing station, and walked through the wall searching for the pink and blue cards with her last name on them.

She found the first one quickly and stood in awe cherishing the beautiful face sleeping peacefully without a care in the world. She was precious, tiny and amassed with monitors, but lovely. Caroline's heart swelled with pride as she whispered a prayer for the safety of her beautiful baby. Her daughter. It felt strange to say that, but she really liked it. In the instant she laid eyes on her child Caroline knew she would go to the ends of the earth to keep her safe. It was instinctual and a fierce emotion that overpowered everything else.

Caroline kissed her fingertips and touched the plastic capsule where her daughter lay. She scoured the room for her son, but he wasn't there.

A familiar lullaby drifted from a figure standing between two mahogany rocking chairs. Rachel swayed back and forth, humming to a dramatically undersized infant in her arms.

Tunnel vision shrank everything around Caroline. Reality crashed over her and her heart split in two, not believing that it could be more broken than it already was. Her son hadn't survived, and her tiny daughter was in intensive care. All while her body was on a completely different floor of the hospital, and her spirit wandered aimlessly through the creepy inner realm of unconsciousness.

Caroline didn't want to exist in this painful hell anymore. She wanted to be happy again. To jump back to a simple life with no pain, no ghosts, no one trying to kill her or her family. . .no sadness. She wished she could return to the moment she told Cade she was pregnant with twins. Remembering the elation in his eyes weighed heavily on her now. Was there no hope then? Would she be stuck here until George succeeded and ruined Eddie's life? Cade's? Caroline clutched her abdomen and doubled over with the despondency that engulfed her as if someone doused her with a hundred gallons of water and extinguished the tiny flame that kept her burning to return to her life.

She wanted to hold her daughter and watch her grow. To tell her about her twin brother. She needed to teach her how to braid, to cook, and to understand the difference between leggings and tights. She wanted to teach her the value of quality make-up and flat irons, and to appreciate a good sturdy bra. That confidence is not the same as arrogance, and to never allow someone to disrespect her. She needed to teach her about Jesus and to never settle for a man who doesn't care about her soul.

Sympathy creased Rachel's features as she offered a reassuring smile. Drifting toward Caroline, she whispered, "I'll take good care of him. Go back to your body now, Caroline. It's not safe without your spirit present." Rachel disappeared into thin air with the baby in her arms.

Caroline never had a chance to hold him.

Caroline forgot how to move, how to breathe. Digesting this revelation, Rachel's last words of warning echoed through her troubled mind. If her spirit couldn't do anything but look at her body, what kind of protection was that? Although, if Rachel could be in this inner realm of consciousness, then George was probably somewhere around here, too.

Was the spirit world like she'd seen in the movies where she could enter a living person's body and control them? Oh, how she'd like to possess April and walk off a cliff. Caroline shuddered. The thought of sharing any molecule with that woman sickened her.

Back in her room, she found her mom alone sitting beside the bed. She'd been crying, her voice thick with emotion.

"I knew something like this would happen. I saw it. I'm sorry, sweetheart. I should have told you about my vision, but it scared me to death. I didn't want to cause you to worry anymore than necessary."

"You saw this? Is that why you started bawling when I told you I was pregnant? Why didn't you tell me?" Caroline shouted.

Emily rested her forehead against Caroline's and held her hand. A faint brush, a tickle, shot across her palm as her mother whispered, "Oh, Caroline, where are you?"

"I'm here, Momma. I'm right here," Caroline screamed. Blinding frustration and panic fueled her hysteria. She couldn't even cry to satisfactorily express the grief from losing half of her heart, her baby boy. "Why can't anyone hear me?" The crippling grief twisted in her empty chest and fury seized her for not knowing how to get back. Exasperated, Caroline growled and shrieked out the boiling emotion.

Emily recoiled and abruptly stood.

"Did you hear me?" Caroline said. "Can you hear me, Momma?"

Emily scanned the room before smoothing the blanket around Caroline's shoulders with her free hand while her other held tight to Caroline's hand. Bewildered and intrigued, confused even, she sat down and quietly prayed.

After all Caroline had witnessed already in this realm, hearing her mother's intimate conversation with God broke her to pieces. Her spirit's eyes pricked with unleashed tears she couldn't release as her mother prayed for Caroline's safe and speedy return, the health of her granddaughter, the safekeeping of her grandson's soul, and for Cade. She thanked God for bringing her family back together and for the new additions to it.

Caroline collapsed in the chair beside her mother, emotionally spent. She wanted her body back. Why was she suspended in this middle ground, this inner realm of unconsciousness? It must be one level deeper than dreaming, but one level above being a ghost. Whatever the classification, it was way better than the scary *outer* realm.

Runway's silent approach surprised them both. Something bothered him, and Caroline held her breath as to what it could be.

"Have you talked to Kristy?" Emily asked.

He nodded slowly. "Yes, ma'am. I just got off the phone with her. Depending on how she feels, she hopes to fly here the day after tomorrow. She's worried about Caroline."

Emily stared at Caroline's face with a mother's admiration. "We all are." She smoothed Caroline's hair back, resting her hand on her forehead as if she was checking for fever. "Oh, Caroline. Come back to us, please."

"I'm trying! Nothing's working!" She threw her arms in the air. "I'm open to suggestions," she quipped, her retort dripping with sarcasm. Again, her mother's head snapped up as if she heard Caroline. Caroline leaned in closer to her mother and studied her eyes. "Can you hear me?"

"Is everything okay, Emily?" Runway noticed her sudden interest in the empty corner.

"Did you hear something?" she asked.

He stood and walked around the room looking out the window and doorway for anyone standing nearby. "No, ma'am. Did you?"

Her eyes narrowed with suspicion as she breathed out the words. "Yes, I did." Her head slowly turned back to Caroline's unconscious face, hand still on her forehead. "Caroline, are you here? Can you hear me?"

"Yes! Yes, Momma, I can hear you." Caroline jumped up and down like a giddy toddler. Finally, some way to communicate with someone.

Emily gasped, and her tears flowed. Runway brooded.

"What's wrong? Is she okay?"

Emily couldn't speak through the emotion, but she nodded, chin quivering, as she studied Caroline's face. She retracted her hand from Caroline's forehead, and covered her gaping mouth. Frightened, she whispered, "Impossible."

Beyond frustrated, Caroline lay on her body again trying to force her spirit to cling or teleport back into her body. It didn't work. She wiggled and squirmed, but it was no use.

Runway handed her mother a tissue, and led her back down to the seat.

"Mrs. Fontenot, are you well?"

"Yes. I'm fine." She took a breath. "I think. . . No. I know I just heard Caroline."

EIGHT

"What are you doing here?" Kenneth barked.

Unaffected, April sashayed into the office and sat, smoothly crossing her long slender legs. "What, a girl can't pay a visit to an old friend?"

"Friends?" Kenneth tossed his reading glasses onto his desk and raised his brow. "Who said we were friends?"

Trevor shifted uncomfortably in the hard conference chair. He hadn't seen April since Louisiana when she'd convinced him Caroline was sleeping with the gardener, and then she tried to seduce him. She was ballsy, he'd give her that. Her piercing gaze fell on him.

"Trevor. Long time no see."

"April," he nodded.

"Sorry I missed your visit last summer. I heard it was quite eventful," she smiled wickedly before glancing at Kenneth. "How about you? Made any trips to the spooky bayou lately?" She laughed.

"What can we do for you, April," Trevor asked. His dad's glaring red face indicated his less-than-welcoming greeting. "You must have a reason for gracing us with your presence."

She nodded thoughtfully, "Actually, you were an added bonus. I was coming to see your father." She crossed her arms. "Marcellino is unhappy with you."

His dad's face paled at the mention of the head of the Louisiana mafia. What trouble had he gotten himself involved in now?

"The mafia, Dad? Again?"

"More like still," April chided. Her ice cold stare landed on Kenneth's glower. "Pops, here, has been working with Angelo Marcellino since before your botched wedding." She mocked surprise, "He hasn't told you?" Her slender fingers covered her mouth. "Uh-oh, have I said too much?"

"You have overstayed your welcome, Mrs. Fontenot. Leave or I'll call security." The brief glimpse of the pale, frightened man faded. His dad transformed into the snarling ogre Trevor knew him to be.

She stood. "Fine, but you need me more than you realize." He cocked a doubtful eyebrow and crossed his arms. "Angelo Marcellino is my godfather. He stepped up in the area that my," she gave him a once over, "*real* father didn't. I might be able to convince him not to sic the dogs on you just yet."

He jerked his head to the side and pressed his lips into a firm line, "And why would you do that? Or should I say how much will that cost me?"

"Thought you'd never ask." Her answering smile faded. "Fifty percent of your company."

Trevor's jaw dropped along with his father's. "You can package that offer up and take it right to hell along with you on your way out."

"No?" April feigned disappointment.

“No.” Kenneth pointed to the door with one hand while he punched numbers on his office phone with the other.

“Suit yourself,” she shrugged. “Hope you have all your affairs in order. You likely won’t make it in tomorrow.” She nodded at Trevor and turned on her heel.

“Wait just a minute,” Kenneth ordered. “What’s he planning?”

“Oh, that’s a nice try, Mr. Callahan. But I know better than to cross a man like Angelo Marcellino.” She walked back to his desk with supermodel grace. “I will talk to him in your favor, but it’s going to cost you.”

“How much, damn it? And don’t even try to barter with my business.”

She smiled, but it reeked of malice. “Does the name Maria Morales mean anything to you?”

Kenneth hesitated for a moment, staring at his desk in thought before his eyes snapped up to meet hers. Trevor recognized that hardened glaze. “Nope. Can’t say that it does.”

April glared in a standoff with him for a full thirty seconds. “Think harder.”

Exasperated, Kenneth paced around his desk and raised his voice. “What else do you want me to say? I don’t know anyone by that name.” Trevor peered at his dad through narrowed eyes. He could always tell when Kenneth was lying.

“Come on, Callahan. You can do better than that.”

"How much will it take to get Marcellino off my back. I’ll pay you right now.” He scribbled on a check and ripped it out. He held it out and she looked at it with disgust. “This should cover it, yes?”

The blue slits of her eyes accented the hiss that slipped from her mouth. “You slimy sack of—”

"Not enough? What do you want from me?" His eyes traveled down her body. "Look, I'm married, but. . ." He glanced at Trevor and cleared his throat. "We can work something out. How much? I'll make it worth your while. You have my word."

Her rigid posture reminded Trevor of Caroline's reaction at their wedding when he insulted her in front of everyone. "Your word?" she spat. "Your word means absolutely nothing to me, you disgusting idiot." She slapped an envelope on his desk and glared at him with fire in her eyes. "You're no more honorable than the fool I married." April spun on her heel headed for the door and shouted over her shoulder. "You have one week."

Trevor studied his father's disgusted face. April had compared him to the one person in the world he would take offense to. Eddie Fontenot. But why? What was in that envelope?

"What was that all about?" Trevor said.

Without speaking, Kenneth opened the envelope and pulled out a single sheet of paper. Trevor waited for an explanation, but his father calmly folded it and put it back. He gathered his jacket, and said, "Lock up when you leave." He didn't look back as he stormed through the door.

NINE

Cade flopped on the couch in Eddie's house in uptown New Orleans. Exhausted didn't come close to an accurate description of how he felt. Whether physically worn or emotionally spent, or both, Cade wanted to sleep for ten years straight. A pick-me-up was in order. He dragged himself to the bathroom, shaved, showered, and dressed, and then sank into the recliner to put on his shoes. The microsuede sofa that he'd spent several nights on last spring while Caroline finished her last semester of college mocked him.

They'd spent hours on that sofa mostly cuddling because her mom slept in the room down the hall. They'd even risked fooling around a couple of times on the white animal skin rug in the middle of the floor. But most of their time was spent talking. It's no wonder she'd been frustrated with him before they married. The nights they'd stayed up talking in this house, they only talked about her.

She was right. He was a foolish, tight-lipped jackass afraid to open up. He had avoided her questions and always changed the subject back to her. Disgusted with himself, he scrubbed his fingers through his wet hair. Runway was right, she deserved to know about his life before her. She'd told him her life story.

He'd tell her everything she ever wanted to know and more if she'd just friggin' come back already. He hoped it wasn't too late.

He pushed the negative thoughts from his mind. Refreshed, he rested his head and thought about everything that had happened in the past few days. His phone jarred him awake. Glancing at his watch, he cursed. He'd been asleep for two hours.

"Yeah, Runway, what's up?"

"Hey, man. Did I wake you?"

"No, it's cool. Is Caroline okay? The baby?"

"Yes, they're both fine." His voice softened. "Well, they're the same at least."

"Oh." Disappointment engulfed him. "You okay? Need a break?"

"No, no, I'm cool. I called because Emily thinks. . . Well, you may want to come back up here and hang out for a while."

Cade's mind raced. "Why? Is something wrong? Something happen?" Cade straightened a decoration on the mantle and blew dust away, fanning it from his face.

"No, nothing's wrong. If Emily is right, then it's great. Just get up here. I'll let her explain it."

"Dude, come on," Cade huffed. "She have another vision or something?"

"Come see for yourself. Trust me."

Cade exhaled a frustrated sigh. Runway had to be dramatic, but when he said trust him, Cade had no choice. He'd trusted him with his life too many times not to. "I'll call Eddie and be there in a few. I'm sure he'll want to know about whatever it is that's got you all worked up."

"Okay. Seriously, Beau, relax." His smile seeped through his inflection, "It's cool."

"Right. Later."

Eddie was equally annoyed that Runway hadn't disclosed more. They arrived at the hospital within minutes of each other. Where had Eddie been? Cade didn't ask as they briskly walked to Caroline's room. Emily stood beside the bed with one hand on her daughter's shoulder and one on her forehead. She perked up when they walked in, and her face split in an exuberant smile.

"I'm glad y'all are here."

Cade frowned and surveyed Caroline. No change. Why was Emily so happy? Caroline still lay unconscious. Until she sat up and talked to him, he wouldn't be smiling.

"What's going on?" Cade shot a look at Runway who leaned casually against the counter grinning smugly.

Emily left Caroline's side and approached them with hands up like she was being arrested. "Okay, y'all know I've been having these crazy visions, right?" He and Eddie glanced at each other and nodded. "Well, before Runway called you, I was talking to Caroline, and," she paused, "I heard something."

Cade studied her hopeful eyes. "I'm sorry, what?" He shifted his weight, and shoved his hands in his pockets. "You *heard* something? Like what?"

"This is going to sound strange, but I think it was Caroline's spirit."

Cade tried not to look at his mother-in-law like she was stark-raving mad.

"I didn't understand it, either." Emily continued. "I thought I was hearing voices that had carried into the room from the hallway, but no one was out there. I asked Caroline a question, and I heard a muffled response as if she'd answered me. I was shocked and confused at first. I asked Runway if he'd heard anything, and he hadn't, so I asked her another question, and I heard her answer me. I know it!"

"What did you ask her?"

"When I thought I'd heard her respond the first time, I asked her if she could hear me. I heard what sounded like 'Yes,' and then a cadence of other words like she was excited that I could hear her, as well."

As much as Cade wanted to believe her, it was a little too outrageous. His tolerance for the strange and unusual was nearly tapped out. His gaze dropped to the floor again, and he spoke calmly so not to insult her intelligence.

"Mrs. Emily, I know how badly you want her to wake up. So do I. More than anything. It's driving me crazy just sitting around waiting for her to come to, and knowing there's nothing I can do to help her. Are you sure you aren't so hopeful for a sign that you might have imagined it?"

Her face fell, and her eyes tightened. For an instant he saw Caroline in her mother's angry, determined expression. "You don't believe me? After all the ghost weirdness with Rachel, I was certain you would be the one to believe me. I know what I heard, Cade. I firmly believe Caroline is in this room with us right now, and she's probably screaming at you for not believing it." She turned to Eddie. "How 'bout you? You think I'm nuts, too?"

Eddie rolled his shoulders back and tilted his head like he needed to crack his neck. "Em, I know you want her to come back. I do, too." He clenched his jaw, the tense muscles rippled. "We all do, but..." The war of whether or not to piss her off by not believing her or whether he should support her flashed across his solemn features.

Cade was running on fumes and his heart was already broken. His tone sounded much harsher than he intended, but a false hope would shatter him. “If that’s the case, then why can’t you hear her right now?” He frowned and pounded his fist against his stuttering heart. “If she’s really here, then why doesn’t she wake up? If she’s in this room right now, why can’t she simply climb into her body and come back to us? To me.” Cade’s eyes burned, and he didn’t want to cry. He whipped around to face the wall with both hands in his hair until he could clear his head.

Runway distracted Emily by asking her to show them. Cade watched their reflection in the windows as Emily placed her hand on Caroline’s forehead. “Caroline, can you hear me, baby?" Emily squealed a moment later. “Oh my goodness! I heard her again.”

Cade rocked his head and closed his eyes before anyone caught him rolling them. His mother-in-law has had one too many visions. Cade bit his tongue before his erratic, uncensored thoughts slipped past his lips.

“Wait, what, honey? Caroline, slow down. Say that again. What’s a zinger? Isn’t that a cupcake or something?"

Cade whirled around and breathlessly whispered, “What did you just say?”

Emily frowned. “Even in a coma, she's craving dessert.” She leaned closer and whispered in Caroline’s ear, but Cade heard her fine. “Caroline, did you mean *singer*? Yes, baby, Cade is here. He’s ready for—okay.” Emily shrugged at Cade with a raised brow. “Does the word zinger mean anything to you?"

Eddie snickered, and Cade rubbed his mouth to hide his smirk. He stared at Caroline’s unconscious body, and slowly shook his head in disbelief. “Well, I’ll be damned.”

Emily smiled. "You believe me now? What does that mean? What's a zinger?"

Eddie grinned and answered for him. "It's Cajun slang for a swamp rat. I called Beau a zinger in front of Caroline the first time those two were together in my house." He turned to Cade and nodded before adding, "What I don't get is the significance of it right now."

"So I would believe she's here," Cade answered. He moved to her bedside, and Emily backed away to allow Cade to whisper in Caroline's ear while caressing her face. "You're a tenacious, stubborn, adorable, crazy girl, you know that?" He pressed his forehead to hers. "I'm thankful for you and your goofy ideas. I love you so much." Tears fell down his cheeks, but he didn't care anymore. Though not in her body, she was here. That was better than nothing. "Okay, sweet Caroline, I got the message." He kissed her forehead and tipped his head to the side again, chuckling. Guess he had to tell the story now.

"When Caroline moved down here after she left Trevor, she'd missed the deadline for the fall semester enrollment at LSU, allowing us several months of quality time together. One night, while sitting in Rachel's original room, we discussed her ghost and how Caroline refused to believe she was being haunted. After finally convincing her that ghosts existed, she got this crazy idea to come up with a signal or a code word in case one of us died and remained stuck on this earth as a ghost." He smiled proudly.

"Some way to let the other one know we were still here watching over them. We wanted a word significant to both of us that no one else would understand. I wanted to go with 'shower' because of how we first met, but she wouldn't hear of it." Cade smiled playfully, ignoring the disapproving glares from both Emily and Eddie.

Emily raised an eyebrow. “I thought you two met in the library?”

“Officially, yes.” He started to explain, but closed his mouth. “I’ll let Caroline tell you the details of our first unofficial meeting after she wakes up. For now, let’s just say that the first time we crossed paths, she caught me with my pants down.” It could’ve been Cade’s imagination, but he’d swear the beeping of Caroline’s heart monitor had sped up. Probably good that he couldn’t hear her because she was certainly cussing him.

“Anyway,” he cleared his throat, “she decided that zinger would be a good word. I had to explain what it meant after Eddie called me that. It was a strangely intimate moment that stuck with us. She adopted that endearing little nickname for me and has used it several times.” Cade pulled her hand to his mouth to kiss it. “I never thought in a million years that we’d end up using it for its intended purpose,” he mumbled before facing Emily. “I’m sorry I doubted you. Lucinda told us that you probably had some manner of psychic abilities. But I never imagined. . .”

Emily’s face crumpled. “What? Who’s Lucinda?”

“A crazy woman we met at a voodoo shop while on our honeymoon in New Orleans.” Eddie shifted uncomfortably as Emily snapped her gaping mouth closed. They didn’t know how strongly Cade despised the subject, but after finding April’s bag in Eddie’s closet with their belongings, then the doll Runway found, voodoo was a touchy subject all around.

Cade held his hands up in surrender. “Believe me, I was livid. I wanted nothing to do with her, but Caroline’s curiosity overruled. Thankfully, this particular woman was not a voodoo priestess but indirectly involved in the practice. Guilty by association, if you will. Her late husband was a voodoo priest whose sister and mother were also priestesses, but evil, ruthless ones."

Cade tilted his head, "She was actually very nice, but, for personal reasons, I still intend to keep my entire family a very good distance from voodooism. Anyway, Lucinda told Caroline she had sensitive abilities, and that she'd probably inherited it from one or both of her parents." Eddie cleared his throat and shifted uncomfortably while Cade nodded to Emily. "Caroline mentioned your visions to the woman, and she agreed that when the can of milk hit your forehead it triggered your sensitive capabilities. I didn't buy into all that nonsense at the time, but now," his eyes fell to Caroline, "I'm not so sure." He smoothed Caroline's hair. "It's obvious you two share a special connection. Pretty amazing, if you ask me." He frowned and choked back the lump threatening to rear its ugly head again. "Why can't she come back already?"

Cade knew what he had to do. Focused and determined, he stood abruptly, kissed Caroline's pale lips once more, and told the curious faces in the room he'd be back in an hour.

"Need any help?" Runway asked.

Cade answered with a quick swivel of his head. He needed to do this on his own.

"Make sure someone is in here with her at all times. Don't leave her alone, okay?" Cade wasn't taking any chances with April still out there.

"You got it. We'll take care of her." Runway winked, understanding Cade was on to something good, and probably relieved to see some life back in him.

A man on a mission, Cade headed for the French Quarter.

TEN

Lucinda waved a bony arm in Caroline's direction. She threw a glance over her shoulder to see who stood behind her, but there was no one. Lucinda smiled knowingly and waved again. Dumbfounded, Caroline pointed to herself. The tiny woman nodded and walked toward her.

Cade must've asked her to wait by the elevators so his mom wouldn't freak out when his family left from visiting Caroline. The men on Angie Beauregard's side of the family had been cursed long ago by a wicked voodoo priestess. If Cade's mom knew about Lucinda she wouldn't hold back if the petite Creole woman came within fifty feet of anyone she loved. Cade mustn't have wanted to take any chances to raise questions.

Caroline swung her head and waved her arms to be more visible. Lucinda really could see her. Amazing. Caroline knew Lucinda could see auras, but she had no idea the woman could see spirits. Maybe she couldn't, perhaps she only saw Caroline's aura waving wildly. After all, it was her spirit, not her body, that emitted an aura. Caroline's heart, or where it should be, fluttered hopefully. What did Cade expect Lucinda to do? Explain how to get back into her body? Being stuck in this frustrating state of existence exhausted her. How many other coma patients in the hospital wandered the hallways, hopelessly stranded? She fought the urge to look around for others in her state of being, and selfishly focused on fixing her own problems.

The strange feeling she had upon sensing Lucinda's presence mimicked an adrenaline rush, like her blood raced, complete with heart palpitations. Would that show up on the monitor? With Cade's hand resting securely on her body's shoulder, she had faith that her body would be safe enough for her to venture toward Lucinda, who watched her approach.

"Lucinda. How are you?"

She didn't respond directly, but pretended to read a poster on the wall. "I can't hear you, child, I can only see you. In quite the predicament, aren't you?" Without smiling, she released an amused chuckle confusing Caroline. She continued speaking while pretending to read the poster. "You are dangling in between worlds. Have you seen your spirit friends?"

Lucinda looked directly at her, and Caroline nodded. "You'll have to make large movements, my dear. I can't see you clearly. You are a colorful, but blurry shape, and I can't see slight movements."

Caroline gave a larger nod.

She closed her eyes, disappointed. "The dark spirit has spoken to you?"

Caroline nodded exaggeratedly again.

"I was afraid of that. His energy is stronger now than when I saw you last. His darkness is spreading around you trying to overwhelm your energy."

"What? How can that happen? What can I do about it? How do I stop him?"

Cade's family bustled out into the hallway toward the elevators. They were leaving, and Cade discretely nodded to

Lucinda as he walked them out. That meant he wasn't touching Caroline's body anymore. She waved for Lucinda to follow as she rushed back to her room. Her mom stood beside the bed with her hand on Caroline's forehead. She'd been trying to communicate, but Caroline wasn't there. Emily popped her head up to Lucinda, standing at the foot of the bed, staring at Caroline's body.

"Can I help you with something?" Emily snapped without removing her hand from Caroline.

"I met your daughter in June while she was on her honeymoon. You must be her mother? My name is Lucinda."

Recognition flushed through her mother. "The voodoo woman."

"In a manner of speaking, yes, ma'am. I assure you I only do pure works, not evil. Your daughter is in grave danger, and I want to help her."

Emily's face fell. "What kind of grave danger? I heard her, she's here with us. Her body is getting stronger."

"Yes, it is. She's here right now. You can hear her?" Lucinda leaned toward Emily, reaching her slender arm in her direction, clearly interested in learning more. "She inherited her sensitivity from you, then. You are the one having visions?"

Caroline's mom nodded. "Yes, but I haven't had any for a while. I can hear Caroline's muffled voice, and only when I'm touching her forehead."

"That is her third eye chakra. It's acting as a portal, or microphone, if you will, for her to communicate with you. What has she said?"

Cade and Runway walked in. Sensing the tension in the room, Cade apprehensively shifted his attention between Emily and Lucinda.

"Eddie said to tell you he would call later. He's going to check on Claire before he heads back to Golden Meadow to be with Remy." He glanced toward Lucinda. "You two have met?"

Emily spoke first. "Yes. Lucinda is the woman you told us about."

Runway's eyes glowed with curiosity as he studied his voodoo-hating friend's reaction to the woman. Cade introduced Lucinda to him, then began his interrogation. "Can you hear or see her?"

Emily interrupted. "Lucinda said Caroline is in grave danger."

"What? How?" Cade's posture went rigid and his face fierce. His sharp eyes studied Lucinda, and Caroline imagined this was his no-nonsense military persona. "Tell me everything you know."

"I cannot hear her." Lucinda squared her shoulders and Caroline grinned. The tiny woman had never been intimidated by Cade, no matter his size, speed, or threatening body language. If only Caroline had a fraction of that bravery, George wouldn't be a problem. There would be no fear for him to feed off of. "But I can see the aura of her spirit. She stands over there."

She pointed to the corner of the room where Caroline stood, and all three heads followed her gaze. Caroline snorted. They looked knowing full well they wouldn't see her.

"Her heart breaks to see you all this sad. She is well, and her spirit is strong, but the dark spirit that has been looming over her is stronger. He now wishes to overwhelm her energy to keep her from making it back to her body. There is one good thing. When we met last year she had two dark spirits in her aura. Now there is only one."

Cade rushed Lucinda, towering over her tiny frame. Again, not intimidated by his size, she didn't falter as he continued to press her for information. “How can she get back to her body? How can she make herself wake up? Can we help her? Can she fight him? Is her energy stronger than his?"

She looked from Caroline’s body to his face. “All I know is that she has seen him and even spoken to him.”

He straightened. “How do you know that? I thought you couldn’t hear her?”

“I asked if she’d seen her spirit friends, and she nodded. Then I asked if she spoke to the dark spirit, and she nodded again, but her color shifted to one of fear. He has threatened or scared her somehow while in his level of existence.”

Caroline recognized the frenzied look in Cade's eyes masked by his superhuman control. “She’s with him now?” he said in a whisper. “What the hell does that mean? He’s dead.” Cade rubbed the back of his neck. “What can he do to her? Can he hurt her?”

“I don’t know. Her heart beats strongly. Her dark spirit is deceased, but has manifested before, which means he exists in the upper etheric reality closer to where angels and spirits live, but below the astral reality which is entirely spiritual." Lucinda studied Caroline's aura in the corner. "She’s still alive, stranded in the lower etheric reality closer to the magnetic aura of the earth. She is here, which means he hasn’t hurt her yet." She smiled at Cade. "Your wife is stubborn, Mr. Beauregard. She is not going to give in without a fight.”

“You got that right.” Caroline chimed in admiring her husband’s playful smirk. He knew her stubbornness all too well.

“Oh!” Emily started. Her hand still rested on Caroline’s forehead. Caroline laughed.

“Don’t you laugh at me. You scared me.” Emily laughed with her, but Cade, Runway and Lucinda curiously watched. “I think

Caroline agreed with you. I wasn't expecting to hear her, and it startled me."

Cade smiled, reassured. "Caroline, have you seen George's spirit?"

"Yes," she answered eagerly. "He meant to attack me to keep me from my body, but I heard you singing and I shifted from the outer realm to the inner realm. I'm scared and ready to come home."

Emily's frantic voice filled the room. "Caroline, I can't understand all that. Your voice is muffled, and you're talking fast. Short sentences and slowly please."

Caroline sighed, frustrated. It was like reading a children's book aloud. "Yes. I saw George."

Emily translated, and Cade's jaw rippled with tension as he balled his fists. "Did he hurt you?"

"Almost, but you saved me."

"She said he almost did but you saved her," Emily said, her voice thick.

Cade's face reflected a plethora of emotions. First, fear and pain that George was trying to hurt Caroline, then anger because he couldn't stop him, followed by relief for saving her.

"How? I-I don't understand."

Caroline touched his befuddled face. "Your song."

Emily translated, and Lucinda told him Caroline was touching his left cheek. He held his hand to his face, and his eyes filled with wonder making her ache for the ability to really touch him.

"You heard my song?" he whispered. He swallowed the emotion building in his throat, and squeezed his eyes closed. "Caroline, I'm sorry. Please come back to me. I won't rest until you're safely in my arms. I can't protect you when you're in this spirit form. It's killing me. You know I need to be able to protect you. I can't breathe until I know you're safe."

Caroline's eyes tingled with tears she was unable to shed. She glanced at her body and caught a tear sliding down her face. "Mom, look at my face."

Emily sucked in a breath. "Cade. She's crying."

He knelt beside her and kissed the moisture trail left by the tear. Their connection stung her spirit's face. Without removing his gaze from Caroline, he spoke just above a whisper.

"Emily," the eerie pause lingered in the air as he swallowed forcefully. "Does she know?" His sad, red-rimmed eyes burned through her. He wanted to know if she knew about their son.

"Yes," she said. Emily nodded, unable to speak through the streaming tears. Caroline's determination to get back to him amplified upon witnessing his distress. It tore her up to see Cade as this broken man crumbling before her. He rested his forehead on Caroline's shoulder for a moment before he stood, determination burning in his hazel eyes. He faced Lucinda. "How can she get back into her body?"

"Her strong vitality is not powerful enough to launch her back into her physical being. This dark spirit is trying to consume her energy, so she won't have the strength to get back to her body. It's the only way he can personally take her life without causing her to have an accident. She's on his turf now, and he doesn't want to let her go."

Cade let out a string of curses and punched the wall, surprising everyone in the room but Runway. While Cade paced the floor, and the women gawked at the size hole his fist left, Runway removed a laminated piece of paper that was taped to the sink reminding everyone to wash their hands, and casually placed it over the hole in the wall. Caroline chuckled. He said he would always have Cade's back. Guess that was one way to do it.

"What can she do to increase her energy? A power surge, if you will," Runway asked.

Lucinda thought for a moment, the crease between her brows deepening. "Well, anger is one of the most powerful emotions the human body can possess, generating the most energy. That's why our hands shake when we're furious. The adrenaline pulses through our veins. The body's fight or flight response generates the most energy." She shrugged, "The flight response when we're scared pumps adrenaline through our body, but we're less likely to pursue someone or something when we're frightened. The fight response tends to be more powerful. When we're angry, our emotions take over, adding to our energy, and we're inclined to push the intense energy from our body."

Runway's brow furrowed. "So we need to do something to make Caroline really mad to get her back into her body?"

Cade stopped pacing like a caged panther and stared at Caroline's face.

Lucinda spoke quietly, "I think it's your best chance of getting her back before the dark spirit consumes hers."

"What pisses you off the most Caroline?" Cade asked playfully. "I know you've got a hot little temper. What can I do to provoke it?"

Her distracted mind couldn't concentrate on anger in the spirit world. In fact, seeing him this excited and fixated, she couldn't take her eyes off of his sculpted body and enlivened eyes. She felt anything but anger. Desire washed over her. Who knew a spirit form could be turned on?

Lucinda cleared her throat and smiled. “Focus, child. There will be plenty of time for *that* once you’re back and your body has healed.”

Cade’s puzzlement morphed into recognition with a boastful smile. “That’s my girl. Too bad that’s not strong enough to pull you back. It’d be a lot more fun.”

Lucinda continued, directing her attention to the issue at hand. “Perhaps there’s something she feels passionate about, or someone who really gets under her skin?” There was only one person Caroline could think of that could make her angry enough, and she really didn’t want to see her right now. She didn’t want her within a hundred yards of her baby or her body.

“Well, Trevor could usually get a pretty good rise out of her. I’m sure he would come down here if you asked him,” Emily suggested.

Cade disagreed. “No, I don’t think she’s angry enough with him anymore for it to work. Maybe Claire? She was pretty upset with her when Claire hatefully announced to Eddie that she wanted to move in with—”

Her name slipped through Caroline’s lips with a surge of hatred before she even realized that Emily, Cade and Runway all said it at the same time.

“April.”

Lucinda smiled. “Uh-huh. The decision is unanimous. I would love to meet this April to see her aura. She seems to have quite an effect on you all.”

Emily rolled her eyes. “Oh, honey, you have no idea.”

“I’m getting a pretty good one right now,” Lucinda said. “Caroline’s aura color has completely changed in response, as well as each of yours. My suggestion is that you call her in and let her provoke Caroline back to consciousness.”

Cade rolled his tense shoulders. "Hell no," he mumbled. "*If* I'd even consider that, which I won't, it wouldn't be that easy. If April thought she'd be helping Caroline, she'd never agree to it. She's the one who put her here in the first place."

Lucinda's eyes narrowed. "She's responsible for Caroline's coma? How, exactly?"

Cade eyed her, contemplating for a few seconds before answering, obviously deciding if he wanted to go there or not. "Voodoo."

Lucinda stood silently, her gaze never leaving Cade, for what seemed like forever. "What is her last name?"

A short, balding, and rather unhealthy looking doctor knocked on the door's frame, flanked by two nurses. Still cleaning his teeth with his tongue from dinner, he smelled like onions.

"Good evening. I'm doctor Hays, and I'll be attending to Caroline tonight. Her lungs were combating with the machines, so we turned the ventilator off completely, and she's been breathing on her own for about an hour. I'm going to remove the tube, so you all need to leave. You can step out in the waiting room, and I'll have a nurse come get you when you're able to return." Caroline snorted. *Great bedside manner, Doc. Let's see how far that tone of voice gets you.*

"I'm staying." Cade squared his broad shoulders and planted his feet.

"I'm sorry, that's against policy. There is a comfortable waiting room just outside the ICU with a phone. We will call if there are any complications. Otherwise a nurse will come get you when we're finished here."

Cade remained solid and crossed his arms. "I'm not leaving her. We will wait outside the room. How long will it take?"

The doctor stared at Cade impassively without answering, and it was clear there was no other option. Cade's glare could wilt a sturdy oak tree.

Runway broke the tension. "Beau, come on, man. Let them do their job. She'll be okay." His fierce, pale green eyes shifted to the doctor. "Isn't that right, doc? She's in good hands?" The implied threat was masked with a politeness only Runway could provide.

Dr. Hays shifted uncomfortably, a sheen of sweat coating his pasty forehead. "Of course. We perform this simple task on a daily basis. She will be fine, but I'm afraid I am going to need you all to step out while we do it." He shrugged, clearly shaken by their hostility. "Hospital rules, not mine."

Cade leaned close to Caroline. "I'm going to drive Lucinda home, and I'll come right back, love. You take care of yourself, do you hear me? Keep your energy strong." He kissed her forehead, nodded at the doctor, and led her mother and Runway out of the room.

Caroline studied the monitors trying to determine if her brain activity reflected any of the frightening or depressing events she'd experienced throughout the day. A few spikes here and there showed activity, but she couldn't tell when they happened. Not that she had any concept of time.

What would Cade tell Lucinda about April when they got to the truck? Her interest in April spiked after she heard voodoo was involved. Caroline would never have pinned April for the black magic type, but when she thought about it, the musky smell brought it all together.

The room in Eddie's house that Caroline had ducked into after eavesdropping on him and Claire the day of their graduation party flashed through her frazzled memories. That was the time Caroline freaked out when someone or something ran a finger up her spine. She remembered the strong, potent cough-inducing smell, and the general feel of that creepy, dark space. Evil. Lucinda's voodoo shop had the same smell.

The musky smell lingered, then shuffling in the room snagged her attention. Waves of sheer hatred from a murderous ice-blue glare assaulted Caroline's helpless body.

Had she conjured April's presence somehow by thinking of her? Why would this woman come visit her when she'd put Caroline in this position, herself? A thousand, tiny, icicles sank into her spirit. *She's here to finish the job.*

ELEVEN

"Thank you for coming with me today." The leather on Cade's steering wheel protested beneath his grip. He liked Lucinda, but he hated voodoo and everything related to its black magic. His nerves were on edge, and he didn't think the petite caramel-colored woman sitting beside him had anything to do with it. No need to take his personal loathing out on her. "You didn't have to, but I'm really glad you did."

"Tell me about this April you're so fond of."

Cade cocked an eyebrow to her satiric grin. "Caroline's step mother. Only, April's not her real name. Perhaps you've heard of her or her family. Her real name is Ana Marie Morales."

Recognition hardened Lucinda's expression. "I see. She goes by Ana-Marie, and her mother was my husband's sister."

"I know," said Cade. "Small world." Her head snapped up to look at him. "I did some checking on you, madam. Surely you didn't think I'd let my wife spend all that time with you before I was positive you weren't a threat?"

She smiled. "Certainly. That is why I fancy you, Mr. Beauregard. You protect those you love, but not to the point of pushing them away. It's a gift."

"You can imagine my dismay and cause for distrust upon discovering your connection to April's family. At first I suspected you were involved with her, so I watched you closely, but you proved yourself by teaching Caroline things that would help her protect herself." Cade cringed, "Guess it's paying off, now."

"Caroline is stronger than you think."

Cade bristled thinking about her fighting off George. He couldn't help her against her spiritual enemies and it ate him up inside. But he *could* do something about the physical threats in her life. "I think Ana-Marie may be taking after her mother and grandmother."

"You're certain?"

"Call it a hunch." Cade explained his encounter with April at Caroline's graduation party when she had some target practice in the woods, as well as the doll at the hospital. He wasn't positive she'd been the one to send it, but Caroline's hairbrush was found in April's duffel bag full of stolen items last summer. She had access to Caroline's hair.

"So you don't know for a fact it was Ana-Marie, you only suspect."

Cade ground his teeth. "I don't need proof. I've seen enough to know."

Lucinda shifted in her seat and crossed her arms as she regarded Cade and squinted her eyes. "Whatcha chewin' on, *teté-boy*?" Her question was laden with a heavy French-Cajun accent.

He frowned. "What do you mean?"

"Something else is eating at you. I told you before, you cannot hide from me. I see your aura, remember?"

He adjusted his mirror, changed the radio station, and looked everywhere but at her. He should keep his mouth shut. She'd already pissed him off by defending April. But she was right, damn it. He didn't have any hard evidence or witnesses that she's the one who sent the doll with the pins. It could've been anybody. Hell, he's the one who ripped the pins out. Caroline was fine 'til he did that.

"I'm not getting any younger. Out with it."

Surely she couldn't read his mind.

Lucinda chuckled, "Your aura is wavering and tinged with anxiety. I sense that you have something to discuss with me. Let's hear it."

He clenched his jaw as he reached into his front pocket and pulled out the gold amulet he took from Caroline before the babies were born. Lucinda's eyes widened when she saw it.

"Well now," she breathed, leaning forward to get a better look. "Where did you get that?"

"What do you know about this pendant?" he asked, looking from her to the road and back.

She studied his face for a moment. "Better still, *le fils*, you tell me how you know about it?"

"I'm cursed, that's what."

"Cursed, you say? Go on." Her chocolate eyes brightened with amusement.

He ground his teeth and looked at the clock. "Fine," he sighed. Cade rubbed his hand over his face into his hair. "When I was ten years old, my best friend was twelve, and we worked in the sugar cane fields every summer. One day on our walk to work we always passed a swamp. We came upon an abandoned old leather bag sitting next to a tree beside the water, and no one was around. I wanted to keep walking, but Colin started digging through it."

Cade shook his head, “I told him not to touch it. To leave it alone, but he didn’t listen to me.” He exhaled, “Colin pulled out glass pill bottles, a mirror, a voodoo doll, and a gold necklace. *This* necklace.” Cade shifted uncomfortably and took a drink of his Coke. He relished the fizzy burn as it trailed down his esophagus. That felt better than rehashing this part of his past.

“Against my objections, Colin knocked me aside and put the chain around his neck before he pulled the voodoo doll out and slung it into the tree. He said, ‘Chicken. Don’t be such a *capon*, Beau. It’s just a stupid doll.’ It wouldn’t stay up there, so he tied it like a piñata with the vines, and then chopped its head off with his sickle. Then he, uh. . .” Cade chewed at his lips thinking of the best way to say the next part. “He threw everything but the necklace back in the bag and pissed all over it.” Lucinda’s face remained expressionless, but Cade’s shame filled the space for both of them. “Colin was a dick. To everyone. But he’d been my best friend since preschool.”

Cade adjusted the air vent. Why was he fidgeting? He’d briefed much more intimidating people than this woman about Top Secret missions. “Anyway, we worked all day, and on our walk home the sun glinted off something up in a tree. A fishing rod that someone had gotten tangled in the vines, but it wasn’t just any fishing rod. It was an Abu Garcia. That’s like the Porsche of fishing rods, especially to a twelve-year-old. I was tired and ready to get home, but Colin insisted we get it because it was worth a lot of money. He climbed the tree with his sickle to cut the branch down, but it was too thick. So, he crawled out on the branch to reach the vines.”

Cade blew a breath making his cheeks puff out. He hadn't talked about this in nearly twenty years. “He was too heavy for the branch. It broke and his neck got tangled in the vines, choking him, but his sickle dangled dangerously on the branch above him. I was just a skinny little kid, but he wasn't very high above the water, so I risked the gators and swam out below him hoping I could reach his feet to give him something to stand on. I wasn't a very strong swimmer then. I couldn't tread water long enough, and he was pushing me under, drowning me. The vines broke under his weight, and he fell, unconscious, on top of me."

Cade practically whispered the next sentence. It was the first time he'd said it aloud since it happened. "I wasn't strong enough to tow him back to shore before the sickle fell."

Cade pulled the sleeve of his T-shirt up to reveal a crescent shaped scar on his deltoid muscle. "I only caught the tip of the sickle. Colin's neck caught the rest." He stopped at a red light and dragged his palm over his face, cupping his chin.

"He bled out in my arms after I finally got him on land, gurgling with each suffocating breath. All while I hugged his head, begging him not to die." Cade rubbed his eyes, sucked in a deep breath, and repeatedly cleared his throat to keep from crying. He hadn't realized the emotion still bottled up from this traumatic experience. "I was just a kid. I freaked out. I didn't know what to do. What would I tell his parents? The police? That a voodoo doll killed him? My best friend was dead in my lap, steadily bleeding all over the swamp bank, and he still had that damned necklace on. I ripped it off and threw it as hard as I could into the swamp."

"You were only a boy," Lucinda said tenderly. "You did everything you could."

Cade ducked his head. "If I had been a better swimmer. . .stronger. . .I could've gotten him out of harm's way before the sickle fell. I could've saved him."

"No. You—"

"Yes!" Cade slammed the heel of his hand on the steering wheel, rattling the whole dashboard. "Do you know what that did to me? He was my best friend, like a brother to me. I've had to live with that image, that whole tragic, disturbing experience for almost twenty years. I can still picture it clear as crystal, and that day I swore I would never be vulnerable again." He gave her a long look. "I became a Navy SEAL, the best of the best in the elite special forces. I'd never be too weak and helpless again." Cade spoke through his teeth, "Yet here I am, weak and helpless, unable to save the most important person in my life."

They both stared out the windshield, neither speaking nor moving.

"I learned later that the bag belonged to an old voodoo woman nearby who allegedly killed three husbands and her son-in-law. *That's* why I detest voodoo. I watched my best friend suffer a brutal, agonizing death and there wasn't a damned thing I could do to stop it. That necklace was cursed, just like the doll. The moment he touched it, he was destined to suffer the same fate. Why else would the bag be abandoned in the middle of a stretch of empty dirt road?"

He searched her face, but she simply shrugged one shoulder. "Perhaps."

"Perhaps, nothing! I threw that thing in the middle of the swamp," Cade said. "How else did it make it back into my life if it isn't a curse on my family? On me?"

"If the curse did to someone what that person did to the necklace, you would've drowned in that swamp after you threw it into the water, no?"

"Maybe. Maybe not. There's been a voodoo doll each time I've come across the necklace. Maybe they're related." He swallowed hard, anger boiling in his chest, lapping at the edges of his control. "I'm the only boy out of five kids in my family. The only Beauregard left to carry on the name. I've had two sons die before they ever had a chance to live. I believe that curse, my punishment for not stopping Colin from stealing or vandalizing those things that day, is why I can't have a son to carry on my legacy."

"Your legacy is more than a simple name. Tell me, how did you get your hands on the necklace this time? Where did you find it?"

His jaw muscles twitched. "Caroline was holding it the day she went into labor. She couldn't remember exactly, but thought it had been delivered with a bouquet of flowers just before I'd gotten there. Maybe the day before. I touched the necklace the day I ripped the pins from a voodoo doll wrapped with Caroline's hair, the same day I lost my second son whose heart was beating strongly until Caroline touched this damned thing."

Cade held the necklace up again and spoke through gritted teeth. "Your turn. Someone's trying to hurt my family. Tell me everything you know about this medallion."

Lucinda took it from him and studied the intricate design. The web of gold in the middle of the circle consisted of four strong lines almost meeting in the middle. It strongly resembled the crosshairs from his scope on his sniper rifle.

"This is part of a family crest. Only a small segment, but an important one."

"Which family?" Cade expected a name he recognized, but she surprised him.

"Aurieux. Before my time, the Aurieux family controlled much of the area merchants. They had their fingers in everything, all underhanded, of course. Armand Aurieux never suffered any consequence for the money he gained illegally, nor for the people he threatened, hurt, or killed."

"What does that have to do with me? Why is this necklace hexed?"

She held up her bony finger. "Ah, now that is the right question. You see, your friend was not the only person to ever cross a voodoo priestess." She held the chain so the amulet dangled and spun in a circle, dancing a mockery of fate in Cade's face. "This piece is a result of a. . .*cunja,* a spell put on someone. My Carlos told me great stories that were passed down through his family. Legends." She stared into the medallion as if reading the story directly from the design, itself.

"Armand Aurieux was born into a prominent family. He was young and arrogant. After his father, an honorable man respected in the city, died unexpectedly, eighteen-year-old Armand expressed his grief by flashing his family crest around town like a lawman's badge to get what he wanted. He lied, cheated, and stole anything he wanted all in his father's name. Eventually, whenever people saw the crest, they feared what would happen to them if they didn't comply with his unreasonable demands. On top of being a thief and a bully, he was also a sociopath. A controlling and unfaithful husband who left his young wife with nothing, no money or children, though he later had several offspring through his mistresses."

She held the necklace up causing the pendant to spin again, and the shiny gold reflected the lights from oncoming traffic.

"This particular section of the crest he was proudest of symbolized, of all things, loyalty." She looked up at Cade, commanding his attention. "Eventually, only this portion of his crest became his calling card. It was all he needed. He branded it on his whores, painted it on buildings he claimed, and signed his threats with it."

Cade pulled up to Lucinda's place and shifted the truck into Park. "That's a fascinating story, but I still don't know what it has to do with me or Caroline."

"Armand's mother remarried, and her new husband was ashamed of his new stepson's behavior. He cut Armand off from everything involving his family. Armand didn't like that much, so he visited Madam Découx." Cade sucked in a breath.

"I know that name. My great-grandfather, his brother, and son had some. . .unfortunate dealings with her."

"Yes," she said. "Madam Découx was my husband's great aunt. A very powerful necromancer, well versed in the occult." She continued, "Armand wanted to make his mother's new husband pay for crossing him. He had Madam Découx put a curse on his stepfather in return for his gold pendant as payment for her services. The curse was cast, and the family suffered the great loss of their young Patriarch to a severe case of pneumonia."

"What about Armand's mother? Where was she during this whole ordeal?"

"She died shortly after. Rumor was a broken heart, but Carlos believed Madam Découx put a *cunja* on the entire family. For Armand grew even more arrogant with his mother and stepfather out of the picture, and he refused to pay Madam Découx, claiming she hadn't done anything, that his stepfather had died of natural causes."

Cade rocked his head back in understanding. "Ah. So Madam Découx cursed his necklace that should have belonged to her, and would surely be handed down through the generations. Let me guess, Armand Aurieux died a tragically slow and painful death?"

Lucinda grinned. "Voodoo can be useful if used appropriately, though some abuse its bounties. Indeed, Armand suffered greatly, but not before his stepsister ripped the infamous calling card from his neck on his death bed, blaming him for ruining her family."

Cade sighed and rubbed his temples. Keeping up with the Jones's was giving him a headache. "And who was the vengeful stepsister?"

"Carlos once told me her name," she tapped her forehead, "but it escapes me now."

Cade walked around to her side of the car and opened her door. "Thank you for all your help."

"Moreau." She smiled proudly. "I remember. Her name was Marie-Emilie Moreau."

The name didn't register with him, and still didn't explain why his buddy Colin suffered. So how did this piece of cursed jewelry find its way back into Cade's life? Had April somehow managed to get her hands on it? Cade had some research to do, but first he needed more eyes on the people he loved.

Lucinda's cold hand interrupted his thoughts. "There's one more thing," she warned. "The necklace may be damned, but you are not. Legends say that after Armand died, Madam Découx altered her *cunja* to remain dormant, restricting its evil to only his descendants. His blood sets the curse in motion whenever it touches the amulet. So unless you are within his bloodline, someone else controls the curse."

Cade racked his brain to think of who, besides himself and Caroline, could have touched the necklace. Colin never knew who his father was. It was possible Cade's best friend had been a descendant through one of Armand's mistresses. But why was it active now? By whom? His mind raced. He had to figure out the mystery before anything else happened. Before Caroline was trapped from returning to her body.

"Young man, you needn't carry the world on your shoulders. You will get through this if you lean on your faith. God will not allow harm come to your family if you trust Him."

Cade forced a smile and tried to keep the bitterness from seeping into his tone as he disagreed. "He already has."

TWELVE

Caroline had never thought of herself as the helpless type, but the malevolent expression in April's eyes as she scowled at Caroline's abandoned, debilitated body instilled the proverbial sitting-duck situation. She was here for one purpose. How long would it take April to finish what she started? How would she do it? Caroline glanced out the windows. Any chance a doctor or a nurse might catch her in time? Caroline wanted to run for help, but had no idea how to communicate with anyone, and her mom and Runway were in the waiting room oblivious that her last breath approached.

Truly helpless, Caroline stood in front of April staring her down and willing her to have a sudden fatal heart attack. April rested her hand on the bed rail near Caroline's head.

"Why. Aren't. You. Dead. Yet?" She hissed through clenched teeth. "What more must I do to rid my life of you, you little pest?" She straightened and smoothed her black fitted sweater over her narrow bony hips. "I never imagined that fool would send you down here for the entire summer. I expected him to come with you for a weekend, meet your father, and be done with it. His idiot father completely dropped the ball on that one." She chuckled without humor. "At first, Eddie played right into my hands by adding you to his will, but then you almost ruined everything with that gardener." She shrugged, "Of course, I can see why. A woman would have to be blind not to notice his rugged sex appeal. And that body. . ." Her stony blue eyes glazed over with a memory as she lusted after Caroline's husband. Caroline hated her.

April sighed. "I would sunbathe in my sexiest bikinis on the days I knew he'd be working, but I never received so much as a glance from him." Her eyes narrowed. "Then you came along like a dog in heat, and, suddenly, he was around all the time. I was sure the rattlesnake I sent to finish you would work, but no. Not with Prince Charming rushing to save the day. How was I to know he was a sniper and would be watching your every move?" April rolled her eyes and huffed. "When I saw him in your bed I knew I had to do something," she spat, "You disgusting little whore."

April's phone rang and she snatched it from her purse before it caught anyone's attention.

"Where is it?" April searched the room, sorting through gift bags, balloons, and flower arrangements. "It's not in here. I thought you said it would be here, you incompetent fool. I never should've involved you. Nothing but trouble. That's all you've caused." She stood bolt upright. "Oh, don't you dare threaten me, you little traitor. I did you a favor. Cross me and I'll sick the real bad boys on you. That gold-plated pedestal will be knocked right out from under you."

Screaming, Caroline clawed at her feeble, distracted mind. She had to do something, but what? She couldn't touch or move anything. A group of nurses laughed boisterously in passing, and April ducked low beside the bed. She continued talking quietly for which Caroline was thankful. Caroline had already learned a lot from April's confession, and her meager spirit light was transforming into a raging fire.

Caroline swung a few times at April's head, but her hands zipped right through. What was she looking for? Who was she talking to?

April ended the call, festering about something. "Where is it?" She visually inspected Caroline's body.

"Eddie's disgraceful impotence regarding all-things-Caroine. . ." she mocked. "I had a plan until you brought your damned, backwoods slut of a mother back with you." April rolled her eyes. "Thirteen years of planning, preparation, kissing-up and pretending to be someone I wasn't to people I loathed. . .all down the drain when your mother came shaking her fat hips in his direction, and he instantly became a hormonal teenager again. He had the nerve to divorce me. All my time and investment wasted." April's scrunched scowl reminded Caroline of the first time she'd tasted her grandpa's bitter black coffee. "Navy sludge the Navy way," he'd proudly said.

April sifted through extra blankets and pillows in the companion chair all while grumbling about a blackmailing traitor.

"My little doll didn't completely do the trick, did it? You still managed to produce another heir to the Fontenot fortune. A little *Beau-peep* to add to your flock of losers. Well, worry not, *stepdaughter*, she'll be joining her brother soon enough." She slammed a cabinet drawer shut in her fumbling, flinching and looking over her shoulder to see if anyone heard. "Soon as I find what I'm looking for." Frustration hissed from her parted lips as she dialed a number. "Yeah. It's not here. I don't know. . .everywhere," she whispered. April's brow angled, cutting the planes of her forehead sharply enough to slice through her faulty composure, “Come find it yourself, then. I’m leaving before anyone sees me."

Caroline needed April to stay just a little longer in order for Cade to find her there. But how? Just for the sake of trying, she punched at April a few more times with the same results. Nothing. She remembered the movie *Ghost* when Patrick Swayze entered Whoopi Goldberg’s body. It was worth a shot. Desperation dominated aversion, and cringing, she squeezed her eyes closed, bracing herself as she literally stepped into April’s shoes.

What she hadn’t counted on was the beastly bout of hatred that devoured her from within April’s baleful essence. Exposed, imperiled, and revolted, Caroline’s spirit rejected the abhorrent limited space like swimming in a vat of hot grease. Her chest cavity burned, longing for oxygen, only to inhale the fiery tear gas from April’s malignant spirit. Caroline escaped the poisonous entrapment as quickly as she’d entered it. Momentarily stunned by the brief invasion, April shivered, confusion clouding her features, and gathered her bag she’d set at the head of the bed.

“Hey! You’re not supposed to be in here,” Dr. Hays shouted. “How did you get past the front desk?” He observed her suspicious positioning over Caroline’s head. “Who are you? Security!”

April’s mouth opened as she scanned the hallway. Fear flashed through her sapphire eyes when they locked onto Cade. In a full sprint headed to the room, he effortlessly wove in between people with the grace of a professional football running back. His crazed face reflected his grip on the doorway, and for a very brief moment Caroline almost felt sorry for April. The promise of pain and suffering enveloped his eyes. She swallowed forcibly, a fly caught in a spider's web as Cade stalked into the room.

Cade glanced at Dr. Hays and collected himself. He straightened and squared his shoulders as he grinned ruthlessly. Always in control of his temper, he was spectacular.

"Doctor, this woman is not to come within a mile of Caroline ever again." His nostrils flared, jaw muscles rippled, and chest swelled with each exaggerated breath. "She's a threat you want nothing to do with. Trust me." Caroline enjoyed witnessing his difficulty in not ripping April's face off, and, just this once, for a fraction of a second, she wished he would break his composure.

Dr. Hays squinted as he sized April up. "Yes, I gathered that. Ma'am, follow me, please."

"I'll see my own way out, thank you." April looped her bag over her head and started out when she paused at the doorway.

April smiled smugly at the doctor. "I think I'll go visit my granddaughter."

"Like hell, you murderous bitch!" Caroline shouted to deaf ears.

Cade and Runway blocked April like the great wall of China. However, Caroline's relief was short lived. Her throat constricted when she remembered April's comment about her daughter joining her brother soon enough. She rushed to the NICU just in time to see the shadowy form of a man standing beside her baby's sleeping body.

"No." Gravel scraped through her tight vocal chords in the weak exclamation. Though the NICU nurses were present, Caroline was the only one who could see the menacing figure leaning over her daughter's tiny frame. Cade had no idea or he would've gone crazy.

"No, you bastard. Get away from my daughter!" Her shrieking only amused him causing his lips to curl and spread across his face. His stringy black hair dangled only inches from her baby's face as he eagerly watched her like a viper stalking a mouse. George Callahan laughed at Caroline's frozen form. What could she do? What would happen if he touched her spirit form? For all she knew she'd spontaneously combust into a million molecules. She would take that chance, though, and skate barefoot through the embers of hell to protect her daughter.

Her mind circled the realization and gravity of her duty. Fury rampaged through every molecule of her being. This baby was hers. "Get the hell away from my daughter! I will never let you have her soul, and I will die protecting her!"

A malevolent grin stretched across the entity's face. "That can be arranged."

Caroline's eyes wobbled, her control slipped. She knew George wanted her body worse than her baby's to use it against Eddie, but he didn't seem picky at this point, and she couldn't protect her baby girl's fragile energy in this spirit form. Caroline needed her body back in order to protect them both. Icebergs would form in hell before she let George Callahan capture anybody's soul, especially her daughter's.

Caroline frantically scanned the room as the hospital walls seemed to crumble into shards around her. No one else moved as the room shook. Only she acknowledged the earthquake. She couldn't control her surroundings. What was happening? The shrill noise blasting from her mouth as fear and rage searched for an escape remained unheard by everyone except the one soul she wished would combust into the broiling underworld. Quicksand pulled at her limbs preventing her from reaching George before everything faded to a blood red tinge, and she lost the ability to focus on anything but her chilled spirit convulsing with raw anger. A bright light, or possibly rage, blinded her, and everything disappeared into the white abyss.

This wasn't like before when she'd passed from the outer realm to the inner realm. This was completely different. Terrifying. She needed to get back to her daughter. She pressed her eyes closed, but the shaking worsened. Thinking about George or April anywhere in the vicinity of her child fueled the inferno scorching her insides. They'd already stolen one of her babies from her, she'd be damned if they got the other. The quaking room spun, and Caroline sat before she fell. She hoped the transfer back to her body would happen before she simply burst into glitter.

The numbness and quivering abruptly halted, and eerie silence thundered in her head. She tried to speak, but nothing came out. She tried to move, but couldn't. What happened? Where was she now? A heaviness crept over her and she succumbed to the cold, inky blackness.

THIRTEEN

The incessant beeping grated on Cade's nerves. Caroline's pulse had sped to an alarming rate for a while before finally settling back to normal. Why wasn't she waking up? What had caused the spike in her heart rate? The doctor said her brain activity was normal, her heart was strong, so what was the hold up? He tapped his fingers in rhythm to the steady beat on the back of her hand until he couldn't stand it anymore. He had to ask again.

"Is she okay? Her heartbeat sounds normal. Think she'll wake up soon?"

Dr. Hays, the jerk-off hospitalist that had been assigned to Caroline, pushed his glasses up the bridge of his nose and rolled his eyes. "Whatever happened before your friend—"

"That woman is no friend of mine, Doc."

Dr. Hays's exasperated sigh ruffled the papers fastened to his clipboard. "As I was saying, whatever happened before your friend took *that woman* downstairs must have flagged down her sub-conscience and brought her back to reality. The large spike in brain activity can prove that, and her body is responding well to my tests. She should wake up any time. She's probably listening to us now."

Cade snapped his teeth together. Lucinda must have been right about the anger pulling Caroline's spirit back to her body. Seeing April probably cycled enough energy to power a nuclear plant. Cade brushed her hair from her forehead. "Come on, baby," he whispered. "Show me those pretty green irises."

Her eyeballs rolled beneath their lids as they sleepily parted. The lights were bright, and she squeezed them shut again.

"Caroline?" Cade snapped his fingers to get Dr. Hays's attention. "Hey, Doc, flip that light switch off, will ya? I think she's waking up." He didn't care about manners or respect, he was only focused on one thing right now. She squeezed his hand and he sucked in a breath. She quickly blinked her eyes open again, frowning, and he couldn't help but rejoice, frown or not.

He looked to the ceiling, "Oh, thank you, Jesus." A jackhammer couldn't pound the smile from his face. "Yes! Caroline, I'm here, baby." He rested his chin on her shoulder. "Hey, beautiful. Welcome back." She moaned. "Thirsty?" He reached for a cup on the bedside table. "Here, have a few ice chips. Dr. Hays said you'd be thirsty, but we can't give you water just yet." She tried to sit up and winced. "No, no, sweetheart. You just had surgery, remember? Lie down and let me take care of you."

Caroline sucked on her ice chip. Judging from her look of ecstasy, it must have hit the spot. Finally, she licked her lips and whispered a single, scratchy syllable.

"Hey." Her lopsided grin melted his heart.

Cade smiled as he scooped another couple of ice chips with a plastic spoon and carefully placed them in her mouth. "Hey, yourself." He wanted to tell her how incredibly happy he was to hear her voice, to see her smile, but he controlled himself. He didn't want to bombard her so quickly.

Caroline's shoulders relaxed, and she absently nodded as if trying to recall a far off memory. "Mom?"

"She's downstairs with Runway."

Cade watched her closely. How much would she remember? When her head snapped up to look at him with a frantic expression, he didn't even have to ask what memory reared its ugly head.

Cade's face hardened. "Runway is making sure April never bothers you in here again." He looked around, "Hopefully, you won't have to be in this hospital much longer."

"Our daughter. Where is she? Is she okay?"

"Yes, she's perfect." Did she remember about their son? Should he tell her, or wait to see if she mentioned it? "Sh-she's in the nursery. Your dad is in there with her. He hasn't taken his hands off her."

"How long have I. . ." She swallowed, confusion creasing her delicate features.

He frowned again, grief piercing his gut. Stalling, he placed a few more ice chips in her mouth. "How long have you been in here?" she nodded. "You were in a coma for three days." His eyes throbbed, the tears threatening to say too much, and he tried brushing it off by rubbing them and clearing the emotion from his throat. He whispered, "Do you. . . Did you see. . ." he had a lot to say, but no idea how to get it all out without overwhelming Caroline. "I was scared, baby. I ain't gonna lie. I thought I'd lost you." He kissed her, relishing her response. "It's great to finally have you kissing me back. I've missed you like crazy. Please don't ever leave me like that again, or I will find a way to come get you, myself."

Caroline's eyes widened, and she started to speak, but Cade covered her lips with one finger.

“Do you remember everything you witnessed while you were unconscious?"

Her brows furrowed. “Not everything, but some of it, yes. Most of it seems like a dream.”

Holding her gaze and seeing the confusion, he closed his eyes and drew in a deep breath. She needed to know. How much, he wasn’t sure, but certainly about their son. “I need to tell you something.” He struggled to find the words, clearing his throat, swallowing, and clearing it again. Anything to control the emotion to allow him calmly break the news.

He reviewed what happened before the babies were born, when he'd ripped the pins from the voodoo doll like an idiot. "I rarely left your side after that." He chuckled, “I pissed off a few doctors, including Dr. Guillory.”

Cade kissed the back of her hand before threading his fingers through hers. “Our daughter is gorgeous.” His heart swelled. “She’s perfect. Tiny, but perfect. Ten fingers, ten toes, and a headful of golden-brown hair. The docs call her the miracle baby because she only needed the machines and feeding tubes for two days.”

Caroline smiled, but tears filled her eyes, and his control slipped. It was no use trying to hide the agony. “Um. . . Our son. . . He, uh. . .he didn’t. . .” He cleared his throat when his voice cracked and cursed his inability to be strong for Caroline. “He didn’t make it.” Cade’s voice quivered on the last two words and the corners of his mouth trembled.

Caroline frowned and swiped her tears away. “I remember that. What. . .what happened, exactly?”

“His placenta had busted, or something. I don’t know. The doctor explained it, but all the terminology escapes me. He was born alive, but his little heart wasn’t strong enough. . .” Unshed tears breached the dam and fell down his cheeks. "He didn't make it." He sucked in a hard breath through trembling lips. She nodded, but her short-lived composure crashed, and she finally lost it.

He caught her in a tender embrace, allowing her to weep against him and use him as a buffer for her sadness while he clung to her for comfort. The petty scuffles, secrets, and stand-offs they'd had throughout the past year didn't matter as they shared their heartbreak over losing a precious soul they'd created and nurtured together. Cade had sung to the babies regularly, Caroline read stories aloud, and now they mourned.

Caroline's shoulders quaked from the staggering grief as she wailed. They mourned for their son's twin sister who would grow up never knowing him, feeling as if a part of her was missing. A part of her heart lost forever. She told Cade about seeing Rachel rocking and singing their son, her promise to protect him, and they vowed to keep his memory alive for all of their sakes. Cade pressed his hand to his chest afraid his heart would bleed out through the gaping hole that had been drilled through his torso. The pain was too strong to be from anything else. Caroline clutched his shirt as she howled into the fabric, asking why this happened. He wished he could give her an answer. He only had one thought blasting through his mind.

"Caroline, I'm sorry," Cade muttered between sobs. "This is my fault." She pushed against him weakly. He raised his head to look at her.

Her husky voice sounded foreign. "This is *not* your fault." He silently disagreed with a tilt of his head. Now wasn't the time to tell her why it was, in fact, his fault. Holding firm, she calmly said it again without taking her eyes off him. "Cade, none of this was *your* fault."

He held her gaze long and hard. “I can’t accept that.” He sat up straight, his busy hands tugged on a loose thread of her blanket. “I could’ve handled things differently. If I had confronted April sooner. . . If I hadn’t pulled the pins out like a fool, you’d still be pregnant with both of our children.”

“I learned about placental abruption in nursing school. Only the basics, but, from what I can remember, I’m lucky to be alive right now."

He swiveled his head and grumbled, “No thanks to me. It doesn’t matter now."

She squeezed his hand about as hard as a toddler squeezing it, and he bit his tongue, cursing himself for letting that slip. “April had that doll with the pins in it two weeks before you touched them, and there’s nothing to say you pulling them out is what caused the abruption.” He gave her a disbelieving look, and she scowled.

“Okay, how about this, what if you *hadn’t* pulled the pins out, and the bleeding continued for two more weeks slowly and effectively killing them both? We would’ve had two stillborn babies instead of one adorable, healthy baby now. If you want to take responsibility for something, let it be saving your daughter from that evil monster.”

He loved her spirit, which was exactly why he couldn’t worry her any further. He’d do whatever it took to get her home and nursed back to health. “Do you have any idea how much I’ve missed you? But you need to calm down. I don’t want your temper stealing you back to wherever you were being held prisoner, away from me. Besides, her name is Ana Morales.”

“What? Who?” Caroline frowned. He could tell she’d caught his not-so-subtle change of subject, but, lucky for him, her curiosity won out.

"April Jones, her maiden name, was an alias. After she married your dad, she became April Fontenot. But her real name is Ana-Marie Morales. I've been researching her."

Closing her gaping jaw, Caroline asked, "April has an alias? For what reason would that woman need two identities? She's bad enough with only one."

He laughed and kissed her forehead. "I agree, but she's hiding something."

"Wait a sec. How long have you known about this?"

Cade tried a nonchalant shrug, "A while." It didn't work. She glared until he finally gave in. "I hadn't told you because you were pregnant, and I wanted to have all of my facts before I said anything. I know how much you hate her, and I didn't want to risk upsetting and potentially harming all three of you." She arched a disbelieving eyebrow. "I promise. There's plenty more to tell, but let's focus on getting you home first, okay?"

"There's more?"

"Yes, but I don't want to talk about it here. Later, I promise." He quickly kissed her lips again, a feeling he would never tire of. " He popped outside the room to speak with a nurse, but kept his eye on her through the doorway.

Cade stopped talking mid-sentence when Caroline's heart monitor grabbed his attention with a staccato rhythm. He rushed over to her bedside scanning over her body and the machines, the heart monitor, blood pressure reading, and everything looked fine until his eyes landed on her blushing face. It reminded him of the time in the library when he'd first met her. He had caught her checking him out while he loaded the microfilm. She looked like she wanted to crawl under the dinosaur machine and die, much like she looked now. A sly smile crept across his face.

"You okay?"

The look she gave was one he'd only seen behind closed doors when she was usually naked, and it stirred the sleeping giant. Damn. It had been forever since he thought about sex, and seeing that look, knowing, or at least hoping Caroline was thinking about it, had him ready to go. "What are you thinking about to cause that lovely pink glow I've missed?"

"You. . .making love to me."

His brows rose, and his cargo shorts grew so tight he was afraid he'd pop the button. Her still-husky voice lowered adding a seductive flavor to it. "I was watching you just now, your muscles flexing in your shoulders and back as you walked around, the things those capable fingers can do. . ." She sighed with a moan, sexy as hell. "I miss your hands on me. Your mouth. . ."

Cade slowly licked his lips attempting to keep his composure and gingerly braced his hands on the bed framing her head. He leaned close to nibble on her earlobe and she arched into him.

"Baby, you can't say things like that to me when you're laid up in a hospital bed. Torture." His labored breathing on her neck caused her to shiver. He kissed a trail down her neck to her chest, ending in that delicate, now heaving, space between her breasts. He worked his way up the other side of her neck.

Runway and Emily walked into the room abruptly ending the sensual moment. Emily's face lit up with tears, and Runway smirked as he took in their heated body language.

"Well, that didn't take long. Beau's girl is back with us." He smiled, amused. "Welcome back, *bella*."

"Thanks. It's good to be back."

"Sweetheart, you had us all worried. I'm so happy you're awake." Emily's voice wavered.

"I'm back now. You can breathe again. You *all* played a part in bringing me home. Thank you." Caroline reached for her mother's hand. "I still can't believe you could hear me. That's insane."

"You're telling me. I thought I'd lost my mind." She gestured to Cade. "So did your husband."

Cade shamefully bowed his head. He *had* thought she was looney, grasping for straws, but thankfully he'd been wrong.

"If it hadn't been for Runway encouraging me," Emily said, "and that crazy code word you came up with, I might have checked *myself* into this hospital."

Caroline shook her head. "No, you're not the crazy one, April is. Maybe it's because it happened right before I came back, but I remember most of what she said to me when she was in here. She's psycho. I can't believe she was in here for that long before anyone found her." Caroline trained her eyes on Runway. "Why did you let her leave?" She looked at Cade. "She was, or is, planning to kill our daughter."

Cade bit his cheek, muffling his thirst for April's blood, while Runway gathered the thin cable he'd placed in the flower arrangement by Caroline's head. "What is that?" Emily asked.

He circled the delicate cable in his capable hands and placed it in a clear plastic bag. Then he reached around behind the plant and pulled out a square, metal, postage stamp-sized device, holding it up for everyone to see. "I'm not worried about April. I had a feeling she would make a visit, and if not her, possibly someone who knew something we needed to know." He casually raised a shoulder. "I bugged the room. Hopefully, the sound is clear."

Cade recalled their intimate conversation just before his best friend and mother-in-law walked in. Caroline's face flushed again, only with humiliation rather than arousal.

"Good thinking. I'm eager to listen to it," Cade quipped, grinning like the cat that ate the canary. "I'm sure it has some good stuff on it." He glanced at Caroline and winked.

Caroline rolled her eyes and shot a stern look at Runway. "How's Kristy?"

He nodded apprehensively. "She's well. I called her just now to let her know you were awake. She sends her love and promises to visit as soon as she can." Runway had told Cade about his confession to Caroline, and now he was clearly worried he'd said too much.

"Good." Caroline smirked, "I'm sure my daughter and I will pale in comparison to the gift you'll have for her when she gets here, right?" He stared blankly until recognition flooded his eyes.

"As if anything could ever outshine you two, but yes, I will have a *sparkling* surprise for her when she arrives."

Caroline winked.

Yep. Cade chuckled. She remembered.

"Don't worry, lover boy. I'll act surprised when I see her." His shoulders relaxed. "She's madly in love with you. She'll say yes. Trust me."

"I do," Runway said.

"Caroline, you told me George tried to hurt you," Emily said.

"Yes," she whispered. "I saw Rachel first, and she told me I was in the outer realm of unconsciousness." Caroline pressed the heel of her hand to her forehead. "Gah! I was spacey and distracted while stuck there. I couldn't focus on anything. She urged me to get back to my body, then she disappeared. George. . . is insane. I'm his revenge. He was planning to keep me from coming back to my body. He wants to watch Eddie grieve and suffer from my death, and then kill him slowly." Caroline's tears streaked her face, and Cade wished he could've protected her from that bastard.

"He was terrifying. I didn't know what else to do, so I prayed. That's when we both heard Cade's voice." Cade winced, an arrow piercing him in the gut for not being able to do more. "He'd been about to come after me. What, I'm not sure, but your singing stopped him." Caroline turned his face to look at her. "Cade, you were the answer to my prayer. Your singing saved me. When George lunged for me, the room spun, and I sank to the ground. The next thing I knew I was sitting next to you while you sang to me."

Emotion overwhelmed him. He couldn't describe the cauldron of feelings boiling inside of him—pain, grief, fear, anger, elation, embarrassment, relief. Cade kissed her, and she mumbled against his lips. "It was a wonderful song." He buried his face into the crook of her neck and hugged her like she might disappear.

Caroline held Cade's head to her bosom gently playing with his hair, and he'd be okay if he never left that position. "I could see y'all. I tried everything to get back into my body. I laid on it, wallowed in it, and I even tried coming up into it from beneath my bed, but nothing worked. I wasn't sticking. It was incredibly frustrating."

Emily dabbed her swollen eyes with a tissue.

"I vaguely remember the moment when you heard me. I remember I was so happy I wanted to kiss you."

Emily nodded, wiping away fresh tears. "Me, too."

Caroline tugged Cade's hair to look up at her. "I know you still blame yourself for everything that happened, and hold yourself personally responsible for the death of our son, for my coma, and for allowing April the opportunity to hurt us. I need you to believe me when I tell you that none of this is your fault. I love you, I'm here with you now, and we have a precious daughter to raise and protect. We'll get through our son's funeral *together*. I will *not* let you shoulder this responsibility or grief alone."

"Caroline, there something—"

"Caden Luke, do you understand me?" He closed his eyes. "Now," she sat up cheerfully, "we have a very important task ahead of us."

Clearing the frog from his throat, he glanced at Emily and Runway. "What's that, love?"

She grinned. "We owe our babies a name, don't you think?"

Everything else on Cade's mind took a backseat. "Indeed, we do."

FOURTEEN

Caroline peacefully rocked her baby girl in the chair that had once belonged to Rachel. The heavens opened again for the fifth day in a row, and Caroline reflected on her experience in the hospital. At least the rain waited for them to get home from New Orleans. She would've hated to expose her preemie to the drenching Gulf Coast rains.

The past five weeks had been crazy and stressful, but Caroline could finally breathe easier now that she was home with her perfect little girl. Because she'd been confined to the incubator in the NICU, Caroline and Cade temporarily moved in to Eddie's house in New Orleans. They ate, they slept, and they drove back and forth to the hospital. Luckily, winter in southeast Louisiana was cold enough to have plants and weeds in hibernation, allowing Cade free time away from his landscaping business. He had quit his part-time shift at the library when Caroline landed herself on bed rest, but he managed to squeeze in a few gigs with his band at several places in the French Quarter.

Watching Cade hold their child like a delicate flower melted Caroline's heart. And, though she was bigger now, his large, strong hands dwarfed her. The emanating joy from him whenever he held her eased the struggle they had bringing their miracle into the world.

They chose a name significant to both families, Danielle Helene Beauregard, Dani for short. She was every bit as marvelous as her given name. Danielle was Caroline's grandmother who died when Caroline was only a child, and Helene belonged in nearly every generation of the Beauregard family.

Caroline retrieved the newspaper clipping of her son's obituary from the side table and brushed her thumb across his name. The funeral for their son was like shoving her battered heart through a meat grinder, but it hadn't killed her, though sometimes the continuous grief came close. She'd trade places with him in a heartbeat if she could. Instead, all she could offer him was his name. Joseph Toutant Beauregard. Joseph was Eddie's middle name as well as Rachel's son, Caroline's G2 grandfather. Her son's unusual middle name, Toutant, had originally been a surname in every generation of boys in the Beauregard family except Cade who had been named after his mother's family. Because Catherine was named after their dad's family, Angie Beauregard wanted to honor her father through her first son's name. She didn't realize she'd never have another boy.

Caroline regretted she hadn't seen baby Joseph as his life began and ended so quickly while she struggled to save her own life. She hadn't seen his body, but Cade insisted that was for the best. She knew if she'd seen him, that mental image would forever be embedded in her mind. She comforted herself by imagining he resembled Dani, only with stronger features and handsome like Cade, as she said her sorrowful goodbyes. Letting go of a child she carried for seven months, and didn't get to see, kiss, or hold, was truly one of the hardest days of her life. She would never see the world the same going forward. Her selfish behavior from the past couple of years weighed heavily on her heart, and she formed a growing mental list of people to apologize to for being such a pushy, immature brat. Nothing forced one to grow up quite like burying her child after almost dying, herself. She wouldn't wish it on her worst enemy, not even April.

Caroline had seen the tears April shed when Remy was shot last year. Though Remy wasn't her biological son, she had raised him. April was his mother for all intents and purposes. However, why would April try to kill Caroline and threaten to kill Dani, too? Caroline wanted to believe there was at least a sliver of goodness in April. What was her motive? Was it all a farce to act as a distraction from a different agenda? To hit left when the enemy was looking right? Or perhaps April really was pure evil infecting anyone who came too close to her. Either way, Caroline didn't want her anywhere near her loved ones.

Delia peeked in the room. "Ms. Caroline? You have a phone call from Dr. Guidry." She smiled down at Dani, "Want me to tell her you'll call her back?"

Delia was the first person Caroline met when she arrived on the Fontenot doorstep nearly two years ago, soaking wet, naïve, and completely clueless. Delia had been Eddie's personal assistant, his caretaker, for years, caring for the house and anything else that needed doing. Though she was only ten years older than Eddie, she adopted the maternal role of the house as the surrogate grandmother, and Caroline couldn't imagine the Fontenot plantation without her.

"No, that's okay. If you don't mind holding Dani I'll take the call."

Delia set the phone on the antique dressing table and held her arms out. “Of course I don’t mind. Come see Maw-maw D, boo boo.” Delia sang to Dani, dancing her around the room.

After Caroline’s unusual experience traipsing around in the spirit world, she’d decided to become a psych nurse. Lucinda believed Caroline had a clairvoyant gift that would come in handy helping others who were lost in their own minds. There was a clinic in Houma and she wanted to work close to home. Perhaps the clinic’s Chief Psychiatrist, Dr. Guidry had some wonderful news.

***

“Hey, have you talked to Kristy?” Cade asked, peeking his head into Eddie’s office where Caroline had gone to take her call. The crease between Cade’s brows seemed like a permanent fixture lately.

“Not since she texted me a picture of the exquisite ring Runway gave her. Have you seen that thing? It’s incredible.”

“No.” His heavy lids, wrinkled forehead, and tight mouth proved his disinterest.

“Everything okay?”

“I can’t get hold of Runway. He’s not answering, and I can’t get this damned bugging contraption he’d set up in your hospital room to work. I should’ve made him show me before he left, but no, not me, I insisted I could do it.” Cade brusquely rubbed the back of his neck. “I tried for three weeks to break the code before I finally realized I had the wrong damned software. I ordered the correct software and it came in last week but I still haven’t figured out how to sync it to my computer. Guess I’ve been out of the game too long. It’s pissing me off,” he scowled.

“I can see that.” She ambled over to him. “Need some cheering up? I know a girl who knows a few things.”

He considered it for a second before giving a peck on her lips and backing up a step. “Not right now. I have some calls to make. Maybe Tonya can help me decode it.”

Bitterness coated her tongue from the stinging rejection. Since she’d been released from the hospital Cade had hardly touched her, not intimately at least. Sure, they’d fooled around, but it was just like before they were married. Heavy petting that he always stopped before things got too steamy. Caroline slipped into her room and positioned the full length mirror to see her whole body.

She raised her shirt and cringed. Wavy red stretch marks curved around the small-but-present lumps of chub she had gained with the pregnancy. She gingerly stroked her finger across the still-tender scar from her Cesarean and back over the squishy skin of her belly. What a difference a tiny baby—or two—could make. She stared in disbelief at her reflection. Dark circles beneath sleepless eyes peered back at her. Her stringy unconditioned hair hadn’t been styled in weeks, and her once voluptuous breasts now sagged shapelessly, having been stretched to the max. She’d been unable to nurse Dani in the NICU. No wonder Cade was keeping his distance. Caroline shoved the mirror backward against the wall, swiping her tears away.

“Caroline? Are you off the phone?” Her mother called from downstairs.

“Yes, I’m coming.” She smoothed her shirt, twisted her hair up in a messy bun, and trotted down the steps. Cade loved her, scars and all.

Caroline nibbled on another salad, choking it down while fantasizing about a bacon cheeseburger. It tasted fine, but she’d actually lost her appetite while pondering everything Cade had told her about April. Tonya Floyd, his FBI friend, had discovered that April, aka Ana Morales, was the illegitimate daughter of Kenneth Callahan. That shocked Caroline more than anything. Never in a million years would she have guessed that. April had hit on Trevor when he was here, which Caroline thought was an act to get a rise out of her, but still, he was her half-brother and April must have known. She shuddered. April's mother, Maria, had listed Kenneth as the biological father on April's birth certificate—hard evidence proving the connection.

It figured, Kenneth Callahan was a prick. It was no surprise that he'd cheated on his wife. Also no surprise he'd never taken responsibility for the baby, the greedy chauvinist that he was. Caroline would bet if April had been a boy instead of a girl, the strapping fruit of his loins to carry on the family name, he would have tried to sue for custody. Cade told her that, at the time, Kenneth Callahan denied having an affair with the woman, then he tried to claim that he was sterile from a case of mumps he'd had as a child. Five years later, Trevor was born.

"Earth to Caroline," Emily said.

"This dahlin's mind is a thousand miles away." Delphine chuckled as she drizzled glaze over her warm rum cake.

"Smells delicious, Delphine."

"Thanks, beb. Gimme ten minutes and I'll cut you a piece."

Caroline held up her hand. "Nope. None for me, thanks."

Emily frowned. "You okay, honey? It's not like you to turn down dessert. Especially rum cake." She rocked side-to-side holding Dani while feeding her a bottle.

"I've got some vanilla ice cream in the freezer, love. It'll go great with it," Delia added. "Delphine baked that cake just for you."

"No, seriously. Y'all are sweet, but I've got to watch my calories if I want to lose this baby weight."

"What baby weight? You look like a million bucks, boo." Delphine cackled, "Hell, I wish I looked as good as you now, and I never had a baby. . .much less two."

Caroline flinched. She tried to hide the sting of Delphine's words, but they all noticed. Instead, she changed the subject.

"Cade's been stressing over the connection between April, Kenneth Callahan, and Angelo Marcellino. He suspects they were working together to get me and Trevor married, but can't figure out why?" Caroline chugged a bottle of water to wash down the remaining bite of salad. "I can't think of any reason April would agree to work with that lying, cheating Callahan except for money."

"Maybe he felt guilty after all this time for abandoning her and offered to give her a cut if she would help him?" Emily offered.

"Yeah, and when that plan bombed they hired professional killers to finish the job," Delia said.

"Cade's friend Tonya is helping him decode the surveillance recording Runway had put in my hospital room. Surely the Federal government can crack the new technology." Caroline glowered, "I can't remember everything she said to me when I was knocked out." She washed out her bowl and put it in the dishwasher. "Apparently Tonya has insight into the mafia, too. Or at least this leader dude. I wouldn't know him if I passed him on the streets."

"Is Cade up in New Orleans now with her?" Emily asked as Dani suckled the last of her bottle.

She nodded, unable to miss the implication in her mother's tone. "I'm just trying to stay out of their way and focus on my new role as a mother." Caroline needed the time to grieve, too. She visited her son's grave a few times a week to refresh the flowers and say a prayer for the safekeeping of his spirit.

"How do you feel about them working together?"

"I trust him." She had no reason to feel threatened by Tonya. She welcomed the alone time with her daughter. Besides, it wasn't like Cade was never around. He only went to New Orleans for a couple of days during the week while she and Dani were safe at home with her family.

"Can't say I like him digging around the Louisiana mafia's business, though." Until she'd met Lucinda, Caroline had never worried about voodoo, hoodoo, or magic, but there was always that lingering doubt in her mind that it could be real. She had absolutely no doubt that organized crime was real. She'd watched *The History Channel* enough to know the kinds of things the mafia was capable of, and she wanted no part of it. She had to trust Cade, and Tonya seemed more than capable of discretion.

"How's Beau holding up, boo?" Delia asked.

Caroline shrugged and sipped her water. She honestly didn't know. "He's taking Joey's death harder than he lets on. He's buried himself in busyness. He's always doing something. Working out, running, gigs with his band, and researching with Tonya. He makes some time for Dani and me, but I can't help but feel he's avoiding something."

"He needs time, sweetheart." Emily smoothed her hand over Caroline's disheveled hair. "Men grieve differently than we do. Maybe if he has nothing to do it will make the pain in his heart worse."

"Yeah. He'll be back to hisself soon, love." Delphine chuckled, "I seen him the other day running wit' no shirt along the highway, muscles slicked with sweat and flexing with every step, and nearly ran into the car in front of me." She took a large bite of rum cake and spoke with her mouth full, "Let him keep workin' out, beb, and keep reapin' the benefits of his therapy."

The women shared a laugh and Emily added, "Hang in there. He's still worried about you, and now he has two women in his life to keep safe. I'm sure once everything has settled down, and the authorities catch whoever is trying to hurt this family, he'll be back to his fun, playful self." She winked, "You'll have your husband back."

"Here's hoping." Caroline grinned and excused herself to put Dani down for a nap. Delphine was right, Cade's gym therapy had buffed him up even more than he was when they'd first met, and she couldn't keep her eyes off him. . .when he was around. Caroline watched her daughter sleep for a few minutes and called Kristy. She needed a pick-me-up, and her best friend always delivered.

"What's up, C? I've missed you like crazy!"

Caroline smiled, Kristy's cheerful voice eased the pain. "I've missed you, too. How's. . .everything?"

Kristy still didn't know Caroline knew she was pregnant, and it was almost funny how she danced around the gigantic white elephant in their relationship. "Um. . .great. Sorry I couldn't fly in while you were in the hospital. Nothing seems to be going my way right now. How about you? How's my baby girl?"

"She's good. I loved the pictures of your new ring. I'm glad Runway finally got his act together and proposed. When's the wedding?"

"Oh, uh, I um," she sighed, "I don't know. My parents are being difficult."

"Well, knowing them, I'm sure they'd rather their grandchild's parents be married before it's born. You'd better hop to it."

Caroline bit her lip not to laugh at the abrupt silence. "What do you mean?"

"Oh come on, Kris. You didn't think I wouldn't figure it out? You would've been over here on the first flight out the second I got out of the hospital if you could've. Plus, you hate going to the doctor and every time I've called lately you're at the doctor's office. Runway was always avoiding my questions. Wasn't too hard to figure out."

"I'm sorry, C. I wanted to tell you, but I didn't want you to be upset and think I was trying to steal your thunder or rub your nose in it." She sniffled. "I was going to tell you after your babies were born, but then you were in a coma. . .then when you came to and I found out about. . ." She blew her nose. "Well, I didn't find the right time to tell you."

"It's okay. Honest. I'm happy for you. So tell me what happened. I thought you were on the pill? Didn't you learn anything from my experience?"

"Girl, please. I've been on birth control since I was sixteen to regulate my periods. I know how to take it. I missed one pill because I dropped it. I was late for work and remembered on my way that I hadn't taken it yet. I tried popping it out of the case while driving, and it fell between my seat and the console. You know how snug the interior of my Audi is. Anyway, I was going to search for it when I got to work, but then my phone blew up with text messages as I pulled into the parking lot. I forgot all about looking for the stupid pill."

Caroline had forgotten how good it felt to laugh. "What'd Runway do when you told him?"

"After the initial shock, he morphed into this protective horny-toad. He won't keep his hands off me. I guess he's not worried about using protection anymore so why not, you know? He says it's because watching my body grow with his child is exhilarating."

Tears flooded Caroline's eyes. The moment she and Cade shared in the hospital was the last time he'd shown interest. First, he said he was afraid he'd hurt her. Now, healed or not, her husband hardly had the time to make love to her.

"Do you know what it is yet?"

Her voice lowered. "A boy."

Caroline choked back the tears and smiled through the pain. "That's great, Kris. I'm excited for you. When is he due?"

"Four more weeks." Kristy's voice softened, "Oh, Caro. I'm so sorry I didn't tell you. I was freaking out and ashamed because Matt and I aren't married. Thank you for not hating me for keeping it a secret. I was stupid and should've told you. Trust me, it killed me not to say anything. I wish you could be here. My blood pressure is high and I'm kind of terrified."

"Don't be. Relax and you'll do just fine. At least you don't have a voodoo witch trying to kill you."

"How are things with you and Cade? I'll bet he's a doting father."

"Yeah. He loves being a daddy. She's already got him wrapped around her little finger."

"Uh-huh. What's this despondency I hear in your voice? Everything okay?"

Caroline breathed, searching for the right words to explain her feelings. "No. I mean, yes, I love watching him with Dani. They're great together. I just. . . I just wish I could have some of his undivided attention."

"Ah. I see." Kristy's tone shifted to the bossy best friend from College. "Girl, you work your body and show that boy what he's missing. He'll come running. He went all the way the hell to Chicago to keep you from marrying someone else. He wants you and only you, so remind him of what he's missing."

"I will. I wish he would open up to me and explain his reluctance. I'm sure it's not my post-baby body, but my insecurities are overwhelming. I need to get over myself, that's all. I'm feeling selfish and throwing a pity party. I'm sure there's a reasonable explanation. I'll talk to him about it."

They ended their conversation on a happy note, and Caroline decided it was time to start working out and improve herself, physically and emotionally, instead of putting all the pressure and responsibility on Cade.

FIFTEEN

"Surprise." Trevor crooned in Caroline's ear.

She fumbled with her phone as her knee bumped the table leg, sloshing gumbo from her bowl. "Trevor! What are you doing here? Geezum! Give me a heart attack, why don't you? You can't just sneak up on a girl like that." She ignored his smirk but took in his sleek appearance. His pressed olive green dress shirt contrasted against his stark white undershirt. His glossy raven hair fell just above his dark eyebrows that shadowed sapphire irises. "What are you doing here?"

"It's great to see you, too, C." His chiseled jaw framed his full lips as the corner of his mouth tipped upward.

His wounded expression pierced her heart. "I'm sorry. You caught me on a rough day. I'm a little on edge."

"I see that." His sharp eyes studied her, unlocking her vulnerability, and she hunched toward the table. "So what brings you back to the spooky bayou?"

He laughed, a sound she used to adore, and his crooked smile reminded her of the handsome guy she'd once fallen for. "Spooky is right. Thank goodness I managed to ditch the ghosties when I left this swamp. Though I can't say the same for my dad. He's been acting crazy like *he's* seen a ghost."

"You look different," he mused. "Better. I didn't realize it was possible for you to be even more alluring."

"You didn't answer my question."

That seemed to snap him back in the moment and he cringed. "Just checking on some things. It's a quick trip. Plus, I wanted to see you."

"Trevor. . ."

"I also wanted to let you know my dad will be in the area soon. I don't know when for sure, but sometime in the next week. He's been out of sorts lately, not himself, and doesn't trust me anymore." He shrugged. "I mostly wanted to see for myself that you were okay."

She eyed him and raised her brow. "Sure. Why wouldn't I be?"

Trevor smiled. "Just checking. My father hasn't exactly been kind to your family, but as far as I know he's no longer trying to kill you or your father. After all, I ruined his revenge when I failed to marry the heir to the long sought-after Fontenot fortune. No need to sic the sniper on him if you see him."

"How did you know Cade was a sniper?"

"I've done a little research of my own. How are things in paradise, by the way?"

"Fine." She cursed herself for the clipped response. Things were fine if she could get over herself. Caroline curbed her jealousy that Cade had been with Tonya in New Orleans all week. She bit her tongue and smoothed her features. No way would she give Trevor the satisfaction of seeing her upset with Cade. "Things are wonderful. How about you and Jessica?"

"We're doing okay. She's on vacation with her parents right now. Apparently every year they go on some two or three week trip together." Caroline flippantly waved her hand in the air,

"Back-packing Europe or some other outrageous dream vacation. This time I think they're on a Caribbean cruise." Trevor's brow furrowed as his crystal eyes inspected her. "He hasn't hurt you has he?"

Shock bubbled up Caroline's chest. "What? Of course he hasn't hurt me. Why would you even imply that?"

Trevor held his hands up in surrender. "I'm just asking a simple question. You can never tell. Some people are not what they seem, is all." He dropped his hands and sat at the table with her. "I know I wasn't perfect, but neither is he."

"Neither am I. No one is perfect, Trevor."

"Has he told you about his past?"

A tremor of rage rattled her bones as she controlled her breathing to speak. "Of course."

"He's told you what he did?"

"He's done a lot of things, Trev." She frowned suspiciously, "Why do you know anything about his past? Why are you snooping around? I'm married to him already, and you can't change that, so back off." Her dukes were up.

"I'm just asking you if you really know who you married? For over two years you were so cautious and hesitant about marrying me, yet you meet this guy and get married in twelve months. After I left Louisiana to come back to Chicago, I did a little background checking to make sure he wasn't playing you." He leaned back in his chair and shrugged one shoulder. "Only fair considering he paid me the same courtesy. I only wish I'd thought to do it *before* you two tied the knot."

Caroline's nostrils flared. "It wouldn't have changed anything!" She squeezed her eyes closed to slow the fire about to spew from her tongue. "Trevor, it's not your job to protect me anymore. Thanks for your concern, but Cade's past is none of your business!"

"Fair enough. Guess I misjudged you, C. I didn't figure you'd be able to overlook cold-blooded murder. But hey, it's your life." His nonchalant tone grated her nerves.

"Be careful, Trevor. He didn't murder anyone in cold blood." She flinched remembering Cade's confession that he'd killed a lot of people during his time as a Navy SEAL.

"He was a sniper! That's all he *did* do."

Her lip curled in anger. "He had orders from the military. He had no choice. Besides, they were all evil men with agendas to harm people or countries."

His voice lowered, "You sure about that?" He played with a toothpick on the table, bouncing it and catching it. "A reliable source told me he killed a young woman. It's why he got out of the Navy."

"Oh, please. He didn't kill any woman. Jenny's death was an accident. You don't know about him, Trevor. He didn't kill her. Her death nearly killed *him*. Just drop it." She stood, gathered her things, but he grabbed her wrist and gently tugged her back to her seat.

"Look, I'm only making sure you know who you married."

She jerked her arm from his grasp. "I know exactly who I married, and it wasn't you," she pointed her finger in his face. "Back off, Trevor." She frowned and crossed her arms. "Cade told me all about his past and it only made me love him more. I know what you're doing, so just stop it! Stop trying to stir the pot." Caroline rubbed her temples. "You have no concept of what he's been through." She swallowed, remembering what a selfish brat she'd been to her husband. "No one does."

He shrugged one shoulder. “Fine, but it can’t hurt for you to check in to it.” He plucked a crouton from her salad and popped it into his mouth. “Better safe than sorry, right?”

“I’m not sorry for anything.” She traced the lines on the table with her fingernail, “We have a daughter.”

Trevor nearly choked on the crouton. She rolled her eyes and pushed her water toward him. “A daughter?” Through his pained coughing, she saw him calculating the months, the numbers practically flashed across his forehead. He avoided eye contact and muttered, “That was quick.”

“Yep. Got pregnant on my honeymoon.” She nudged him. “Apparently, I’m pretty fertile. Guess it’s a good thing we never consummated our relationship or you’d probably have a toddler by now.”

Remorse flooded his features, dripping from his downcast lashes into a sea of anguish. “I don't think I’d mind a child if it was with you.” Her gaze fell to the straw wrapper she was annihilating. When they were together she dreamed of having his blue-eyed babies, but he’d always detested the idea of a large family. He’d led her to believe she would be lucky to have one child with, much less several. He tilted his head. “What’d I say?”

“Nothing,” she mumbled.

“No, you’re upset. What’s wrong?”

“Well. . .there were two. Twins.”

“Were?”

“Yeah.” Caroline’s mellow voice was saturated with grief as she scraped her fingernail across a gash in the table. “A boy and a girl.” She took her glass of water back from him to ease her dry mouth. She did *not* want to cry anymore. “The boy didn’t make it.”

He took her hand in his and spoke tenderly. She couldn't hold the tears. "Oh, Caroline. I'm sorry. What happened?"

She pulled away and dried her face with her napkin. "I don't really want to talk about this right now. The pain is too. . .raw. I can't, I'm not exactly sure how to mourn. It's heartbreaking to even think about." She took another drink. "I'm certain talking about it with my ex is not the thing to do. I should probably get back, anyway."

"I'm more than just your ex, C. I'm your friend." She stood, and he pulled her back down again. "Don't go. I wanted some gumbo, and I came all the way down here to eat at. . ." he looked around until his eyes landed on the restaurant sign. "What's this place called again?"

"Barrios."

His brow furrowed in confusion. "Wait, I thought it had a different name. This is the place that has the best gumbo in town, right?"

She nodded. "It used to be Dupree's, but he sold it." She leaned back and twisted her hair up in a ponytail. "The food's even better now if you can believe that."

He flashed his heart-stopping smile. "No, I can't." He looked at her thoughtfully, as if trying to read her mind. "You are so beautiful."

"Trev. . ." she grabbed her purse to stand. "You know, they have restaurants with great gumbo in New Orleans. You could've saved yourself the two-hour drive and eaten up there." She didn't know what he was up to, but no way would she fall into the Trevor Callahan trap.

His face fell, "Stay with me. Please."

She sighed, "Fine." Cade would lose his mind if he saw her there with Trevor, but he was working with Tonya today, so she pointed her finger at Trevor and circled it around. “But you have to quit that.”

“Quit what?”

“Quit being. . .” she motioned all around him, “you.”

He laughed with a perplexed expression. “OK. I’ll try to work on that. . .this.”

They laughed together for a few moments, and when the awkward silence reared its ugly head Trevor asked, "Does she look like you?”

Caroline nodded. “Mmmm, she’s kind of a mixture of Cade and me. Thick golden-brown hair, my nose, and I think she’ll have my eyes, but it’s still early to tell just yet. She’s perfect.”

“How could she not be? Her mother’s gorgeous.”

“See, there you go with that again. Stop it.”

He held his hands up in defense. “What? I can’t compliment you anymore? You *are* beautiful, anyone with two eyes and half a brain can see that.”

Caroline detected an envious undertone in his words. Trevor was jealous.

“How about you and Jessica? Any wedding bells in your future?”

He chuckled darkly. “Uh, no. I’m a little gun-shy about marriage these days. Last time didn’t go so well for me.”

Caroline had wondered how long it would be before that came up. “I’m really sorry about that, Trev. I never meant to hurt you like that. I shouldn’t have let it get that far. I know you were humiliated.” Relief washed over her. She’d felt terrible for years, and now she had closure with this apology. She’d tried to apologize when he was down last summer, but Trevor was three sheets to the wind with dirty martinis. Jessica swooped in to save the day, and Caroline had missed her chance.

"Humiliated? You think that was my problem? Am I really so shallow that you think the embarrassment was the worst part for me? Don't get me wrong, I certainly didn't enjoy that part, but—"

"No, Trevor, I knew you detested public humiliation. Being left at the altar is quite humiliating, not to mention that nosy reporter from *The Chicago Tribune* who captured your heartbroken face for all the world to see."

"Caroline, I couldn't care less about that. I can't. . ." He expelled an exasperated sigh. "I can't believe that's how you thought of me. I swear if I'd known that, I would have swallowed my pride and come crawling back to you sooner," he complained. "Maybe then I could've caught you before. . ."

"I'm sorry, I don't understand," Caroline admitted. "You were very clear with your continuous reminders, mixed in with the not-so-nice accusations and insults, at the altar about not embarrassing you. And let's not forget that you hit me!"

"Caroline, I was upset because I lost you. It didn't have anything to do with public humiliation. Granted, I wasn't thrilled to have an audience for my temper tantrum, but ultimately I was hurt. You're right, I don't like public humiliation, but that wasn't what I was the most angry about, and I never intended to hurt you. I'd never hit a woman in my life until that moment. I thought you had lied to me about being with the gardener—"

"Cade," she interrupted.

"Whatever." His temper shone through, and Caroline's old shield reactivated. "I thought you had cheated on me after all, and then he showed up to steal you away from me on our *wedding* day."

"Stop." Caroline held her palm up. "I don't want to rehash painful old memories. I was there. I know what happened. We were both at fault. Can we just accept each other's apologies and move on?" She slowly pulled her hand away. "We weren't meant to be together."

"I can't accept that. I would have to believe in fate to accept that theory. I believe in creating my own destiny. We had a good thing, Caroline. I should never have sent you down here on your own and expected that men wouldn't see your value. Any red-blooded man alive would be a fool to not notice you, and I just let you go without protecting my investment."

Another surge of anger pulsed through her veins. "I was not your investment," she fumed.

"Weren't you? You were my girl, my fiancée, and I delivered you into a pit of horny rattlesnakes. Well, at least *one* horny rattlesnake anyway," he grumbled.

"Do you hear yourself right now? My goodness, have you *always* been like this? How did I not see it? I mean, I knew you hated the no sex rule, but I never realized your pitiful regard for me." She drew in a deep breath to control her flaring temper. "I should've known better. A leopard never changes its spots. It was great to see you again. I wish you the best—"

"My God." He dropped his face to his hands, "Forgive me, Caroline." He stroked his fingers through his raven hair. "This swampland makes me crazy, I don't know what it is. I didn't mean it the way it sounded. I need to know that you understand I had nothing to do with my dad's stupid revenge plan. You believe me, right?"

"I *want* to, but. . ." Brutal honesty. It was the only way to handle a chauvinistic man. She had to be firm with the boundaries of their friendship otherwise anything she said could be misconstrued.

"I really wish you would." His pleading eyes begged her to understand. "Please, Caroline. I had no idea what he was planning. All I know is that he suggested I meet you and sweep you off your feet. I brushed him off until I realized you were as amazing on the inside as on the outside. I knew then that *I* was the lucky one. You swept me off my feet, C. Plain and simple, I fell hopelessly in love with you. Sure, the no-sex rule was frustrating, but it gave me something to look forward to, and when I bought your ring, it took me five months of searching before I found the perfect one. I proposed before I ever knew anything about any of this crap between our families or my dad's ridiculous plan."

Though his heartfelt confession was believable, Caroline couldn't see why it mattered now.

"Trevor, I believe you had nothing to do with the plan, initially at least, but I don't understand why you didn't simply tell me once you found out. Why did you have to keep it from me? A lie of omission is still a lie." She sat back in her chair and took a long pull on her straw, the refreshing cool liquid chilling her throat. "Anyway, it's a moot point now. I'm very happily married with a beautiful child." Maybe he needed closure worse than she did. His defeated look tugged at her heart.

"You should work things out with Jessica. She's pretty and crazy about you." Maybe he was bored with Jessica. Caroline hoped that wasn't the case. She really needed Jessica to keep his attention.

"Maybe you're right." He kissed the back of her hand. "Look, I know we're not married, but I still love you. I'm leaving for Chicago tomorrow, but I'm only a phone call away if there's ever anything you need. Even if it's a simple ear to lend."

"Thanks. I appreciate that." She stood and stepped far enough away that he couldn't stop her this time. "I should really get going now. Great to see you, Trev."

"Oh, one more thing. Speaking of lies of omission. . . ask your husband about what I told you. I knew nothing about anyone named Jenny. I don't think he's told you everything from his past. Ask him about Khatira Shillings. She's the *real* reason he got out of the Navy."

She left the restaurant, her mind spinning in a whirlpool of emotions. She scribbled the name on a receipt in her purse to remember it. Who was Khatira Shillings, and why did Caroline want to throw up thinking about her? Was Trevor just stirring the pot, or had Cade lied to her about his reason for getting out of the military? Did it really matter? Caroline cursed herself for not being able to let it go.

SIXTEEN

Caroline walked into the foyer of the plantation house just in time to see her father and younger brother, Remy arguing over who held Dani next. For someone who'd been shot and nearly died, Remy had handled his experience and rehabilitation like a champion.

"So who's gonna fight to hold me?" Caroline teased.

"Caroline!" Remy limped over to her, still recovering from where the bullet had nicked his spinal cord. He hugged her and kissed her cheek. "Dad's hogging her."

"What else is new?" Caroline eyed his blue and silver walking stick. "New hardware? It's nice."

"Yeah, my Physical Therapist found a hiking staff and tweaked it a little to look more athletic. School colors. Gotta represent."

"Still with your girlfriend?"

"Which one?" Eddie snorted a laugh. "Boy's found a way to milk the sympathy vote. Got the girls fighting over him."

Remy's cheeks flushed, complemented by his twinkling eyes and shy smile. He'd filled out in the past year into a handsome sixteen-year-old.

Caroline playfully shoved his forehead, ruffling his hair. "You little stud." She admired his structured cheekbones and squared jaw. "You look great, Remy. No wonder the girls are all over you," she winked. "It's great to see you looking all healthy and strong."

"Me? What about you, Sleeping Beauty? I didn't think you'd ever wake up."

"You and me, both."

Her dad paced the room with his granddaughter humming a lullaby to her and Emily stood in the corner with a wistful gleam in her eyes. She tossed a glance at Caroline before escaping the room without a sound.

"He's great with her, isn't he?" Remy said quietly, watching Eddie sway and coo with Dani.

Caroline swallowed the bulge in her throat and nodded. "He is," she whispered. "Both of them." She kissed his cheek, "Great to see you, Remy. Excuse me, please."

Caroline saw a spark between her mom and dad that hadn't been there, at least not so dominantly, before she had the babies. She followed her mother to the formal living room where Emily stood in the dark sobbing into her hands.

Caroline slipped an arm around her. "Hey, Momma."

Emily hugged her back. "I'd forgotten how amazing he is with babies." She cleared her throat. "I haven't seen him this happy since you were born." She wiped her face, staring blankly at the wall. "I could have guilted him in to it, you know. Guilted him into taking care of you." She smiled, but it didn't reach her eyes. "He'd have done it. He would have stayed with us, but I needed him to be your father because he *wanted* to, not because I was forcing him to." She buried her face in her hands. "He loved you to the moon and back, but he was miserable. We were both immature. Both too young to raise a baby." She shrugged. "I pushed him away," she whispered.

Emily caught her reflection in the mirror and flinched. She pulled a tissue from the box and dabbed at the smudged mascara beneath her eyes. "Plus, I was furious with him for not wanting me, and I couldn't stand to say his name, much less look at him. I didn't want him anywhere near you. I was prideful, but suppose part of it was jealousy that he loved you more than me, and I wanted to punish him. That wasn't fair to either of us." She caressed Caroline's face. "I'm sorry, sweetheart. I guess it was fate that brought you here so I'd eventually have to face your father again. After all these years. . .after we both had time and experience to grow up."

"How does it feel to be dating again?"

Emily's cheeks lifted with her answering smile, this time reaching full wattage. "Weird. But nice. Eddie is the romantic young boy I met so long ago. . .long walks, holding hands, candlelit dinners, flowers. . ." Emily sighed. "It's surreal. My first love all over again. My only love."

"I'm happy for you, Mom. Dad's had a pep in his step lately, too. You both deserve to be happy."

Emily hugged her. "Thank you."

"Lord knows Dad does after living with April for over a decade. I'm glad he finally kicked her to the curb."

"Mmm, *that* bitch. . ." Emily swung her head in disbelief.

"Mom!" Caroline's jaw dropped and she laughed.

"I'm tellin' ya, I wouldn't count her out just yet. Women like that don't tuck their tails and run. After all, she fought tooth and nail to contest that divorce. For whatever reason, she didn't want to let him go. I have a feeling she'll pop up when we least expect her to." Emily laughed. "She's lucky Cade didn't gut and skin her at the hospital that day. If you could've seen the look on his face. . ." Emily shuddered.

Caroline had seen his look, but the memory was vague. Caroline wished she could remember everything April said to her in the hospital, and hoped Cade was able to lift it from the recording device Runway had planted.

"How's Kristy?"

Caroline's heart fluttered thinking about her best friend. "She's good. She said Runway is more nervous than she is." Caroline twisted the zipper pull on her hoodie. "Her parents still won't talk to her, though. They are disgusted that she's having a baby out of wedlock. They don't seem to care that they're engaged. Her dad called their baby a bastard."

Emily rubbed her hand along Caroline's back. "Give them some time. They are pretty set in their ways. I imagine this is a shock for them. But, all parents want to be in their kids and grandkids lives. When your baby is having a baby, it's a wonderful, exhilarating, terrifying reality, and they'll get over their judgment the second they see that sweet, tiny, handsome face."

"And he will be dazzling. Look at his parents. How could he not be? It's like God hand-picked the perfect genes."

"I think you and Cade did pretty well making a knock-out little girl. She's the prettiest little thing I've ever seen." She winked, "No offense."

Caroline grinned. "None taken."

"Their baby will be abundantly loved and admired by many people."

"And very well dressed," Caroline added.

“Am I interrupting?” Cade’s smooth voice caressed her ears. His handsome face and his curious expression piqued her interest.

“Hey, handsome. Welcome to the party.” She looked at him expecting an announcement or explanation for his mischievous grin, but he only added to the mystery.

“What’d you do for lunch?”

Caroline’s stomach flopped. Had he seen her at Barrios with Trevor? Surely not, but so what if he had. She'd done nothing wrong.

“I ate already. Why?”

“Dinner plans?”

Something was wrong. “None that I’m aware of. What are you up to?” She eyed him speculatively, pathetically trying to muffle her guilty conscience.

He ducked his cleft chin and smiled, but something beneath his peculiar expression contradicted his excitement. His smile was forced, and the glow from behind the hazel color she’d quickly fallen in love with burned with embers of a smoldering fire. She saw right through his façade. His show may have fooled her mother, but not her.

“You okay?”

“Never better. I’d like take you and Dani to visit my parents,” Cade’s grin stretched bigger, his brooding eyes twinkling from her expression, “and then I have a surprise for you." The last time he said this to her, almost verbatim, she received a marriage proposal.

Caroline’s uncanny intuition sounded a warning blow like a fog horn in the depths of her brain.

SEVENTEEN

They drove in unusual silence to Cade's parents house. Any other day, Caroline would be talking his ears off. But not today. She knew something was wrong, and he couldn't lie to her, but he didn't exactly want to spill it just yet. Instead, he quietly stared through the windshield until she couldn't stand the silence any more.

"So what's my surprise?"

He smiled, but he didn't have to look at her to know Caroline caught his hesitation. Her nearly inaudible intake of breath never released as she waited for his reaction. He smirked. His wife was an open book, easy to read. Adorable.

"Well, it's warmer today, and it's been a while since I've taken you out to enjoy the spirits of the bayou. I figured we could go out on a boat today, you know, see some swamps." She stared at him with a blank expression causing him to second guess his plan. "If. . .if that sounds good to you?"

She giggled, his ears rejoicing with the sweet music. "You don't think I've seen enough *spirits* of the bayou in the last year and a half?" He pursed his lips and frowned. She had a good point. He nodded, about to reply, but she beat him to the punch.

“I wouldn’t mind going out on a boat, though. Will we see alligators?”

“Possibly.” He grinned when her shoulders dropped a fraction. “Probably. Ty is coming with us just in case. Besides, it’s his boat.”

“Oh, that’s cool. How’s he doing, anyway?”

Cade shrugged and stared straight ahead. “He’s fine.” The gaping pause after his statement hung in the air like a heavy smog, and he knew he should add more, but didn’t know how to word it. "I think he’s jealous that I've been working with Tonya. He's had a thing for her since our first deployment."

"Hmmm," Caroline mumbled. Cade knew Caroline was more jealous than Ty, but for a much different reason, and he didn't know how else to show her he had no feelings for Tonya in that way. "I've never seen him show interest in anyone." She stared out the window, thoughtfully. "She must be pretty special. Is she hot?"

Warning! Loaded question. Answer with extreme caution. Cade's jaw tightened. If he hesitated too long Caroline would hone in on that and he'd be in a mess.

He shrugged and made a less-than-impressed roll of his lips. "Meh. Sure, she's pretty, but she's a typical jarhead. Too damned cocky for her own good." Cade laughed, but Caroline barely smiled.

"What's she look like?"

He shrugged. "Blonde hair, blue eyes, petite. Not my type, but she can take Ty down and it drives him crazy. She knows all the pressure points that can make a tank like him buckle with the slightest squeeze. I don't think she realizes how much he wants her."

"Maybe he lets her take him down. Does she like him?" Cade didn't miss the wistfulness in her voice. She was worried. "Oh yeah, she just won't admit it." He squeezed Caroline's hand. "She might be more stubborn than you."

"You have a type?"

And here it is. . .

"Only one. You."

Caroline's laughter rang like wind chimes through the cab. A sound he'd missed more than breath in his lungs. "That is the right answer." She sighed. "Where are we going?"

"Myrtle Grove."

She rolled her eyes, sarcasm dripping from her tone, "Gee, that's helpful. I have no idea where that is. Are we talking ten more minutes or two more hours? What's in Myrtle Grove?"

"Alligators and swamps." He replied, matching her sarcasm. "It's not far."

"Are you okay?"

He stole a glance, sensing her continued frustration."Yeah, why?"

"You seem upset. Or angry." She wrinkled her nose in that cute way he loved. "You're kind of moody."

He genuinely grinned this time and it felt great. It had been too long since he relaxed. "*Moody?* Like a chick?" He mocked offense and smiled, garnering a breathtaking smile from her.

"Precisely. Like a woman on a PMS wrath." He laughed louder than was necessary, anything to avoid her interrogation, but she didn't fall for it. "Seriously, Cade, what's going on? I can tell something is bothering you and I want to know what it is."

"I don't know. Just a little mellow today, you know? I'm okay." He cocked an eyebrow and grinned wickedly, "Maybe you can help perk me up a little later." The second it slipped through his lips, he regretted saying it. Her arms defiantly crossed. He'd screwed up.

Once, while staying at Eddie's house in New Orleans right before Dani was released from the NICU, they were into some deep foreplay, and Cade was completely lost in sensation, lost in her, when a car backfired. He'd nearly lost control, scaring the crap out of himself and her. From that point on, he stopped things before they started, or at least until after Caroline had been sated. Aside from being terrified that she would get pregnant again, risking the complications and being at the mercy of invisible monsters he couldn't protect her from, the amount of stress he'd been dealing with was dragging up some demons of his own that he thought he'd buried and burned long ago. PTSD was no joke, and Cade hadn't been himself lately. He would live a cold, celibate life before he risked hurting Caroline again.

"Excuse me? I've all but tied you up and forced you to make love to me over the past few weeks. You've hardly touched me since I got out of the hospital," she scolded. His heart sank when she self-consciously crossed her arms over her belly. "I mean, I know I have some baby weight to lose, but there's nothing wrong with my. . .other parts." He cursed himself for causing the shamed flush across her face. She thought she wasn't sexy anymore. That he didn't desire her because of her body.

"Caroline, you are—"

"Beautiful. Yes, you tell me that all the time, and I love it. But just once I'd like for you to show me. Every time I start trying anything deeper than kissing, you stop me with the excuse that I've not healed enough. Don't act all sexy now just because you're avoiding telling me something. I want you, but I want to know what's eating you first. I don't want our first sexual experience after having a baby to be a reward for a champion diversion."

He rolled to a stop at a red light and looked at Dani sleeping soundly in her car seat. He gently rubbed a finger down her velvety cheek. They made some pretty babies. He wished they could have five more just like her. Dani started at his touch, her arm shooting straight up in the empty air, and he chuckled. "I'm grateful for you and Dani, that's all." His neck cramped the way it always did in the field, a warning when something bad was on the horizon. "Just don't be annoyed with me if I seem overprotective of y'all for the next few weeks."

"Why? What's going on? Did something happen?"

"It's carnival season. Things get crazy during Mardi Gras."

Thankfully they pulled up to his parents house just in time for him to avoid answering any more questions as his mom and sister rushed out to meet them.

"Dibs! I got dibs on feeding her first!" Catherine exclaimed.

Cade's mom rolled her eyes and smiled. "Don't worry about a thing, y'all. This beauty will be the safest, most spoiled little princess in Louisiana. She'll never leave our arms."

"I never doubted that for an instant," Caroline said.

Liar. Caroline's stiff shoulders and hesitation to hand Dani over contradicted her cheerful tone. Her eyes met his for a split second before he had to look away. She was probing him for information, and he knew he'd have to explain his surly mood once they were alone.

"We'll be back in time for dinner."

"I really wish you would tell me what's bugging you. I'm sure my thoughts are much worse than. . ." She cleared her throat. "At least I hope they are," she murmured.

Pondering her comment through a furrowed brow, Cade didn’t say anything for a good sixty-seconds. He couldn't find the right words, so he finally mumbled, “It’s nothing.”

“Bull.”

She scowled. He frowned back. “What?”

She had no idea how badly he wanted to pull the truck over and show her exactly how ready he was to make love to her. But he couldn’t. Not right now. Not in this frame of mind. “Baby—”

“Please don’t lie to me.”

He frowned again, only this time he was angry. “What? Caroline, I’m not lying to you. You *are* beautiful. I want you every single day. Every time you lick your lips. Every time you look at me with those sexy cat eyes! Trust me, I’m having to use every ounce of my self-control not to pull over and take you right now!”

She silently watched the trees whizzing by out the window. He didn't have to ask to know she didn’t fully believe him.

“Caroline.” He tapped his thumb on the steering wheel, thinking of how to explain his problem. “When that snake had you trapped, I didn’t hesitate to kill it. I’d have wrestled it with my bare hands to protect you from it. I was ready to beat the hell out of one of my childhood buddies for threatening you. I never knew what he said, but I didn’t care, I was ready to kill him.” He gripped the steering wheel tighter, the leather groaned and protested.

“When Callahan got physical with you, I saw red and had to hold back to keep from killing him.”

He grabbed her hand and rubbed his thumb across her knuckles. “When you fell into the duck pond, I was scared. I jumped in to get you, and the massive amount of blood terrified me. I was already in love with you then, and had been since that first day I met you in the library. I tried to respect your engagement and not pressure you, but the more I learned about your situation, the more I realized you needed me as much as I needed you."

He tilted her chin to look into his eyes. "I've seen nasty, frightening, unimaginable things during my time in the military. Things you can't begin to imagine. I've been scared, terrified, even, but I've never in my entire life been more scared than I was while you were lost in whatever realm of unconsciousness that kept you away from me."

She swallowed and blinked back the moisture pooling in her deep emerald eyes. He tempered his voice and went in for the kill.

"I've dealt with the deaths of innocent strangers as well as intimate loved ones. As a sniper, I was responsible for taking some of those lives. But seeing my wife, my children, helpless and dying because of some stupid move I made without thinking. . . I will never ever forget that or forgive myself."

"Cade, that was not your—"

He placed a finger over her mouth. "I'm not finished." He said, smiling. "It wasn't the voodoo doll or the surgery, or even losing Joseph, that scared me the most. You being stuck in a coma being chased by some evil spirit trying to kill you, prevent you from returning you to your body, was horrifying. *That* left me feeling helpless and impotent with nothing I could do to help or protect you."

"May I speak now?" she muttered through her lips pressed by his finger.

"Sure," he smirked.

"None of that was your fault, and you did help me when I was in a coma. If it hadn't been for your song I never would have found my way back, or even had the will to get back. Your voice, the pleading, loving tone is what brought me back. At least to the inner realm and away from the immediate threat of George. I don't remember everything I observed in spirit form, but I remember that much."

"At least I was able to contribute something. But until I'm convinced that you're healed, safe, and ready, I will not put you at risk. April and Kenneth Callahan are still out there. Whoever shot Remy is still on the loose. George Callahan, Rachel, and God knows who else still haunt you from the great beyond. And I. . ." How could he say this without scaring her or sounding like a lame excuse? "I haven't been myself lately. I'm stressed to the max, and it kills me to admit it, but my PTSD is resurfacing. I would never be able to live with myself if I hurt you."

She blinked. What was she thinking? Instead of asking, he simply smiled with the satisfaction of rendering her speechless, which was not something that happened often.

"Will you at least answer my question? What is bothering you today? Don't you dare say it's nothing because I know it's *something*. I want to know what it is. I can see it in your eyes, and in your distractions."

He sighed, resigned, as he stared out the windshield. "You are observant, aren't you?" He mumbled. "That's good, I'll need those observation skills today."

She raised her brows, "With alligators? Are we hunting them?"

He pictured her handling the line, or worse, shooting the gun with a gator fighting at the other end. That wouldn't end well for any parties involved.

"No, but that's a great visual." He smoothed her hair. "As hot as it would be to see you get your hands dirty, I would never put you in that kind of danger. So, no, we're not hunting gators today." He drew in a deep breath and cleared his throat. "I need you to keep a look out for anything. . .unusual. Spiritually speaking."

Confusion creased her features. "Huh?"

He sighed and ran his fingers through his hair. Again, words were not his friend today. How could he explain this without sounding like a selfish moron? "I know what you've been through, and I would never ask you to do anything like this if it wasn't important. I need you to try to get in touch with your spiritually sensitive capabilities while we're on the water. I don't know how to tell you to do it because I don't understand it myself, but whatever gifts you and your mom have that allowed you to communicate with each other while you were in a coma. . .that's special. And today I need you to try to tap into those extrasensory abilities if you can." He caressed her face. "Something terrible has happened, and I think you can help."

EIGHTEEN

"That's not something I can control. Why? What am I supposed to be looking for? I can't just freely tap into that realm of my sub-conscience, even if I wanted to." She stopped twisting her fingers, looked into his tormented eyes. Cade hated himself for asking her to do this. "I didn't particularly enjoy it when I was there last time. I want to help, but I don't know how."

Cade rested his forehead on the steering wheel after coming to a stop in front of Ty's small wooden house. "I know. You're absolutely right. I thought since you'd been working with Lucinda that you may have some things you could try, but that's a lot of pressure to put on you." He squeezed her leg just above the knee without moving his head. "I'm sorry. I shouldn't have even asked."

Caroline brought his hand to her mouth and kissed it. She scooted closer and wrapped her arm around his neck to comb her fingers through the silky strands of his hair while he sat quietly, brooding with worry.

"Baby, you have to tell me what is wrong. It's killing me. I can see it in your face, but if you don't tell me what's going on, there's no way I can help you," Caroline begged. He closed his eyes and sucked in a breath while she continued pleading with him. “Okay, I’ll try,” she said. He turned to her, probing her face with his sharp gaze. She traced her fingertip along the creases between his eyes. “Whatever it is you want me to do, I promise I’ll try, just tell me what’s causing these frown lines.”

Cade shook his head. “Forget I even brought it up. It’s too dangerous, and I’m taking you back home where you’ll be safe.”

Where I’ll be safe? Caroline frowned and turned the engine off quickly taking the key and hiding it behind her back. “No. It’s obviously important or you wouldn’t have asked me. Tell me why we’re here."

He tugged her across his lap into his arms and kissed her like he was afraid she’d disappear. Old leather, minty breath, soap, and Cade swirled around in her head and scrambled her senses as she gripped the back of his head to hold him in place. He pulled back, stared into her eyes as his chest heaved to catch his breath. She watched a battle ensue in his apprehensive hazel eyes, his clenched jaw, and rigid lip as his decision to tell her wobbled on its fulcrum.

“Okay, now you *have* to tell me. You can’t kiss me like that and not explain what’s going on.”

He held the keys up and grinned before putting them back in the ignition. He’d snatched them from her hands while distracting her with his luscious mouth. The boy didn’t fight fair. She launched herself into his lap, straddling his hips while blocking him from the steering wheel. She cradled his face and ran the tip of her tongue along his jaw before she captured his mouth with hers.

“Tell me now before I rip your clothes off and finish what you just started,” she whispered. It had been almost six weeks, her incision was healed, and her libido ached for attention. She didn't care if Ty witnessed or not, she was ready to remind her husband just how sexy she could be.

His crooked smile and twinkling hazel eyes nearly pushed her over the edge as she gyrated her hips against his pelvis and pressed her face into the crook of his neck, inhaling his scent. She nipped at his warm, sensitive skin with her teeth. But a knock on the window interrupted their seductive play. The burly friend she'd grown attached to last summer sheepishly grinned, knowing he'd interrupted their intimate moment. Caroline smiled back and rolled the window down.

"Ty, I don't think your attire is appropriate for alligator hunting, I think you need to go change clothes. Please, take your time."

His baffled expression shifted from her to Cade and back when a salacious grin stretched across his handsome face. "Gator huntin', huh? Looks to me like you were huntin' a snake." He laughed loud enough that the sound bounced back from the surrounding trees. Caroline's face burned betraying her intentions.

After they hooked the boat trailer to Cade's truck, Ty shoved her farther into the middle of the bench seat while he occupied his space and half of hers with his massive body. She didn't mind being pressed against Cade's warmth, smelling his tantalizing, fresh, woodsy scent."Have you heard anything from Chris's mom?" Ty asked.

Cade shook his head without speaking.

"Talked to his girlfriend yesterday. She hasn't seen him in two weeks."

The muscles in Cade's jaw rolled beneath the skin. His anger just below the surface hinted he was capable of cold-blooded murder. Trevor's words echoed in Caroline's head again. She squashed them and placed her hand on his.

"Is that what this is about? You're looking for Chris?" she whispered.

"Yeah. His mom called the police about two weeks ago after he didn't come home from work. They blew it off thinking he'd spent the night with his girlfriend again without telling her. After four days with no contact, the police became concerned. A buddy of mine from the station called to let me know and to ask if I'd heard from him."

"So why are we out here?"

He glanced down at her and smirked, but it wasn't with amusement. "Gator hunting isn't easy work, love. They're strong, deadly animals. That's why we usually go with two or three in the boat. Chris was stupid and would sometimes go out alone."

"Why would he do that?" The rhetorical question hung in the stale air as Caroline gazed out the window at the bare stumps of trees zooming past. The usually stunning swamp with its draping Spanish moss and lush greenery looked weepy and mournful today. Now, in the winter months, the bare, gray, empty marshland held an eeriness that prickled her spine. Her body danced on the chills that cloaked her skin, but not from the cold. "What exactly are we looking for? If he's been out here for two weeks wouldn't he have died from dehydration by now?"

"Don't let me miss the turn. I've only been by here once before," Cade said, ignoring her.

"Okay, you're gonna turn left at the next road and then Bayou Voodoo is about two miles down. You'll see the entrance on the right."

"Bayou what?" She couldn't believe her ears. When Cade's leg tensed beneath her hand, she knew he hadn't intended for her to know the name of the place they were going. He shot a murderous glare at Ty who shrugged apologetically. "Bayou *Voodoo*?"

Ty tried to cover his verbal slip. "Just a nickname. No one hunts out here 'cause this particular bayou is too shallow. Only time we can get in here's when it's rained for a few weeks without stopping. Some superstitious people coined the nickname after several unlucky boats got stuck in the marsh."

She didn't fully believe him and as they parked to unload the boat an uneasy feeling consumed her. Caroline's ribs ached from the mosh pit in her belly. What exactly was Cade's purpose for bringing her here, and what could she possibly do to help him? Ignoring the goose bumps forming a protective shell over her skin, she shuddered and concentrated on Chris, picturing his face. He'd been Cade's talkative friend when she met him at the daiquiri shop two years ago. The one most willing to dish about his mysterious, enigmatic buddy. If she hoped to find a spiritual connection with him, concentration was imperative.

Who was she kidding? She had no idea how to do this. Caroline wasn't clairvoyant, just a freak of nature whose grandmother chose to haunt and invade her dreams with her own agenda. This was crazy.

Caroline hurried out of the truck and the men eased the boat into the water. She stared into the murky swamp trying to make sense of Cade's hesitant explanation. He wasn't telling her everything and she knew it. But why? To protect her from something?

"You have to tell me what's going on before I agree to get in that boat with you. I know you're keeping something from me, and if you want my cooperation you're gonna have to spill it, *zinger*. What's going on with Chris?"

He let out a breath and smiled. "You ever thought about going into law enforcement? Your knack for knowing when you're not getting the full story would be handy." She stared him down until he continued. "Alright, I promise I'll tell you everything, just get in the boat so we can get moving before we lose anymore daylight." When she resisted, Cade tugged her closer and tucked her into the safety of his muscular chest, his mouth stopping mere inches from her face. "I promise," his hot breath tickled her skin before he pressed his lips to her forehead. "I'll tell you everything."

Caroline conceded, letting him scoop her up and place her in the small aluminum boat to avoid getting her shoes muddy. He slid into the boat barely rocking it. Ty drove while Cade explained.

"I confronted Chris this past summer when I suspected he was working with April. I'd overheard her on the phone just before your graduation party chewing someone out for wanting to back out on their deal. She mentioned something about hunting alligators." His shoulders sagged. "I knew in my gut that it could only be one of two people who would betray me and your dad."

Though she'd mastered the art of disguising shock from her face, she still struggled to hide if from her voice. Her response slinked out in a choked squeak. "Chris and. . ." She swallowed the fear from her next thought. "Henry?" Her last memory of Henry, Cade's quiet friend whom she'd met at the daiquiri shop her first summer here, was when he'd accosted her in front of Cade's cabin. He'd cornered Caroline with the intent of molesting her until Cade stopped him just in time. Cade had been her own personal hero that summer. Caroline shuddered. She'd expected Henry to be the type to work with April, but not Chris. He was sweet, fun, and friendly. "Why?" she whispered. "Why would he work for April? I thought he liked me?"

"He did. He does." Cade huffed. "He's a good guy. He'd gotten his girlfriend pregnant, and, like most greedy people, he was momentarily blinded by the promise of a large sum of money. When he realized what she wanted him to do for it, his conscience took over and he decided no amount of money was worth murder. Especially one of his best friends."

Caroline's blood cooled in her veins. "Wait. . .he was going to kill *you*?"

Cade looked out over the water, clearly trying to decide how much more he wanted to tell her. She was about to remind him that he promised, but he continued. "April wanted him to kill me after he killed your dad."

Bile burned Caroline's throat as her abdominal mosh pit broke out into a full blown brawl, threatening to expel what was left of her lunch. But then anger dominated. "Well, there you go! There's the evidence you need to put her in jail. A solicitation to commit murder."

He swiveled his head slowly as he stared at the water. "No evidence. April was meticulous and careful about covering her tracks, making sure nothing could be linked back to her. She's got some pretty serious connections with Angelo Marcellino's people. Furious with Chris for backing out of their agreement, she'd tried to blackmail him. When that didn't work, she obviously moved on to someone else to do her dirty work." Cade stared out through the passing trees. "Now, I'm afraid he's suffered the consequence of his betrayal."

"You think April killed him?"

"I think she had her mafia thugs take him out. I won't know for sure until we find him, but my gut is telling me this was a professional job, and that he won't be walking into the police station to give an official statement."

"And you want me to try to see his spirit?" The panicked shriek returned. "I don't know how to do that, Cade. I don't know how I've been able to do any of this crazy stuff!"

"Caroline." Ty commanded her attention. "Do you remember the first time we met when you learned about voodoo?" She nodded. "Remember how you thought it was all nonsense and called us a bunch of superstitious pirates?" She smirked and nodded again. "After your most recent experiences, do you believe us now?"

She chewed on his comments for a moment. He was right. When she'd first moved down here she didn't believe in ghosts or voodoo. Since then, she'd witnessed that both actually exist and are more powerful than she ever thought possible. "Yes. But that doesn't mean I'll be able to see anything."

He smiled. "Just open your mind to the possibilities. Maybe you'll see something that me and Beau miss. Maybe you'll sense something, or see a flash that could lead us in the right direction to find Chris."

"Maybe you could ask Rachel to help?" Cade suggested.

Caroline snorted, "If Rachel helped upon my request, I'd already know who shot Remy, who April was scheming with, how to get rid of George, and why he was hell bent on ruining my life. Needless to say she hasn't been extremely helpful lately."

Cade moved across the flat bottom aluminum boat until he knelt in front of Caroline. He cupped her face. "I don't want you to do anything you're uncomfortable with, I'm just asking you to open your sixth sense, or whatever it is that you and Lucinda have been working on, and help us search for Chris. That's all. If you don't see anything, it's okay, we'll keep looking. If you do see something, we'll check it out."

She stared into his pleading eyes, willing him to understand her self-doubt. "What if it doesn't work? What if I don't *really* see anything and it ends up leading us on a wild goose chase?"

He smiled, "Then I guess we'll be chasing some geese. Either way, it can't hurt. You've got something unique, something I've never seen or heard of before, and I believe in you. I believe you can help in a way that no one else can. Just try, please. For me?"

He believed in her, and if ever anyone could talk her into doing the impossible, making herself look like a crazy loon, it was him. Lucinda had taught her about scrying, the practice of looking into something clear, like crystals, glass, mirrors, or water to see spiritual visions, and she'd been able to do it with a bowl of clear water, but only once and when she was in a trance. She felt foolish doing it, though. Like a gypsy with a crystal ball. She sighed and rolled her eyes to the heavens silently praying for some divine intervention.

"Fine." Cade pressed his cheek against hers and whispered, "Thanks, sweet Caroline. I'll happily repay you soon for your troubles." He winked and kissed her nose. "Promise."

A flutter of desire coursed through her chest.

Remembering Lucinda's instructions, she closed her eyes and pressed her fingertips to her temples. She concentrated on the whirr of the boat motor and the gentle lapping of the waves to try to fall into a trance. She pictured Chris's face and imagined herself flying over the swamps searching for him. It was useless. She felt ridiculous. She looked up in frustration to find both of them staring at her just as the heat flooded her face.

"Okay, if I'm going to have any success with this, you're both going to have to pretend I'm not even here."

Silently, they swept their eyes across the banks for any sign of Chris or his belongings. For the first time Caroline fully observed her surroundings. Abandoned boats littered the steep, muddy banks causing it to look and feel like a barren boat graveyard. Super creepy. Where squirrels and birds usually traipsed through the branches, chirping and chattering, an eerie silence hung low with the chill in the air. The crisp breeze slithered through the barren trees, and the murky water lapped at the desolate cypress trunks. Mosquitoes swarmed them as the approaching dusk crept in with its looming shadows.

"What's the story with this bayou, anyway?"

Ty's muted voice intensified the haunting feel the dreary waters already possessed. "The locals believe this bayou is cursed. Too many boats come in and don't make it back out. They either run aground or quit operating for some unexplained reason."

"What, like the Bermuda Triangle?"

He smiled crookedly. "Something like that. When it happens, the owners leave their boats and make a run for it without coming back. Some don't make it home. They either get lost in the bayou and die from dehydration or get cornered by an angry alligator. Either way, people respect their superstitions enough not to bother this bayou too much. It's great for hunting 'cause the gators that live here rarely get caught. They get to be pretty dang big. Only the bravest, or the dumbest, swamp people come here for their catch."

"So if it's cursed, and people generally avoid it, why are we out here right now?"

Ty shrugged. "Chris has always liked coming here to hunt. He's competitive, cocky, and always tries for the biggest gators to be considered the *Swamp Champ*. Only that idiot would come here alone. He ain't the brightest light in the harbor, that's for sure."

Caroline's arms tingled with the little hairs standing upright, and a chill slithered down her spine. She swatted a mosquito trying to tap into her carotid artery. A foreboding damper settled through the restless energy of the dismal swamp, the heaviness weighing on Caroline's shoulders like sandbags. She shoved off her unease, closed her eyes again, and zoned in on her purpose. She silently asked Rachel to throw her a bone, and tossed up a little prayer for some help.

As the purr of the boat motor and the gentle, chilly breeze relaxed her into a meditative state, her mind wandered—like dreaming, only still aware of her surroundings. The sounds she had missed before now resounded like a squealing toddler in an empty basketball gym. Birds chirped and fluttered in the trees, jumping from branch-to-branch. Bullfrogs croaked in the hollow cypress trunks jutting from the swampy water, and the crickets played their own jazz melodies.

In the midst of her daydream a quick flash of a red and blue striped object flitted through her mind. She asked Ty to stop the engine and stared into the dark water. The flash had been too fast to distinguish what the object was, but the image of a long, cylindrical shape formed in the ripples of the water. When she described it to Cade and Ty their eyes lit up with interest.

"Chris's new airboat was blue with a three inch red stripe down the side of it," Ty said.

Cade nodded once, solemn and vigilant, probably figuring they'd be pulling his friend's body from the swamps today.

Caroline's heart ached for both of them.The gravity of the situation, their sense of duty and penchant for taking responsibility, the raw fear of losing a childhood friend. One more agonizing tragedy her already-overwhelmed husband would have to endure. She closed her eyes again and focused on the sounds around them. It was easier to drift into the meditative state again, becoming more familiar with it—like driving mile after mile on a long deserted highway.

Fully aware and tuned in to her surroundings, Caroline was now in a trance. Chris surfaced again, only he wasn't the smiling, joking Chris she knew. His face. . .it was gruesome. She flinched.

"You okay?" Cade asked, his voice strained with concern.

"Yeah. Just saw something." Caroline admitted, breathlessly.

"What'd you see?" Ty asked.

"Chris. Busted up like he'd been in a fight. Bleeding from his forehead, nose, and mouth, and. . ." She swallowed, unable to continue.

"What is it? What else did you see?"

"His, um, his eyes were closed. It was only a flash, I didn't see much. I could have misinterpreted it."

Cade placed his hand on her shoulders and stared straight into her soul. "Caroline, I need you to try again and see if you can notice the place where you saw him. Try to find a landmark or something significant we can search for."

"All of these places down here look the same to me. A swamp is a swamp. There's no way I could distinguish a location that you would recognize. I'm sorry, I'm really trying, but I'm afraid I'm not much help with this."

"Yes, you are. I believe you can, Caroline. You've already given us something. Keep trying. We'll leave you alone to concentrate, just try not to jump out of the boat if you can help it."

Why couldn't she believe in herself as much as he believed in her. She leaned forward with her elbows on her knees and face in her hands.

Soon, she had a vision she was up in a tree, hiding behind the moss draping from the branches. Alone in the swamp with only the sounds of the critters scurrying to find shelter for the coming night, she heard whimpering in the distance. She floated toward it, hovering like a superhero assessing the mayhem of the charred remains of a city he'd sworn to protect.

As she neared the sound, the accompanying stench, musky with a trace of road kill, churned her insides. The putrid smell of rotting flesh baking in the sun overpowered the all-too-familiar smell of stagnant water and algae, and Caroline knew she'd found the murder scene. She searched the area below, unsure where she'd traveled. Among the many abandoned boats, one in particular stood out.

Nestled across the swamp beneath a fork-shaped tree that had been purposefully trimmed for the drooping power lines cutting through the middle, the blue and red boat. It didn't look like an airboat to her. There was no propeller attached to the back of it. The metal structure, the part she assumed was called rigging, was where it should be, but the motor-controlled propeller was missing. The pungent odor grew stronger reminding Caroline of her gluttony at lunch that afternoon. A flash interrupted her vision again with a horrifying image.

Caroline twisted to the side of the boat and emptied the contents of her stomach into the swamp.

NINETEEN

Cade rubbed Caroline's back to comfort her, but trepidation pulsed through his veins. He had a good idea of what she'd seen, but refused to believe it until he saw it for himself. Caroline sat straight and wiped her mouth.

"You good? Squared away?" She dipped her chin. "Was it as bad as I imagined?" He eyed her warily trying to decide if she would vomit again or cry. She squeezed her eyes closed, the faint lines in her forehead deepening. Damn. This was bad. Exactly what he feared. "Alright, then." Cade sucked air into his lungs and held it for a moment before reluctantly expelling it. "Where are we headed?"

After she'd explained about the tree and what they needed to be looking for, Caroline made a conscious effort to breathe only through her mouth. He couldn't believe she'd been able to see anything, but that's what he got for doubting her. She kept claiming it was her imagination, but his gut told him differently.

They rounded a bend toward the power lines, and a grisly sensation clamped on the muscles between his shoulders, prickling his neck. Blood rushed to his ears sounding like water gushing through a porthole. It was the same feeling he'd get while overseas when death was imminent. They were close. His skin crawled. Evil surrounded them, without a doubt.

"Slow down, Ty. It's right there." Caroline pointed to an embankment up ahead with a trembling finger.

The gurgle of the motor slowed, adding to the macabre atmosphere. All the surrounding critters were still and silent as they stalked the quiet shore. In the distance, a fork-shaped tree came into view. If they found what Caroline described near that tree, it proved that her sensitive qualities had transformed into more powerful, and apparently controllable, clairvoyant abilities. And that his friend was dead.

The remains of a red and blue airboat that had been picked apart were hidden behind a screen of overgrown brush near the forked tree. It was badly dented as if someone took a crowbar to it, and just like she'd described from her vision, the motorized propeller was missing. Cade swore under his breath. Ty cut the motor and hopped out to drag the boat onto the bank. Caroline stayed frozen on the bench seat, continuing with her mouth breathing.

Cade eyed her warily. "You okay?"

"Does it stink?"

Ty answered her question without breaking eye contact with Cade. "Like nothing you've ever smelled before."

Though he tried to be subtle, Ty's concentrated interest in Cade's reaction gave him away.

Cade rounded the trunk of the tree and spewed a strain of curse words he hadn't uttered since he'd been in hell. He kicked a piece of scrap metal that flew twenty yards and lodged into the side of a tree. He glanced at Caroline who wore a brave face, but he knew she was scared out of her mind. He'd never fully lost his temper around her, and now he couldn't control it. His limbs had a mind of their own. Rage bubbled from the pits of his body he'd sealed off from the world, and now he couldn't contain it.

Heat scorched across his face and anger plumed through his voice as it thundered across the bayou, bouncing off trees and frightening the nosy critters surrounding them. Birds fluttered from branches, squirrels and chipmunks scurried to safety, leaping from the tree Cade kicked repeatedly. He punched the side of Chris's boat, ignoring the blinding pain that radiated from his wrist, scoring the bones in his right forearm. He screamed again, his pent up rage finally finding release.

Cade stalked behind the tree out of Caroline's sight and pulled the Bowie knife from his boot holster. He furiously slashed at the vines hanging around the tattered airboat, careful not to get too close and destroy the crime scene, but enough to sate his wrath before stabbing the forked tree over, and over, and over until he'd pierced a gaping hole. Blood pulsed in his forehead, throbbing as he panted to control his frenzy, but his brain and his temper weren't on speaking terms at the moment.

Cade shouted expletives in the first foreign language that popped in his head as he inspected the carnage of what used to be one of his best friends. He cursed even more, black spots clouding his vision through the blazing rage. He spoke several different languages as part of his SEAL training for the advantage of blending in with his surroundings, but he hadn't spoken Thai in years. It came back easily, like riding a bike, but didn't make him feel better. Not enough, at least.

His pounding heart raced as he stalked around the area, keyed up, a live wire, naked and exposed to his rage. He pulled his Glock .45 from his hip holster and fired six rounds into the murky water. The deafening shots echoed through the empty marshland ensuring their privacy from wildlife.

Ty didn't flinch at Cade's behavior. He simply pulled his shirt up to cover his nose and took pictures of the crime scene with his phone, but Cade didn't miss his wary eye. His buddy worried about his sanity, and normally that would piss him off, but lately he'd been on edge. Probably best to have a steady watchman monitoring his unstable behavior. Cade pulled out his phone to call the police station.

"Yeah, it's Beau. My signal sucks out here, dude, but you need to send someone out to Voodoo Bayou to pick up the body. . ." he swallowed, damning himself for letting emotion get in the way, ". . . of Chris Broussard." He paused, closing his eyes to clear a disturbing memory from his mind, and coughed out a breath. "Yeah, I'm absolutely sure he's dead." Cade forcefully cleared his throat. "He's been chopped and dismembered by the propeller from his airboat." He lowered his voice. "He's in pieces."

Cade listened to the rookie deputy on the other line spouting regulation BS, and his temper surged. His lips curled over his teeth and he angled the phone so the microphone was directly in front of his mouth. "I don't know how long he's been out here, I'm not a coroner!"

He demanded to talk to his buddy on the force. He needed someone who understood his position. Finally after more cursing in the background from his friend, he heard the deep voice of the Police Chief. A guy he'd known since they were teenagers. "Yeah, dude. I don't know how long he's been out here, but I can tell you the stench would knock the buzzards right out of the sky." He lowered his voice. "I haven't smelled anything like this since I was overseas." He spun around to look at the body again and rubbed his palm to his forehead. "Yeah, it looks like what's left of him has been picked apart by animals. It's nasty, bro.

Tragic. Just get someone out here to gather him up before something finishes him off. He's got family that will want to give him a proper burial." Cade slid his phone back in his pocket as he rushed to the boat to check on Caroline.

He labored to control his anger. "She's going down. If it's the last thing I do on this earth, Ana Morales will pay dearly." Caroline agreed much too quickly to be believable. He appraised her with concern. "You sure you're okay?" She nodded again. Unconvinced, he swung his leg into the boat.

"No, Cade, I'm fine. Go help Ty."

He hesitated, trying to decide if she was, indeed, all right.

"Go," she insisted.

He hurried back to where Ty was examining and photographing the battered airboat.

"It looks like they removed the protective outer grid, put it underneath him, and rigged his propeller engine with a motion sensor," Cade grumbled, assessing the scene. "With the way he's hanging, *damn. . .*"

"I know, man. They planned it so if he moved it set off the motion sensor which started the engine of the propeller. The more he moved the more he swung bringing him closer and closer each time until he eventually started getting chopped to pieces starting with his toes." Ty whispered. "The mosquitoes alone would've made that happen."

"All we can hope is that he passed out before anything else got to him. Before he suffered too much. I can't imagine the pain. . ." Cade heard the agony in his own voice. Chris was one of his closest friends.

"Beau, you alright, man?"

Cade ignored him, not interested in discussing his stability. "Looks like his upper extremities were snapped off by a gator or something else with big, powerful jaws and sharp teeth. Look at that. . .are those claw marks?" *Mercy*. "You ever seen anything like this before?" Cade's voice cracked. *He* had.

"Nope. Never." After a brief but noticeable pause, recognition flooded Ty's face and his compassion morphed into a firm, vehement scolding. "Uh-uh. No way. I know what you're thinking, and, man, you can cut that crap out right now. This ain't the same kind of thing." His voice lowered so Caroline wouldn't hear. "What happened over there was completely different. That village didn't know what was coming for them, and *she* was. . ." Ty let out a frustrated sigh. "And *you*. . . Beau, man, you can't. . . Just. . .don't! I will *not* let you take responsibility for this. Listen, Chris knew exactly what he was getting himself into, and there was nothing you or me could've done to warn him or prevent this."

Cade mumbled a warning in Cajun so Caroline wouldn't understand it. He didn't need a lecture right now. Cade was well aware of what Ty was referring to.

Ty brushed it off and continued assessing the scene.

"This is definitely a professional job." Cade looked up at the wires drooping sadly above them. "No accident that he wound up under these power lines. Whoever rigged it up knew about wires and electricity because this panel here," Cade kicked the metal control panel. "This is wired to those two cables hanging over the power line. It jump-starts the motor to the propeller when the motion detector is activated. Like I said, the mosquitoes. . ." Cade cursed. "And if a wild animal approached him, as low as he's hanging, I'd imagine he flipped out." Cade quavered his head and spit the repulsive taste from his mouth.

"This is brutal," Ty said. "I'd bet whoever did it has either done it before or really put a lot of thought into it."

Cade glanced at Caroline again. She sat still as a statue, pale and calm, scanning over the water. She must be going into shock. She was way too calm. He told himself she was simply watching for alligators, but he worried she'd seen too much. Suddenly she became instantly alert and focused on a particular area across the bayou water. He followed her gaze a good seventy-five feet from the bank on the other side but saw nothing.

"Caroline, what is it? What's wrong?"

She sat frozen, hands covering her mouth, and Cade nearly came undone until she finally spoke. "It's a cloudy, white, glowing figure over there." She pointed, but he still saw nothing but cypress trees and underbrush. "A ghost. It has to be. I can see through it!"

"Who is it, can you tell?" The last thing he needed right now was an invisible enemy he couldn't protect them from.

"I think it's Rachel." She swallowed hard. "I mean, I've seen her before, but this is the first time while conscious." She stiffened and clutched her chest, and looked panicked as she scanned the walls of trees as if they were closing in on her.

"Easy, baby. You're safe."

"If Rachel's here, then George could be, too." She scoured the darkening woods, her chest heaving, emphasizing the V-shape of the muscles in her throat as she struggled to breathe.

He held her shoulders and forced her to look at him. "Look at my eyes, Caroline. Me and Ty are right here with you, and we're about to head back to the truck. We're gonna get you out of here. Breathe." She needed to calm down before she had a full-blown panic attack. She sucked in deep breaths through her nose and out her mouth, but her attention shifted back to their surroundings. "Better?" Anxiety emanated off her petite frame. "Caroline?"

"I'm okay, just a little dizzy." Caroline gasped and stared into the trees. She clutched her throat, and released a shrill, ear-piercing scream that bounced through the trees.

TWENTY

While Cade drove back to Ty's house, Caroline peered out the window allowing the passing landscape to hypnotize her as she sank deep in thought. Chris's distraught mother's howling sobs replayed through her mind. Caroline missed her son and she never even had the chance to meet him. She couldn't imagine losing a son after twenty-eight years, and so brutally. Ty and Cade spared her the gory details of her son's death, but she knew he'd been murdered. Caroline was glad she could help find him.

Rachel was helping, after all. Had she put the images in Caroline's head to help them find Chris, or was it the scrying Lucinda had taught her how to do? Both, maybe? It wasn't such a stretch that Rachel helped considering she'd managed to manipulate Caroline's dreams before. But how could Caroline see her now when she couldn't before while trying to solve Rachel's mystery? Did it have to do with Caroline's recent visit to the outer and inner realms of unconsciousness? Was she more attuned to Rachel because of that?

Maybe her grandmother's spirit gained more energy from Caroline's now that she was getting in touch with her sensitive capabilities. This was all too confusing and hard to believe. Did Rachel have more in store for Caroline? It's one thing to invade someone's dreams when she's not awake or aware, but seeing the ghost and feeling her presence?

Caroline shivered and Cade noticed, gently squeezing her hand as he clicked the heat up a notch. She snuggled closer to him while her train of thought kept chugging along.

Still. . .why the evasion? Why wouldn't Rachel come to her since Caroline was finally able to see her? As scary as that would be, it would make things a thousand times more helpful. In the woods today, Rachel was running from something or someone, and then, as if that wasn't terrifying enough, she spread her arms wide and threw her head back just before she dissipated into thin air. Had her pursuer captured her? Was she sending a message?

An uneasy tightness balled up in Caroline's chest. If Rachel still lingered around her, what about George? Was he still lurking? Feeding off her energy like a vampire?

Caroline vaguely remembered Rachel telling her she wasn't finished with her yet, and that she was trying to distract George. *Perhaps she's running to keep his attention on her rather than me?* Maybe her message was for Caroline to hold on to her faith? The biggest question still remained. Where was George Callahan?

A gentle nudge and a tender swipe across Caroline's cheek woke her, and she moaned in protest, blinking her heavy eyelids. Cade's chest rumbled with subdued laughter. "Wake up, sleepy head. Dani is probably ready to see her momma." That commanded her attention better than his tender touch as her dreams calculated that sensation in an entirely different context.

Outside her in-laws' home, flashing lightening bugs flittered through the unusually warm February air. The crickets and frogs joined in with their evening symphony.

Her gaze fell upon Cade's supple lips curved into a pleasant smile.

"What are you grinning at, Cheshire cat?" she asked playfully.

"You, little Alice. And your difficulty waking up. You were sleeping very soundly on the drive home. Ty tried to mess with you by tickling your nose with your hair and you hardly moved. If it hadn't been for the snoring, I would have thought you passed out on me." He snickered.

Caroline sat up and stared at him in horror. "I was snoring?"

His eyes crinkled at the corners with amusement. "Yes, but it was cute. You didn't sound like a trucker, so relax. I kinda liked it. I'm actually a little jealous."

She raised an eyebrow. "You're jealous of my snoring?"

He suppressed a bigger smile. "Yes. I haven't slept that soundly in a bed, but you were dead to the world riding in my bumpy truck through the gravel back roads of the bayou. Must be nice."

"It's only because I was against you the whole time. I could sleep anywhere with you by my side."

He wrapped his arm around her shoulders and squeezed her closer, cloaking her with his warmth as he kissed her hair. A distant memory trickled into the back of her brain like a dream. Runway had asked Cade about sleep, and images from their discussion flashed like a slideshow in her head. PTSD and night terrors, and something that had happened to Cade. Something he desperately didn't want her to know.

His phone vibrated. He checked it, quickly closing the screen and tucked it back in his pocket.

"Who was that?"

He kissed her nose. "Nobody important. Let's go get Dani and go home."

Caroline wanted to press for more, but fatigue and uncertainty plagued her self-confidence. Whoever had called or texted, Cade didn't want her to know. More secrets. Trevor's stupid words sounded through her mind again about that girl, Khatira whoever. Caroline's uncomplicated husband now seemed like a Rubik's cube that she couldn't seem to solve. Too bad she couldn't cheat like she used to with the cube and just move the stickers to be where she needed them.

***

"Did Runway call you today?" Caroline asked with elation.

"No, why?" Cade frowned. "Is Kristy okay?" He emptied his pockets onto the nightstand. It had been a rough couple of days, and Cade and Ty continued searching for clues about Chris's death, but Cade seemed more distracted than ever. He peeled off his T-shirt and rubbed the material over his damp hair, tousling the locks into a beautiful mess. Then, he bent over to untie his boots and loosen them before pushing against the heel of one with the toe of the other to slip it off.

He looked like a stripper, bare-chested and glossy as he removed his clothing, one article at a time. He swiftly tugged his belt from the loops with a swish, sending whiffs of leather, sweat, and woodsy smells her way. Caroline salivated from the sexy gesture. The muscle definition of his chest and abs glistened, providing a sheen of manliness like no other. Lust stirred deep in her belly. He glanced up when she didn't answer him, concern etched into his features.

He sat on the edge of the bed and took off his socks without removing his eyes from hers, waiting for an answer. She sauntered toward him, commanding his attention. She settled between his knees, blocking him from continuing his undressing.

His tense, exhausted features smoothed with desire, kindling the passion at Caroline's core.

She straddled his lap, which had incidentally become her signature move, and slowly kissed him with every bit of sexual frustration she'd stored up over the past couple of months. He eagerly reciprocated. Their kisses burned with the passion, their chemistry a warm blanket covering their frigid worries, shielding them from the outside world. She tangled her fingers into his thick hair and tugged to lift his face toward her. Caroline ground her hips into him back and forth on his lap, her blood thrumming through her body. She feverishly kissed his jaw, trailing a blazing path beneath his ear down the length of his neck, while her hands massaged his tense shoulders. He panted, his chest heaving with each breath. It had been so long, Caroline thought she might explode in his lap before he laid a hand on her.

She was hot for him, her husband, the father of her child. . .well, children. He stoked a scorching, charring wildfire deep in her soul, extinguished only by his touch, his passion, his pleasure.

Her fingers explored his sculpted chest, resting on the scar over his heart. The branding that he and his SEAL team brothers had inflicted upon themselves as a reminder to always protect one another. A tribute to a fallen brother. Caroline lowered her mouth to his precious scar and kissed it while her hands found the button on his jeans.

She pushed him back to lie down while she tugged at his pants, but his body became a rigid frame as he grasped her hands to stop the progress. Had she done something wrong? Cade knew her intentions, and his body responded accordingly, deliciously, but his restraint suggested otherwise.

"What's wrong?" she whispered to prevent her voice from cracking with emotion.

Still lying down, he glanced anxiously at the bassinet. "What about Dani?"

Perched above his hips, Caroline answered with a rock of her pelvis. The luxurious bulge strategically placed between her thighs twitched. "She's asleep. Won't hear a thing."

She hadn't expected more hesitation. "Cade, what is it?" She pointed at the bassinet. "Look. She's fine. At this age, all babies do is eat, sleep, and poop. She'll have no clue what we're doing. Promise." Caroline winked. "I'll be quiet." She bit her lip and looked him up and down. "Well, quiet*er.*"

He sat up with his hands wrapped around her hips, closed his eyes and sighed, resting his forehead on her breastbone. Caroline's heart sank. The last time he did this, in this exact position, he'd rejected her eager, though impulsive, sensual advances. Honorably, but no less humiliating. He'd said he couldn't make love to her while she was engaged to another man. She'd appreciated his all-powerful control and respect then, and he knew she wanted to stay pure until marriage, but that wasn't the case now. With no valid reason not to make love to her, Caroline didn't understand his hesitation, and her imagination soared with horrid insecurities.

"Not tonight, okay, love? I'm exhausted and dirty from being in the swamps all day, and I'd rather not make love when Dani's in the room with us."

She stared down at her hands, nervously picking her nails. "When?" His head popped up in surprise, probably from her tone, and his confusion sparked her temper. "Cade, it's been seven weeks since my surgery. And over ten weeks since we've made love."

"You just had two humans cut out of your abdomen. I don't want to hurt you." He rubbed his fingertip across her lips and smiled. "We have the rest of our lives to—"

"Oh, no you don't." Her temper flared as she dismounted Cade's lap to pace in front of him. "I'm well aware I've just had twins." She yanked her shirt up to reveal the stretch marks upon her belly. "I have to look at this road map every single day." Having his eyes zeroed in on her soft, shapeless mid-section only made her more self-conscious. "Cade, I know my body. I'm healed. I'm ready."

He opened his mouth to reply, but she interrupted him by bending at the waist to be nose-to-nose with him and braced her hands on his massive, rock-solid thighs. He snapped his mouth shut and leaned back propping himself on his hands. No way would she let him weasel his way out of this. "If all you're worried about is hurting me, we don't have to have intercourse."

She sweetened her tone. "If you're tired, then relax and let me have all the fun." With a lifted eyebrow and a grin, she scraped her fingernail against the coarse denim threads stretched across his swollen shaft. Cade's stomach muscles contracted and his eyes rolled back as he closed them, lifting his face to the ceiling with an exhale. He swallowed, and his Adam's apple bobbed up and down. Something she found incredibly sexy.

"Ahh, Caroline. You're killing me."

She kissed her way down his torso headed for his sweet spot. "When I get. . .through with you. . .you'll feel like. . .you died and went to heaven." She looked up and wickedly licked the saltiness from her lips. "Just let me please you. Let me help you release some tension." She tugged at the denim with her teeth, but he led her face back up to his.

"Baby, I'm nasty." He brushed her hair back with long fingers and smirked. "As much as I would love to feel your mouth on me right now, I don't particularly want you tasting the swamp tonight."

Resigned, and frankly tired of rejection, a fun idea popped in her head. "We could shower together," she suggested, crawling back up his body. "I'd be happy to wash your back." She trailed a finger down the valley between his chiseled pectorals and rippled abs. Her finger looped over his waistband and she pulled as her gaze slowly rose to his with a wicked invitation. "And your front," she breathed.

Caroline trained her eyes on his mouth with a thousand memories of ways that bewitching, talented, succulent organ could pleasure her. Her other hand, the one that wasn't mere centimeters from his erection, scratched its nails suggestively down his back. With Cade's breath hot on her face, she drifted forward to lightly touch her lips to his. *Please open up to me.*

Molten hazel irises carefully watched her, daring her bravery. Then, a simple flick of his teasing tongue flipped her sanity, and she captured his mouth with hers, kissing him ferociously while tugging on his bottom lip with her teeth. Cade moaned, deep and throaty, and devoured her advances as he flipped her onto her back. He pinned her down and kissed her like he'd never tasted her before. His hands gripped her breasts and squeezed almost to the point of pain, and she released a mewling whimper while tangling her hands in his curls.

"Mmm. . .I've missed you." She triumphantly arched into him. "Make love to me," she whispered.

He suckled on her neck with his sizzling mouth as she gyrated against his weight. One of his hands remained on her breast while the other slinked beneath her, flattening against her lower back to pull her pelvis closer against his arousal. She swallowed the pinching twinge of pain from her incision, refusing to let him know of her discomfort where he pressed against her pubic bone. His movement slowed, resting his face in the crook of her neck. When he paused two seconds too long, she knew that was as far as he'd go tonight. *Dammit!* Beyond frustrated, she went limp, unable to believe he could stop that easily in the heat of the moment while she burned with extreme lust from the inside out.

He attempted a reassuring smile, but the solid reluctance bleeding through his expression directly contradicted it. He had no intention of letting her have her way.

"I really need a shower."

Her insecurities took hold, and Caroline lost her nerve to fight back. She slipped from beneath him and walked to the far side of the room.

Cade quickly closed the distance between them. "I'm sorry, baby. I'm beat. I'm about to crash."

She felt like she already had. Refusing to be the victim, she faced him, but couldn't hide the dejection seeping from her tear-filled eyes.

"Caroline, please, don't look at me like that. I want to be with you," he framed his straining zipper with his hands, "See? Proof! You're sexy. I want you, I do! Just not tonight." He rubbed the back of his neck, "My head's all over the place, and I'm worried as hell about you and Dani. I've got a lot on my mind, and. . ." He heaved a frustrated breath. "Look, I'm not myself right now, and I know that's a lame excuse, but I don't want to take my frustrations out on you. Plus, I'm afraid if we make love. . ." He ran both hands through his hair while he turned his back to her, and an exasperated sigh hissed through his teeth. He quieted his voice, and when he turned around, his eyes pierced right through her. “I’m afraid I won’t be in the moment completely.” He caressed her face, tipping her chin up to look at him. “And you deserve to have *all* of me every time we make love.”

She nodded, blinking back her traitor tears. His words made sense, but the rejection stung, and she didn’t know how to deal with it. She refused to believe the fears tap, tap, tapping Morse Code directly into her self-doubt that he wasn’t as in to her. She’d experienced firsthand thirty-seconds ago how hot he was for her, but it didn’t make it any easier to swallow the stinging rejection.

The suffocating pain stole her breath, and the shards of her shattered heart sliced her postpartum self-esteem to bits. Caroline choked back her insecurity and offered her own lame reassurance.

“It’s fine.” She kissed his cheek. “Go shower and get some rest.”

His eyes grew wide with sincerity. “I love you.”

Resisting the urge to scream, she mumbled, “See you in the morning,” and turned to walk away.

“Wait.”

Caroline stopped and looked back with false hope that he’d changed his mind.

“What were you going to tell me about Runway and Kristy?”

Deflated, Caroline shrugged to hide the crushing pain in her chest. “Kristy’s in labor."

She walked away, unsure of where exactly she was headed. She needed to get away for a few minutes, hours, and lick her wounds.

Caroline didn’t know what time she finally crawled into bed, sometime after Dani’s midnight feeding, but her brain wouldn’t shut down and let her weary body rest. From the moment she walked into her room, a constant unease sank into her bones, and she couldn't catch her breath for the tightness in her chest.

Caroline slinked between the smooth, cool sheets, careful not to disturb her sleeping husband, and replayed over and over in her mind what happened earlier. She'd only had two or three serious boyfriends before Cade, and never such a physical relationship. This type of dismissal was new to her.

For half of a second she considered that he may be having an affair, but not likely. Cade was loyal to the core. It bugged her that he wouldn't tell her who called the other night in the truck. Why not? Who was it that he couldn't just tell her? She'd caught a glimpse of a T on the screen when he slipped it from his pocket, but that could've been anyone. Ty, Tonya, Tommy Dupree. . .there were endless possibilities considering her husband knew everyone in this town. Maybe it was the stress, like he said. The last thing she wanted to do was be another trigger for his PTSD.

Images of airboat propellers, blue eyes, and Runway scolding Cade in the hospital flashed through her exhausted mind. Finally, a vision of Kristy holding a newborn baby glowed warmly in her thoughts. She smiled as she fell into a peaceful, dreamless sleep.

Caroline couldn't breathe. She'd crawled under her car to get something. What, she couldn't remember, but the extreme pressure on her chest prevented her from taking a deep breath. Like inhaling thick, suffocating smoke. She tried to stretch to reach it, but an invisible force kept her from moving her arms. She struggled for release, but the heaviness only increased until finally she was gasping for air. Her eyes popped open. She wasn't dreaming. Something was crushing her chest, pushing her deeper into the mattress and stealing her breath. It felt like a hand clutched her throat and squeezed, squeezed, squeezed until she was near blacking out.

“Cade,” she wheezed. He didn’t stir. She peered from the corner of her eye, unable to turn her head to see why, but he wasn’t there. She coughed out his name again using the remainder of her oxygen and wildly kicked her feet beneath the covers. Spots flashed in her vision and darkness crept in. Suddenly, hands jolted her awake and jerked her from the clutches of darkness.

Cade held her close. “What is it? What happened?”

Caroline sucked in the precious air, her chest expanding with each breath in panic. “I don’t know. I was dreaming, and then I felt like something was squishing and choking me, and when I woke up it didn’t go away. I couldn’t yell your name.” She buried her face in his neck, relishing the clean, comforting warmth. “Where were you?”

“Couldn’t sleep."

She frowned. "I thought you were exhausted?"

"I was. I am," he said, rubbing his eyes. "I had a nightmare. I was downstairs reading. I heard muffled sounds and flew up the stairs as fast as I could. Are you okay?”

She nodded. “I was terrified.”

Cade’s jaw moved as he gnashed his teeth. “George?”

“I don’t know,” she whispered. “I was uneasy before I went to bed, like something wasn’t right, but I thought it was just from earlier when. . .you know.” Cade tensed. “I wasn’t in the best of moods. I’m sure my negative energy was rampant. Guess it’s possible he latched on to that.”

Cade pressed her cheek against his chest and rocked. "I'm sick of this, baby," he said with a groan. "How the hell can we get rid of this asshole?"

She shrugged one shoulder. "I'm not sure, but he's getting stronger," she whispered.

"Well, I'm going to find a way if it kills me." Cade kissed her head. "And we're going to send that demon back to hell where he belongs."

Caroline fixated on his pulse and calmed her breathing. She didn't know how George managed to physically harm her, but she'd underestimated his strength. Good thing Cade was there to pull her from his trap. She shivered and Cade tightened his hold, rubbing his hand up her arm to warm her. For the moment, she relished the protective shield of his embrace. She hoped nothing like this happened again, but tomorrow she'd clear the room of any sharp objects. Just in case George tried again. No need to make it easy for him.

TWENTY-ONE

"You're acting weird." Trevor observed his dad fumbling with the sugar packet before he dumped it into his coffee. "What's going on?"

Kenneth feigned innocence as he looked around the bustling crowd in the bistro. "I don't know what you mean." A large woman carrying an umbrella half her size barged in between them to gather condiments to dress her breakfast sandwich and coffee.

He patiently waited for the woman to move. Totally uncharacteristic of him. "Dad, you dropped that sugar packet three times before you finally got it opened. Your slacks don't match your shirt or your jacket, your hair's a mess, and you didn't just insult or curse at that woman to get the hell out of your way. Tell me what's up."

"Just having a rough day, son. You know about those quite well, I believe."

"Nice." Trevor bristled at the cheap shot. His father never fought fair. He was a Callahan. Callahan men didn't understand the meaning of fair. Lie, cheat, steal, and step on the man who's down, it didn't matter as long as you come out on top. Something had his dad frazzled, and Trevor wanted to know what, exactly.

They headed for a small table in the corner near the window. Trevor hated sitting in the blinding morning sun, but it was the only seat available in the busy restaurant.

"You're not in deep with the mafia again are you?" He squinted. "Has April Fontenot's threat gotten to you?"

"Course not. Don't be ridiculous." Kenneth Callahan was known for his poker face, but Trevor knew that he held his breath when he lied. He was lying now.

"Dad, whatever it is, if Caroline Fontenot is involved, or if she gets hurt, just remember I'm the one responsible for choosing your nursing home." He clapped his dad's shoulder as they pulled out their chairs to sit. "Don't disappoint me."

"Don't be ridiculous. You're not foolish enough to think I don't already have that taken care of."

Trevor tilted his head in amusement. "Do you?"

"Hell yes. Bought and handled, in the hands of my lawyer."

"Impressive."

Trevor still didn't understand why his dad insisted carrying out the family feud. Kenneth would have an aneurism if he knew Trevor was working with Beau to build Caroline's future house on Callahan property. The notion to divulge that information briefly tempted Trevor to see exactly what would happen, but he thought better of it.

"What do you care about her anymore? She dumped you and ran off with the gardener. You should want her to suffer as much as anyone."

Trevor held up a finger. "Ah, but you see, I don't. I want her to be happy. I still care about her. Like a gentleman, but you know nothing of that, do you, Father?"

Kenneth flashed his steely blue eyes at Trevor beneath a coal black brow. "Easy, boy. Watch your tongue. I demand respect, especially from my flesh and blood." He sipped his coffee, wincing as the hot liquid singed his tongue.

"Why? Will you sic your thugs on me, too?" Trevor challenged.

Normally, Kenneth would get huffy and fight back. This time he simply shrugged. "If I had any thugs, I certainly wouldn't sic them on my own son."

Trevor watched him suspiciously—sweaty brow, trembling hands, constantly looking over his shoulder, checking his phone, and avoiding calls from his office.

"Seriously, Dad. Have you gotten yourself into trouble? You're acting like you're running from someone."

Kenneth laughed boisterously, too loud to be authentic, and nudged him. "You worry too much. You're too young to be concerned with my well-being. Worry about that woman of yours. Where is she, anyway?"

"She extended her vacation to meet up with her brother in Cancun. He took off for Mardi Gras, and his family wants to spend time with him."

Kenneth avoided eye contact. "I'm going on a little vacation, myself. I'll be out for a few weeks. You can call my secretary if you need anything."

"You're not taking your phone with you? Where are you going?"

"Of course I'm taking my phone with me. What, am I an imbecile? I'm just not answering any work calls."

Trevor breathed in through his nose to control his rising temper. "Dad, I'm not a work call. I'm your son. Chances are if I'm calling your cell it's because I need you, not your business." Trevor sat back in his chair and clasped his hands together. "You didn't answer my question. Where are you going?"

He waved his hands about and stammered. “Oh, a few places. Nowhere in particular. More of a road trip. Sight-seeing, you know? I'm getting older, and there's too much I haven't seen yet.”

Trevor narrowed his eyes. His dad was holding his breath again. “Louisiana wouldn’t happen to be a stop on this road trip, would it?” Kenneth shook his head hard enough that his hair tumbled across his forehead and stuck to the sweat beading on his skin. “Okay, really, you don’t have to lie to me. I checked with your secretary before I met you today. I thought it was odd that you invited me to breakfast for no reason, and I checked your schedule.”

His father’s face reddened, and Trevor thought he might squeeze his cardboard coffee cup until it burst. “Checking up on me, eh? Best be careful you don’t stumble across something you can’t *un*see.”

Trevor leaned across the table with his best no-nonsense tone. “Ease up, Dad. Drop the crap and tell me what’s going on. It's winter. Nobody travels to sight-see in the snow and ice. You’ve canceled all your meetings and prospective clients for the rest of the year, signed off on all the work in your cue, and set up an open-ended out-of-office email response message. Didn’t you think I’d find that suspicious? Are you retiring?” Trevor flopped back in his chair, his nostrils flaring and head throbbing. “Why did you buy a one-way ticket to New Orleans? Are you not planning to come back?”

Kenneth picked at his croissant. “I’ve sold the property I purchased in the bayou.” He pulled his cup to his lips and mumbled. It’s worthless marshland, anyway.”

“What?” Trevor clenched his fist. It’s a good damn thing he took what he could when he did for Caroline and Beau.

Otherwise his dad would have sold it right out from under their feet.

"You heard me. I'm washing my hands of it." Kenneth pointed a stubby finger at him. "And if you know what's good for yourself, you'll stay the hell away from that woman and that whole damned state."

"Does this have anything to do with April Fontenot?"

Kenneth looked genuinely surprised. "I have no business with that trifling snake. She offered to buy my property and I told her where she could strategically place her offer. I'll die before a Fontenot gets the best of me."

Trevor shook his head and sipped his coffee. His father was a child. "Who's buying it?"

His father flippantly waved his hand as he poured more cream into his coffee, spilling some on the table as he did so. "Someone by the name Moreau. I haven't met him yet, but we've corresponded through email. He made a fair offer, and I accepted. All that's left is going down there to clear the land of my equipment and compensate the crew who have worked on the property already. Frankly, I'll be glad to be rid of it."

He took a large bite of his croissant, scrambled egg shooting from his mouth as he spoke with it full. "I can't wait to see the look on Eddie Fontenot's face when I tell him." Kenneth scoffed, "Bastard thought he had me over a barrel. I've got his barrel right here." Kenneth's lewd gesture would've humiliated Trevor had anyone seen it. He looked around at the faces paying them no attention.

"Really, Dad? Are we fifteen?"

Kenneth smugly grinned and shrugged it off. "Need to relax, Trev. Life's too short."

Something was definitely wrong. His dad was giving him advice about relaxing and enjoying life. He glowered. "Who are you and what have you done with my father?"

Kenneth snorted. "Don't be stupid. I've had to learn things the hard way. I don't want you to suffer the same mistakes I have." He shot a stern look at Trevor. "Listen to me when I tell you to stay the hell away from Louisiana and that girl." He ate the last bite of his breakfast and wiped his mouth before mumbling in his cup again. "At least for the next few weeks."

"Come again?"

"Nothing." He raised his eyebrows and looked at the empty dishes. "Finished?"

"What happens in the next few weeks?"

"Nothing." Kenneth stood and gathered his coat. "Forget I said that."

Trevor bolted upright and jerked his arms into the sleeves of his wool overcoat. "No, I want to know what you meant by that. Caroline matters to me, and if she's in danger I want to know." He grabbed his father's arm. "What have you done?"

Kenneth looked at Trevor's hand on his arm and narrowed his cold blue gaze upon him. "Nothing that concerns you." He ripped his arm from Trevor's grasp and noticed concerned stares from a few diners. He put on a fake smile and said loudly, "Besides, it's Mardi Gras season. You don't want to go down there and fight the tourists, do you?" He buttoned his coat and lowered his voice. "Now let's go. I have some things to take care of, and I don't need your whining right now."

Trevor's stomach roiled. He'd been right to worry about Caroline, but she seemed fine when he saw her. Did Beau know something was about to happen? Was he deliberately keeping Trevor in the dark? Regardless, he should warn Beau just in case.

But of what? He didn't know any more now than he did before he walked into this place an hour ago. Only that something was going down in the next few weeks.

TWENTY-TWO

Cade pinched the bridge of his nose. "When?" he asked, quietly.

"Day after tomorrow. I called you the other day to give you more notice, but you never called me back. I need you up here today if you can swing it. Plus, I've got your disk with the surveillance recording." Tonya's authoritative tone blasted through the phone to his sleep-deprived ears.

"Yeah, sorry. Marcellino's planning something day after tomorrow?" Cade's brain hurt. "On a Monday?"

"Yeah. The day before Fat Tuesday when everybody who's anybody will be in the city celebrating Mardi Gras. It's perfect, actually. The buzz is that he'll be at the Endymion Extravaganza tonight. I need you to go undercover with me to try to get a better tip of his plans."

"Tonya, I'm not in the Bureau. Don't they frown upon outsiders nosing around their cases?"

"This is off the record. I'm not trusting my coworkers right now. Can you meet me at my office to go over what I found and work out a game plan before we go to the dome tonight?"

Cade looked at his watch. Four o'clock. He sighed. "I'll be there to catch the sunrise. Have the coffee ready."

“Bring nice clothes and guitar. You’re filling in for a band member tonight.”

The F.B.I. office bustled with people scurrying around, screeching old school dot matrix printers, ringing phones, and televisions blasting the breaking news stories. Much too busy for the early hour. Of course, if he’d slept better, he’d probably be in a better mood. Sleep evaded him, torturing and punishing him with the haunting evils from his past. Why must the painful memories resurface now? He thought he’d buried them long ago.

Last night something happened. He didn’t know exactly what, but Caroline woke again in a panic, this time screaming. He couldn’t see anything, but she gasped for air like someone was choking her. Just like the time before, only that time someone was also crushing her chest. She assured him she was fine, but he didn’t get a lick of sleep after that. Damn ghosts. He was fighting her demons right along with his own, and hers liked to attack while she slept. All the stress had made him a time bomb, and not being able to see the spirits trying to hurt Caroline was worse than walking through a minefield. He had to play it safe, for both of their sakes.

Denying her physically tortured him as much as it did her. Especially when she came on so strong. He’d almost given in when she dropped to her knees. If he’d been clean, he would have. Cade shifted in his seat recalling that searing hot moment, his body responding again with the simple memory. She looked smoking hot staring up at him through her long lashes, those green eyes shining. But he’d been in the nasty swamp all day, and would be damned if he let her put her sexy mouth on his filthy body.

He didn't lie to her, not completely, anyway. His mind really was all over the place, and as much as he'd love to lose himself in her and forget about everything else, he couldn't take the chance. Several things lately had triggered painful memories, and Cade knew his Post Traumatic Stress Disorder had returned full swing. Completely unpredictable, it terrified him to be in the heated throes of passion when something sparked it. A smell, sound, whatever, could send him over the edge and he'd find himself doing something awful like choking the life out of the one person in this world he couldn't live without. The ghosts were bad enough, but the last person he wanted to have to protect Caroline from was himself.

Cade waited patiently in Tonya's fancy office while she finished up some paperwork at the copier. Exhaustion weighted his senses. It took everything he had not to fall asleep in the plastic chair. Leaving the house before dawn to get there at the same time as Tonya had caught up to him. The punishing fatigue had him hallucinating, thinking he was moving when he was really sitting still, or nervously glancing around when he thought something moved in his peripheral vision, but saw nothing. He was losing it.

Tonya brushed past him when entering her office, making him flinch. "Okay, I was *finally* able to figure out h—" She stopped after getting a good look at him. Her eyes widened and then instantly narrowed into slits as she scowled. "Dude, you look like living hell. Have you slept at all in the past week?" she scolded.

Cade grinned. Apart from his time away in the military, he'd spent his entire life around women. One would think he'd be used to the lectures by now.

"What the hell are you grinning at? I didn't say anything funny. I'm serious, Beau. You look like you're about to pass out right here. I can't entrust you with this mission if I think you might blow it and get us both killed. Your wife would probably be the first one after us. Does she know you drove up here like this?"

Nearly delirious with fatigue, his sluggish tongue slurred his speech. "My wife. Yesss, she prolly wouldn't be too thrilled," he laughed.

Tonya stared for a moment, or maybe it was an hour, before her shoulders squared and chin lifted. She was right. He couldn't operate like this. Sleep deprivation was likened to intoxication when behind the wheel. Or walking. Or talking.

"That's it, you're taking a nap."

"No." Cade stood, swaying until he'd had to lean against the wall to steady himself. "I can't sleep. Why do you think I'm in this condition to start with?"

Her stern face mellowed. He groaned. He didn't want her pity. "Beau, have you been having the nightmares again?"

Anger pulsed through him causing his tone to be harsher than he'd intended. "Does it matter? Plus, my wife just had a baby. I've taken the past few middle-of-the-night bottle feeding duties." Cade rolled his burning eyes when she stared impassively at him. "I'll rest easy when this case is solved. What did you find in the recordings? Anything to bring Ana Morales down?"

She crossed her arms and her stubborn jaw tilted up. "I'm not telling you anything until you get some rest."

"I'm fine."

She slapped her papers on the desk and pointed at him. "Bullshit. You're taking a nap, right here, right now, until you're squared away. I need you on your game tonight. I'll make you sleep if I have to."

He wobbled his head. "Nope. Not gonna happen, jarhead. Might as well quit while you're ahead. I can assure you what I see in my sleep is a hell of a lot scarier than you are."

She stepped closer and he shifted his weight away from her. "You need help," she whispered. "Let me help you."

Cade peered down his nose at her, mildly uncomfortable with her proximity. If Caroline walked in and saw them she'd blow her top. He stood his ground and spoke blandly. "How? Nothing short of a lobotomy to erase the memories will help."

"Sit," she commanded. He did, but only to keep from eventually falling. The tank of adrenaline he'd been running on was just about depleted.

"Have you tried combat naps?" Tonya asked.

He nodded, puckering his lips and blinking longer than necessary. It felt too good to close his eyes, so he raised his brows to pull them back open. "'S what got me through while Caroline was in the hospital." He over-enunciated so not to slur his words, but it was no use. He sounded drunk. "I've managed a few in the passs c'ple o' weeks, but iss apparently still not 'nough."

She smirked and pulled an object the size of a postage stamp along with headphones from her desk drawer. She looked at him with careful eyes. "Humor me."

Snapping back in the moment, he eyed her warily. She waited for permission, so he gave a quick nod. "Come sit in my comfortable chair. That plastic one you're in is crap." Cade sluggishly moved to her squishy leather chair that rocked back with his weight into a slight recline. He exhaled, relieved with the comfort it provided.

"Remember, you said you would humor me." Tonya reminded him as she held up the tiny square device. "My iPod. I keep it here for stressful times when I need to relax or just shut out my surroundings. Sax music. I'm thinking, *hoping*, that when you fall asleep," she glanced at her watch, "which should only take about three-seconds after you close your eyes, while the baritone sax whispers sweet nothings in your ears, it might just relax you enough to keep the nightmares at bay. At least long enough for a substantial, rejuvenating power nap. That alone will allow low-level comprehension and let you function properly." She placed the headphones over his ears and he grabbed her hand.

"Promise to tell me er'thing after I resss?" he slurred. She silently agreed. "How long you makin' me sleep?"

Shrugging, she casually replied, "Oh, I don't know, at least one of the *twelve* hours you need. Let's see if this works first. I'll remove my letter opener and any other sharp objects you could use as a weapon in case you wake up screaming, ready to annihilate the first poor S.O.B. you come across." After she disconnected her desk phone, she winked, and pulled the door behind her, pausing as his sand-filled eyes closed. "I'll lock you in here so you'll be undisturbed. Sleep well, my friend." She turned the light off and closed the door, a faint click following.

The first familiar tune on her playlist surprisingly relaxed him. He allowed the muscles in his face to succumb to the weights pulling him farther into the squishy leather chair, much like his eyelids had already done, sealing out any light or disturbing images. Almost instantly he was floating down the Mississippi River relaxing in the lounge on the Steamboat Natchez while the tall, lanky cat on the saxophone played his solo. Gentle waves rocked the boat as the music called to him.

The next thing Cade knew, something gently nudged his shoulder. When he opened his eyes, Tonya was standing a good four feet away clutching the very tip of a yard stick that she pushed against his shoulder with her outstretched arm. Feeling refreshed, he smiled, amused by her innovative method of waking him.

She answered his smile with a bright one of her own. "You look much better. How you feelin'?" she asked.

"Like a different person." Cade arched his back and stretched his arms above his head. The popping and cracking of joints filled the quiet room, and he realized the open space outside of her office was dark. His stomach dropped and he jumped up. "What time is it?" he shrieked.

"Five o'clock," Tonya calmly replied, unaffected by his abrupt movement.

A stream of curse words hissed through Cade's teeth. Caroline would flip out. "Damn it, Tonya! I didn't get here at the butt-crack of dawn to take a ten-hour nap. Why didn't you wake me sooner?" He fumbled with the things on her desk, disoriented and unsure why he'd come in the first place, or how he even got here.

"Easy, Beau. Everyone left early because it's Saturday." She held out a CD in a slim case. "Here's your recording." She pulled it back when he reached for it, and ire squeezed his throat. He tilted his chin in warning and sucked in a slow breath. Didn't seem to faze her. "I let you sleep because you desperately needed it. I want you sharp tonight at the Endymion Extravaganza. Go get changed. We leave in twenty."

Crap. Cade had forgotten he agreed to go to that. Hopefully Caroline got the note he'd scribbled and left on the counter this morning.

Cade tore his hands through his hair to avoid using them to strangle Tonya. Dangerously close to losing control, he snatched the case from her hands, spun on his heel, and mumbled his thanks as he raced to the truck. He called Caroline to apologize for being late, and prayed she would be understanding, but she didn't answer. He left a message asking her to call him back so he could explain.

Cade stared anxiously at the silver disk in his hands, almost twitching with excitement. He hated April with a passion and hoped this held the evidence he needed to bring her down. Listening to it would surely reopen the wounds of losing Joseph and his impotence of protecting Caroline from the invisible evil haunting her in the spirit world. Cade checked his watch and cursed. He didn't have time to listen to it tonight. He slipped the CD under his seat and grabbed his clothes and guitar. Tonya would need to disclose their plan on the way because they were almost out of time.

TWENTY-THREE

"You look hot," Catherine said with a gleaming smile. "My brother will kill me if he knows I let you out in public wearing that dress. Red is definitely your color."

Caroline's cheeks warmed as she smoothed her hand down the satin material. "Thanks. It's exquisite. Revealing, but dazzling. Thank you for letting me borrow it."

"You're welcome. It's too short for me. You can keep it since it looks better on you, anyway. And it's only revealing in all the right places."

"Catherine," her voice lowered, "thanks for getting me out of the house. I needed this."

She squealed, "Your first Mardi Gras ball!" Cade's sister fluffed her curls and checked her lip gloss in the mirror before she put the car in gear headed for New Orleans. "It's no problem, honey. I had an extra ticket, and there's no reason you should hole yourself up just because you're a mommy now." She cranked the music up. "It's time for some fun!"

Caroline glowed. Catherine had come over just after Caroline found Cade's note saying he would be working with Tonya tonight. She noticed Caroline's surly mood and forced her to go shopping, get her hair and nails done, and a thorough body waxing. Caroline was as primped now as she'd been for her wedding night, and she had every intention of using that to her advantage the next time she laid eyes on her husband.

Eddie had been adamant before she left about her taking it easy on Cade. He explained how important the safety of his family was to a man, and how difficult this must be for Cade to fight someone he can't see. He was used to being the silent protector hidden in the bushes or desert, but now he was exposed and vulnerable with no way to protect his wife and daughter. Tack on the death of another child and April's threats, and Cade was a walking nuclear weapon. Caroline understood, and she agreed to lay off, she just wished he would let her in. Let her help him in the only way she knew how. By loving him. Pleasing him.

"Penny for your thoughts." Catherine's smooth voice sliced through the silence.

Caroline smiled shyly. "Oh, you caught me. I'm just thinking about Cade."

"Well, that's sweet, but this is a girl's night out. Time to relax. Chill out, drink, and dance with me, and you can worry about my brother tomorrow."

Caroline saluted her. "Yes, ma'am."

"We're crashing at my friend's place uptown tonight so we don't have to make the drive back. Cade won't bust a vein when you don't come home tonight, right?"

"No, but I should text him to let him know."

Catherine laughed. "Probably a good idea. He worries too much."

Caroline cringed when her screen wouldn't light up. She'd forgotten to charge it, and they'd been shopping most of the day. "My phone is dead. Can I use yours?"

Catherine handed it to her. “Tell him you're with me, but don’t tell him where we’re going. I don’t need my overprotective brother following us around and spoiling our fun.” Caroline considered it for a moment before Catherine added, “We’ll be safe, I promise. My friend’s boyfriend and his brother are going to be with us, and they’re big beefy guys. We’ll be fine.”

She agreed, but worried about Cade’s reaction if he found out. He wouldn’t be thrilled that she was in the city during Mardi Gras without him, especially knowing someone was still out there trying to hurt their family. It ate at her that he was spending all his time with Tonya. He wasn’t the jealous type, but she sure was. She’d never met Tonya, had no clue what she looked like.

“You found something you liked at the boutique this afternoon?”

Caroline nodded. “Yep. Something your brother’s gonna like a lot, too. At least I hope so.”

A wicked grin dressed Catherine’s feminine features. “Oh, I saw it. You’ll be lucky if it stays in one piece.”

Caroline laughed and smacked her arm playfully. “Catherine!”

Catherine shrugged. “I’m tellin’ ya. I know my brother. And you bought lace up stilettos. Men are suckers for hot chicks in stilettos. They make your butt look fantastic.”

Catherine’s compliments worked wonders for her self-esteem. “Yeah?”

She rocked her head slowly. “Oh, yeah. Why do you think strippers wear them? Just you wait. That little black teddy won’t last five minutes.”

They parked near Catherine’s friend Melanie’s house on St. Charles Avenue and caught a cab for the French Quarter to indulge in a nice dinner at a popular restaurant on Royal Street. As they passed through the city, she marveled at the action around them.

Ladders lined St. Charles Avenue with children perched in make-shift baskets atop them, ready to catch throws at the parades. Crowds of people wearing purple, green, and gold feather boas and blinking beads stood six bodies deep through the neutral ground from the street.

"What are all these people here for?"

"St. Charles is on the parade route for Endymion. It starts soon." Catherine groaned, "We're about to see some serious traffic."

Caroline marveled at all the beads hanging sorrowfully from the tree branches and power lines, never making it into the hands of elated children or drunk tourists. Now they were simply shimmering evidence of the former parade floats. As they rode through the city, random performers capped the street corners playing catchy jazz tunes with their saxophones, clarinets, trumpets, and bucket drums lighting up the city with the spirits of Carnival.

Laughter from crowds gathered on balconies, adorned with hanging ferns, filtered through background music trickling from the interior of their homes. The sounds floated across the charged air like the haunting whispers of long-dead Krewe members and their royalty. The patchy cobblestone streets of the French Quarter were illuminated by flickering gas lanterns casting long shadows across the narrow pathways. She now truly understood the magic of Mardi Gras.

Caroline shivered with one breath, and laughed aloud with the next when one group of musicians at the corner of Chartres Street and Canal in the French Quarter played the Mardi Gras anthem, "Iko-Iko." As if rehearsed, the surrounding crowd busted into celebratory group dancing and sang along.

The taxi driver honked along with the beat as they passed and everyone lifted their drinks and called out to them. It was happy madness like she'd never seen before, and she loved it. How could one city be so much fun in so many different ways.

"Do we get to watch the parade?" Excitement bubbled from Caroline's core. She hadn't gone to Endymion or Bacchus last year because she'd had a stomach virus all weekend. She really wanted to see the parade.

"Of course." Catherine smiled, her perfect teeth gleaming. "It winds through the city and ends at the Superdome where it drives around the inside. That's what makes the Extravaganza so special. In the meantime, we'll be drinking and dancing to the live bands until the floats show up around nine-thirty."

"What bands will be there?"

"A couple of locals. *The Blue Tarps*, a chick band called *The Mardi Bras*, the young country duo *Brass and Sass*, and Rock Anthony is the special guest star."

"Ooh, I love Rock Anthony. Kristy and I used to dance all night to his album."

"I know. His music was the soundtrack to my rage workouts after my ex-fiancé tried to kill me. I punched and kicked my share of seventy pound *Everlast* bags with Rock's voice providing a worthy anthem."

Caroline was more thrilled than ever. Not just for the famous bands, but for the local bands, too. New Orleans was a diamond mine of raw, undiscovered talent. Her heart ached for Cade. He would've loved to be here with her. She wondered if his band had ever had the opportunity to play at the Extravaganza.

After dinner they crossed Bourbon street on their way to hail a cab to the Superdome. Along their trek, Caroline witnessed a crowd cheering and throwing beads to a woman on the balcony who flashed her boobs.

"Tourists," Catherine mumbled with a shake of her head.

Next, they passed two men peeing on the side of a building, a cat fight between three women wearing glittering feathered masks, and a group dressed in Wizard of Oz costumes.

"I love their costumes," Catherine said. "Gay men have all the fun."

"No way. Those are guys?" Caroline asked, shocked. "Man, I'd be lying if I said I didn't envy Dorothy's long shapely legs. He wears those ruby slippers better than I ever could."

They found their table in the dome, and Melanie's boyfriend, Mark, and his brother, Alex, immediately served them each a shot of Goldschläger.

"Cheers to our lovely lady friends. Happy Mardi Gras." They clinked their glasses, and after knocking them back, Catherine cheered, "*Laissez les bons temps rouler*!"

"Man, I love Cajuns," Alex retorted with a face-splitting smile. He was a good looking guy with broad shoulders, dark hair, and a handsome face, and it didn't take a genius to know he was hot for Catherine. But Caroline's sister-in-law trusted only two men. Her father and brother. And the likes of that ever changing were slim to none.

Catherine gestured toward the stage where *The Mardi Bras* were performing. "Let's go dance," she shouted.

Caroline smiled and took her hand. "I'll follow you."

***

Cade scanned the massive crowd piling into the huge Superdome. He'd never played for an audience this huge. He'd met the local band he was filling in for tonight, *The Blue Tarps*, and they were cool. One of their guitarists broke his arm in a fight the day before and the band needed someone in a pinch. Tonya told them Cade could play the rhythm guitar. That led to a forty-five minute jam session in the parking garage. Cade picked up the bars pretty quickly. Mostly basic rhythms and chords, and he knew their songs, so they offered him the luxury of improvising if need be.

"How am I going to be much help to you if I'm on the stage? What do you even need me to do?"

"Relax, will ya? The band is only going to be on stage for an hour to fill the gap for when Rock Anthony comes out. You'll be fine. I mostly need you to be my eyes, and the stage is the best place for that. Keep your eyes open and scanning the faces for Marcellino. You'll have a much better chance at seeing him from the elevated stage than I will through the sea of bodies." Tonya tugged at the glittery gold material of her strapless dress before slipping a beaded necklace over her head. A small but deadly dagger hung from the strand.

Where did she plan to hide that in her gown and still have access to it? She offered Cade a sly grin as she slid the weapon into a sheath concealed in the bones of her bodice, the bejeweled handle mingling with the beads for the perfect disguise.

"Just in case." She patted the weapon.

She tightened her nude-colored thigh holster through the high slit in her chiffon skirt and checked the safety on her Walter PPK. She'd have made a perfect *Bond* girl. Cade would've awarded her a sexist remark if only Tonya wasn't so proficient with those weapons she'd just strapped on.

"And if I spot him? How the hell am I supposed to tell you? Both my arms will be busy."

"Easy," she smiled, fluffing the filmy material of her skirt over the holster. "Blow me a kiss and nod in his direction. Come on, Beau, where's your creativity and romance?"

"In the bayou with my wife," he muttered.

"Yeah, yeah, Romeo. You can afford one night suffering through a little fun." She rolled her eyes as she plopped a fedora on his head. She'd worn a long black wig and a gold mask to conceal her own identity. Marcellino would certainly recognize her otherwise.

"Whatever you do, don't let him recognize you. You can bet that April has told him about your interference, and he's probably had eyes on you for a while now. I just need you to be my back up in case I get made."

"What are you going to do when you get close to him?"

"Well, I'm not going to risk bugging him personally, he's much too clever for that. You know as well as I do that Angelo Marcellino never gets his hands dirty. But his right hand man does, and he's a dumbass. Joey Terrebonne is all brawn and no brain, ya know what I'm sayin'?" Tonya twirled her finger around her ear, her Georgian accent seeping through. "Anyway he's always on his phone. So, I've got this little gadget." She held up a black, flat instrument that resembled a small Smartphone, "My brother sent it to me. He's been working with the nerd squad of the CIA to develop a technology that will electronically latch on to any Smartphone you want it to just by getting close."

"Like a Bluetooth?"

"Precisely. I've programmed it to track his calls, location, and pictures, and everything else he does." Tonya smiled. "He's our best bet. Trust me, Marcellino doesn't take a dump without this guy guarding the door." She smacked Cade's cheek a couple of times, "Okay, y'all are on in ten. I'm going to take my place serving drinks to the tables. Look for me every few minutes and signal me if you see him."

What a disaster. Cade's edgy nerves primed him for the lashing he'd give his guitar. Something felt off, but he found comfort in knowing Caroline and Dani were safe and sound in Golden Meadow.

He settled into position and within minutes strummed out the intro to *The Blue Tarps* hit song, *Here To Stay*. He'd never admit it, but the nap had helped. His sharp eyes scanned the faces in the crowd searching for any sign of Marcellino as he released his pent up frustration through the music. Surely Marcellino would have his entourage with him. Bastard didn't go anywhere alone. Cade bobbed his head, rocking out to the music, and focused on keeping rhythm while he watched Tonya gracefully weave through the white tablecloths.

About three quarters of the way through their set, a large group laughed loudly enough that Cade heard it over the subwoofer, and his attention shot stage right. Marcellino and his crew made quite an entrance with their flashy pinstriped suits and gowns with precious jewels. Cade scanned the plethora of people around the stage. Where the hell was Tonya?

He kept his eyes moving from Marcellino to the faces all around until he finally found Tonya and blew her a kiss. He signaled to his right, and she'd already replenished her tray of glasses, headed in that direction. Most people brought their own booze and food, but occasionally for VIPs, a caterer was provided.

The slime made his way through the women surrounding him, placing his hands lower on their backs more than he should, leaning in to whisper in their ears while provocatively brushing their hair back. Cade hated the man as he watched his every move, his idiot sidekick perched next to him and texting someone. Cade laughed. Tonya was right. That must be Joey Terrebonne.

After making his presence known, Marcellino and his shadow sauntered their way to another group a few tables over, and his body language shifted slightly. He looked over his shoulder more, shared silent communication with his companions, and indicated toward a young woman in a skintight red dress that barely covered her curvy attributes. Something about her was familiar, and Cade wished she would turn around. His teeth throbbed from the massive vibrations the amp created beside him as the lead guitarist busted out in his solo, scraping the pick across the high-pitched E-string.

Whoever this chick was, she'd captivated the don's attention, and the predatory way he watched her infuriated Cade. Marcellino didn't move, but his minion did.

His strumming intensified, but he managed to stay with the beat, shredding the strings a bit for added pleasure. The bass player glanced back at him a couple of times, but Cade didn't care.

Joey startled the young woman when he traced his fingertips down her bare porcelain back before pulling her gloved hand to his mouth. Her shoulders tensed, and, as far as Cade could tell, she didn't seem to enjoy the thug's close proximity.

While Terrebonne hit on the woman, clearly complimenting her slinky gown, Cade tore his eyes from them to find Tonya. She had been stopped a few times on her way to that side of the room and only had a few glasses of champagne left on her tray. Cade's focus shifted back to the woman in the red dress and noticed her friend had joined them. That made him feel a little better, but he still couldn't see their faces. The taller woman, whose purple gown wasn't nearly as revealing, used exaggerated hand motions and long curly hair reminding Cade of his sister.

A chill skittered through him. He hadn't spoken to Catherine in a couple of weeks. She wouldn't be at the Extravaganza, would she? Marcellino had joined them now, and Cade scanned the area for Tonya. Frazzled, he missed a couple of bars, garnering dirty looks from the bass player. He got back on track and found Marcellino with Terrebonne and the two women now. Marcellino responded to his sidekick with a dip of his chin and sipped his champagne. They were up to something and Tonya hadn't made her connection yet. Just then, the curly-haired woman tossed her head back in laughter and Cade recognized his sister. She clearly didn't know she was talking to two of the most dangerous men in the country. Unable to do anything from his current undercover position, he slashed his pick across the strings in frustration.

Cade furiously ripped through the bars and added a few unscripted chords, his fingers creating magic and infinitely improving the song, but he caught the rest of the band's attention as well as Tonya's. She glared at him from across the room, a warning, but she had no idea what was happening. Cover or not, he needed to get his sister away from those two. Cade needed to make it through the rest of this song.

Tonya slinked in that direction with a fresh tray of champagne, and Cade's temper surged when Terrebonne pulled his sister back to him and groped her.

The crowd cheered for an encore, but Cade's eyes never left stage right. He cursed as the band started their encore song. Marcellino held his glass up to toast the stage, looked directly at Cade, and smiled as he took a sip.

TWENTY-FOUR

"First Extravaganza?"

Caroline started at the older man's voice in her ear. She hadn't seen him approach her, and his palm inappropriately rested just above her tailbone. She pushed his hand away and leaned back to look at him. "Yes, it's fantastic." His eyes were kind, but guarded and somewhat hidden by his black fedora, as was his salt-n-pepper hair. And his smile hinted at an agenda she had no interest in accepting. Caroline looked for her sister-in-law, but she had rushed to the dance floor with Alex to escape the creepy guy who'd been pawing at her moments ago.

The man grasped and pulled at Caroline's white-gloved hand to kiss it. She hesitantly allowed it, thinking it a harmless, but flattering gesture.

"Surely you aren't here unaccompanied?" he asked with sophistication. Though charming, Caroline's intuition had her uncomfortably stepping back and squeezing her clutch a little tighter beneath her arm.

"Of course not," she said, dryly. Caroline politely faced him, but looked around for her friends hoping they would rudely interrupt. His intrusive gaze along her scarcely-covered body blanketed her with unease. She regretted wearing Catherine's revealing dress. How badly she wished she could disappear into the crowd, yet she felt like a spotlight shone on her.

"Lovely gown, Miss. . .?" he said, waiting for her response. His stare practically burned a hole through the material.

"*Mrs.* Thanks, it's not mine."

Shock crossed his handsome features. "Really?" He inspected her body from her elegant up-do to her freshly polished toes, and the exposure assaulted her insecurities. The provocative dress exuded sex appeal, but he made her feel dirty. She grabbed her clutch from beneath her arm and shifted to the side to move around him, but he mistook her movement as acceptance and slinked his arm around her waist and pulled her a little too close for comfort. "I'd have bet a fortune it was made for only you."

She took a step back and looked at him. He looked like he had a fortune to spend. Who was this guy? "And you are?"

"Call me Don."

"It's been a pleasure, Don. I should go." She turned to leave, but he tugged her back again.

Unfazed, he smiled, "Enjoying the music?"

Caroline blinked and nodded at him, thankful the crowd cheering for an encore was too loud to talk over. She didn't know what to say to get away from this man.

"That guy on rhythm guitar is intense." He looked to the stage and held up his glass as if toasting the band.

"I need to find the restroom. Excuse—"

"You see that clown face up there?" he interrupted, pointing to a large decoration hanging from the rafters, "the court jester?" She rolled her eyes and sighed in frustration as she looked for Catherine. "That damn thing is here every year and it creeps me out. Everything about it screams psycho, you know?"

"Yep. It's the stuff nightmares are made of."

"Isn't it?" He grinned. "You know, fear is not always a bad thing." He leaned in closely. Too close. "Fear can be exhilarating. Exciting," he murmured through wet lips that grazed her ear causing her to recoil. He squared his shoulders. "That's why people enjoy scary movies and ghost stories. Gets the adrenaline flowing, the heart pumping, and, if executed properly, can sometimes release endorphins." He looked up at the band again and sipped his drink. "Much like sex," he mumbled against the glass still at his mouth.

Caroline snapped her gaze up to his and then over to the man who'd been hovering behind her inappropriate admirer. He wasn't looking, but he was obviously listening as he stifled a chuckle.

"I don't make a habit of discussing my sex life with strangers."

A wicked smile stretched across the older man's face, and he bent down so his lips brushed her ear again. "Madam, I said nothing about *your* sex life. But if that's an invitation, I'd be foolish to decline."

She turned to walk away when he gripped her hand and pulled her back, handing her a champagne flute. "You look positively *ravishing* in this dress." His gaze slinked up her body as he held on to her hand and spun her around.

She hadn't finished one revolution before a woman with long black hair stumbled between them spilling a tray of filled glasses all over the creepy guy who had hit on Catherine. Glass shattered as it crashed to the floor splashing champagne on Caroline's dress and her unwanted pursuers' crisply pressed suits.

"Oh my Lawd, excuse me! I'm so sorry!" Her severe accent seeped through the words. "Somebody pushed me and I tripped over all the feet. And these heels. . . It's a wonder I didn't break my neck. Everybody okay?" The voluptuous woman obnoxiously dabbed a towel over Don's pants, but he shoved her away. She moved to the hovering gnat beside him. The creepy guy allowed her to touch all over him, enjoying her fondling, but the death glare shooting from the older man's chocolate eyes would've strangled the woman if looks could kill.

Having never released Caroline's hand, Don pulled her along with him as he moved to the other side of the table, and offered her a new glass of champagne.

She tugged against his hold, declined his offer and held up her glass. "Still have some." She tried backing away again. "I really need to go find my friends."

"Stay, Caroline." His grip on her wrist tightened. "I insist."

"How—how did you know my name?" Fear slipped its icy hand through her ribcage and clenched its death fingers around her palpitating heart.

He smiled, "You told me." He gestured to the glass in her hand, "Don't you remember?"

Caroline didn't appreciate his implication and shook her head. She was not drunk. Not even close. She pulled harder against his clutches. "No, I didn't." She jerked her hand from his grasp. "Enjoy the party."

He didn't try to stop her as he calmly watched her retreat, but she refused to turn her back to him. She kept walking backwards until she ran into a brick wall. At least it seemed that way until she looked up into the most beautiful, liquid gold irises. Furious golden irises. "Cade." *What the heck is he doing here?* Caroline was busted but ultimately thankful he was there.

In a flash he observed her skimpy gown before his eyes narrowed on Don. "I see you've met my wife."

Don smiled, unaffected by Cade's threatening presence. "Ah, the famous, or should I say *in*famous, Caden Beauregard."

"Wait. You know each other?" Caroline was seriously confused.

Don casually looked at her before sipping his champagne. "Of course. Who doesn't know this guy?" he laughed.

Cade's arm tightened around her waist.

"He told me his name was Don."

Cade scoffed. "Right." The older man tipped his hat. "Caroline, meet Angelo Marcellino. The head of the Louisiana mafia." Caroline's heart leaped into her throat and piggybacked her voice box preventing her from speaking, so she nodded and finished off her champagne. So this was the guy Cade had been stressing about.

Marcellino put a finger to his lips. "Shh, not too loudly," he mocked, "you'll scare somebody." He set his empty glass on the table and snatched another from a passing tray. "Congratulations, by the way, and welcome back to the conscious world. I sent flowers to the hospital. Though I'm sure it was lost in the sea of get well gifts from your loved ones."

"How did you. . ." Caroline's voice trailed off as she realized how he must've known.

"Dear girl, I have more ways than most of getting information." He winked at Cade. "No one's secrets are safe." He took a sip and smacked his lips as he swallowed. "Tell me, Beau, did you ever get that mess settled with the Navy regarding the Shillings girl?"

Caroline thought she might swallow her tongue. That name! Trevor had been right.

Cade shrugged. "Aww, *Don*, you should know by now that I'm not at liberty to say."

Marcellino rocked his head back, pursing his lips. "Ah, indeed I do. Your family? Are they well?"

"Sure. Yours? Ana-Marie?"

Caroline's gaze bounced between the two men trading barbs. Cade participated in the charade while Marcellino showed no emotion.

"Wonderful. Never better." Marcellino scowled at the floor and tapped his forehead. "What about your childhood friend, what was his name? Colin?" Cade tensed ever so slightly, and a devious grin stretched across Marcellino's features. "Did they ever discover his cause of death?"

Cade hesitated, holding his breath a moment before answering. He'd never mentioned anyone named Colin to her before. "No."

Marcellino took a step forward. "That's a shame." But his intimidation was lost on Cade. "And what of your friend Chris? I heard he recently suffered quite a brutal death as well. Any leads?"

Cade crossed his arms. "Nope. Still looking. Though I'll be happy to accept new intel, your involvement would remain classified, of course."

Marcellino winked and tossed Cade's words back at him. "Aww, *Beau*. You should know by now that I'm no snitch." To the untrained eye his condescending tone had no affect on Cade, but Caroline knew her husband's every breath, twitch, and sniffle. He was pissed. Marcellino held his hands up and took a step back. "My hands are clean. But I'll be sure to keep my eyes open for you."

Cade stared him down, his handsome face stone-cold sober. "We'll see."

After a few awkward moments of sizing each other up, Marcellino moved to Caroline and reached out to touch her face. He didn't flinch from Cade's lightening fast movement when he gripped Marcellino's forearm to stop him.

"Be cautious, madam. Everything this man touches, every person he cares for. . . they all suffer a horrific, untimely death." With his other hand, the one Cade didn't have a death grip on, he brushed some loose strands of hair from Caroline's face and she recoiled, cringing away from him. "I'd really hate to see anything happen to you."

Caroline pierced him with her own warning gaze and batted his hand away. "I'll take my chances."

Marcellino shrugged. "Suit yourself." He knocked back the remainder of his champagne and set the glass on the table. "Joey."

"Yeah, boss."

"Get the car. This party's a bust." He looked at her and Cade one last time. "Send Rock Anthony a bottle of Cristal and invite him to my place after the Extravaganza. There's no one else here worth wasting my time for." He turned, but stopped and held a finger up. "Oh, and Joey. . ." Marcellino looked toward the dance floor at Catherine when he spoke to his assistant, "tell Mr. Anthony I'll have a nice leggy surprise waiting for him when he arrives." He glanced back at Cade and laughed loudly as they walked away.

TWENTY-FIVE

"Will Catherine be okay?"

"I told her to get back to her car and go straight home. Whether she'll listen to me or not, I don't know." Cade had never wanted to hurt his sister more than he had tonight. "So stubborn." He'd warned her to stay out of the Quarter until he'd taken care of this mess. Cade inserted the disk Tonya had given him into his truck stereo, but it wouldn't play. Frustrated, he punched random buttons and swore under his breath.

"Don't be too hard on her." Caroline's hand covered his, pulling it into her lap and entwining her fingers through his. She'd taken her gloves off and wasn't wearing her rings. It bothered him more than it probably should have. "She was only trying to get me out of the house for some fun."

"What were y'all doing there? She knows what all is going on and how I've been killing myself to keep you and Dani safe." He eyed his stereo again wondering why it wouldn't play. "She knew better than to bring you to the city during Mardi Gras." He stole a glance, taking in her appearance. His body stirred, appreciating the scarlet scraps of material she wore. The rise and fall of Caroline's chest with each breath accentuated her full breasts, her cleavage glistening through the keyhole opening of the slinky gown.

"And exactly where did you get that dress?" She shrank away from him. *Damn.* "I'm sorry, baby." Cade rubbed his face. "I'm on edge right now, and seeing that bastard with his hands on you. . ." He tilted his chin, "I might have gone to prison for murder if he'd continued his pursuit."

He offered her a smile, but it did no good. "You look sexy as hell in that gown. Every man in the Superdome was wishing they were in my shoes."

She tried to hide her smirk, but failed miserably. "Thanks. Your sister gave it to me." She peered from the corner of her eye. "Pretty strong reaction for someone who claims not to be the jealous type."

He put his hand on her slender, toned leg, appreciating the silky fabric against her warm skin. "Tonight I was. You look so hot. Like a goddess straight out of my fantasies." He smiled, "I'm a *damn* lucky man." Caroline's cheeks flushed with color as she shyly dipped her chin.

"So what was up with you and Marcellino, anyway? I was aware that you knew him, but it blew me away when he knew you. Knew private details, even."

Cade shrugged, not sure how far into Marcellino he wanted to go with her. "I had a run in with him after my first tour overseas when Tonya lost her father. Marcellino had been responsible. It was clear as day to anyone who knew about him." Cade's grip on the wheel tightened. "But not a speck or sliver of evidence to pin him for the murder."

"Tonya's dad was murdered?" Caroline masked her horror. "No wonder she hates him."

"Mm-hmm," Cade agreed. "That's why Tonya is also terrified of Marcellino. He's slick, crafty, and completely evil."

"What happened to your childhood friend? Colin was his name?"

Cade's chest throbbed thinking about that horrid day. Digging up a long-buried memory of something that had left him traumatized as a child punctured his lungs and stole his breath. On top of everything else going on, this wasn't something he'd wanted to revisit. "I was ten years old when I saw him die." Caroline's eyebrows rose and her jaw dropped. Cade forced a reassuring smile. "Freak accident," he cut his eyes to her, "but one that involved a voodoo doll and a cursed necklace."

She grimaced. "A necklace like the one you ripped from my hands in the hospital?"

Man, she didn't miss anything. Cade drew in a cleansing breath. "The very same."

"That explains a lot. You know, you could've told me. I would've understood." He would've told her if she hadn't been on bed rest at the time, but he wasn't taking any chances upsetting her and further complicating things. So much for that theory.

"Hard for you to talk about it?"

He nodded. "Honestly, I hadn't even *thought* about it until I recognized that medallion." He licked his lips and huffed, "It was like Colin had risen from the dead and was haunting me, himself. I almost lost my mind right then and there when I saw you holding it."

"Someday will you tell me the story?"

"Someday."

They sat quietly for a few minutes as Cade navigated through the city that never sleeps. The wind had picked up and storm clouds were quickly rolling in. Cade smelled the moisture in the air. The tempestuous weather added tension to their morose conversation.

"Cade. . ." Caroline's whole demeanor shifted and she fidgeted with the clasp of her purse. Cade knew that look. He'd seen it often having four sisters. He dreaded whatever was about to slip from her luscious pout. "Who is Khatira Shillings?"

Cade withdrew his hand back to the steering wheel. Had he told her about that? Marcellino mentioned it, but had only said her last name. So how did Caroline know her first name? Hearing her full name unexpectedly evoked reminders and images that he did *not* want to associate with Caroline. Cade opened his mouth, but clamped it shut again.

He didn't know what to say. This was one thing he didn't want to rehash, and he desperately wanted to know how she knew anything about it. But he didn't want to fight with her tonight. He hadn't revealed much about that time in his life, but he could probably tell her enough to satisfy her curiosity. The same sense of curiosity that he fell in love with.

"Did you love her?"

Cade snapped his head over to see if she was serious. "What? No." The drawn corners of her mouth and glistening eyes confused him. "Why would you even ask. . . How. . . No. I didn't." He smiled. "Sweet girl, I told you, the only women I've ever loved, apart from family, in my entire life are you and Jenny."

She acknowledged, chewing on her lip, and those breathtaking green eyes penetrated his soul. "You don't have to tell me about her if you don't want to."

He pulled in front of Eddie's house Uptown and shifted into Park before ejecting the disk and snapping it back in the case.

"We'll stay here tonight. I don't want to leave the city until I know Catherine is safe." He checked his watch. "I need to run this to my buddy with the Police Department. Tonya said she thought she had a mole in the FBI office, but this," he held the CD case up, "is the recording from the hospital. It happened in the NOPD's jurisdiction, and I have enough on my plate to worry about. I'll pass the baton to my boy Tony and let him handle April."

"Who's Tony?"

"He's the Private Investigator who helped me get the intel that stopped you from marrying Callahan." He kissed her hand. "I owe him a lifetime for that." He smiled and walked her to the door. "Lock it and don't open it for anyone. Tony only lives a couple of miles from here. I'll be back in twenty minutes."

A quick peek inside to make sure it was safe, and a peck from Caroline, Cade trotted back to the car, hopping across the broken sidewalk. She waved and closed the door, but he didn't pull away until he heard the click of the lock.

He leaned back against the headrest and rubbed his jaw as he zipped past Audubon Park. People were still going strong, not bothered by the threat of the impending storm. Cade laughed as a strong wind circled around a woman, nearly strangling her with her feather boa while her skirt lifted with the gust revealing an embarrassing pair of granny panties. She'll never live that one down.

Cade thought about what to tell Caroline. He wasn't ready to dig up old bones from his past, but he doubted she would let it rest. Plus, he didn't want another ghost intruding in his relationship. There were already too many of those as it was.

He'd tell her about Khatira Shillings, and then anything else she wanted to know. It was time for him to open the pages for his wife. She needed him, and he'd been selfish to close her out. They hadn't been married a year and had already suffered the loss of a child, the almost-loss of each other, and he'd be damned if refusing to open old wounds would be the cause of any more pain in their lives. His phone chimed with a text from Catherine.

"I'm safe with Melanie and her two body guards. Now stop worrying about me and go enjoy your wife!"

He grinned. *"Good. Go straight home and lock your doors. I mean it."*

"Yes, sir! Bossy. Don't forget who's older."

Cade smiled and put his phone away. Catherine was less than a year older than him, but they acted like twins their whole lives. He was protective of all of them, but closer to Cat than his other sisters. After Catherine's fiancé raped and nearly killed her, Cade became overprotective. He'd made sure that bastard wouldn't hurt anyone else again. Cade had plenty of pent up rage to release then, and the asshole just happened to be the perfect outlet.

"Aw, look out, now. Call the animal control. Someone done let 'dem frogs loose in the city again." Tony's booming voice matched his giant physique. "Whatcha did now, podnah?" His wide ultra-white smile contrasted his black skin, and Cade held out his hand to greet his long-time friend.

"Man, you don't even wanna know."

Tony's laughter echoed off the trees. "You probably right, son. Great to see you, Beau." He pulled Cade into a tight, back-slapping hug, "It's been too long."

"I know. How's your family?"

"Good, good. My boy's on the varsity track team. Been breakin' records and breakin' hearts. Good thing he quick." Tony shook his head, "I tell ya, brother, I got a new lil' girl callin' my house every other day." They shared a laugh before Tony sobered up. "How's Caroline? I was real sorry to hear about your son. We keepin' y'all in our prayers."

Cade bowed his chin, "Thank you. Caroline's doing well. Great actually. And Dani is as perfect as can be. She looks like her momma."

"Good thing she didn't get her daddy's ugly mug."

After more therapeutic laughter, Cade finally pulled the disk from his pocket. "I have something for you."

Tony squared his shoulders. "Sure, sure." He scanned their surroundings, "Come on inside."

"I can't stay. Caroline's waiting for me." Tony nodded. "Look, I don't know what exactly is on this disk because it wouldn't play in my truck stereo, but I'm pretty sure it's enough for you to at least pull April Fontenot, or Ana Morales, in for questioning."

"Regarding?"

"I don't know. She's up to something, and I am certain she had a hand in what happened to Caroline and my son, I just can't prove it. I can feel it in my gut, though."

Tony signaled his understanding again with pressed lips. "I've always trusted your gut. If there's something there, I'll find it. Thanks, Beau."

"No, thank you. Thanks for always having my back."

Tony pulled him into another hug, "Course. It's what brothers do. Don't wait another year before you come see me again, ya hear? Now get back to ya girl before the storm hits."

Cade headed back to Caroline, feeling better, though still wary of discussing his past, specifically Khatira Schillings. Raindrops sporadically smacked his windshield, but didn't break his thoughts. What *had* April been doing in Caroline's hospital room? Why was she there, and if the doctor hadn't interrupted her, what would she have done? Why was Marcellino interested in Catherine? Cade had personally dragged his sister from the dome while her friends retrieved their car. He didn't want to let her go with them, but she insisted. It still didn't explain Marcellino's interest in her. Was it to get to him? And if that was the case, why the hell was he all over Caroline?

Cade glanced in his rearview mirror periodically, making sure he didn't have a tail. No one followed him. He called Tonya to get an update, but she didn't answer. She'd texted him shortly after he had left with Caroline and told him Marcellino was gone and her plant was successful. Tonya could take care of herself, but he didn't like ending the stressful evening with only a reassuring text message. He wanted to hear her say she was fine. Cade exhaled and rubbed his tense shoulders.

He needed more help. Marcellino intended to play dirty, April would always be a threat as long as she was breathing, he wasn't convinced Kenneth Callahan wouldn't pop in unexpectedly, and, to top all that, Cade couldn't see all the damned ghosts threatening his loved ones. With Runway in California, he didn't have extra eyes and ears and Cade couldn't stretch himself this thin any longer. He made a few calls to his old SEAL buddies and relaxed after he got off the phone. Help would arrive before lunch tomorrow.

It was storming now, the drops angrily pounding the windshield. He parked and sprinted through the torrent to the porch. Cade braced himself for a long night of storytelling and skeletons in the closet as he turned the key in the lock. He never expected the sensual treat that awaited him, knocking him clean off his feet.

TWENTY-SIX

"What the. . .?" Cade's slack jaw said all Caroline needed to hear.

"Welcome home, lover," Caroline licked her lips, her voice raspy with longing, and gave him her best salacious smile. She'd hoped using the same words she had after their honeymoon would clarify her intentions—assuming her black lace chemise missed the mark.

His genuine reaction boosted her confidence as she lay across the sofa on her side, her torso curved and dipped at the waist. She dropped her head back, released her long hair from the tightly-pinned French twist, and she caressed her hand over the slope of her hips, sliding her top leg slightly up her other calf. Her lace-up stilettos pinching her pedicured toes elongated her legs. She'd once seen a nearly-naked supermodel in this very pose advertising a high-end perfume and she stole the idea. With his hooded eyes and liquid gold irises, Caroline felt incredibly sexy.

"Sweet baby Jesus." The metal keys clanged on the wooden floor as they slipped from his grasp and the door slammed shut behind him.

Before she could respond, the flames of the candles she'd lit flickered from his movement and he was upon her. His mouth devoured her neck as he slid his hand beneath her back and pulled her against him. His body hovered over hers and he smelled like rain and masculinity. How was he supporting himself while both hands ferociously roamed her curves? Maybe he wasn't, and she simply couldn't feel his weight for her light-as-the-air bliss.

"Don't tell me you had this outfit crammed into your tiny little purse," he whispered, his breath hot on her skin, "'cause I know those vixen heels weren't on your feet when I left you here." His scorching mouth singed every inch of her neck while his palms tantalized her sensitive, touch-deprived skin, tugging at the dainty bowties on her straps.

"I bought it this afternoon. Your sister stopped by tonight just after you left and dropped it off. I'd planned to wear it tomorrow. . ." She panted, for his lips kissed places they hadn't touched in months.

"Tomorrow my ass." He pulled her up from the couch. "Let me see you." Cade slowly walked her to the middle of the floor. "Perfection. God must be an artist because you truly are a masterpiece." The normal her would've blushed, laughed at his cheesy line, maybe even fidgeted a little. But not tonight. Tonight, she was a sizzling, sensuous temptress, and nothing would stop her.

The powerful energy between them buzzed sparking the reminder of how badly she needed him. She pressed her eyes closed and swallowed as she savored his touch.

"Do you remember our first kiss?"

"Yes, ma'am, I do." He drawled, plucking at her earlobe with his lips.

"You won the bet." She said, feeling his cheeks tighten against hers with a smile.

“Fair and square, mind you,” he teased.

“I don’t know, I think you may have cheated. I clearly remember you guessing wrong and then quickly changing your answer after asking when my birthday was. The rules didn’t clarify that you could have two guesses.” She dropped her head to the side as he nipped at the tingling skin on the back of her neck. “I think I wanted you to win, anyway,” she added, softly.

“Me, too,” he agreed and switched sides. His lips felt so good on her, and she cherished the attention.

The storm outside had strengthened and the rain pelted against the window. Thunder rumbled a baritone sonnet in the distance.

“My favorite part was when you asked to kiss me again to see if it was as magical as the first time.”

Cade’s nose traced along her jaw, his mouth hovering above her parted lips. “I remember it like it was yesterday.”

“That was an amazing kiss,” she whispered.

“You’re amazing.” He crushed his mouth to hers.

Their tongues moved synchronously, dancing an erotic waltz to the simultaneous beat of their hearts. Walls were crumbling, and the pent up frustration and emotion from the past few months was dissipating with each heated breath. Time ceased to exist as Caroline’s heart was swept away with Cade’s flavor and passion.

He dropped to his knees in front of her, his eyes just below her cleavage, and his fingers trailed searing paths up her smooth legs.

“So damn sexy.” He breathed deeply, and moaned. “You smell incredible.” As the room stopped spinning, Caroline gripped his shoulders and applauded herself for buying the expensive body oil that she’d nearly talked herself out of because of the price. Cade rested his forehead against her belly and whispered, “I can’t. . .” He sighed as he pulled her body closer to his face and inhaled her scent again. "Baby, what if I hurt you? I'd never forgive myself."

She thread her fingers through his hair and squeezed, pulling his head back to look up at her. "Let me show you how ready I am for this." She captured his mouth with hers and fervently kissed him while rubbing her palm down his chiseled chest, deftly unbuttoning it as she went. She dragged her nails back up his bare skin to his face. A growl slipped from his throat as he fell backward to the floor.

"My body is yours, love," he crooned. "I'm next."

Thrill ignited a faucet between her thighs as hot liquid pooled, preparing her for the ride of her life. "That's if you can still move after I'm through with you."

"I accept that challenge." Cade grinned.

"Pants," she pointed with her manicured finger. "Take them off."

"Yes, ma'am." His elated smile accentuated the dimple in his chin, and Caroline stifled her overwhelming desire to kiss it. She was in control and waited for him to lie back down, naked on the floor in front of her, before slowly walking around him. A lioness stalking her prey.

Caroline straddled his body, the stripper heels empowering her confidence, and bent at the waist to relieve him of his remaining clothes.

"Speaking of a masterpiece. . ." She knelt beside him and smacked his hand away as he tried to touch her. "Uh-uh. My turn."She traced each of his scars with her fingertip, reveling in the goose bumps she provoked, and finally replaced her nails with her tongue. She scraped her teeth across his pebbled nipples, smiling when he flinched. He tasted salty, his clean musk driving her senses wild. Michelangelo could only have dreamed to construct a statue of this body. David had nothing on Cade Beauregard.

On all fours, Caroline crawled between his legs. She massaged his thighs, stopping just below his primed and ready manhood, and crept a little higher to his abdomen. Her wavy tresses swept across his flesh, his arousal eagerly pulsating with his vast approval. Cade groaned, rolled his head from side-to-side, and rubbed his face as Caroline grazed her tongue along a trail to his collarbone. He opened his smoldering eyes and invaded her soul.

"Do you have any idea how much I love you?"

She placed a long, red-polished finger over his lips and stood, one stiletto on each side of his hips. His eyes grew wide along with his open mouth. "How does it feel to be the only one in the room completely exposed?" she asked.

He smiled, "As long as you're the one standing over me wearing that, I'll be exposed any day." He reached up for her, his clenching abs whetting her need for him, but she dodged his grasp. Cade playfully growled, dropping his head back, rolling his eyes and covering his face. "You're killing me."

Caroline dropped to her knees and crawled up his body, flicking her tongue over his wanting lips and smiled. "Oh, I'm just getting started."

She slinked her way back down his body, wrapped her slender fingers around his girth, and flicked her tongue across the tip of his ultra-sensitive flesh. Cade sucked in a breath, and his entire body tightened. She relished in his impassioned reaction and took him deeper, pushing herself to work harder for more extreme responses. Caroline peeked up through her lashes at Cade's hard body, every swell of muscle, chiseled pecs, and washboard abs. He was a sight to behold. She suckled and pulled with all her might, rolling his delicate sac in her palm, squeezing gently, delighting in his groans and squirms until he finally sat up and cradled her head.

"Caroline, wait," he pleaded. "I'm close." His tan skin glistened with a sheen of sweat.

She hummed her response and his head dropped back. "Holy hell, Caroline. The vibrations. If you don't stop. . ." He growled. "Baby, I'm—" She moaned and his body stiffened as he cried out in ecstasy. He needed the release worse than she did, and she'd never felt such satisfaction by pleasing him, not even on their honeymoon. She was a new woman now. More experienced, more mature, more appreciative of her blessings in life. Cade was her blessing, and she fully intended to enjoy every rock-hard inch of him.

After she milked his body for everything he had, she sat back on her knees, appraising her sexy husband's reactions to her touch. His six-pack abs contracted with each breath, his chest rose and fell, and his Adam's apple bobbed while he regained his composure. He peeked out from beneath his muscular arms and the playful smile she adored stole her breath.

She started to speak, but before a sound could escape, he'd launched himself forward and captured her mouth with his. He'd silently established the understanding that it was his turn to pleasure her. While never breaking their connection, he lifted her to stand with him and ended the kiss by pressing his cheek to hers.

"Strip for me."

She pulled back to look at him and blinked. "What?"

A sly, crooked grin crept across his handsome features, and his eyelids drooped. "You heard me. I want to see you strip." He grabbed his phone and scrolled through his playlist for a slow, seductive song. His finger tugged on the lace of her bodice. “Feel the music, let it inside and dance for me. Slow and sexy.” He settled on the sofa, stark naked on a blanket, with his hands behind his head and waited for her to begin.

She could do this. Forget about her insecurities to entice her husband. Right? If a show was what he wanted, she would give him one he’d never forget.

“Alright, zinger. Buckle your seatbelt.”

Caroline sashayed, and swayed around the living room, bending and dropping to the floor like a stripper without a pole as she slowly removed one article at a time, starting with her earrings. Cade watched her intently with hooded, molten eyes, and occasionally he’d pucker his lips in satisfaction. The springing response of his recently-satiated arousal brought gratification and inspired more creative dance moves in her sky-high stilettos. She reached to untie the laces of one, and his voice cut into her concentration.

“Wait.” He stood and flashed a carnal smile. “Leave the shoes on.”

His lean, muscular body flexed as he prowled around her, inspecting her naked body and moaned. “So sexy,” he said. He led her to the fireplace and turned a metal key to ignite the flames. Heat feathered in her proximity, tightening her skin with its radiating fever. “Turn around.” Sweat beads traced her hairline, and she wasn’t sure if it was from the licking flames or the sizzling anticipation of Cade in control.

He gently placed each of her hands on the mantle and used his feet to spread her legs apart. “Are you going to frisk me?” she asked.

His lips brushed her ear causing her to shiver. “In a manner of speaking.”

Cade trailed his fingers down the length of her arms, across her ribs and down her back until his hands cupped her naked rear. His lips were still at her ear as he spoke in French, probably describing what he had in store for her. Oh, how she wished she was more fluent in the exotic language. His accent skyrocketed her libido and his hands only teased her further. She wanted, desired, craved his touch. The need was almost too much.

"Cade," she whimpered, "I'm ready. I want you."

"Soon," he whispered, and continued with the French sweet-nothings. "Close your eyes."

She tried, but she kept looking at him over her shoulder, so he slipped the velvet curtain pull from the window treatment and secured it over her eyes with a glittering Mardi Gras mask he plucked from the mantle. Her other senses were heightened once her sight was stolen.

When his hand crept down her abdomen she held her breath, hoping he couldn't feel the squishy stretch marks. When his lips suddenly brushed her Cesarean scar she yelped.

"Sorry." His fingertips grazed the tender area as his warm breath tickled against her skin.

She answered with a slight shake of her head. "No, you just. . .surprised me." The incision site itself was still numb, but the extra-sensitive skin around it tingled with his hot breath taking her by surprise.

"Now we both have special scars," he said, tenderly.

Caroline swallowed back the emotion creeping up her throat. Her heart swelled with his sweet words that touched every insecurity she had about her body. She desperately wanted to be able to relax, to let him have his way with every physical part, even the ugly ones. "Cade, I—"

She lost her breath when his scorching mouth covered her throbbing heat, and her knees buckled. Cade's capable hands braced her thighs.

"*Laissez aller pour moi, bébé*. Let go for me." His words, the rumble of his voice, and the puffs of air from his speech combined had Caroline writhing and moaning with pleasure taking her to erotic heights she'd never reached before. Naughty phrases escaped her lips. Who was this bold woman?

It didn't take long until she was screaming his name while he spun her into a frenzy with his skilled tongue and fingers, and he positioned himself directly behind her as she clung to the mantle for support.

His hands snaked around and cupped her heavy breasts, and his severe need teased her from behind. His lips brushed her ears. "I love seeing you like this." He pushed her shoulders forward and pulled her hips back to him, and she quivered with anticipation. His fingers gripped her curves, his calluses bit into her flesh, and he paused.

Her breath stilled to shallow pants, flutters bubbling up in her stomach as Cade slowly rocked his hips forward sliding himself across her wet sex, and Caroline nearly came undone waiting for penetration. The teasing was maddening. She moaned, her raspy voice unrecognizable. "Cade. . ."

"Tell me what you want."

"Make love to me," she said.

His rocking intensified until she was panting and arching her back to give him easier access. And then he thrust into her, filling her to the brim, her breath escaping with a heaving *whoosh*. Pleasure clutched deep in her belly as her body adjusted to his erotic invasion, clamping and encompassing his girth. Her insecurities crumbled, empowering her.

"*Ay, si serré!*" he grunted through clenched teeth. "So tight. It's good! *Ca c'est bon!*"

Caroline extended her head back and exhaled, reveling in the uninhibited expressions spouting from his mouth in different languages, and she eagerly showed her appreciation for his translations by clenching her muscles around him. His excitable reactions fueled her sensuality, and she responded accordingly to his vocal appreciation with moans and mewls.

He slowly and sensually made love to her from this position until the heat building from the pit of her belly exploded and her legs couldn't hold her anymore. Stars burst before her eyes and Caroline's limbs went slack.

Cade scooped her into his arms to lay her on the furry white rug in the middle of the floor. When he pulled the mask from her eyes, she refused to open them, afraid the endorphins would stop the fireworks show behind her lids.

"Open your eyes, love." Cade's velvety, melodic voice caressed her ears, and she didn't know which was better, looking at him or listening to him. She lazily fluttered her eyes open.

"Wow," she muttered with a smile. "You really know what you're doing."

"Hardly." He kissed her earnestly and passionately before moving to tend to her breasts. Her sensitive, taut buds peaked to reach him. His fingers found her other sweet spot. "You're soaked, *cher*."

She wrapped her legs around his waist and pulled her hips up to him. She'd been sated—twice, but he hadn't since she'd had her turn. He was due.

"More," she said.

He sat back on his haunches and studied her face as his palms skimmed down her silky legs tracing circles, massaging her liquid muscles. "You sure?"

She bit her lip and bucked her hips to answer.

His fingers curled around the spiky heels of her stilettos and a wicked smile brightened his face. "I really love these shoes."

She smiled back. "I'll be sure to wear them several times a week."

With a rumble deep from his chest. "God, I love you." He pushed her feet forward until her knees rested against her chest and positioned himself in front of her. She eagerly pulled on his arms.

"I want you inside me," she begged. "All of you."

Cade's pupils dilated and quickly shrank to pin holes beneath heavy lids. "Damn woman, you keep talking like that and this'll be over before it starts." He flashed his playful smile, "I love you."

"I love you, too," she purred.

He went slowly at first, but when she gyrated her hips his head fell back. "Girl. . ." Cade pushed her knees to her chest again and increased his speed. She loved this position. She could see Cade's handsome face, witness his responses. The exhilaration of watching her always-in-control husband lose himself within her thrilled Caroline more than anything else. The muscles in his jaw rippled as his eyes rolled back and closed, yet he paid careful attention to her comfort while completely rocking her world. Best of all, he shouted his pleasure in French-Creole as he spilled his seed inside her.

"*Mon Dieu, tu es incroyable.*" He flopped on the rug beside her.

"Translate, please." Caroline smiled through her own satiated fog.

"You're incredible. Amazing. Unbelievable. Delicious. Irresistible," he rolled to his side and kissed her, "and mine."

"Yours," she granted. "Always."

After a few minutes of contented silence, Cade rolled to his side again and began tracing patterns on her upper arm.

"Caroline, I'm ready to talk about things from my past."

She froze, crystallizing into a statue for fear he'd stop talking. "Only if you want to. I don't want to push."

"No, it's okay. I want you to know." He huffed out a forced chuckle. "I think I *need* you to know."

Caroline propped herself on one arm and ran her fingers through his hair. "Okay. I'm here for you. I'm listening."

"About Khatira Schillings. . ." Cade pulled her hand from his hair and stroked her knuckles. "Well. . ." he exhaled.

"Yes?" Caroline breathed, barely audible to her own ears.

"I killed her."

TWENTY-SEVEN

"I don't care what he told you to tell me. Where is my father?"

"Um, he didn't give me details of his destination, sir. . ." Trevor squeezed his eyes closed as his father's secretary fumbled through papers on her ridiculously messy desk.

"You know, if you would actually *use* those filing cabinets behind you then you *might* be able to find something in this *century*!" He spun on his heel and storming out. Kenneth Callahan didn't do anything without a purpose, and if anyone could figure out what he was scheming, it would be his equally conniving son.

Yesterday his dear ol' dad said he was going to Washington state to try out fly fishing. His father hated fishing. He hated anything to do with the outdoors, nature, or animals. And the sweat beading up on his dad's forehead when he stammered over his reasoning was a sure sign he was lying.

Trevor knew in his gut this had something to do with the Fontenot's, and he would be the one to make sure nothing happened to them. He needed to check on his construction crew in Louisiana and meet with Beau, anyway, and Jess would be getting back from her trip this weekend. He fired a text to Beau with his flight details, and drove through Chicago like a mad man.

The unease rippling through his mind set off a sense of urgency he couldn't fight. He impatiently tapped the steering wheel while stopped at a red light and revved his engine when it took too long to change. The roar of the motor when the light finally changed turned a few heads, but he didn't care. He was already pissed that he couldn't get out of O'Hare today because of the snow storm. The skies were projected to be clear tomorrow. If not, he'd drive the whole damned way.

Without warning, something heavy smacked into his windshield. Cracks webbed across the fractured glass. Trevor cursed, fear coursing through his blood as he slammed on the brakes and jerked the wheel toward the curb. His heart pounded as he came to a stop. Trevor peered through his broken windshield for witnesses or any sign of what had fallen, until finally stepping out of the Acura's warm cocoon. He cursed again when the frigid blast of air sliced through his wool overcoat. He pinched the collar together and braved the blinding snow as passing cars blew their horns and gave him the finger as they swerved around him.

Trevor surveyed the damage and spouted a few more strains of Oscar-worthy cursing before finally escaping back to his warm car. Something had fallen from the overpass, or someone threw a brick. He couldn't determine the exact cause of the destruction. At least his heater still worked and the damage was confined to the passenger side.

As he pulled into traffic, soliciting more unfriendly honks, Trevor drove more carefully to get to his street. Traffic moved slowly through the blankets of snow. Visibility couldn't be more than arm's length. The icy road denied his tires the stability needed to stay in his lane, and he drifted into oncoming traffic. Headlights zipped past him, horns blaring, until finally he'd managed to get back to his side of the road. When he pumped the brake to turn onto the road leading to his apartment, nothing happened.

"What the. . .?" What was happening? He hadn't had any trouble when he left work. Trevor wasn't much of an auto mechanic, but surely the windshield cracking couldn't have altered his brakes?

He slammed his foot on the brake pedal but it may as well have been the gas. His car continued on track, speeding up in the process. When he pulled up the emergency brake, the car slowed only marginally, the metal screeching, but not enough to make a difference on the slick roads.

Panic gripped his throat. A frisson of terror shot through to his fingertips tightly wrapped around the steering wheel, and up the back of his neck. His scalp tingled, legs went numb, and waves of nausea twisted his insides. He tried to steer the runaway car into a light pole simply to stop its course, but the wheel locked in position. The gas pedal jammed to the floor and soon his Acura was flying uncontrollably down East Illinois Street toward the Navy Pier. Trevor grabbed his phone, prepared to jump from the car, but the locked door wouldn't open. A menacing chuckle resounded through the sound system followed by a whispered, "Traitor." He fumbled with the automatic locks as his black sports car barreled toward the empty pier.

Trevor shoved the door open against the wind resistance and stinging snow pelting his face with needles. He braced his hands against the door frame and launched himself from the speeding car hoping he didn't die on impact. His face smacked the frozen ground leaving a contrasting trail of crimson against the fresh white snow. He sat up quickly, his cheekbone throbbing, and watched his vehicle plummet into the icy harbor. Shock settled deep in his bones and he realized, though bloody and beaten, how lucky he truly was to get the car door open in time. What had just happened? Who caused it? He didn't want to admit that a ghost tried to kill him. Trevor spat the metallic liquid pooling in his mouth, and the red saliva stained the snowbank. This asshole had moved past simplistic haunting. He was out for blood.

By this point several passersby stopped to help him, offering their scarves for warmth. One lady wanted to take him to the Emergency Room. He respectfully declined her offer, thanked her for her help, and limped his way home. Too pissed off and freaked out about his near-death experience, he'd deal with his car disaster later.

Nearly frozen from the four-block trek in negative degree wind chill, Trevor staggered up to his flat. He retrieved the spare key he'd hidden under the hallway fire hydrant for nights he'd stumbled home drunk and unlocked his apartment door. He slammed the door shut, threw his phone against the wall, and kicked his ottoman across the room. He couldn't believe what just happened, nor why or how. But deep down he knew exactly who.

"Show yourself, coward!" Trevor shouted with his hands spread wide as he spun in a slow circle in his living room. "You call me a disgrace to the Callahan name, but you're the disgrace."

Trevor's stereo came on and he snapped his attention to the receiver box. He quickly unplugged the stereo, but refused to show how scared he truly was, though his heaving chest was evidence enough. The stereo crackled with static. A scratchy voice reverberated through the white noise. “Traitor.”

“Bullshit!” Trevor grabbed a hockey stick from the wall and shouted, “Show yourself!” He raised the blade in the air. “You’re not the only Callahan with a temper!” He smashed his entertainment console with the ferocity of a jackhammer to stop the eerie, unexplainable voice. Sweating and exhausted, Trevor slumped to the floor and leaned against the wall. Guess he hadn’t left his ghost in Louisiana, after all. The longer he sat thinking, the angrier he became.

“Traitor,” he spat. “You who committed cold-blooded murder because you couldn’t handle a simple rejection from someone who wasn’t yours to begin with.” Trevor laughed. “And then you didn’t even own up to it. You whined like a bitch about a double cross, moved across the country, and pretended you had nothing to do with it.”

He sneered, “Don’t call *me* the traitor. At least I’m man enough to admit when I have no shot, and I own my defeat. You’re the spineless bastard who ruined the Callahan name with all your childish damned revenge plots that you pounded into your descendants, you arrogant fool.” Trevor scoffed, “You can’t even let it go in the afterlife.”

He stood and limped to the bathroom. “It’s over. Caroline is happily married now, and Eddie is alive and well. Your efforts are wasted here, so go haunt somebody else. Someone who isn’t ashamed to share your blood. I’m through with you and all your inane scare tactics.” Trevor held his finger in the air. “Better yet, go to Hell where you belong.”

The lights in his apartment flickered, mirrors shattered, the smoke alarms beeped, and his security alarm activated simultaneously for thirty seconds or more. Then. . .silence.

Trevor blanched when his phone rang from the kitchen, and he hobbled his way toward the sound. The alarm company wanted to check on him. He assured them there was no threat and asked to be connected to the police department to report a car in the Chicago harbor.

Trevor shook his head at the damage he'd caused his electronics. This day couldn't get any worse. Who would ever believe a ghost was the reason for his insanity? Maybe he *was* losing his mind. At least he was leaving the frozen Tundra tomorrow for warmer temperatures. Dealing with the gardener was better than this crap, and then the possibility of seeing Caroline. She always brightened his mood.

Just after he hung up with the police, his phone chimed with a text. He picked up the contraption, surprised it still worked after smacking against the wall. His screen was cracked, but it was still readable. All flights from O'Hare were delayed by three hours tomorrow. And his car was sitting at the bottom of Chicago Harbor. Guess the jinx was true. Don't ever ask what else could go wrong. Trevor cursed, texted Beau again with the update, and went to pack his things. When he realized the blueprints for Beau and Caroline's house had been in his back seat he screamed and pulled at his hair while shouting every curse word known to man.

He stalked into the kitchen, pulled out the bottle of vodka and poured a glass with a splash of cranberry juice. Then he rolled out fresh paper on his drafting table, fired up his computer, and took a long, burning drink from his highball glass. He knew what he'd be doing for the rest of the night, might as well enjoy it. Assuming his poltergeist didn't make a comeback for round two.

TWENTY-EIGHT

"I had to."

Cade dropped his voice to just above a whisper, wondering if he'd jumped the gun on offering to tell Caroline his darkest secret. Remembering this time in his life was like slitting open old wounds that never quite healed properly. "It was dark, around twenty-three-hundred hours. Runway and I were on our way up the mountain to get to our post to prepare for when our target emerged from his hole in the early hours of the morning. We needed to get downwind, but high enough to be out of sight. Runway had to stop to take a piss. He stepped behind a tree to do his business, and I heard screaming. I crept through the underbrush until I could see the source, and wished I hadn't."

Cade swallowed. This was harder than he thought it would be. "A young woman was tied to a tree branch, hanging by her wrists with her arms stretched above her head. She was naked, bloody, and they were beating her like a punching bag." Cade glanced at Caroline to see if she was still following or if she'd fallen asleep. No such luck. Her large eyes hung on his every word.

"There were about five guys. Runway buried his bladder bag and returned, urging me to keep moving." Cade pressed his lips together. "But I couldn't leave her there. She was just a kid. A teenager. The same approximate age as my sister, Carly. And she was Caucasian." The vice squeezing his lungs tightened as he struggled to breathe. Memories flashed through his mind disturbing the dust that had settled and petrified over the past five years.

"What did you do?" Caroline whispered. Cade could tell the suspense was killing her. She had no concept of what he'd witnessed, and he had no intention of describing all the gory details. Just enough to drive home the impact it had on him.

"Runway and I watched for a while until I couldn't stand it any longer. He insisted we keep moving, that there was nothing we could do to help her, but I couldn't tear my eyes away. I established comms with my Team Leader for help or permission to act, but was told to disregard. When I explained who I thought she was, he told me to wait one while he contacted our Commanding Officer. He came back and told us to proceed with necessary force, but to do it silently." Cade flinched from the recollection. "She was a rag doll. Her tortured screams turned to muffled sobs like she had checked out. Like she couldn't feel anything, anymore. But then. . ."

The muscles between Cade's shoulders twisted into knots at the memory and he sat up. He tore his fingers through his hair and breathed into his hands as he rubbed his face.

"Cade, you don't have to—"

"I was only to kill the men, and rescue her, but before we made it to them, her blood curdling scream was cut short. Too short." He swallowed, forcefully. Cade observed Caroline for a moment, unable to stop the sadness from seeping through his voice. "The guy had a blade to her throat as he pounded into her, thrust for thrust from the front, while another raped her from the back. They kept her from screaming as he and his buddy double-teamed her." Caroline covered her mouth. "She was raped, sodomized, and beaten, simultaneously. They laughed it up after they'd all taken turns violating her in every possible way." A wicked grin creased his features. "At least until Runway and I got hold of them.

"We had to move fast, and quietly, we couldn't risk revealing our location and blowing the mission, but by the time we got through them to rescue the girl. . ." Cade coughed to clear the blockage in his throat. "She, uh. . .she was bleeding pretty badly. They'd stabbed her liver so she would slowly bleed out while they used her like a blowup doll. She was innocent, and they. . ." His lips curled over his teeth and he closed his eyes to inhale a deep, cleansing breath.

"So what did you do?"

Cade stared blankly at his trembling hands, remembering the terrified look in Khatira's vacant eyes. The pleading look from her, begging him to stop the pain. Those eyes haunted his nightmares for years and continue to do so.

"I killed her."

"How. . ."

Cade raised a skeptic eyebrow. "Do you really want to know that?" She turned her face to the side and dropped her gaze to her twisting fingers in her lap.

"No, I guess not." Caroline rubbed her hand along the tense muscles in his back. Her touch may as well have been razor-sharp briars scraping his electrified skin, but he forced himself to accept her comforting gesture, reminding himself that she wasn't the enemy.

"So your Team Leader gave you permission to kill those guys? You said you recognized who she might be. Who was she?"

"An American who had been kidnapped on her way back to the Embassy."

"You couldn't save her?"

"No." Cade stood to pace. He couldn't sit still anymore. His body jolted with the fight or flight impulse like he'd just experienced this yesterday. "We had to get to our post to fulfill our mission or risk compromising everything. Our whole team. Our target was much more dangerous and worth taking out than risking everything for a missing child. No matter who she was. But they'd tortured her so badly, she was dying slowly, anyway." Cade tore his hands through his hair. He'd relived this dilemma so many times, replayed it in his head of what he should have done, what he could've done differently. He would always wonder if there was any way they could've saved her.

"I had to end her suffering. I couldn't shoot her, for the same reason I couldn't shoot the monsters torturing her. I couldn't risk revealing our position. But I had to do something. I couldn't save her, but I also couldn't let her just hang there dying a slow, torturous, painful death."

"No honorable person would have. You did the right thing."

Cade clenched his jaw. "Yeah, well, if I hadn't waited so long, I might have been able to get to her before they stabbed her. I could've saved her."

"But you don't know that," Caroline insisted.

"I could've at least stopped them from barbarically molesting her. And there's always the chance she wouldn't have bled out. That we could've brought her with us until we took out our target and then tried to get her to safety. . .to help. But not me, not the hero." He threw his hands in the air and continued walking a hole in the floor as he ranted. "I gave in to her pleas to stop her pain. She begged me to finish her. To kill her. I took an innocent girl's life, and I have to look at my reflection and live with being a murderer for the rest of my life." Cade hadn't meant to raise his voice, but she was defending him, and he didn't want justification for his actions. She hadn't watched the life drain from Khatira's tortured eyes..

"I'm sorry." Caroline hugged her legs. He'd upset her.

"No, I'm sorry. I didn't mean to go off on you. I'm still pretty torn up about this, so it's a touchy subject for me."

"I understand."

She had no idea. He sat on the floor beside her again.

"So what was Marcellino talking about? When he asked you if it had gotten the mess settled with the Navy?"

Cade sat quietly, contemplating how he wanted to answer. Did he want to tell her everything? Could he?

"Khatira Shillings was the American Ambassador's stepdaughter. He was working closely with my Commander when his daughter went missing."

Caroline's eyes widened and her mouth popped open. "Oh no."

Cade brushed the hair from her worried face and placed a finger under her chin to close her mouth. "Yeah. I only had permission to kill the terrorist and the five guys holding her captive. Khatira wasn't on that list."

"Did you and Runway get into trouble?"

"Yes and no. I told my Team Leader and Commander it was all my idea and insisted that Runway had no part in it. As you can imagine, the girl's father was very unhappy, but my CO explained to him in private what had happened to her. The Ambassador thanked me for finding his daughter and trying to rescue her, claimed I acted out of duty to protect one of our own, and that his daughter had died from the extensive injuries sustained from the torture of her captors."

"And they just believed him?"

"Runway was the only witness, and he insisted to the authorities that the girl had already passed away by the time we reached her."

Cade searched her eyes, imploring her to understand the depth of his shame. "But I knew better. And I'll have to live with that decision for the rest of my life. It still haunts me."

Caroline responded with a slight bow of her head, but quietly twisted a lock of her hair while chewing on her lip. He waited patiently for her to get it off her chest, whatever was eating at her. "Is she why you got out of the Navy?"

Cade smiled. "No. She certainly helped make the decision, but she wasn't the sole reason. I wanted to have a family. I was tired of playing politics and having someone keep me from being there for the ones I loved." Cade stood and held his hand out to help Caroline off the floor.

"When I got back, and everything happened with Jenny. . . I lost it. I was a mess. But, it's Khatira's tragically haunted, empty eyes I see in my nightmares. She's the reason I can't bear to let anything happen to you. She showed me what kind of monsters were out there and the pain they can inflict on innocent lives who were stuck in the middle of a very bad situation, in the wrong place at the wrong time. I will never be able to take back what happened that day, but I can do everything possible to prevent it from happening to anyone else I come across."

"Thank you."

"For what?"

"For opening up to me. I know it had to be hard to bring all that up again."

He agreed, puckering his lips, thoughtfully. “It was. But it feels really good to have that off my chest. Maybe it explains why I am the way I am a little better for you.”

“I didn’t think it was possible to love you even more than I did before, but I do.”

Cade pulled her on top of him as they stretched out on the couch. She nestled her body against his and sighed contentedly.

“I love you, sweet Caroline. More than you’ll ever know.” He kissed the top of her head and hummed a love song while playing with her hair. A smile slowly stretched across his face when faint snoring filled the room. His angel was sleeping.

TWENTY-NINE

Caroline hung up the phone with her mom and smiled, thankful she had family to depend on for help. Dani was doing well. Emily and Eddie were spoiling her as grandparents should. Caroline set her phone down next to the coffee pot and poured another cup.

Her eyes blurred on the smooth brown liquid as she daydreamed a replay of the romantic evening she shared with Cade. They had connected more than just physically. He'd finally opened up to her about his past. He'd revealed his darkest secret about Khatira Shillings.

She knew he hadn't disclosed all the details, only that he was still haunted by her eyes and her screams. She understood a little better why he suffered from PTSD. Stuff like that didn't simply disappear from a person's memory, nor did a career of killing people or watching close friends die.

She didn't press Cade for more information. It was a mercy killing; Khatira would've died, anyway. He and Runway had made it safely to their post without compromising their mission, and Runway had saved Cade from getting in trouble over it. The tragedy with Khatira Shillings had been his deciding factor to get out of the Navy. Having a family was important to Cade.

What was he like after Jenny died? Alone. . .feeling like everything he'd worked for in his life was gone and he'd wasted his best years. . .his purpose in life crumbling. . .until he met Caroline.

She smiled remembering that day. She'd crept into his cabin, trespassing, but seeking relief from the excruciating humidity. She'd snooped into his room, heard the shower shutting off, and crashed into his naked body while frantically trying to escape unnoticed. It was one of the most terrifying and humiliating moments of her life, second only to the day in the restaurant when he'd pieced together the clues through her quiet mortification that she was the trespasser who had fallen face-first into his bare wet hips.

Caroline's heart did a little flop hearing him talk about Jenny and the love they'd shared. Did he wish things had worked out differently? She squashed that idea. If they had, she and Cade wouldn't have Dani, and she was the best thing either of them had ever done in their lives.

A faint dinging sound caught her attention, so she zipped back to the bedroom searching for the noisemaker. She found Cade's phone in his coat pocket and scurried out into the hallway before glancing at the screen. She'd been too late to answer it, but her eyes narrowed when she read the caller's name. Her stomach twisted. *Why in the world would Trevor be calling Cade?* Before she could dial him back, Cade's phone dinged again, this time with a text.

"Picking me up or do I need a rental?"

Caroline heard the shower still running, so she texted Trevor back before Cade got out. *"Will pick you up."*

"Good. Thanks. I'm beat. Didn't feel like driving today."

Curiosity nibbled at her, so she responded again. *"Really? Why?"*

"Wouldn't believe me. Arrival time 10:50."

"See you then."

Strong hands gripped her waist from behind. "Hey, sexy. I love this lingerie. You can wear black lace for me any time." His lips grazed her shoulder. "How are you feeling?"

"Great!" She answered a little too enthusiastically and spun around with her hands behind her back. He smiled, but eyed her suspiciously.

"Mm-hmm. What's up?"

"Nothing." She dropped her other hand to her side but left the one with his phone behind her back.

"Caroline, what's in your hand?"

She hadn't had time to delete the text, so he'd know she answered for him. "Your phone." He held out his hand for it, but she crossed her arms instead, pushing her breasts up to peak over the lace. "Why is Trevor texting you?"

He pressed his lips together. "What'd he say?"

"He'll be here at 10:50 and wants us to pick him up at the airport." She tossed him the phone and watched as he checked the message with a scowl.

"He wants *me* to pick him up."

"Since when are you and Trevor BFF's? I'm going with you."

Cade shook his head and frowned, clearly put out with her. "Of course you are."

"What does that mean?"

"It means that it doesn't matter how much I object, you wouldn't listen, anyway." Cade's clipped tone reflected his annoyance.

"You're right." Caroline felt guilty that he automatically assumed that, and he was spot on. She'd been trying hard to not be so stubborn. "But I still don't understand why you and Trevor have been texting each other and now he's coming to visit you? I thought you hated him?"

Cade sighed and let his towel fall from his bare hips. He casually walked over to her, a smile playing at the corner of his mouth. "You are impossible to surprise."

"What?" she swallowed, but her throat was dry. It was hard to not become distracted by his nakedness.

He swept the hair from her face and brushed his thumb over her lips. "Will your curiosity ever be satisfied enough for me to successfully surprise you before you snoop around to figure it out?"

"What are you talking about? I wasn't snoop—"

He cut her off with a panty-busting kiss that his body quickly caught up to, and her heart raced with the thought of a live replay. "Trevor is helping me with your anniversary present."

She glowered in confusion. "How could Trevor help? What, are you building us a house or something?" When his lips pursed and his nostrils flared, Caroline raised her eyebrows and screeched, "What? You're building us a house?" Joy bubbled inside her and she jumped in his arms, wrapping her legs around his naked hips.

"Yes. Now can you leave it at that and not ask any more questions, or do I need to thoroughly distract you?"

She pondered it for half a second before licking her lips. "Distract me, and then I'll consider it."

Their heated moment was interrupted by Cade's phone again. He tore his lips from hers and reached for the annoying device ready to turn it off, but urgency stopped his arm midway the second he saw who it was. He practically dropped Caroline where they stood.

"Troy, tell me you got something."

Caroline could hear the excitable voice of Cade's police buddy filtering through the earpiece and watched as Cade's muscular chest rose and fell with each heavy breath. The lust gone, she cursed Troy for interrupting their passionate exchange. She hadn't gotten enough of her husband last night, and wasn't sure when his *good senses* would kick in again to protect her from himself. She wanted to jump on the chance when she had it. Quite literally.

"Well spit it out, man. I'm aging here." Troy's volume lowered, but judging by Cade's reaction it wasn't good news. "What kind of paper?" Whatever Troy said next caused Cade to mumble words she didn't hear from him often. "Don't count your chickens yet, dude. There are a lot of fingers dipped in this pie, *big* fingers. Keep me in the loop." He hung up the phone and dialed another number. When whoever he called didn't answer Cade slapped the phone upon the table.

"Dammit!"

Caroline jumped. "What is it?"

"The Medical Examiner found something wedged in Chris's throat. A sliver of paper."

"Okay. . ."

"From a KC Real Estate flyer." A Kenneth Callahan real estate flyer? Dread saturated the questions running rampant in her mind. "It was a message. Clearly one expected to be found." Cade rubbed his face and muttered, "But was it to throw us off the trail or to warn us?"

She grasped for answers. "Maybe Chris knew who was trying to kill him and he swallowed it on purpose to leave a clue about his killer?"

"Maybe. They're testing it for prints and DNA, but they put an APB out for Kenneth Callahan to bring him in for questioning. His secretary said he was away on business, but she didn't know where."

"You think he has something to do with Chris's death?"

Cade shrugged. "I don't know. It seems too easy. He could've been framed. It could've been April. Could've been Marcellino's guys. Or both. Or neither." Cade slipped into his jeans. "Could've been anybody, but my money's on April. She's the one who was mad at Chris for backing out of their deal. He made her look bad. Incompetent." Cade shrugged into his dress shirt and his phone rang again. He answered, said one word that made no sense, and grabbed his keys.

"Where are you going?" Caroline sipped her coffee, trying to look unaffected by his rush to leave.

"Tonya needs help." Cade checked at his watch. "Crap. Callahan. I have to meet someone at the Lakefront airport at eleven o'clock. I won't be able to make it to both places in time." He clenched his teeth.

"I can pick Trevor up."

"I don't know about that, *cher*. Marcellino is still out there, and now that Kenneth Callahan is apparently involved. . ."

"I'm sure nothing will happen to me in a busy airport. Too many witnesses. Besides, I won't even have to get out of the truck.

"I'll text him to let him know you'll be the one meeting him." Cade rolled his eyes. "I'm sure he'll be thrilled."

"Wait, I don't have a car."

Cade swore under his breath. "You're right." He dialed another number and paced the floor while he spoke. Caroline sipped her coffee, breathing in the rich aroma, and watched him prowl around the room trying to find anyone else possible to help him with his errands today. He hung up and pulled her into his arms causing her to almost spill her hot coffee.

"Tony's going to lend me his car, so you can have my truck." He kissed her forehead. "Be careful with Trevor. I don't like this. Letting you out of my sight was not on my agenda today, but I don't have another choice. Everyone I know is busy with other things and can't get away. I don't know where Kenneth Callahan is, and he may not be directly involved, but if he knows his son will be in the area he may try something, okay? Just keep your eyes open."

Caroline saluted and groaned as she hooked a finger over his waistband and tugged on the button of his jeans, "Do you have to leave so soon?"

He lifted her onto the countertop and nestled his body between her thighs. "I could probably spare a few minutes," he said, kissing her chest down the valley of her cleavage. He grunted. "Won't take long with you wearing that."

She slipped the slinky chemise over her head and tossed it to the side, leaving only a black G-string. "It'll take even less time with me wearing this."

"Have mercy," he crooned. She wrapped her legs around his waist and hooked her ankles as he lifted her from the counter and carried her back to the bedroom, whisking her away to paradise one last time before they faced the day.

Caroline waved to Trevor as he searched through the waiting faces in Baggage Claim. She couldn't help but laugh when he had as much luggage as Kristy had when she stayed for the whole summer. His beaming smile upon seeing her tweaked her heart. Though she no longer had romantic feelings for him, he was still special to her. He set his massive suitcases down and gave Caroline a bear hug.

"Um, hello. Hashtag high maintenance."

He shrugged, innocently. "What?"

"Did you leave any clothes in your closet?" She was thankful she'd left some extra clothes at her dad's place in the city. Otherwise she'd have been wearing her gown and heels from the night before.

Trevor laughed. "Of course. This isn't even half of it."

"So what brings you back so soon? Here to check on me again?" she winked.

His shoulders stiffened, and his mouth turned down at the corners. "Yes and no."

She playfully punched his arm as they approached the truck and he loaded the bags. "You don't have to lie. Cade told me why you were coming."

He scowled. "He did?" Trevor shook his head and mumbled under his breath. "Damn Cajun can't keep his mouth shut."

"Actually, I am the one who texted you back this morning. He was in the shower, so I intercepted your message. Good thing you didn't say anything bad about me, huh?"

"I guess. Did he tell you anything else?"

Caroline buckled her seatbelt and slipped her sunglasses on. "Wow, Trev. All business and no fun today." She saluted him. "Negative, Captain. He only told me that you were helping him build a house for my anniversary gift. He gave no details or descriptions. I don't even know where it will be."

"Good." Trevor propped his elbow on the door panel and rubbed his chin. His dark brows shadowed those pretty blue eyes.

Caroline frowned. "What's wrong?"

Trevor looked around, glancing in the mirror. "Well," he dramatically sighed, "I had a bit of unfortunate paranormal activity yesterday with my dear, ghostly grandfather."

Caroline's eyes widened and she clamped her slack jaw shut. "George?"

"I'm assuming. He never formally introduced himself. So rude."

Caroline laughed, though it really wasn't funny. It was nice that Trevor could find humor in it. "What happened?"

"Other than trying to kill me, calling me a traitor, and destroying my car and apartment, it went well, I think."

Caroline listened intently to his ghost story wishing she could've seen George's face when Trevor stood up to him.

"The bastard owes me a new car. How do you sue someone who's been dead for over a century?"

"You've got me. I have no idea. I'm still trying to figure out how to get rid of him." Caroline glanced nervously in the rearview mirror at a dark-colored vehicle that nearly clipped her. She sped up and merged into the traffic flowing from the airport.

"Maybe between the two of us we could perform an exorcism."

"That'd be YouTube worthy for sure!"

After a good laugh and a few moments of silence, Caroline said, "Thank you for what you're doing. I'm thrilled that you're helping Cade design my home. I can't think of anyone else I'd rather have do it."

"I am pretty amazing, aren't I?" He flashed his million-dollar smile.

"And humble to boot!" She grabbed his hand, " I know things didn't end so well between us, but I'm happy we were able to get past all that and remain close."

His mouth tilted upward on one side, her favorite crooked smile, "Me, too. I'd rather have you in my life as my friend than not have you at all." He took her hand and kissed the back of it. "You were my first love, Caro. You always will be."

"How come Jessica didn't pick you up at the airport?" Caroline checked the mirror again. The same car that had almost hit her was still behind her. A dark SUV with blacked out windows. Alarm crept up her spine and prickled the hairs on her neck.

"She's on a vacation with her family. They'll be back this weekend."

"Ah, I see. Things still going well between y'all?"

Trevor shrugged. "I guess."

"Really? That's it? No huge sparks or bells and whistles?"

"She's great. Really." His sad eyes pricked her heart. "But she's not you."

To avoid a much-too-deep awkward conversation, Caroline changed the subject. "So what else is bothering you? And don't lie, because I can tell you're holding something inside. Your jaw is twitching, so fess up. Why did you *really* come down here this time?"

Trevor breathed out heavily through his nose and slid his fingers through his shiny black tresses. He shifted uncomfortably in his seat before finally leaning forward to rest his elbows on his knees.

"Oh man, this can't be good. Worse than the ghost?"

"My dad left day before yesterday and nobody seems to know where he went. I came down here to make sure he's not doing anything stupid or threatening to your family."

Caroline swallowed forcefully and verified the same suspicious vehicle was still closely following her. Kenneth Callahan was looking guiltier and guiltier. "What if he has? What can you do to stop him?"

Trevor stared out the window, pinching his lip between his fingers. "I don't know." He turned toward her and grabbed her hand. "But I couldn't just sit in my apartment, snowed in, and wait to hear the bad news after the fact." He gently squeezed her fingers. "I'll do whatever it takes to keep him from hurting anyone."

"Well thank you, but I'm well protected."

Trevor leaned back and flicked his hand in the air, "I know you've got your very own *G.I. Beau* to protect you, but another set of eyes and ears won't hurt."

Caroline agreed and glanced in her mirror again. Unfortunately, her protector had too much on his plate.

"Speaking of said hero, where is he?"

"He had to meet a couple of his SEAL buddies. He told me to pick you up and head down to the bayou."

Trevor rocked his head back, and his lips formed an exaggerated O shape. "Calling in reinforcements, eh? Must've been difficult for him, asking for help and all. Dampens his superhero status."

Caroline bristled. "I wish you'd lay off. Cade is a great guy, and your snide comments really get on my nerves."

"I'm sure he is a great guy, but he stole my fiancée. I have a right to dislike him."

Caroline watched her rearview mirror. “Then why are you working with him.”

“I assure you I’m not doing it for him.”

Caroline scowled in the mirror again. “Man, this dude has been on my bumper since we left the airport. It’s starting to piss me off.” She slowed down hoping the car would pass her, but he slowed down, too. “Seriously?” she huffed. Fear spiked through her limbs. “Trev, I think we’re being followed.”

Trevor discreetly peeked in the side mirror. “Change lanes.” She did and the SUV followed. “Yep, we’ve got a tail. Take the next turn.” She turned and so did their follower.

“Again. See if you can lose him.” Trevor scouted out the back window, squinting his eyes. “I can’t see any faces for the dark tint. The driver’s wearing sunglasses. Take the next turn.”

“We’re following the river! There aren’t many places we can go.” They caught a red light. “No, no, no!” Caroline banged the steering wheel as she slowed.

“Run it.”

“What? I can’t run it, what if there are cars com—” The car rammed them from behind and Caroline screamed.

“Run the damn light, Caroline!”

She zipped through the intersection with the SUV right behind her. She floored it, but Cade’s older truck couldn’t compete with the newer SUV ramming them from behind again, this time pushing them off the road. The truck careened across the bumpy neutral ground, narrowly missing an oncoming moving truck, until it finally slammed against a utility pole. Pain radiated across her face as it smashed into the airbag.

Before she could register what had happened, someone jerked open both of their doors and pulled them from the mangled vehicle.

"Trevor!" She winced at the pain and coughing through the white powder from the airbag floating in the air. It hurt to talk, to move. "Trevor?"

He groaned. "Caroline." His muffled voice was strained, and he sounded equally disoriented, but then she only heard the smacking and popping of bones crunching as his captor beat him until he was unconscious. Caroline screamed, but another attacker placed a cloth over her nose and mouth until everything turned black.

THIRTY

Cade called his sister, but she didn't answer. Frustrated, he tried Tonya again. She didn't answer. He knew something was up. She would've normally briefed him by now. Why hadn't these stubborn women called him back? He'd grown worried he hadn't heard from either of them, but especially Tonya. Her one word call earlier was their code for distress, but he needed to know where she was. He assumed she was at her office, but he couldn't bank on that, and he didn't have time to drive all over town looking for her. He called her again. This time she answered on the first ring.

"Yeah, Voodoo. You close?" She hadn't called him by that name in years. She knew he loathed it, and her clipped tone confirmed she was in trouble.

"Be there in twenty. I'm in Tony's Chrysler. You okay?"

"Yep. Stinks in here. We'll have to go out for lunch 'cause I can't enjoy a meal in this atmosphere."

Code talking was a bad sign. Her phone or office had been bugged. "No problem. I could go for some beignets and coffee. I'm almost there."

When Cade pulled up, Tonya was waiting outside the Bureau wearing her emotionless combat face. Cade had seen the look many times. There weren't many things that scared Tonya Floyd. He was anxious for what had her so shaken up. Her trembling hands twisted in her lap after she slammed the door shut and told Cade to drive.

"Everything okay?"

She whipped her head side-to-side and unzipped her boots.

"What are you doing?"

She ignored him as she kicked them off and then stripped out of her shirt down to her pink lace bra. Cade's eyes nearly popped from his head as he alternated looking from her to the road.

"Whoa! What the—"

"I'm starving." She shushed him with a finger to her lips before shimmying her slacks off her hips revealing a matching pink thong. "How about some Chinese." She pointed to a trash can on the next block as she nervously inspected behind them.

Cade clenched his teeth and focused on the road as he pulled over. "Sure. Chinese sounds good."

She rolled her window down before emptying her wallet in the floorboard. Tonya tucked a picture of a young girl and lip balm into her bra, and then dumped her belongings into the trash bin. Including her phone.

She rolled up her window and shivered. "Now I feel a little better."

"You wanna tell me what the hell is going on?" Cade unbuttoned and shrugged out of his shirt and handed it to her. "Put this on. I can't have you showing up to my house in your bra and panties. Caroline would castrate me."

Tonya slipped her arms into the sleeves and bundled into his shirt.

"Spill it, Floyd."

Tonya finished buttoning his shirt that swallowed her and pretended to smooth her make-up in the mirror while checking for a tail. "Someone broke into my office and wiped my computer clean, stole my paper files from my locked filing cabinet, and bugged my office." Her quiet voice slipped through barely moving lips. "It's a good thing I'm obsessive and bring my work home with me. My jump drive is locked away in a safe deposit box." She wistfully stared out the side window. "Gotta have a mole in the office. It's the only explanation."

"Marcellino?" Cade mumbled.

She shrugged. "Maybe. Probably one of his henchmen he planted to cover his tracks."

"Okay, but that doesn't explain the impromptu strip tease. Why'd you dump your clothes? And your phone?"

She tilted her head to the side, not removing her eyes from the road. "They were in my house, Beau." She blinked at him through watery, terrified blue eyes. "Nothing I have is safe now. Marcellino is on to me and he won't stop until he has me."

Cade ground his teeth. "You're coming back to the Bayou. I called in some of my team for help. They're on the way down now. We're headed to the Lakefront to pick up Falcon. He flew out of Atlanta first thing this morning. Hammer, Crooner, and Rattler are on their way to my place now. Ty is going to meet us there, too." Tonya's chin lifted at the mention of Ty's name.

"Chief's coming, too?" Ty's call name was Chief because of his Native American heritage, but that was also what everyone back home called his dad. Only his closest friends called him by his given name.

Cade smirked. "Yeah. He's gonna love your new attire. Caroline, however. . ."

Tonya smiled. "I'm sure she'll understand after we explain."

Cade shook his head and puckered his lips. “Hope so.”

On the way to his cabin, Cade stopped at the plantation house first so he could grab Tonya some of Caroline’s clothes.

“You want to wait in the car?”

“No, I’ll be quick,” Tonya said.

A chill crept over Cade’s flesh. The South was typically a warm climate, but even the bayou was nippy in February. The bite of the crisp air from the cold front the rain had brought pebbled his skin with goose bumps. He dreaded leaving the warmth of the car.

“How ’bout you?” he asked Falcon. Cade’s mentor shook his head and stared out the window.

“Nope. I’ll stay right here in the warmth while y’all handle that.” Cade was glad he’d been in Tony’s car rather than his truck with a bench seat. That would’ve made for a crunched, uncomfortable drive home.

Always a gentleman, Falcon had kept pretty quiet about Cade and Tonya’s awkward situation when they picked him up, commenting only once. Falcon laughed and said, “Man, I didn’t see nothing. What I don’t do or say, my wife can’t kill me for. Y’all don’t know pain ’til you deal with a mad black woman. I’m keeping my eyes forward and my mouth shut.”

“Okay, here goes nothing,” Cade said as he opened the door. They scurried to the porch, and Cade groaned upon hearing the crowd of voices gathered in the foyer.

“Damn. They’re all here,” he grumbled. “I told them to meet me at the cabin.” He closed his eyes and dropped his head back. “Last chance, Tonya. You can run back to the truck and I’ll go grab you some clothes.”

"Oh, whatever," she snapped, her teeth chattering. "You'll still have to explain why you're shirtless. It's freezing. Let's just go in. I'm sure they'll rib us a little, but once we explain it'll be fine."

He doubted Caroline would understand. She was already pissed with the amount of time he spent with Tonya. One look, and forget about the straw breaking its back, the whole damn camel would explode. Cade waved for Falcon to come inside. This might take a while.

When he opened the door, heads turned and mouths closed. And dropped. There he stood, half naked, with Tonya following in only his oversized dress shirt.

"Cade, what in the world. . ." Emily glared as she took in Tonya's attire.

His buddies stood and crossed their arms, some with suppressed smiles, others not. Ty, in particular, could've stopped a raging bull with his fierce expression.

"'Sup, T? I thought married men weren't your thing," Rattler teased.

"Oh, eat it, dickweed," she spat. "It ain't what it seems." Her pleading eyes found Ty.

"When did y'all get here?" Cade asked. "I thought you were. . ."

An unexpected yet familiar smiling face parted through the crowd to greet Cade with a brotherly hug.

"Runway!" Relief washed over Cade upon seeing his best friend. "I thought you couldn't come?"

"We arrived last night. Kristy wanted to surprise you and Caroline, otherwise I would've called. It seems you're in more trouble than you thought, yes?" Runway's eyes shifted behind Cade. He tipped his chin, "Ciao, Tonya."

Cade sighed. “Maybe. But the guys came in to help me keep watch.” He glanced at Eddie who seemed to be sizing up Cade and Tonya’s uncomfortable dilemma as Falcon slipped inside quietly behind them. “Something’s about to go down,” Cade warned. “I can feel it. I just don’t know when or where.”

Runway assented. “I’ve got your back. Tell me what you need.”

“Where’s Kristy?”

“She’s putting the baby down for—”

“Oh, hell no!” Kristy’s voice boomed through the foyer. “I sure hope you have a good story, or else your auburn-haired fireball is gonna blow her copper top when she gets home and sees this.” Kristy smiled as she reached for a hug, but Cade didn’t mistake the warning in her big brown eyes.

“Caroline’s not here yet?” Cade fretted.

“Nope.” She popped the p. “Not yet.” Kristy’s eyes probed his naked chest and Tonya’s bare legs.

“I do have an explanation.” Cade regarded Tonya while searching for how to begin.

“I have a mole in my office, and everything I owned was compromised.” Tonya flipped her hand in the air, unthreatened by Kristy’s scrutiny. “Including my clothes. I didn’t know what was bugged or traced and what wasn’t, so I dumped everything.” She glanced at Cade before turning back to the wondering eyes. “Beau was nice enough to lend me his shirt.”

Kristy’s forced cheerfulness broke through the awkward silence. “Okay then. You must be freezing.” She held out her hand, “I’m Kristy. Caroline’s best friend, and Matteo’s fiancée.”

Tonya smiled and took her hand. “Pleasure to meet you,” she said with her Georgia twang.

"Clothes are my thing, so let's get you upstairs and changed into something warmer and a little more. . .decent."

"We thought you bailed on us," Hammer said. "We have a little story of our own to share." He laughed, his ash blue eyes dancing. His blonde hair brushed the tops of his broad shoulders, and, with his red shirt with the silver jacket, he resembled a super hero.

"Oh yeah?" Cade smiled. "Let's hear it."

"On the way down here we passed a car flipped on its side still running, so we checked the woods around it."

"Find anything?" Cade asked, his eyes scanning the other faces in the room.

Hammer struggled to contain his amusement. "Yeah. Two twitchy dudes who claimed they'd seen a ghost."

Cade huffed out a laugh and checked his watch. "Not surprising around these parts." Where the hell was Caroline?

"It gets better." Crooner chimed in, his smile spreading wide across his thin face. "They were in shock. Said it was the ghost of your wife." Crooner chortled. Cade smirked, back in the day Crooner would've improvised a song out of that. It's how he got his name. "After we strongly persuaded them to talk, they admitted that they'd been sent to ruffle her up, bring her in, but that someone else had already gotten to her."

"The driver said she'd entered his body and made him spin the car until it flipped." Hammer smiled. "Said she took advantage of his good senses and violated him."

Cade forced a grin, but Caroline had him worried. He met Runway's knowing gaze. Rachel must still be watching out for them, but those guys had been after Caroline. Something was wrong. He needed to call her. Cade's buddies continued laughing about the thugs, but he didn't find much humor in it considering

Caroline was still out there somewhere. "Where are the guys now?"

Ty stepped forward, all serious, the gravity of the situation creasing his features. "We hog tied them with some dummy cord and strapped them to a deer stand on the grounds near your cabin. Crooner wired 'em up real good so they won't try to escape."

"Yeah, I don't know which was funnier. Their faces when they talked about a ghost, or when I strapped a few chemical IEDs strategically wired to their backs that'll blow from just the vibrations of their voices." Crooner's chest puffed with pride. "My own design."

"Nice. I have a feeling those aren't the last thugs we'll see, though." Cade rubbed the tension from his brow and noticed Eddie leaning against the door frame watching his every move with concern etched in his features. Emily stood next to Eddie with her hands politely clasped in front of her, and Cade realized he hadn't made any introductions. "Have y'all met my family yet?" he asked the guys. Cade checked his watch again.

"Um, not officially. We introduced ourselves, but didn't explain why we were here," Rattler said.

Cade stifled his urge to call Caroline until after introductions. After all, she was with Trevor and he was no limp noodle. Cade remembered how well Callahan held his own in their brief fight two summers ago. But still. . .

Cade held his hand out to his family, trying not to sound rushed, "Eddie and Emily Fontenot, my in-laws." The guys shook their hands as Cade gestured behind them. "Delia and Delphine take care of everything around the house," Cade's stomach growled, "including that delicious aroma wafting from the kitchen."

Delphine smiled. “Yeah, beb. We got plenty crawfish étouffée for lunch, ya heard? Y’all come help ya’selves.”

Delia smiled at each burly man occupying the large foyer making it seem small. “If y’all need anything, I’m your girl,” she blushed. “I mean, I’ll accommodate you however you’d like.”

Everyone laughed as she scurried out of the room, giggling with Delphine like a couple of teenage girls.

“Emily and Eddie, these guys were part of my SEAL team. I trust them with my life. Quick introductions,” he pointed to his buddies. “I’ll stick to call names to eliminate any confusion. Falcon, Rattler, Hammer, Crooner, and y’all already know Ty.”

Their names are pretty fitting to their personalities. Especially Crooner. He thinks he’s in the Rat Pack and sings *all* the damned time.”

“Almost as much as you,” Crooner quipped, and the room broke out in laughter.

“Yeah, maybe someday you’ll be as awesome as me.” Cade winked. “Anyway,” he turned back to Emily and Eddie, “he’d give Sinatra a run for his money.”

“Oh, I’d love to hear that!” Emily said excitedly. After everyone’s attention focused on her, she blushed. Cade smiled, reminded of his beautiful wife, and glanced at his watch. She really should be here by now. His nerves were raw, his intuition screaming, and he knew trouble was brewing. Cade flicked his hands out at his sides like he was flinging water and clenched them into fists. He wouldn’t relax until she was safely in his arms again. “I mean, s-sometime later,” Emily stuttered. “You obviously don’t have to sing right now, of course.”

“Don’t let him fool you, Ms. Emily. Crooner’s skills go far beyond his big mouth. His specialty is actually demolition. He can blow up anything above or below water and control the blast so that nothing around the explosion site has so much as a scratch on it." Cade tipped his head toward his buddy. "It's quite impressive."

"Aw, Beau, you're making me blush."

Cade rolled his eyes. "As if that was even possible."

"It's a pleasure to have y'all here. We appreciate your help, and if there is anything you need at any time, please don't hesitate to ask," said Eddie.

"Where is Caroline? Has anyone heard from her?" Beau asked, not finishing the introductions. He couldn't wait any longer. He needed to know where his wife was.

"No. We all thought she was with you," Emily's face creased with worry.

The lingering fear spread throughout Cade's chest. "No, she took my truck to pick up Trevor from the airport." He looked at his watch again. "She should've been back by now. Something's wrong." He pulled out his phone and paced the floor as he called her, but she didn't answer. Panic seized his heart and his limbs felt like lead. The sinking worry that had been teetering on the edge of disaster all day crashed to the flaming pits of his paranoia. A dozen different possible reasons for her not answering her phone flashed through Cade's head. He dialed Trevor's number. When it went straight to voicemail, Cade approached Emily and whispered, "You haven't had any visions today or yesterday, have you?"

"No, why?"

"Something doesn't feel right." He called Troy at the station to see if he'd heard anything.

"Beau, I was about to call you to see if you were okay, man."

"Why wouldn't I be? What's happened?"

"Oh. Where are you? Still in town?"

"No, I'm back in the bayou. Have you heard from Caroline?"

"Well, no, but. . ." he paused.

"Give it to me straight, dude. I don't have time for procedure."

"Your truck was found wrapped around a telephone pole near River Road."

Cade swallowed, "Is Caroline okay? Callahan?"

"Beau, the truck was empty. Caroline's purse was still in the cab."

Cade cursed a blue streak and thanked his friend, asking him to call with any updates as he ran out the door.

"Beau, wait! Where are you going?" Runway and Eddie shouted, chasing after him.

"My truck was wrecked and Caroline and Trevor are missing. I have to go find them."

"I'm coming with you," Runway said.

"No, wait, I need you here." Cade cringed. He hadn't had time to brief the guys on what he needed them to do. "You know what's going on better than the guys inside. Give them a rundown on the situation and post them. Send Hammer to find Catherine. She's not answering her phone and Marcellino had his sights set on her last night."

"I'm not letting you go alone," Eddie demanded. "Emily and Kristy will take care of the babies with Delia and Delphine. If Caroline's in trouble I'm coming with you."

Cade acknowledged. "She's in trouble." He pointed at Runway as he walked backwards to Tony's car. "Post Falcon at the house to guard the home front. Keep your phone on you."

As they pulled out, Cade filled Eddie in on the details.

"Let's just pray that Caroline is wearing the watch I gave her."

"Why?"

"It has a GPS embedded in it." He had helped her clasp it on her wrist that morning, and hoped it was still where he'd left it. "If she's wearing it, we'll be able to find her, hopefully before it's too late." He pressed the pedal harder and prayed. "I knew that thing would come in handy someday."

Cade called his parents who were on their way to Lafayette to stay with his grandparents for a week, and he warned them not to come home early. He racked his brain to think of anyone else he loved that Marcellino could harm, but everyone was safely out of harm's way except Catherine. He tried her cell again and it went straight to voicemail, so this time he left a message.

"Damn it, Cat! Where the hell are you and why aren't you answering your phone? I'm sending Hammer to find you and bring you home. He's a pretty-boy, huge with blonde hair, and his name is David." Catherine would not be receptive to a large, strange man trying to make her come with him. "Don't freak out," Cade paused a moment, "And don't trust anyone else," he added.

"What's Hammer's specialty?" Eddie asked. Cade knew he was trying to distract him. He'd overheard Runway at the hospital back when Caroline was unconscious telling Eddie the symptoms for PTSD. Eddie was clearly questioning his control at the moment.

"He's a Hospital Corpsman. A field medic. The best there is. He got his nickname because he does everything fast and strong. Walking, talking, eating, and especially running. He could sprint from person to person patching them up in a matter of seconds without getting wounded, himself. And he's a beast. Seriously strong." Cade huffed, "We tease him for being pretty, but I tell ya, I wouldn't want to cross him. He got in fight once at a bar in

Coronado, and the poor guy had a broken nose, broken ribs, a bleeding ear, and missing teeth before he ever got the first swing in."

"Wow," Eddie exclaimed. "What'd the guy do to deserve that beating?"

"A young woman had accused him of date rape, and the guy blew her off telling her she asked for it. When she slapped him, the guy slapped her back. Hammer has zero tolerance for guys who hit women or sexually abuse them." Cade shifted uncomfortably, trying to decide how much to tell. "His mother was date raped when she was younger and he was the result. She loved him and raised him as a single mother while teaching him how to respect a woman."

"Sounds like he taught that guy a good lesson. I'm surprised you weren't in on that."

Cade thoughtfully tilted his chin. "Yeah, I think that was before what happened to my sister. What I did to her fiancé was nothing compared to what Hammer would've done if he'd gotten hold of him."

"It's getting dark. Where do you think Caroline is?" Eddie asked. The worry resonated in his voice, sinking clean into Cade's bones. He checked his phone app to find the watch signal and slammed on the brakes.

Eddie gripped the dash, "What is it?"

"She's this way."

He spun out and headed for the location of the pulsating dot on his app, praying she was okay. It was stationary, and he had a sinking suspicion he knew where they were. "I need to call Runway and let him know."

While waiting for Runway to answer, Eddie's phone rang. Cade told Runway to get the guys together with their equipment and meet him in the field where they had found April last summer before Caroline's graduation party. When he hung up and focused on following the dot again, he noticed Eddie silence. He risked a glance and blanched at Eddie's stark white face.

"What's wrong? Who was that?"

Eddie slowly raised his eyes to Cade's. "Claire. They've got her, too."

THIRTY-ONE

"Trevor?" Caroline croaked through dry, cracking lips. Parched didn't begin to cover her state of being. Everything hurt. Her wrists were tied together behind her and her back pressed tightly against a cold metal post. Urgency filled her as she remembered what happened before she blacked out. "Trevor!" she frantically whispered.

"Yeah." He groaned. "I feel like I've been hit by a Mack truck. Are you okay?"

"I think so." Caroline opened her eyes as wide as they would go, but she couldn't see much from the slivers of light filtering in through cracks in the walls. "Where are we?"

Trevor huffed and whispered. "Hell if I know. This is *your* neck of the woods, remember?"

"This is a dirt floor. I've been here before, I think. In a dream."

"Okay, Cinderella, where are we then?" Trevor's sardonic tone infuriated her.

"Seriously. I think this is one of the out buildings on my dad's property. I had seen it in a dream last year and I searched the grounds for it to see if I was crazy. It's almost like a barn, but I think my dad said back in the day they used it to store the plow carts and wheelbarrows."

"Who brought us here?"

"I don't know. But I'm sure Cade is looking for us by now."

"Let's hope so. His knack for always showing up to save the day might actually be helpful for once."

"I'm sorry, Trev. I tried to keep the truck on the road as long as I could. I lost control."

"It's not your fault, C. Are you okay?"

"Yeah. The right side of my face burns. Glad I had the airbag." Caroline licked her lips, but it didn't do any good. Her tongue was just as dry. "How 'bout you? I saw, well, mostly *heard* the beating you took."

Trevor spit in the dirt. Caroline wished she had some spit. Her teeth stuck to her lips. "Yeah, son of a bitch got me good. I think my nose is broken." Trevor scuffled around. "All I know is we've got to get out of here. Whoever went through such drastic measures to capture and tie us up in here isn't going to want to talk it out. We have to get out before they come back."

Caroline pulled on the rope binding her wrists. "It's really tight. It's cutting into my skin."

Trevor swore under his breath. "Mine, too."

Caroline shimmied up the pole to stand, and tried to turn, but it painfully twisted her arms and she had to turn back around. "I don't think we're going to find a way out of this. Hopefully Cade will think to look in these abandoned buildings. He knows these grounds better than anyone."

"I wonder how long we were knocked out? You picked me up around lunch time, and if we're on your dad's property, that was a few hours driving. The light coming through those boards isn't very bright. . . I'd guess it's probably going to be dark soon. Why would Beau think to look here? As far as he knows we're still in New Orleans. If he's heard about the wreck, he's probably looking at the nearby hospitals, not down here in the bayou."

Trevor was right. Cade would think they were still in the city. She slumped back to the ground. "Well, at least we won't die alone."

"You're not going to die today. Not if I can help it."

The cold musty air stung Caroline's nose. "I don't see how you can."

They sat in silence listening for any noise, voices, or clues as to who had them and what their plans were. Nothing but chirping crickets, cicadas, and bull frogs. All the sounds she used to love about the country now sang her impending death symphony.

"Caroline?"

"Yeah?"

"For what it's worth, I never cheated on you."

Caroline swallowed the lump growing in her throat. Last confessions.

"I was faithful to you until the very end." A laugh hissed through his teeth. "I know I was a player before, but that ended when I met you. Sure, I'd get frustrated when you'd say no, but. . ." He coughed. Was he covering his emotion the same way Cade always did? "You were worth waiting for."

"Thank you. That means a lot to me." More than Trevor would ever know.

A noise caught her attention in the corner of the structure. "I hope that's not a rat. If it is I will probably develop super human strength and break these binds. I hate rodents." Caroline's feeble attempt at levity wasn't wasted.

Trevor chuckled. "But you married a swamp rat."

"For what it's worth, I didn't cheat on you either." Trevor sat still, clearly waiting for her to continue. "I almost did," she whispered, squeezing her eyes closed with the admission. "I actually tried to." She heard the soft intake of breath he tried to hide. "I was angry with you for acting so weird, for being so controlling, and I wanted to give you a taste of your own medicine. But, Cade stopped me."

Trevor snorted, "Whatever."

"No, he did. It was humiliating. I came on to him, and he told me he couldn't do it. That he couldn't make love to me while I was still engaged to you. He didn't want to be the *other* guy. Out of respect for me, himself, and even you, he couldn't do it." Caroline leaned her head against the metal post and blinked, letting the pool of tears breach her eyelids. She hadn't expected the memories to elicit such strong emotions.

"I was ashamed, as I should have been, and thankful Cade had put things into perspective for me. When I got back to my dad's house, you were there, waiting for me on my bed." Caroline licked the tear that teetered on the edge of her top lip. "I was genuinely happy to see you."

"I forgive you, Caroline," Trevor tenderly replied. "I only hope you can forgive me for being such a jerk. Beau had more self-control than I would have had." Trevor huffed. "When he showed up on our wedding day, my jealous rage took over, and I. . ." he exhaled. "Anger, humiliation, resentment. I have no excuse. I was an ass. I'm. . . I am my father's son." Trevor released a cynical laugh, "And apparently my great, great, great grandfather's son. And I'm incredibly sorry."

"It's okay, Trev. I forgive you, too. Everything happens for a reason."

"Yeah? So why are we here?"

"I don't know," she said, thoughtfully. "But I have to believe that we're going to be okay." Caroline wished Rachel would do something magical to get them out of here.

"You were the best thing I almost had," Trevor murmured.

"You still have me. Just in a different context."

Rustling leaves from outside echoed through the hollow structure and Caroline nearly swallowed her heart. Her pulse pounded in her ears as she waited to see who walked through the doors. Cool air rushed in, and the dusk sky offered a shred of light, but she could only see two figures approaching holding flashlights.

"Well, look who finally came to. Welcome back, sweetheart," the shorter one said. Caroline squinted to make out his face, but all she could see was his shape.

"Sorry we late. Rip Van Winkle over here fell asleep keeping watch. We almost missed da party."

What party?

The shorter guy, the one untying her, shined the flashlight in her face. She jerked back and smacked her head on the pole, cringing from the blinding pain. "Oh, looks like your careless driving left a nasty mark. Hope it don't scar dat pretty face. Not dat it matters. How your guy looks, Joe?"

Caroline caught a glimpse of Trevor's battered face when his captor shined the light on him.

"Oh, he won't be winnin' no beauty contest, dat's fuh sure." Trevor fought against the ties. "Oh, oh, Roy, we got us a fighter, here. Dis one's feisty." He grabbed the bridge of Trevor's nose and squeezed. Trevor's howl reverberated through the still night air.

"Stop! Please, stop!" Caroline screeched. "You coward! He can't even defend himself with his hands tied. Leave him alone."

The guy shuffled across the dirt floor over to her and put the light to his face, "Speakin' of feisty." A sinister smile crept across his oily face. "Remember me, doll?"

She grimaced. "Should I?"

He briefly appeared wounded that she hadn't recognized him, but then a hardened glaze covered his eyes. "Let's get 'em over to da field. Boss'll wanna know they ready. But be quiet so we don't draw no unwanted attention. I don't want dat bitch in my ear no more."

April. Had to be April. Caroline had her fill of that woman. If she could manage to untie her hands she'd show her stepmother just how much.

It was dusk, difficult to tell if it was early morning just after sunrise, or late afternoon just before sunset, as the creeps led them through the wooded, tree-filled area sounding like a herd of buffalo stomping through the dry leaves. Cade would've been twitching from the noise these idiots made while trying to be stealthy. Maybe it was a good thing. Caroline faked a sneeze that bounced off the trunks surrounding them, and asked loudly, "Where are you taking us?"

"Don't worry 'bout it. Now shut ya mouth before I put somethin' in it." His buddy laughed at the lewd innuendo and Trevor gnashed his teeth as he drug his feet. The impressive trail he'd left behind would surely lead Cade or at least one of his SEAL buddies to them. The sun had gone down behind the trees, but Cade always said Navy SEALs worked best in the dark.

Please hurry, Cade.

When the idiots leading them finally stopped, Caroline had no idea where they were. It was a small clearing with not a building in sight.

"Where we at? You got us lost?" the shorter one called Roy asked.

"No, stupid. Dis is da place. See, dere she goes." The taller one, Joey, pointed toward a cluster of trees. Although she knew who they were talking about, fear and vulnerability clutched her throat and her insides burned. Caroline tugged at the ropes still binding her wrists and squinted through the dusk to see better. All she could make out was the blonde hair, but that was enough to activate her heightened gag reflex. She spilled the contents of her stomach.

THIRTY-TWO

"A two-for-one special. It must be my lucky day." April's voice startled Caroline as it came from her left. She snapped her head to see the evil woman bringing Cade and Eddie at gunpoint into the clearing. "I didn't expect to see the ex in the mix. The love triangle is complete." She smiled wickedly at Caroline. "Do control yourself, Caroline." April glared at the incompetent captors. "Took you long enough."

"Dey put up a fight. We got here quick as we could," Roy lied.

April slowly shook her head at the man. "You disgust me, you flagrant waste of cells. I don't know why *parrain* even tolerates you." She scowled at the taller man. "Joey, where's Callahan?" He pointed to Trevor. "Not that one, you idiot. His father."

Joey shrugged. "I dunno. You was 'sposed to tell him where to meet, not me."

Caroline's blood slowed upon hearing that Trevor's dad would be joining them, and she peered back in the direction of the blonde she'd seen first. Her eyes must've been playing tricks on her in the dim light. She would swear she saw April straight ahead.

Eddie looked over her, frantically searching the perimeter of the property, but Caroline's heart seized when she saw blood trickling from Cade's fingers from the metal wire April had used to bind his wrists. How had April had been able to subdue both strong men by herself? The only thing that would've kept either of them from ripping April apart limb from limb was if she'd used Caroline or Dani as leverage. Where were all of Cade's Navy SEAL friends? He'd said he was calling in backup, so how had he been captured?

"Cade. . .," Caroline whispered as her fury swirled behind her eyes. "April, why are you doing this? What did we ever do to you?"

April pouted her lips and mocked. "Oh, you mean besides breathing?" She reduced her crystal eyes to slits. "You ruin everything. All of you." She shoved them forward. "You two stand over there with the others so I can make sure you don't try anything stupid."

Cade's jaw rippled when he caught sight of Caroline's face, his eyes focusing on her scraped cheek, then he got a good look at Trevor's bloodied face. "Gee, Callahan, you didn't have to get all made up just for me," he joked.

Trevor smirked. "Only the best for you."

"Aww, isn't this nice?" April mocked. "One big happy family. You could always keep them both, Caroline. Wife to one, whore to the other."

"Jealous, April?" Caroline taunted.

April withdrew something from her pocket and smoothed her thumb across it. "Nice watch."

Her watch. Caroline hadn't realized it was missing. They must have taken it from her after they knocked her out.

"You know, relationships are based on trust. Don't you agree, Beau?" She paced. "I knew this stupid thing would lead you right to me. You can't resist being the knight in shining armor. The hero."

April pointed the hand holding the watch at Caroline while her other hand kept her weapon steadily aimed at them. Specifically Cade. He was the bigger threat. "Did you know your darling husband had a trace on you?" She threw the watch against a tree.

"Had a GPS in it the whole time so he could rush to the rescue and save his damsel in distress whenever she needed him. Valiant, right?" April's eyes narrowed. "Or untrusting. It's also a good way to keep tabs on you wherever you go," her eyes flashed to Trevor, "or whoever you're with. . ."

"April," Eddie started, but she cut him off with the barrel of her gun when she pointed it at his head and cocked it.

"*You* shut up."

"Where is Claire?" He exhaled. "Just let them go. Your beef is with me. Especially the girls. Caroline and Claire are—"

April's shrill laughter echoed through the forest. "You think this is all about you?" Her chin jutted out as she twisted her head to the side. "You're such an arrogant prick." She rubbed the back of her free hand across her forehead. "All those years I wasted on you, raising your little misfits. And for what? My plan turned to shit when the prodigal daughter showed up. And then your other daughter with her pathetic blackmail attempt."

"Claire?" Eddie asked.

April huffed. "Oh yeah. After everything I'd done for that little troll, she tried blackmailing me by using my own words against me. She's smarter than you ever gave her credit for. " April squinted her steely eyes at him. "I handled her, though."

"Where is she, April?" Eddie spat. "I know you have her. She called me."

"Oh, I know." She laughed.

Caroline looked to Cade for a signal of what they should do. He was scanning the trees around them, probably searching for his SEAL buddies. He glanced at her and slightly nodded his reassurance. She trusted him, but it didn't make her any less terrified.

"Why the hell you chose this swampy muck over an abandoned shack in the city, I'll never understand." Kenneth Callahan's brusque voice sliced through the tension like a hot knife through butter. "Ruined. A three-hundred-dollar pair of shoes completely destroyed." He came up from behind them and slung his foot in the air. Clumps of mud plopped into the leaves, but Caroline focused on the large pistol in his hand.

"Why the—" He froze when he saw Trevor. His furious blue eyes centered on April. "What's the meaning of this? Why is my son here?"

April twirled her hand in the air. "Oh, this just keeps getting better and better. Welcome to the party, pops. Stop whining and help keep an eye on Junior and his playmates so they don't get out of hand."

"Did you do that to his face? This wasn't part of my plan."

April tilted her head and mockingly puckered. "Your plan? Oh, did you think you were calling the shots?" Her face hardened. "Of course you did."

"Of course I'm calling the shots. I handled your little rogue swamp puppet, didn't I?" Caroline looked at Cade whose body vibrated with rage. Kenneth had to be talking about Chris. "It was more than you could do. You couldn't control a kitten." He laughed before his cold eyes centered on April. "You may have decided when and where by slapping that envelope on my desk last week, but this was my idea. My land. My revenge. Trevor had nothing to do with my plans."

"Wrong again," April chided.

"How dare you pull my son in to this."

"Oh, believe me, you did that all on your own," April said.

"Trevor, get over here by me. This bitch is crazy."

"No, I think I'll stay right where I am. Thanks, anyway."

"What? Don't be ridiculous." Kenneth's infuriated expression turned worrisome. "Trevor?

"Why, Dad? And don't give me the revenge BS. You've pulled innocent lives, including your own flesh and blood, into harm's way. Why?"

"This is Callahan territory. It should've rightfully been ours over a hundred years ago, and I'm finally on the cusp of having it. This is what our ancestors wanted. You are my son. My heir. And it's time we take back what has belonged to us from the beginning. This land justly belongs to the Callahan family, and Callahan's take care of their own. I'm doing you a favor—"

"It *did* belong to a Callahan until your son ruined everything by not sealing the deal with his fiancée," April interrupted.

Kenneth bristled. "Excuse me?"

"Instead, he sent her down here right into the arms of her boy toy." April's gaze raked over Trevor's body. "Hmm. I would've thought he could satisfy her enough to keep her out of another man's bed." Her eyes hardened. "Guess not." Her focus returned to Kenneth Callahan. "But this land was in the hands of a Callahan until you blew it."

"Nonsense. You're insane," Kenneth spat.

"Maybe not by name," she raised her gun toward Kenneth, "but by blood."

He raised his weapon back at her. “Careful with that firearm, Ms. Fontenot. You’re treading on dangerous ground.”

“Maria Morales,” April shouted.

“Oh, please.” He scoured the trees impatiently. "Are we on this again? I told you already. Never heard of her," Kenneth callously replied, stubborn chin raised high.

“She was my mother. The woman you knocked up and refused to associate with, or even acknowledge, after she had *your* baby.” April took a step closer to him. “The woman you forced to raise a fatherless child and live on her own as a maid, a servant, to support *your* child.” April sneered. “Tell me, Kenneth, how does that fit into your ‘Callahan’s take care of their own’ motto?”

April aimed her gun back to Caroline, Trevor, Cade and Eddie. “My plan was so sweet until you four ruined it. I had it all worked out. Trevor would marry Caroline and own half of her inherited fortune she gained after her no-longer-estranged father’s death. I would get my part of the inheritance as his beloved wife and guardian of his then-underage children.”

April pulled a necklace from her pocket, the same one Cade had ripped from Caroline’s grasp at the hospital, and let it dangle from her finger. Cade swore under his breath.

“And then,” she continued, “after a tragic accident involving Kenneth, Trevor and Trevor’s dear mother, as the only living Callahan, a matching DNA test provided, of course, I would inherit everything the Callahan and Fontenot families ever owned. Thereby, succeeding in the revenge plot the Callahan men could never seem to pull off.”

She sighed. “If only you weren’t so misogynistic I might have forgiven you for never claiming me as your child, and we could’ve made a great team.” April’s eyes brightened. “Though, just when I thought all hope was lost, a new opportunity presented itself. A better one from someone not very different from her mother."

"That necklace belongs to me." A voice boomed from across the field.

April's eyes widened and she swallowed back whatever biting remark she'd been about to spew.

All heads turned to see who had the power to shut April up, and Caroline nearly swallowed her tongue.

No way!

THIRTY-THREE

"Claire! Go! Run now!" Caroline shouted to her sister, but she kept walking toward them. Was she the blonde Caroline had seen before. What was her sister doing?

"That is my necklace. Give it back," Claire spat.

April sighed, clutched the medallion and cut her eyes at Claire. "No."

"Don't make me use it against you," Claire threatened.

April sneered. "Fine, but it won't do any good."

"Claire?" Eddie muttered. "What are you doing here?"

"Oh, Daddy. You have no idea. Let's just say I'm not the little girl you raised." She scoffed, "Or made April raise."

"Are you kidding me?" Eddie said, shocked.

She crossed her arms and raised her brow. "April told me everything."

"What did she tell you?" Eddie asked.

"When Caroline and Trevor's wedding fell apart, I overheard April plotting with someone about her plans to kill you. I told her I was going to turn her in. That's when she told me the truth." Unshed tears glistened in Claire's eyes, but she blinked them back.

"What truth?"

"About how you never wanted kids, but only adopted Remy and me because Elizabeth, your second wife, the woman who *actually* wanted us, begged you to. And after she died, you were desperate to get married just to find someone who would raise your annoying children that you never wanted to begin with."

Claire's voice trembled with emotion. "Deep down I think I knew it. I always tried so hard to be a good kid. To stay out of trouble and not stress you out. But you never paid attention to me." Claire straightened. "I chalked it up to you being an emotionally distant, workaholic father." She pointed to Caroline. "And then *she* came along."

Claire's face distorted in anger. "And suddenly you became this doting father obsessed with your wonderful new daughter. At first I liked Caroline, I was excited to have a sister, but April told me about your plans to change your will, cutting me and Remy out completely to leave everything to your biological child. I didn't believe her, but I withdrew from you to test and see for myself if you'd even miss me when I wasn't around." Claire crossed her arms like a defiant child. "You failed the test." She walked to stand next to April. "Then she told me about my *real* mom and gave me this." Claire snatched the necklace from April's hand and held it up.

"Claire, I never considered you and Remy an inconvenience. I love you both very much. Sure, I was screwed up after Elizabeth died, I'll admit that, but y'all were my world." Eddie tipped his head toward April. "And I sure as hell didn't marry her just to take care of you. She couldn't keep a houseplant alive."

Trevor chuckled and April shot daggers at him with her eyes.

"Lies. Stop lying to me!" Claire screamed.

"I'm not lying, baby. And I didn't change my will. I only added Caroline to it. You will still get a third of everything I have."

Claire flashed a brazen grin. One that held deeper meaning than what showed on the surface. "It doesn't matter anymore. I have power you never knew existed!"

"Power you don't know how to handle," April argued.

"I've managed a few things you couldn't do," Claire countered.

"Yeah, until you shot your own brother." Claire's eyes widened while April's tightened. "Go ahead, Claire. Tell him the rest of your genius plan."

No way! Caroline's heart sank. Claire wouldn't shoot her own brother, would she? Cade had said the shooter was an amateur, but Claire and Remy were very close. Eddie's head fell upon seeing Claire's mortification. Her panic-stricken, wide eyes frantically observed the faces staring back at her. Her youth and immaturity shone through the hardened mask she first appeared with.

"Claire, tell me you're not the one who shot Remy," Eddie pleaded.

Claire's nerves and uncontrolled emotions took over. "That was an accident."

"He's just a kid. . .your *brother*. He loves you," Eddie said.

"I didn't mean to shoot him," she screeched through the building tears. "I swear!" In complete hysterics, Claire bawled. "It was supposed to be you!"

"You see, that's what happens when you work with children. They let their emotions get the best of them." April retorted, rolling her eyes. "Control yourself, Claire." April turned back to Kenneth and Eddie. "So, instead of outing me for conspiracy of murder, my cunning stepdaughter thought of an ingenious plan that would benefit us both. An offer I couldn't refuse. Caroline and Eddie for half of the Fontenot fortune and assets."

April cut her eyes to Claire and back to Eddie as she distanced herself from her stepdaughter. "You see, she thought she no longer had claim to any of your fortune, but I knew better. I made her believe she was from a magical lineage with the power to curse people with a medallion only controlled by the family who hexed it." A wicked smile played on her lips. "But it was my great grandmother, Marie Emilie, who held that power, created that curse, and passed the medallion down to me."

"Wait, what? You lied to me?" Claire snapped.

"Shocker," Caroline retorted.

Kenneth's voice boomed as he scolded Claire. "This whole family reunion thing is just great." His inflection blasted throughout the clearing. "And cheers to you, doll, for being the brains of the whole operation." Kenneth praised Claire, waving his gun about while it was still pointed at April. "But you interrupted something much more important, so step aside and let the adults finish talking."

Claire glowered at him while April seethed, "You are unbelievable."

Kenneth glared at her. "*You* are ridiculous. Let's get one thing straight. I never slept with anyone named Maria Morales, and I certainly never had a child I didn't support."

"Liar!" April screamed and her two thugs snickered at her expense. Clearly, they enjoyed seeing her upset. How much respect and power could April possibly have over them? They didn't seem fond of her at all. What would it take for them to turn on her? "How can you stand face-to-face with me and still deny it after I showed you the DNA test results? Your saliva from a coffee cup I swiped from your office trash can proved that your blood runs through my veins. And you denied me everything I should've had! Your name is on my birth certificate, and I *will* get what is coming to me. What is mine. *My* revenge" A sinister smile spread across April's face. "In fact, I already have."

"What are you talking about?" Kenneth hissed. Caroline surveyed the crowd gathered in the small clearing. Eddie stood motionless, his face weighted down with remorse and sadness. Cade's feet were planted, but his eyes never stopped scanning the trees. Trevor watched Caroline. His eyes never left her unless they flickered to April's weapon. Kenneth and April continued their heated standoff as everyone watched, intently, waiting to see who lost their mind first.

"You sold your property last week to someone by the name of Moreau. Jog any memories now," April ribbed.

Cade shifted, and April turned the gun on their group, lunging her weapon at each of them. "I would've had it all, the Callahan *and* the Fontenot fortune! If *you,*" she pointed the weapon at Trevor, "had a backbone." She moved to Cade. "And *you* had stayed out of it." The gun settled on Caroline. "And *you,* if only you and your slut mother had kept your damn legs closed!"

"That's ludicrous!" Kenneth barked.

"This is getting out of hand," Trevor murmured under his breath.

With Cade on one side of her and Trevor on the other, they both took an undetected half step in front of Caroline to shield her. She appreciated their protection, but who was protecting them?

April pointed the gun back at Kenneth and pulled an envelope from her back pocket. "You faxed me the signed deed last week. Don't you remember? We emailed about it?" Kenneth's dumbfounded expression evoked a triumphant smile from April while Claire sniffled, wiping her nose on her sleeve as she slowly backed toward the trees. "Isn't technology great?" April said with a celebratory smirk. "Thanks, Dad."

"You stupid bitch." Kenneth's bellowing laughter filled the open night air, and chills coated Caroline's arms. "That was all fabricated for this set up." He laughed harder, wheezing in between cackles. "Do you really think I'm that stupid. . .that desperate?" He shook his head, "And you were the one I was duping the whole time." He doubled over laughing. "It's perfect."

April screeched like a banshee, pointed the gun at Kenneth's face and pulled the trigger. Time stood still as everything happened at once. Claire ran into the trees as Eddie slammed his defenseless body into the thug closest to him and took him down. Trevor and Cade both lunged in front of Caroline as April moved her aim to Cade, her frenzied eyes full of panicked rage.

Deafening shots from all around them rang out simultaneously. Cade tackled Caroline and smashed her already bruised face into the moist earth, jamming her shoulder painfully into the socket. A century passed, or maybe seconds, she couldn't tell, before someone clipped through the bindings on her wrists.

She exhaled with the relief it brought, and winced from the pain in her shoulder. The unmoving weight on top of her set off alarms in her head. "No!" The weight lifted, and Caroline groaned from the physical assault.

"Cade! Trevor! Dad!" Her eyes opened wide in the eerily shadowed woods. It wasn't completely dark yet, but difficult to discern identities of the people scurrying around her. If anyone answered her calls, she didn't know it because the ringing in her ears rattled her brain. Caroline crawled on all fours to the two bodies squatting with their backs to her. The movement of everyone rushing around among the shadows disoriented her. She couldn't recognize them, only that neither were anyone she knew. She took a good look at the large mass and realized it wasn't plural. Only one gigantic man blocked her view of whoever he was working on, and Caroline recoiled as a petite blonde woman firmly pulled her to her feet. She wore a black long sleeved shirt with a small picture of a razorback on the front, and black cargo pants with a holstered gun strapped to a very familiar belt. "Why are you wearing my clothes?"

"Are you okay?" The woman's lips moved, but Caroline couldn't hear it through the painful horn blasting through her throbbing head.

She gave a quick nod and cast her panicked attention to each face in the crowd of people she didn't know, mostly law enforcement officers, some dressed in black with their faces painted camouflage, scurrying around them tending to the bodies on the ground. Nothing made sense. Shock. She must be in shock. "Where's Cade?" Caroline asked.

The woman pointed in the direction of a human wall hunched around a single body lying on the ground.

THIRTY-FOUR

"Cade," Caroline frantically screamed. Or at least she thought she had. "Cade!"

His head peeked around the black shirt-clad bodies and he limped over to her. He held his abdomen, his hand bloodied against the front of his soaked shirt.

"What just happened?"

"It's over," he whispered. "You okay?"

"What's over? Why are you bleeding?" She pulled his shirt up to inspect his body, but he pushed her hands down.

"Shh, it's okay. I'm fine. I'm fine." She studied his face, but his expression baffled her. He seemed. . .remorseful.

"What is it?" She immediately glanced around searching the other faces and bodies in the field to see what had happened, but everything was a blur. "Where's my dad? Where's Trevor?"

The designer slacks belonging to the body still on the ground sent tears rushing to her eyes, blurring her vision. "No!"

Caroline hurried to his side. A large man held his hand pressed against Trevor's chest to staunch the flow of blood. Trevor's labored breathing broke her resolve. She scooted up by his head and cradled his cheek.

"Trevor, no," she choked. "No, no! This wasn't supposed to happen."

He smiled, lazily, piercing what was left of her heart. "Did I miss the grand finale?"

"No, I'd say you were right in the middle of it."

"I did it."

"What?" Caroline didn't bother holding back the tears.

"I saved him for you, C. So you can live a long and happy life. With him and your daughter."

Caroline sobbed through quivering lips. "Yeah, you did. You stupid, stupid beautiful man. You saved him." She kissed his forehead and then his lips. "Thank you," she whispered.

Cade knelt beside Caroline. "Thanks, Callahan."

One corner of Trevor's mouth curved up as he slurred, "Who's the hero now, gardener?"

"You are," Cade said, nodding.

Trevor smiled, his blinking slowed and breathing hitched. "Say it again," he wheezed.

"Trevor," Caroline objected.

"I wanna hear the words come outta the Navy SEAL's mouth."

Cade coughed out a laugh. "Alright, fine, you're a real hero."

"Take care of her," Trevor breathed, his voice barely audible.

"Trevor, wait." Caroline begged. "I have so much left to say to you."

Trevor reached up to wipe her tears and caress her cheek. "Nothin' left to say, Caro. I love you, and I always will."

Caroline squeezed her eyes closed, holding his palm to her cheek and willing the pain to stop. "I love you, too, Trevor. Always." When she opened her eyes, she caught one last glimpse of his magnificent blue eyes before he closed them and his smile faded.

With his last breath, Trevor whispered, "I'll keep him away from you."

The words swirled with the sudden breeze rustling the leaves and blowing her hair.

"No, Trevor!" The large man who'd been holding pressure to Trevor's wound silently stepped away. Caroline pressed her forehead to his chest and wept. She didn't care if she got blood on her, or if he was no longer with his body. She wasn't ready to let him go.

Cade rubbed his hand along her back to comfort her.

"Rest in peace, Trevor," Eddie said, quietly.

Muted sobbing drew her attention to the right, close to the trees, where Claire stood with two police officers. She started bawling as they read her rights to her. Procedural chatter from the men standing to her left pulled Caroline back to reality, and, for the first time, she took in her surroundings. Bodies littered the leaf-covered terrain.

Caroline collected herself and limped away from the blood bath in a stupor. She watched as the paramedics carried Trevor's body toward their trucks.

"I sure hope George leaves him alone," Caroline said. "He deserves to go into the light and not be stuck here in misery."

"If anyone could stand up to George, it would be Trevor. He'll never let him hurt you again," Cade said, clearing his throat. "I've been on the receiving end of his punches."

"Is Kenneth dead?" Caroline asked.

"Yes. And so are April and her thugs."

Realization sank in. “With Kenneth and April gone, and now Trevor, that’s the end of the Callahan bloodline. George has no reason to stay here, and no outlet left to work through.”

The wind suddenly howled, ferociously swirling and blowing leaves in a whirlwind only around the clearing. Several trees broke midway up their trunks, filling the emptiness with popping and crackling sounds, and an explosion nearby rocked the ground and filled the air with charged heat. And as immediately as it began, it ended.

Caroline imagined that was Trevor chasing George into the fiery depths of hell.

One of Cade’s SEAL buddies gave a high-five to another one standing nearby and cheered. “Hell yeah! That’s damn fine wiring if I do say so, myself. Those bastards didn’t stand a chance against my handiwork. Guess I’d better go brief the 5-0 on my genius rat trap and give ’em a few pointers.” The guy started loudly singing the Sinatra tune, *That’s Life*. Caroline looked questioningly at Cade who simply grinned.

“That’s Crooner. I’ll introduce you later.”

“Well, y’all made my job easy. You got ’em all here in one place for me.” The blonde woman who had helped Caroline to her feet held her hand out. “You must be Caroline. I’m Special Agent Tonya Floyd. I’ll get your clothes cleaned and back to you as soon as possible.”

Caroline took her hand. “Nice to finally meet you. And thank you. I think we would have all met our maker if y’all hadn’t been there to intervene.”

“Thank your husband. He’s the one who felt it coming. I learned a long time ago to trust his gut.”

Caroline beamed proudly at her husband. “I get that a lot.”

"Mr. Fontenot, can I talk to you for a minute?" A police officer called to her father as he held Claire in custody. Remorse emanated off of Claire in waves. She'd gotten in way over her head with April, and April's manipulations and betrayals caused Claire to almost kill her brother. She could've just asked Eddie if April's allegations were true.

Eddie approached Claire with slumped shoulders and a bowed head. Caroline wanted to hug him. His sorrowful, defeated expression called to her compassion and immense love for her father and she wanted to reach out and comfort him.

"What's going to happen to Claire?" Caroline asked Tonya.

"She's eighteen, so she'll be tried as an adult with a fair trial and probably be charged with a few felonies. Aggravated battery for Remy's gunshot wound, for sure. Also conspiracy to commit first degree murder, or maybe even attempted first degree murder. The DA has the discretion to charge as he sees fit."

"She'll get what she deserves. Excuse me for a moment." Cade walked away from them, approached Claire and said something into her ear. She scowled as he pulled the necklace from her front pocket.

"What's with that necklace?" Caroline asked him when he returned.

"I'll tell you the story later, but first I need to tie up some loose ends."

"I feel bad for Claire. She's so young. It's really sad," Caroline lamented. "She's ruined her young life over jealousy and self-pity."

Cade pulled her in to a hug. "It didn't help that she had a snake in her ear spouting evil manipulations."

"True." She raised up on her tip toes to kiss him. "Let's go home. I want to hold our daughter."

Cade smiled. "I have a surprise for you."

***

When they entered the foyer, Kristy launched herself into Caroline's arms.

"Oh my gosh, Caroline! I've missed you so much! Thank goodness you're okay." She pulled back and took in Caroline's appearance, her hands on her face and hair, patting down her body. "You are okay, right? No holes or cuts? No broken bones?"

When it dawned on Caroline who was groping her, she bounded back to Kristy with a bear hug, and the endless supply of tears flowed. Sniffles from Emily, Delphine and Delia came from beside them. Caroline's shoulders quivered with each jarring sob.

"Caroline, what's the matter? Talk to me." Kristy smoothed her hair. What is it? Honey, what has you all up in the full-fledged ugly cry?" Caroline's face distorted as she opened her mouth to answer, but she couldn't speak. She wailed and buried her face in Kristy's shoulder again. "Caroline, I—"

"Trevor," Caroline managed to get out.

"What about him?"

Caroline took a step back, hiccuping as she wiped her hand down her sodden face. She considered and appreciated her best friend's concern, and tried to regain her control, but shook her head as the emotion overruled her body again. She dropped to her knees and buried her face into her hands. Kristy dropped with her and wrapped her arms around her.

"Oh my gosh! That can't be! Are you sure?"

Caroline confirmed and snorted with her intake of air.

"Cade?" Kristy asked, searching for an understandable explanation of what happened.

Her husband's voice didn't do much to soothe the burning crater in Caroline's heart as he explained how Trevor valiantly died by jumping in front of him to protect him from April's bullet. Caroline didn't think it was possible to cry harder, but she did when Cade repeated Trevor's last words to protect her from George.

Kristy's lips were at her ear. "Oh, sweetie, I get it. I'm so sorry." She cried right along with Caroline, matching her sob for sob. When they finally calmed down, able to look at each other without losing it, Kristy and Caroline made it into the living room where Eddie, Emily, Cade and Runway gathered with a group of faces Caroline didn't recognize.

"When did you get here, Kris? Where's your baby?"

"Ben's asleep upstairs in Dani's bassinet. She's in the crib next to him. We got here last night. We wanted to surprise you and Cade, but I never imagined you'd be in this much danger."

"Oh, you named him Ben? I love it!"

Kristy smiled and pulled Caroline to the sofa to sit beside her. "That's something Matteo and I wanted to talk to you about."

"Okay, sure. Why?"

Kristy smiled and peeked up at Runway who stood proudly behind her. "Well, we wanted to pick something special, so we named him Benito Joseph. After your precious angel baby." Kristy held Caroline's trembling hands. "I hope that's okay with you and Cade."

More tears streamed down Caroline's cheeks as she approved with a slight bob of her head, speechless.

"Of course it's okay, Kristy," Cade said. "Thank you for the tribute." He squeezed Caroline's shoulder. "We love it."

Kristy smiled through her own tears. "Okay, great. I hoped you would."

"Where did the name Benito come from?" Caroline asked.

"Matteo's father. Everyone called him Nito. I pushed for Ben," Kristy added with big eyes and a raised brow. "No need to get the poor boy beaten up on the playground with a name like *Nito*," she emphasized.

"Totally," Caroline laughed. "I love it, Kris. I really do. Can I go see him?"

Kristy breathed. "Of course." She stood and scanned the interested faces watching them, fanning herself. "Whew, the massive bodies and overwhelming sense of testosterone in this room is suffocating."

Still seated, Caroline looked around at Cade's intimidating SEAL buddies who all watched her and Kristy with fascination. She suddenly became very shy. "Um, hi. Thank you for your help today."

They responded with chin dips and bows as Cade stood. "Guys, this is Caroline." Cade held his hand out for her to take. When she accepted it and stood beside him, he pulled her close and gazed upon her face. "My beautiful wife." Caroline's cheeks burned as he fervently kissed her in front of the captive audience.

He rested his forehead to hers and whispered through closed eyes. "I thought I'd lost you."

"Nah, man. We wouldn't've let that happen," said the broad-shouldered tall man standing in the corner. "We were on the ready with our weapons waiting for Tonya's signal, but she took all four of them out before we even got to play."

"Not surprising," Cade said.

"It's alright. At least we had some fun with the two stragglers earlier today."

"Caroline, this is Scott Mason. We call him Rattler because he's from Texas. He's fast and deadly just like a rattle snake. He can blend in anywhere, and, like a rattler with his tail, he lures people in with his looks and charm. He's friendly and charismatic, and the more you talk to him the more you'll realize you're drawn to him in some way you can't explain."

Cade lifted his chin and clapped a hand on Rattler's shoulder, clearly impressed by his friend, and used his other hand for emphasis. Caroline smiled at the awe in her husband's voice. She'd never seen him this way.

"Let me tell you, this guy can go undercover and people from all over naturally trust him without understanding why. They relax and start talking, unsure why they are revealing their secrets to a perfect stranger." Cade laughed. "He's like a bartender, or a barber, people just start talking and disclose everything but their shoe size." Cade's eyes danced with excitement. "We've gotten a lot of good intel depending on those masterful skills."

Rattler winked at Caroline and Kristy, his gray eyes twinkling, "Glad to see someone finally tamed these two knuckleheads." His face-splitting smile revealed a dimple, and Caroline could see how he'd gain trust from people. His welcoming demeanor and handsome face really pulled her in. His nickname fit him well.

Cade pointed toward the other two guys, a tall black man who filled the oversized lounger, and a more slender, but still solidly built blonde guy standing behind the chair. "Falcon, my mentor. He is from southern Georgia, an Atlanta Falcon's fan, and can drive, sail, or fly anything. Transportation is his thing." The seated man greeted her, his stark-white teeth contrasting with his dark skin as he smiled, while Cade pointed to the smirking blonde guy behind him. "And that's Crooner, he's—"

"Caden Luke Beauregard." The front door swung open as Catherine stormed though the foyer. "You have some explaining to do, little brother." She gracefully wove through the furniture and standing bodies with a handsome beast-of-a-man on her heels.

Cade suppressed his grin. "Catherine. Glad to see you're alive and well. Is your phone broken?" he asked, sarcastically.

She bared her teeth. "I appreciate your protectiveness, I do, but," she jutted her thumb to the man behind her, "what the hell is this?"

"That's Hammer. I needed to make sure Marcellino hadn't gotten hold of you. I left you a message."

She sucked in an angry breath through her nose, crossed her arms and tapped her toe as she held up her phone. "I didn't get your message because my phone is dead as a doornail. I stayed at Melanie's yesterday to sleep off my hangover and forgot my charge cord. I didn't know you were gonna send *Thor*," she held her hand out, palm up, toward Hammer, "to sweep me off my feet while claiming to be 'escorting' me back home."

Catherine rubbed her temples before her fierce blue eyes popped open and punctured holes through Cade's head. "What are you laughing at?" She scrutinized all the amused faces in the room, "What's so damned funny?"

"Sweep you off your feet, huh?"

"Oh, shut up. You know what I meant. He accosted me and threw me in his car, while leaving mine at Melanie's," Catherine huffed, "which I still have to go back to town and get."

"I don't think Hammer accosted you, Cat," Cade said. "He doesn't have an aggressive bone in his body when it comes to women. Especially my sister."

"Well, he forced me to accompany him," she sulked. "The hell kind of name is Hammer, anyway?"

Cade shrugged one shoulder. "It's his call name. He's a medic. He does everything fast. Walks, talks, eats, runs. . . He got the name from the trucker phrase, 'put the hammer down,' but I'm thinking Thor is a more fitting reason now." Everyone laughed.

Hammer's smooth baritone voice filled the room. "I don't do *every*thing fast," he announced, before dipping his chin toward Catherine and lowering his voice. "Some things are worth savoring."

Whoops and hollers filled the entry of the Fontenot plantation as Catherine blinked, speechless, at Hammer's innuendo. She rolled her eyes and searched the faces in the room, stopping on Caroline. When she took in the damage from the airbag, her eyes grew wide, "Caroline! What happened to you?"

"Long story," Caroline said. "I'll tell you later. Right now I just want to go hug my baby girl and watch her dream."

"I'll fill her in," Cade said. "Go grab a shower and get some rest, love." Cade kissed her and walked her and Kristy to the foot of the stairs. "Tomorrow is a new day."

A new day.

Caroline beamed over Ben, held her sweet daughter and kissed her almost to the point of waking her up, before finally sinking into her fluffy canopy bed to attempt sleep. Flashes of the night's horror filled her exhausted mind. Kenneth Callahan's hatred emanating toward April as she revealed her murder plot. Claire's spiteful face while revealing her true immaturity and selfishness. Trevor's compassion-filled blue eyes as he whispered his final words to keep her safe.

Caroline drifted into unconsciousness. Rachel's joyful face comforted her, leading her through a colorful field of silky wildflowers. She didn't speak, but she glowed. Literally. She had a golden aura around her as if she stood in front of the sun, a blockade in front of the blinding ball of fire, which radiated warmth and life. As she ascended, she held her palm out to wave goodbye, and blew a kiss. Then both of her hands dropped to her side, held the hands of two children, and walked into the shining abyss.

THIRTY-FIVE

"Delphine, these chocolate chip pancakes are the bomb!" Kristy exclaimed as she shoved the last bite of her third pancake into her mouth. "I swear I could eat three more. But I won't because I'm saving room for more of that incredible coffee." Kristy poured another cup and drank it black. "Mmm," she inhaled. "I've dreamed about this stuff since I left last year."

Caroline walked in to the kitchen with a toothy grin. "I could hear you from upstairs."

Kristy raised her eyebrows and shrugged as she shoved a piece of bacon in her mouth and smacked, "My daddy didn't call me the *Mouth of the South* for nothing when I was little."

Caroline smiled at her best friend as she sipped the fresh cup of coffee her mother placed in front of her. "I'm really happy you're here, Kris. I've missed you like crazy."

"Me, too. There's no place I'd rather be."

Caroline tilted her head to the side groaning from the pull of her neck, and no sooner than she had, a firm hand massaged the tense muscle she'd been stretching. Relief oozed through her knotted muscles as Cade's strong fingers worked out the built-up stress, and tingles radiated across her entire body as her blood flowed more freely with the release.

Cade's hands stilled just as Caroline realized the excessive moaning she heard was her own, and her eyes popped open to see the amused faces watching her carnal enjoyment. The small gathering had grown as all of Cade's SEAL buddies and her father witnessed her bawdy reaction to her husband's touch. Her hand snapped to her mouth and she looked at Cade, whose flushed cheeks framed a sheepish grin.

"Hooyah!" cheered Crooner.

"Hooyah," the rest agreed.

Crooner broke out into Michael Bublé's reinvention of Sinatra's classic about feeling good, and Cade joined him as they harmonized and put on a show for everyone in the kitchen. Caroline didn't even care that it was at her expense, she enjoyed seeing her husband carefree and singing again. It truly was a new dawn, and she fully intended to have more "feeling good" days in her immediate future. Starting with today.

***

"I'd like to make a toast," Eddie said as he clinked his fork against his glass. "I want to thank Barrios for accommodating our family and friends to enjoy this beautiful day. The weather warmed up, the sun is shining, and the air is clear. This is truly an occasion to celebrate overcoming adversity, both seen and unseen, new and old friendships, and family." Eddie tipped his glass to Cade and Caroline. "Good always conquers bad in the end. Beau, you've been there from the beginning watching out for Caroline and me. For all of us. I owe you more than I'll ever be able to pay. Thank you for helping my family get our happily ever after."

"Here, here," the table toasted.

Cade stood and held his own glass toward Eddie. "You owe me nothing, Mr. Fontenot. You and Ms. Emily have given me everything simply by breathing life into this amazing woman sitting beside me. For that I am forever grateful."

Cade swallowed and glanced down at Caroline before continuing. "I'd like to toast to someone else. Someone I despised before I ever knew him. A man who annoyed and amused me in the same sentence, and eventually convinced me he wasn't the waste of breath I originally thought he was. Someone who fought for what he wanted, stood up to anyone who got in his way, and, in the end, protected what he cherished."

Cade's voice mellowed. "I've been in war. I've seen heroes and cowards alike. I've witnessed good and evil come together. Trevor Callahan should be honored for his last brave act. He anticipated April's next move and didn't hesitate to push me and Caroline out of the way, and because of that he lost his own life. He sacrificed himself, something he once held in higher regard than anything else, and for that he is a true hero." He held his glass up to the entire table and smiled at Caroline, taking her breath away. "Cheers to Trevor for securing our happily ever after."

As everyone toasted, Caroline sipped her water with Trevor in mind. He would've liked Cade's thoughtful tribute to him. He always loved being the center of attention, but he'd have especially enjoyed hearing Cade announce to the crowd of Navy SEALs that he was a true hero.

"That was great," Kristy whispered to Caroline as everyone settled in to eat. Caroline agreed, unable to speak for the lump lodged in her throat. "So, whatever happened to your friend?" Kristy asked Cade. "The one who had been bugged."

"She found hard evidence that the mole in her office was Marcellino's son. The one person in this world he was most protective of. So she contacted Marcellino and worked out a deal that she wouldn't mention anything about it if he would agree to leave everyone down here alone and let it drop. April and his thugs were gone now, so there was nothing left for him to protect regarding the Fontenot's, and if it meant keeping his son out of prison he would do anything."

"That's it?" Kristy asked, dumfounded. "That's all it takes to keep the head of the mafia off your back?"

Cade sipped his drink and winked. "Oh, she's no fool. She also told him she had copies of the evidence, complete with audio and video surveillance, against his son hidden away where he'd never find it, and it was to be delivered to the head of the FBI in the event of her sudden death."

Cade shrugged. "He has no issue with us because we aren't the ones who killed his people. Tonya shot them all within the FBI's jurisdiction with the local law enforcement present, so we did nothing wrong. That doesn't mean I won't keep my head on a swivel, but I don't feel the need to stress over it."

"What about that necklace you told me about, Caroline? The one Claire thought was cursed."

"It wasn't cursed. April lied to her to make her think it was so she could trick her into doing her dirty work."

Cade cleared his throat, "Actually, it was, but it's not anymore."

"What?" Caroline asked, nearly choking on her cracker.

"I took it to Lucinda so she could put a counter-curse on it."

"It's really cursed? Claire had powers with that thing?"

"No. I've done some research since that day in the hospital. It affected Claire, but not in the way April led her to believe. It was April's grandmother's, so April had all the power. She could cause bad things to happen to whomever she wanted."

"That explains the sudden bout of rotten luck I had upon my arrival in this city," Caroline said.

"You know when you asked me about my friend Colin?"

Caroline and Kristy listened intently as Cade told them the horrific story from his childhood, skirting over the graphic details, of course.

"The curse was cast on all of Armand Aurieux's descendants who came in physical contact with the amulet. April led Claire to believe she held the power to curse others while in possession of that necklace, but Claire's biological mother was a direct descendant of Aurieux. April knew this and used Claire to keep hold of it while she used its power. April's grandmother was a descendant of the voodoo woman who cursed it, so she held the true power of the medallion."

"Creepy," Kristy said. "So where is the medallion now?"

"I've handed it over to Lucinda so she could put a counter-curse on it. Her mother-in-law was April's aunt, so she knows how to do just that." Cade smiled proudly. "Lucinda is taking care of it. It's out of our lives forever."

"See," Caroline nudged him, "Lucinda wasn't so bad after all."

"This really is the best gumbo I've ever tasted." Kristy inspected Runway's plate, "What'd you get?"

"Crab bisque. Want some?" he offered.

"Mmmm, yes." Kristy slurped from his spoon as Caroline watched in wonder.

"How can you eat like that and never gain any weight?"

The restaurant door swung open and Jessica Robicheaux rushed to her table. Caroline's heart sank. Trevor had mentioned she would be getting back from a cruise vacation with her family this weekend.

"Hey!" she said, brightly. "Have you seen Trevor? He's not answering his phone."

"Jess," Caroline started, her eyes welling with tears.

Jessica's face creased with worry. "What's wrong? Are you okay?"

Caroline nodded. "Have you talked to your brother today?" Caroline figured Jessica's brother, the state trooper, would've broken the news before anyone else had the opportunity.

"No, he was on vacation with us. His lazy butt's still knocked out." Jessica laughed, "He's enjoying his last day of vacation by sleeping off a monster hangover. I tried to give him my secret hangover cure, and the shoe that narrowly missed my head was a clear refusal. Why?"

"Let's go talk outside."

Caroline led the tall, lithe woman outside and searched her frenzied mind for how she would explain what happened. After explaining everything, ugly truth and all, Jessica pressed her back to the wall and slid down to the ground.

"Are you okay? I know this is a lot to take in at once." Caroline sank to the ground with her.

Jessica pressed her face to her hands and sobbed. "I didn't get to say goodbye."

Caroline blinked through the blurry tears and wept with her. "I'm so sorry, Jess. It all happened so fast. But he was very heroic. He saved Cade's life. And mine."

Jess sobbed for a few moments without speaking before she looked up at Caroline with a mascara-streaked face. "Caroline," she whispered, "I'm pregnant."

THIRTY-SIX

Four years later. . .

"We're here!" Caroline chimed to Dani in the back seat as she pulled up to Jessica's shotgun house.

"Yay! Let's go see Trey," Dani exclaimed.

"I'm sure Trey will be excited to see you, too." Caroline held a gift bag in one hand, and Dani's hand in the other. She stopped and squatted down to Dani's level. "Danielle Helene, you listen to me. Best behavior. We're at Trey's house for his birthday party, so you let *him* open his presents. He doesn't need your help."

"Yes, ma'am," Dani said. Caroline watched her daughter's strawberry blonde pigtails bounce as she bounded up the steps to Jessica's front door. "Ms. Jessica, we here to play!"

"We'll see how long that lasts," Cade said, chuckling. "I don't think she'll be able to resist. How 'bout you?" Cade kissed the forehead of their eighteen-month-old son after pulling him from the car seat.

"You know, we could've offered to host his party at our house since Trevor did design it."

Cade observed the lack of cars in the drive. “I don’t think we’re going to have to worry about overcrowding, love. I think we’re the only ones here.”

“I wonder how Jessica’s been doing?” Caroline asked, worry crumpling her features.

“We’ll see soon enough. I bumped in to her at the grocery the other day and she seemed happy.”

“I hope you’re right. She told me last week that Trey has been struggling to make friends. He doesn’t want to play with any other kids, or even play with his toys. She said all he ever does is sit in his room alone and talk to himself while he draws pictures.”

“What kind of pictures?”

“Self portraits, mostly.”

“He is his father’s son,” Cade teased.

“That’s not very nice.”

“I’m only kidding,” Cade said. “But he does look just like Trevor,” he added.

“Spitting image. I told her I’d work with him today after the party.”

“Well, you’ve been a psych nurse for four years, and you have a connection with the subconscious that most people don’t,” Cade gave her a sweet peck on the lips. “If anyone can get through to him it’s you.”

“Hey guys, come on in,” Jessica called. “Trey, look who’s here!” she said, excitedly as she flipped her long dark hair over her shoulder and bent down with her hands on her knees. Trey kept his distance and waved shyly before retreating to his room. Jessica apologized. “Sorry. This is how it’s been for a while now.

Caroline cringed at the Elmo decorations. "You too, huh?" Dani loved Elmo, too, but if Caroline had to sit through one more chorus of the *Elmo's World* song she might just become violent.

"Oh yeah. He could watch it and sing to it all day if I'd let him."

"Look, Dani, they have hand puppets. Go see if Trey wants to put on a puppet show with you."

"Thanks," Jessica said. "I don't know what's gotten in to him lately. When he's not watching television, or engrossed in a game on my tablet, he's mopey. Getting him down for a nap or bedtime is a challenge all in itself. He wants to sleep with me every night." She lowered her voice. "And I usually let him because I can't bear to see those sad baby blues begging me not to leave him in the dark room alone."

Cade plopped down in the cushy leather recliner while their son, Matthew, pulled at the streamers hanging from the coffee table. Cade tried to distract him with the extra-large Legos from the toy box, but Matthew was much more interested in the bright decorations.

"Can I get y'all some punch or sweet tea?"

"Tea for me, please," Cade said.

"I'll have punch, thank you." Caroline sank into a rounded cushion of the dining room chair.

"When he does stay in his room, he has to sleep with every light on and the doors open."

"We went through that for a while until Matthew came along. Now Dani wants to sleep in his room so she can take care of him like a little mother hen." Caroline smiled and squeezed Jessica's shoulder. "It's just a phase. He'll grow out of it."

"I sure hope so. He hasn't made too many friends at his preschool. His teacher said he mostly plays by himself." Jessica cleared her throat. "He's created an imaginary friend. The doctor says that's perfectly normal for only children, and that I shouldn't be worried."

"I had an imaginary friend when I was little," Caroline said. "And I was an only child, too. Experts say it's a sign of creativity and genius."

"Well, he does draw and color a lot." Jessica's face fell. "There's one other thing that happened. Yesterday Trey was crying when I picked him up from preschool. It was Donuts with Dad day, and he was the only kid without his dad there." Jessica bowed her head. "I mean, my dad went with him, so it's not like he didn't have anybody. He had his pawpaw, but I still felt bad for him."

Caroline's heart broke. "Aw, poor baby. Has he asked about Trevor at all?"

Jessica nodded, pursing her lips to control the quiver. "Yeah. All the time. He wants to know everything about him. The hardest is when he asks me why his friends all have daddies and he doesn't." Jessica blinked, pushing the pool of tears over the ledge of her eyelids. "I tell him all the time that God needed his daddy more than we did, but Trevor's always watching over him." She pulled a napkin from the table and wiped the moisture from her face. "Breaks my heart. He just seems so sad all the time, you know?"

Caroline watched Trevor's son play with her own. "Trevor would have loved to see this."

"He would've also loved that you named your son after him. Matthew Trevor is a great name."

Caroline smiled and smoothed her son's golden curls. "It's the least we could do considering Trevor saved both our lives."

Caroline peeked into the living room where Trey and Dani were playing.

They were fine until Trey instinctively looked up as if she'd said his name and caught her watching him. He dropped the toy he'd been playing with and ran into his room.

"May I go talk to him?" Caroline asked Jessica.

Jess exaggeratedly waved her hands toward him. "Please. Be my guest."

Caroline asked Dani to join her, that maybe Trey felt more comfortable in the solace of his room, but Dani dramatically shook her head.

"I not going in dere wit him. I stay here an play wit Elmo and Dorothy."

Caroline put her ear to the door and heard Trey talking to someone. She knocked softly and walked in to find him coloring.

"Hey, buddy. Whatcha coloring?"

"A picture."

"Who you talkin' to?"

"My friend."

"Oh, that's nice." Careful not to make a big deal about his friend, she peeked over his shoulder to see his picture. "Oh, this boy has pretty blue eyes just like you. Did you know your daddy had pretty blue eyes, too?"

Trey nodded. "I seen a picture. My mom shows me." He offered the same crooked smile Trevor always had. "We have the same eyes."

She smiled, fighting back the emotion swelling in her chest. "Yes, you do. Same face, even. The spitting image."

"I wish he was here. I see him in my dreams sometimes."

Caroline's skin pebbled with goosebumps. "You do?" This child's articulation impressed her. Incredible for a three-year-old.

"Yeah. He likes my pictures."

"I'll bet he does." She swiped his dark hair off his forehead. "I'm sure he's very proud of you."

Trey shrugged and moved to his train set and started playing and making chugging sounds.

"So tell me about your friend."

"Whaddya wanna know?" he asked.

"What's he look like?"

"Like me."

"Can anyone else see him?" Trey shook his head. "Does he like to play with you?"

Trey shrugged. "I guess."

"What does your invisible friend like to do?"

"Build things."

"Oh, neat. Like your daddy. Did you know he built things?" Caroline used her hands and raised the tone of her voice to exaggerate and sound fun. "He designed big, huge buildings that looked like they stretched all the way up to the sky."

"I know."

"What kind of things do you build?"

"Blocks and stuff. He knocks over my toys and makes a big mess. Momma gets mad."

"Oh, he gets you in trouble?" Trey nodded. Imaginary friends were commonly used as the scapegoat for misbehavior in only children so they wouldn't get in as much trouble. She used to use that all the time against her mother.

"You know, when I was little I had a special friend, too. We would color on the walls and I would get in trouble for it." Trey smiled. "So, does your friend talk back to you when you talk to him?"

"Yeah. I say I can't play with him at school. My teacher don't like it when he comes."

"Does he make you feel safe? Maybe when you're scared or upset?" Trey shook his head and moved back to the table to color. Caroline walked around looking at the different drawings he'd created. He was quite the artist, his creations were messy but identifiable. The pictures ranged from cityscapes, to bulldozers, to Trey yielding a sword in front of a structure with bars, maybe a cage, battling a large creature that resembled a smoking dragon with flames shooting up around them. Caroline squinted her eyes to study the last one better. Were those bars? Or columns?

"How about your mommy, or your friends? Does he like them?"

"He don't like you."

"Hmm. Maybe because I'm a girl. Is this a 'boys only' room?"

"Nope."

Caroline peeked out the door into the living room where Matthew and Dani played with the party balloons while Cade and Jessica watched them. "Well, I'm an adult, like your teacher and your mommy. I know my special friend would get shy whenever adults were around. She never came out to play when I wanted her to. You think that could be it?"

Trey studied at the corner of the room for a moment, and then up at her before his eyes fell again to the paper he colored. "No."

She stubbornly crossed her arms, "Well maybe I can talk to him. Once he gets to know me, he might like me."

"I don't tink so."

Sensing a challenge, and determined to get through to Trey, Caroline sat in the tiny chair across from him. "Then I'll ask him, myself. What's his name?"

"George."

The End

AUTHOR'S NOTE

The Bayou Secrets Saga is a set of three consecutive books titled, DEADLINE (Book 1), LIFELINE (Book 2), and FLATLINE (Book 3). While they are stand-alone books, if you haven't read them in order, I encourage you to do so. You will better understand the characters, their back stories, and why they do the things they do.

Book 1 - Deadline

Book 2 - Lifeline

ABOUT THE AUTHOR

The Bigger Picture Photography
Location Credit to House Plantation in Hockley, TX.

Judy McDonough is an Arkansas native and a United States Navy Veteran. Her first military duty station was in New Orleans where she met her husband, Mike, a native of the Big Easy. During that time she fell in love with the architecture, cuisine, and haunting vibe of southeastern Louisiana, and, though they've moved around quite a bit, the magic of New Orleans stuck with her. In thirteen years, they've lived in Louisiana, Tennessee, and Texas.

A recent job opportunity has brought their family farther north than any of them have ever lived, and they look forward to experiencing four seasons in Ohio with their three young boys. It's fun to see the reactions of locals when they hear her southern accent, and she loves the scenery, but Judy's heart will always belong to the South.

Join her mailing list to keep up with the latest updates and new releases. She only sends it out quarterly, so no worries about cluttering inboxes. The link to sign up is:

http://eepurl.com/yuIVX

Visit her website for more information.

www.Judy-McDonough.com

Also, construction is underway for a fun character website for all things Bayou Secrets where you can read blog posts from random characters, see outfits and character pictures, participate in contests, and interact through email.

www.bayousecrets.com

Judy posts regularly on her social media platforms, so follow her if you haven't already.

facebook.com/JudyMcDonoughAuthor
twitter.com/JudyMcDonough
goodreads.com/JudyMcDonough
pinterest.com/Judy_McDonough

As always, please be kind enough to leave a review to let others know how you enjoyed the Bayou Secrets Saga and share your love of the bayou with your friends.

Made in the USA
Middletown, DE
06 March 2017